P9-CQA-123

Lying with Strangers

APR 2009

Lying with Strangers

James Grippando

3 1150 01152 3707

HarperCollins*Publishers*

BOISE PUBLIC LIBRARY

This is a work of fiction. The characters, incidents, and dialogues are products of the author's imagination and are not to be construed as real. Any resemblance to actual persons, living or dead, is entirely coincidental.

LYING WITH STRANGERS. Copyright © 2007 by James Grippando. All rights reserved. Printed in the United States of America. No part of this book may be used or reproduced in any manner whatsoever without written permission except in the case of brief quotations embodied in critical articles and reviews. For information, address HarperCollins Publishers, 10 East 53rd Street, New York, NY 10022.

HarperCollins books may be purchased for educational, business, or sales promotional use. For information, please write: Special Markets Department, HarperCollins Publishers, 10 East 53rd Street, New York, NY 10022.

Originally published in a slightly different form in 2006 by Madison Park Press. First HarperCollins edition published in 2007.

FIRST EDITION

Designed by William Ruoto

Library of Congress Cataloging-in-Publication Data

Grippando, James.
    Lying with strangers / by James Grippando.—1st ed.
    p. cm.
    ISBN: 978-0-06-113838-6
    ISBN-10: 0-06-113838-X
    1. Stalking victims—Fiction. 2. Trust—Fiction.
    PS3557.R534 L95   2007
    813'.5—dc22   2006050956

07 08 09 10 11 ID/RRD 10 9 8 7 6 5 4 3 2 1

For Tiffany—Always and forever

Many people claim to be loyal,
but it is hard to find a trustworthy person.

—Proverbs 20:6

Prologue

SHE WANTED HIM. FIVE MINUTES ON THE SUBWAY, AND HE WAS SURE of it. Rudy had a gift for detecting the most subtle signals.

The train was crowded, and he made a point of standing between her and the nearest exit. His eyes barely moved in her direction. He just leaned against the pole and read the *Wall Street Journal*. At least he pretended to read. It was all pretense, from the polished black wing tips to the Armani necktie, from the pinstripe suit to the tortoiseshell eyeglasses.

The train stopped and the doors opened. She started for the exit—right toward him. A long winter coat concealed her body, but the face was attractive. Nice mouth.

"Excuse me," she said as she passed.

She looked straight ahead, never making eye contact, but she hadn't fooled him. Her tone of voice, the way she'd passed just slowly enough to let him drink in the sweet scent of her perfume, were calculated steps in the age-old mating dance. Bottom line, no one had forced her to use the nearest exit; the other set of doors worked just as well. Surely it was no accident that her long brown hair had brushed against his coat as she passed. Most telling of all, she'd opened her mouth, parted those lovely lips, and actually spoken. *Excuse me.* A powerful message wrapped in precious few words. In one brief but electric moment, she had initiated the connection. Rudy could have said something back, and she would have been receptive. They would have talked. Who knows where it might have led?

The chime sounded, signaling that the sliding doors were about to close. It wasn't his stop, but on impulse he hopped off. The train pulled away, leaving Rudy alone on the platform. He'd seized her invitation, but she was gone.

Another worthless tease.

He shook off his anger, climbed the stairs, and emerged at a dark street corner. Downtown was cold and almost deserted at this late hour. He took a moment to choose his path. Throughout Boston's financial district, meandering cross streets intersected at angles and intervals that defied logic, still patterned after old village lanes that only centuries later happened to be lined with forty-story office towers. It was a maze to most, but Rudy knew his way around. Years ago he used to cut through here on his way to the Combat Zone, a two-block area off lower Washington Street that was once infamous for its nude-dancing bars and porno shops. The area had since been cleaned up, and with the pornographic bonanza on the Internet, he didn't even miss the old jaunts downtown. No more trudging through the snow with an aching hard-on in his pants. No more glares from picketers who wanted the smut out of their neighborhood. No more fear of being arrested for jerking off in a dark adult movie theater.

He buttoned his coat and started down the sidewalk, bucking the wind as the salted ice crunched beneath his feet. It was a long walk to Back Bay. He'd exited the subway several stops too early, thanks to the fetching looks of Little Miss Excuse Me. It was just as well he'd lost her. He had to remain focused. He had an entirely different job to do tonight.

Her name was Peyton Shields.

Peyton would be asleep by now, he knew, assuming the time on the flashing bank marquee was correct. Just to be sure, he killed a good hour walking her neighborhood, up Comm. Ave., down Newbury, and finally cutting over on Clarendon to Magnolia. It was her jogging route, and on countless warmer nights he'd watched her blaze down the sidewalks in her flimsy shorts and matching tank top that hugged the glorious shape of her body. They had never said hello, never even made eye contact. But he had passed her many times without her knowing it. She had always been in another world, caught up with the music from the iPod fastened to her belt. Rudy loved the iPod. A set of headphones could rob anyone of her usual alertness. Find a woman with headphones and you could follow her anywhere, practically crawl inside her panties before she even noticed you.

The cold night air stung his cheeks as he neared her apartment. Short hot breaths steamed from his mouth. He stopped beneath the bare magnolia tree across the street, his eyes locking onto her front door. He knew her husband was out of town tonight. Rudy had followed him to the airport. That meant Peyton was inside alone. Just her. And him.

Rudy crossed the street, careful not to stand in any one place too long and draw attention to himself. He walked neither fast nor slow. The street was deserted, but he knew better than to sneak around like a prowler. You never knew when someone was watching—he knew that better than anyone. His heart pounded as he reached her front steps. He felt some fear but mostly excitement. A little fear was healthy. It helped prevent mistakes.

He climbed one step at a time, the right foot, then the left. Every muscle in his body suddenly seemed in sync, the voluntary and the involuntary, the landing of each footstep seeming to match the beating of his heart. He had played this scene over in his mind at least a hundred times. He had studied his surveillance photographs of the front steps and porch. He had memorized the lighting conditions, both with the porch light on and the porch light off. Tonight, she had left it off. The steps were lighted only by the glow of a street lamp forty feet away. Forty-one, to be exact.

Gloves on, he reached inside his pocket for the house key. It had been easy enough to get it. Peyton's husband valeted his car at the same restaurant every Thursday and was stupid enough to hand over his whole set of keys. Rudy had taken a job there just long enough to trace the key to their front door.

His hand shook only slightly. This was a huge step, but he was ready. He grasped the key firmly and aimed it at the lock. Gently, he touched the key to the metal and circled the opening, as if teasing before entering. With a steady hand he guided the tip to the opening and let it fall into the hole just the slightest bit, barely inside, and held it there for several seconds. He felt a sudden urge to ram it home but didn't. He drew a deep breath and inserted it slowly, one click of the lock's tumblers at a time. The adrenaline flowed as the fit grew tighter. A perfect union, so gratifying, so metaphorical. His eyes closed as it slid past the halfway point, deeper and deeper with each passing second. When the tips of his gloved fingers touched the metal casing of the lock he knew he was in. All the way in. Never in his life had he felt so connected to another human being, just knowing she was on the other side. The sensation was almost unbelievable, so he touched himself to make sure and nearly groaned with delight: He was *enormous*.

His eyes opened, and a thin smile crept to his lips. Slowly, but a little faster than he had entered, he pulled out the key and gave it a gentle kiss before tucking it away. His heart pounded, and he could feel the change inside him. He was losing all fear of doing the things that he knew she wanted done to her. His only remaining fear was that he might yet be less than perfect.

He could wait for perfection.

"Good night, Peyton," he said softly. Then quietly, he climbed down the steps and vanished into the night.

Part I

WINTER

PEYTON SHIELDS COULD FEEL IT COMING. NO ONE HAD TIPPED HER off. No neon lights were blinking. But her sixth sense was in high gear.

Peyton was in her first year of residency in pediatric medicine at Children's Hospital, Boston, one of an elite thirty-seven interns chosen from premier medical schools around the world. She'd vaulted to the top through relentless drive, stellar academic credentials, and a mountain of debt to Harvard Medical School. Good instincts, too, were part of the successful package, and at the moment they were telling her that something strange lay ahead.

She parked her car in the space marked PHYSICIAN outside the North Shore clinic, about thirty miles north of Boston in the city of Haverhill. Peyton was at that stage of her professional training where pediatric residents spent three or four days each month at an outlying clinic to broaden their experience. Haverhill was somewhat of a plum as far as clinical assignments went, situated in the affluent Merrimack Valley. Driving out in any direction, you were virtually guaranteed to run smack into a quaint, three-hundred-year-old town whose 98 percent white population earned more than double the state's median annual income. Though not the most charming in the valley, the city was an interesting mix of one of the finest Queen Anne–style streetscapes in America and blue-collar housing that had grown from the once-prominent shoe industry. With roughly 10 percent of its population living below the poverty level, the routine medical needs of its Medicaid children were served primarily by the clinic. Today, that meant primarily by Peyton.

"What are you two doing outside?" asked Peyton as she stepped out of the car.

It was a fair question. Even though it was a sunny fifty-six degrees—a heat wave for late February—it was highly irregular for Felicia and Leticia Browning to be caught chitchatting outside the front door at nine-thirty in the morning. The clinic's two full-time nurses were identical twins with polar-opposite personalities. Felicia was the more serious sister and a frequent pain in the neck.

"Power's out," said Leticia, giggling as usual.

"That's weird. All the traffic lights were working on my way over here."

"Cuz you was coming from the south," said Felicia. "Power's out from here north."

"What happened?"

"Earthquake," said Leticia. More giggles.

"Very funny."

"No joke," said Felicia. "We're on the southern edge of what they call the active zone, thirty miles north of Boston and on up to Clinton. Two dozen quakes in the last twenty-one years. Usually little bitty ones, like this."

"How do you know all that?"

"We'll always know more than you," said Felicia, only half-kidding. "We're nurses."

Leticia pulled a battery-powered radio from her sister's coat pocket. "They just interviewed a Boston College seismologist on the air."

"Shut up, fool," said Felicia.

"Ah," said Peyton, seeing they really weren't yanking her chain. "I take it there's no backup generator for this place."

Leticia just laughed. Her sister said, "Dr. Simons canceled his morning appointments and went home over an hour ago."

Good ol' Doc Simons. He ran the clinic, but hands-on he was not. To him, carpe diem meant "seize the day *off*."

The three women looked at each other in silence, as if soliciting ideas on how to keep busy. Peyton was about to walk inside when a car sped into the parking lot and screeched to a halt. The driver's-side door flew open and a teenage girl jumped out with a baby in her arms.

"Somebody—help my son!" She looked barely old enough to drive and sounded even younger. Peyton ran to her and gathered the baby in her arms.

"How old is he?"

"Twenty-one months," she said in a panicky voice. "His name's TJ. He got stuck with a needle."

"Are you his mother?"

"Yeah. My name's Grace."

"Take him to Room A," said Felicia. "It's got plenty of sunlight."

Peyton hurried inside, stepping carefully through the dimly lit hall. The baby's cry was weak, as if he'd wailed to the point of exhaustion. They slid the examination table closer to the window to take advantage of the streaming sunlight, then laid the boy on it.

"Needle went in right there," said Grace, pointing at his leg.

Felicia aimed a flashlight. Peyton noticed a minor puncture wound inside the thigh. "What kind of needle was it?"

"Sewing needle. About an inch long."

"Did you bring it with you?"

"It's still in his leg."

Peyton looked closely but still didn't see it. "You sure?"

"The very tip was sticking out at first. I tried to work it out, you know, like a sliver. But it disappeared inside him."

Leticia slipped a small blood-pressure cuff onto the boy's right arm and pumped it. "You're sure it was a sewing needle, child?"

"What else would it be?"

Felicia grabbed the girl's wrists and rolled up her sleeves. "Show me your arms."

Grace resisted, but Felicia was much stronger. "I'm no druggy. Leave me alone."

The arms were trackless, but Felicia wasn't finished. "You shoot between your toes, girl? Or is it your boyfriend who does the drugs and leaves his needles laying around?"

"Nobody is on drugs, so just go to hell!"

Peyton was about to side with the girl, but then she noticed the marks on the backs of her legs just below the hemline of her skirt. "Is that blood behind your knees?"

Grace backed away. The nurse grabbed her and hiked up her skirt. The backs of her thighs were pockmarked with bloody needle holes.

"What is going on here, child?" said Felicia.

"My boyfriend did it."

"Did what?" asked Peyton.

"We got in a fight. He started jabbing me with this stick of his, so I grabbed TJ and ran out the door. He got TJ in the leg, and the needle broke off when I jerked away."

"What kind of stick has a sewing needle on it?"

"He made it himself. A broomstick with a needle on the end of it. He uses it when I jog."

"Excuse me?"

She lowered her eyes, as if embarrassed. "I got fat when I was pregnant and couldn't lose it after TJ was born. So he makes me jog. He uses the stick to keep me going."

"You mean like a cattle prod?" asked Leticia.

"Who the hell is your boyfriend?" said Peyton. "I want to meet this chump."

"Believe me. You don't want to meet him."

The baby started crying. Peyton sterilized her hands and gently palpated the leg, starting at the entry wound and inching her way up. "Does it hurt here, little fella?"

"What are you doing?" Grace asked.

"Trying to locate the needle. It seems to have traveled beneath the skin away from the point of entry. It if doesn't exit on its own, it might work its way into the bloodstream."

"Gross," said Grace, grimacing. "It'll rip up his little veins."

She was still too much of a kid to grasp the gravity of it. Peyton said, "My real concern is that it could travel to his heart."

"Then you gotta get it out."

Leticia said, "We can't X-ray without electricity. He has to go to the hospital."

"No way," said Grace. "It could hit his little heart by the time I get him there."

"Hold on," said Peyton. "I think I got it." Gently, she pressed two fingers against his inner thigh. TJ cried as it poked from beneath. Peyton could feel the blunt end of the needle just below the skin.

"Get me a little lidocaine, please."

"You're not going to cut him open," said Felicia.

"With his mother's consent, I will. Just a teeny incision, and it will pop right out."

"Do it," said Grace.

"Don't you dare," said Felicia. "You're an intern in pediatric medicine. Even surgical residents can't do surgery without a supervisory physician."

"This isn't surgery. You're being silly."

"Silly is a know-it-all doctor who oversteps her authority and puts this clinic at risk of losing its malpractice coverage."

Peyton simply injected the local anesthetic and said, "Scalpel, please."

"This is your neck," said Felicia. "You know this is against the rules."

Leticia held the flashlight. Peyton made a minuscule opening, more of a poke than a slice. It barely bled. With the slightest encouragement, the needle's eye emerged.

"Tweezers," said Peyton. She grabbed the end and pulled it straight out, then placed it on the table in front of Felicia. "There you go. I think I'm ready to move on to kidney transplants now, don't you?"

"Go for it," said Felicia. "I'll add it to my incident report." She left the room in a huff.

Peyton shook her head and finished the job. The baby's crying was plentiful, but the bleeding was minimal. A Band-Aid might have been sufficient, but to be safe, Peyton closed the small incision with liquid stitches. It took only a minute. Leticia dressed it with sterile gauze.

Grace hugged her. "Thank you. You saved TJ's life."

"Well, I wouldn't exactly say that."

The young mother held her son tightly. His crying soon turned to coos.

Their contentment ended with a skidding sound from the gravel parking lot outside, followed by the slamming of a car door. Grace ran to the window.

"It's Jake!"

"Grace!" he shouted as he started across the parking lot.

"Hide me. He's crazy!"

Peyton glanced outside. A young, muscular man was charging toward the door, armed with that infamous pointy stick. "In the closet," said Peyton. She pushed the mother and her baby inside and shut the door.

"I know you're in here, Grace!" He was in the reception area.

Leticia grabbed Peyton's cell phone. "I'm calling nine-one-one."

Grace shouted from inside the closet, "We'll all be dead by the time they get here!"

Peyton feared she was right. She knew Doc Simons had faced situations like this before, and she knew where he kept his gun. She hesitated for an instant, then ran to his office and unlocked the drawer. There was barely enough light, but she found the Smith & Wesson. She checked, and it was loaded.

"What are you doing?" asked Felicia, her eyes wide with panic.

"We can't stand by and watch a teenage mother get beat to death with a stick."

"You're crazy to get in the middle of this."

Grace screamed in the next room. Peyton wasn't a big fan of guns, but there was no time to wait for the police. "Maybe I am," she said, almost to herself.

She ran as fast as she could only to find Jake—all six foot six of him—yanking Grace from the closet, poised to slam her head against the wall.

"Stop right there!" Peyton held the gun with both hands, aiming at his chest.

He released his grip. Grace grabbed her crying baby and rushed to Peyton's side. Jake took a half-step forward, challenging them.

"Not another move!" said Peyton.

"As if you know how to use that thing," Jake said, smirking.

"The jar!" she shouted, and with one quick move she fired a shot that shattered the jar of cotton balls resting on the shelf behind his ear.

His eyes turned the size of silver dollars.

"My daddy was a cop, jerk. Now get down on the floor, face-first."

He quickly complied. "How much do you weigh?" Peyton demanded.

"Huh?"

"Just answer the question."

"Two-seventy."

"Leticia!"

"What?" came the muffled reply. She was hiding under a desk.

"Get me the secobarbital sodium. Full adult dosage plus five milliliters."

In thirty seconds, Leticia had the syringe in hand. "Stick him," said Peyton.

The nurse glanced at Grace and her needle-pricked baby. "With pleasure," she said, then gave him a good jolt to the right buttock.

He flinched and muttered a few obscenities, and then his body slowly relaxed. The room fell silent. It seemed to take a long time, but in ninety seconds he was out.

"Thank you," said Grace.

Peyton began to shake, finally hit by the full impact of what she'd just done. "Where the hell are the cops?"

"I'll call nine-one-one again," said Leticia. "Must be lots of calls with the power outage."

A groan suddenly emerged from Dr. Simons's office down the hall, followed by intense cursing. Peyton hurried out, opened the unlocked door, and froze. Felicia was hunched over the examination table, feet on the floor. Her pants were pulled halfway down her large buttocks, and she was applying gauze to the left side. Across the room, Peyton noticed the waist-high bullet hole in the wallpaper. The warning shot she'd fired at the jar of cotton balls had passed through two interior walls. It couldn't have been traveling very fast by the time it reached Dr. Simons's office on the other side of the clinic, but evidently it had been going fast enough.

"You shot me in the ass," said Felicia, groaning.

"Let me help you."

"Stay away. It barely nicked me. Lucky for you."

She didn't feel lucky. Just the fact that it could have been serious made her queasy. "It was . . . an accident," she said, her voice cracking. "I didn't want to hurt anybody. He was coming at me. If I hadn't fired a warning shot, he might have grabbed the gun from me."

"You should have thought of that before you went running for the gun in the first place."

"Felicia, I am so sorry."

"Don't give me sorry."

Peyton stepped into the hall, as if driven back by Felicia's glare. Outside were police sirens, finally. Peyton held her breath, dreading what Felicia might tell them.

"Oh, boy," she said quietly, dying inside.

"GANGWAY!"

A nurse rushed by with a girl in a wheelchair. Peyton quickly dodged out of the way with a nifty little two-step. It was a familiar dance in these busy halls. Emergency was no place for lead feet.

Children's Hospital was one of the largest emergency/trauma centers in New England, each year treating more than 12,000 injured children and recording more than 50,000 patient visits in its emergency department. Peyton felt like 49,000 of them had been recorded in the last week, though this morning was relatively quiet. A teenager in Exam 1 was vomiting nonstop, partly into a big green bucket, mostly onto an intern. The little girl in Exam 2 was crying with a broken arm. The infant in triage was screaming inconsolably, her concerned mother rocking her in her arms. Experience had taught Peyton to enjoy the occasional morning lull, the one time of day when staffing was relatively high and the caseload might actually approach some level of sanity. Like it or not, the emergency department was one of thirteen required rotations for interns over the course of the year. Peyton was just one week into it with three more to go. Her only break so far had been the one-day trip to Haverhill and Nurse Felicia. Some break.

It had been four days since the shooting at the clinic. Felicia's butt was fine, but she was after Peyton's in a big way. Nothing like being on the wrong end of a million-dollar civil lawsuit to launch a young doctor's career. The fight was now in the hands of lawyers. She'd be reassigned to a new clinic, for sure. She just prayed to God she wouldn't get fired.

She reached for a patient chart, but a senior resident beat her to it.

"I got it," he said. "Dr. Landau is looking for you."

Her heart sank. Landau was the residency program director. "What for?"

"I don't know. I just ran into him in the lounge. He was grumbling to Dr. Sheffield about some meeting you missed. Not in a good mood."

Sheffield was the chief resident. This wasn't looking good.

"If you hurry you might catch them."

Butterflies churned in her belly. *This is it. I'm getting canned.*

She crossed the main lobby, passing the huge saltwater aquarium and the life-size ceramic giraffe that was perched behind the reception desk. The giraffe usually made her smile, but too much was on her mind as she opened the door and entered the pavilion lounge.

"Surprise!"

Peyton started, then smiled at the group of nurses and doctors that had squeezed into the small lounge to surprise her. Inflated latex gloves dangled from the ceiling as makeshift balloons. A computer-printed banner from the billing department read HAPPY BIRTHDAY, PEYTON! She recognized almost everyone, a few from the ER but most of them from prior rotations.

"My birthday was last week," said Peyton.

"But then you wouldn't have been surprised," said one of the interns.

"Good point." She smiled, then subtly rolled her eyes. "Sort of."

A nurse poured her a glass of sparkling grape juice, the on-duty version of champagne. The door swung open, and in marched a clown to a round of applause. Clowns were a common sight at Children's, where laughter was a proven therapy for ailing children. This one was a mime dressed in a black tuxedo with a matching bow tie and cummerbund of red-and-white polka dots. The hair was slicked back. His face was painted white with stars on both cheeks.

He set his boom box on the floor and, without a word, pointed to Peyton from across the lounge. With encouragement from her friends, she stepped forward. The mime switched on the music—the tango.

Peyton shrank with embarrassment at the thought of tangoing with, literally, a clown. But he was suddenly Valentino, circling her, giving her the eye. From inside his jacket he snatched a single red rose. Down on one knee, he presented it to Peyton.

"Go for it, girl!" a nurse shouted.

As if on cue, she assumed the classic tango pose, the rose clenched between her teeth. Her friends roared as, cheek to cheek, the dancers darted from one end of the room to the other in surprisingly smooth tango steps. He laid her back over his arm for the final pretend kiss.

The crowd hooted. The chief resident smiled and said, "Peyton, please, this *is* a children's hospital."

The mime snatched the rose and, like magic, handed her a cupcake with a burning candle. The impressed crowd ooohed and broke into an impromptu rendition of "Happy Birthday" in various keys. Peyton blew out the candle to more applause.

"Thank you, all of you."

The door swung open once more, this time for one of the trauma nurses who'd stayed behind in the ER. The expression on her face said it all. "Auto accident. Looks pretty bad. Four kids, one adult. Paramedics are bringing them inside."

The fizz was suddenly gone from their sparkling grape juice. Peyton's trauma-team leader said, "Fun while it lasted. Let's go."

The others stayed put as the ER folks quickly dispersed. Peyton rushed for the door with the rest of them. Out of the corner of her eye she caught sight of the mime, his bemused expression evident even through the thick clown makeup and painted-on stars.

"Thanks," said Peyton.

He just looked at her, ever silent. The lack of response made her slightly uncomfortable, but she kept moving forward. On her way out, she glanced back. He was still watching her.

She sprinted across the main lobby to the ER. The adrenaline kicked in immediately, sparked by the paramedic's announcement of the first victim's arrival: "Eleven-year-old white male. Head trauma, numerous lacerations, broken right fibula."

"Shields, with me! Trauma One."

Nearly at full speed, Peyton followed a team of paramedics wheeling the gurney down the wide hall. Behind her, a cold winter wind poured in from the open emergency entrance, where another ambulance was pulling up. Ahead, the team leader shouted out commands and led the way to the trauma center. In her mind Peyton was already envisioning the patient, the injuries, the treatment. Just before her team made the final turn around the corner, however, she spotted him again.

Her birthday mime was standing outside the hospital's main entrance, peering into the ER through the curved wall of plate-glass windows that lined the separate ER waiting room. She kept moving, trying to focus on the crisis at hand, somewhat unsettled by all that staring. Perhaps he was just intrigued by the general chaos, though he seemed fixated on her, the way she could almost feel his gaze.

"Shields!"

She started at the sound of her team leader's voice, then ducked into the trauma room, no more distractions, no more looking back.

3

NO ONE DIED TONIGHT, AT LEAST NOT ON HER WATCH. THAT MADE the second half of her twenty-hour day a success, Peyton supposed. The first half was another story. They'd lost an eleven-year-old boy. A wonderful euphemism, "lost." As if he were a misplaced mitten or a hapless tourist. He wasn't somehow going to find his way back and miraculously reappear. There was no way to wordsmith around the permanence of such events. She knew that. She had called the code herself.

Time of death, 10:37 A.M.

Long before she'd set foot in the hospital, even before she'd entered Harvard Medical School, Peyton knew that she wanted to practice pediatric medicine. She'd chosen Children's Hospital for her residency because it was the best. As her proud father boasted daily to the world, they'd chosen Peyton for the exact same reason. Even the best, however, occasionally lost a patient.

There it was again, that fudge word. *He's dead, Peyton.* Two days before his twelfth birthday. Seat belts couldn't save everyone. Neither could she.

The wiper blades squeaked across the windshield, pushing the slushy mess aside. Big wet flakes were falling in the darkness, perfect white crystals that splattered on the glass like nature's little kamikazes. It was the first substantial snowfall of the year, and Peyton was one of the first to feel its icy grip on the streets. She was the lone motorist, a little unusual even for three A.M. Two hours of steadily falling snow and the threat of up to twelve inches more in the next twenty-four hours had left the streets more deserted than she'd ever seen them. Peyton wouldn't have ventured outdoors either, if her parents hadn't lived right there in Brookline. With her husband out of town on business, she decided to ride out the storm at her folks' house. Talking to her dad would do her some good after an exhausting shift that had included her first . . . fatality.

There, she'd said it. In her mind at least. Long ago she had come to terms with the fact that a career in pediatrics wasn't all smiles and lollipops. She knew there would be dead children, some patients of her own. This one, however, had affected her deeply, and not just because it was her first. Medically speaking, she and her supervisory physician had done all they could for the boy. No mistakes. There was nothing they wished they had done differently. Dealing with the kid's parents, however, was another story.

She wished she hadn't told them their son would be all right.

She stopped at the traffic light, entranced by the *wump-wump* rhythm of the snow-laden wipers. There was little cross traffic on Avenue Pasteur. Drivers were clearly heeding the winter-storm advisory. Still, she had to stop at a red light that some idiot had programmed to turn red for no reason at all. It must have been a traffic engineer who'd conceived managed care.

The unexpected stop was a chance to dial in for messages on her cell phone. She tried once and got "no service." The storm, she figured. She tried again and reached her voice mail. The first three messages were unimportant. The fourth was from her husband, a quick reminder that he would be in Providence until the following afternoon, so she didn't have to worry about him traveling home in the bad weather. The guilt set in. Yesterday morning, the last thing they'd talked about was how they used to make a real effort to spend time together before he went out of town on business. Now it was a bonus if she was even home to kiss him goodbye as he headed off to the airport.

And tonight he'd gone to bed in some lonely hotel room without her even returning his phone call to say good night.

She was debating whether it would be spontaneous or obnoxious to wake him at 3:00 A.M. to say *I love you*, but the next message killed the moment, hitting her like ice water. It was Felicia from the Haverhill clinic.

"I just thought it would be fair to give you a heads-up. I've decided to file criminal charges against you. Reckless endangerment. If you have any questions, have your lawyer call mine."

The smugness galled her. Felicia obviously had herself one clever lawyer, someone who wouldn't think twice about trampling a young doctor's career to extort a larger settlement from the hospital Peyton worked for. She wished now that she had spoken to Dr. Simons. He was a man of reason. Perhaps he could have nipped this in the bud before Felicia had picked up the phone and dialed 1-800-LAWSUIT. Maybe it wasn't too late. She would drive out to the clinic and talk to him personally, first thing in the morning. But that didn't seem soon enough. Patience was not one of Peyton's virtues. She needed to do something *right now* to atone for not having done enough earlier. About all she could think of was a call to Dr. Simons's answering service to let him know she would be there when the clinic opened.

The traffic light changed as the call went through. She accelerated slowly as she turned through the snowy intersection, holding the phone in one hand, steering with the other.

"Hello, this is Dr. Peyton Shields."

"The clinic is closed now."

"Yes, I know. Could you connect me with Dr. Simons's voice mail, please?"

"One moment," she said, then switched Peyton over.

This is Dr. Hugh Simons . . .

As Peyton listened to the recorded greeting, a large vehicle zipped past her at weather-defying speed, spewing a wave of road slush that covered her entire car. It had nearly sideswiped her. Just as the greeting ended and the tone sounded, she muttered, "Asshole."

She froze, realizing it was on tape.

Peyton, you idiot!

She debated whether to start over, but whenever she felt herself getting in too deep, she remembered what her father referred to as the first rule of holes: stop digging. She switched off the phone, tossed it on the passenger seat, and gripped the wheel with both hands.

She was driving south on Jamaicaway, a winding two-lane road that hugged the eastern perimeter of Olmsted Park. The area was one of old wealth with parks created by the likes of Frederick Law Olmsted, famed designer of New York's Central Park. Peyton's parents lived just beyond the Country Club—literally, *the* country club, forerunner of hundreds of such establishments across the nation. This was not the neighborhood Peyton had grown up in, not with a cop for a father. But her mother was a savvy real estate agent who had traded up all her life. By the time Peyton was seventeen, the family had finally arrived, dragged by her mother. Peyton would have just as soon moved back to the South End, where neighbors weren't afflicted with acute "Ima-itis," as in "I'm a Clayborn" or "I'm a Walpole." As if she cared.

The street only darkened as she continued along the park's tree-lined border. Jamaica Pond was somewhere beyond the blinding snowfall. Traffic was nonexistent, but ahead in the distance she noticed a pair of glowing fuzzy dots that soon revealed themselves as taillights. Perhaps the snow was playing tricks on her, but they seemed to be approaching at a high rate of speed *in reverse*—a dangerous move under any weather conditions on winding Jamaicaway, utter madness tonight. Peyton slowed her own car, though not too suddenly, fearing that she might send herself into a tail-spin. The wet snow fell even harder against the windshield. The wind was kicking up. She adjusted the wiper speed, and just as she did, the vehicle was gone. Strange. She hadn't noticed it back into a driveway or a side street. She flipped her lights to high beam and spotted him just a hundred yards ahead, coming even faster. Her heart leapt to her throat. The headlamps were off.

Peyton flashed her lights, fearing he was drunk. No response, but the car kept coming. Just a half block away, she flashed her lights again. A return of the high beams nearly blinded her. She averted her eyes, but it was impossible to escape. The lights hit her squarely in the face. Squarely.

He's in my lane!

She laid on the horn as the car bore down at even greater speed, seemingly determined to strike her head-on. In a panic she hit the accelerator and swerved to the right, which instantly sent her car spinning in circles on the icy road, completely out of control. The car sped past her, steady on its course, seeming to retrace her tire tracks in the snow. Peyton's car bounced off a guardrail. The air bag exploded in her face, then collapsed in her lap, but her car kept sliding to the opposite side of the street. It was as if she were peering out from the center of a spiraling tornado—spinning, swirling, the headlights cutting across the black night and blinding snow. The front end slammed into a concrete abutment, but momentum carried the whole car right over the top. It tipped and nearly rolled over, righted itself, then skidded down the snow-covered embankment.

Peyton's arms flailed, her whole body jerked, her head slammed forward and back against the headrest. Glass shattered all around her—the side windows, the windshield, an explosion of sharp pellets. Her face was suddenly tingling, wet and warm. She could see nothing, hear nothing, not even her own screams. The rolling and skidding stopped with an ominous thud, but the impact seemed cushioned, as if the battered vehicle had landed in a snowbank. Peyton couldn't tell if she was right side up, wasn't even sure she was conscious. It was as if she were drifting, still moving in slow motion. Her feet felt cold, then her ankles and shins too. It was that wet feeling again. Not the hot, wet feeling that had enveloped her face. This was cold, icy cold. Her car had landed in no snow bank. She was indeed floating. Water was everywhere.

The pond!

She splashed her face to clear away the blood and was suddenly wide awake. The frigid flood was already knee-deep, and still more was seeping in through the doors and floor. The water had a distinct reddish tint that she realized was her own blood. In a moment of panic she tried the door, but it wouldn't budge. She released the seat belt but couldn't move. Her leg was pinned beneath the wreckage somewhere below the steering wheel. She pulled hard, harder still. The dashboard lights flickered on and off, then out for good. Blood continued to seep into her eyes, effectively blinding her, but with the car lights dead it was too dark to see anyway. The water was rising, the car was sinking. Though her limbs were going numb she kept pulling, fighting with every ounce of strength to loosen her trapped foot. The water inched upward to the top of her thighs, the hips. She screamed for help, "Somebody, please!" But it was hardly a scream. With little strength left, she was shivering, minutes away from shock. She tried another cry for help, but her voice only cracked. She felt herself slipping away, then she rebounded once more as that cold, wet sensation rose to her waist. It chilled her belly, the slightly protruding tummy, unleashing tears and one final plea in a voice barely audible.

"*Help me*," she said as she slumped over the wheel.

A pounding noise startled her. She could barely lift her head, but out of the corner of her eye she saw someone beside her. He was standing waist-deep in the frigid water, pulling hard at the twisted car door. She wanted to say something. She felt her mouth moving, but it was an uncontrolled movement, as if her body no longer would follow commands. She reached inside for strength and tried to focus, but her vision was still blurred by the blood that was now freezing to her face. The car door opened a few inches but wouldn't budge any farther. The window was gone; the glass had been shattered in the crash. She suddenly felt a strong grip around her shoulders. Her body lifted from the seat, which made her cry out in pain. Her foot was still caught down below, somewhere beneath the cold, rising water. Her leg straightened. The pulling continued. The foot wouldn't budge, but the pain was gone. The man was gone, too.

Help me! she heard herself cry, though she doubted anyone heard it.

The man was suddenly back, this time at the passenger side. Her sight seemed better on this side, the right eye less obscured by the blood. The door opened, but no water rushed in. The car was only half submerged, she realized, the rear end clinging to the snowy shoreline. Still, the water had risen above her waist. All sensation in her feet was gone. She felt as though she were floating, as though the vehicle no longer had a grip on her.

With a sudden jerk the foot dislodged. She exploded from the seat, her whole body sailing across the front seat and out the open passenger door. She was moving, being carried, she knew, but she was limp in his arms. She felt the wind and snow on her face, but the sense of movement ceased. She lay on her back in a blanket of fresh snow. In the darkness she could discern the image of the man standing over her. Her vision was nearly gone. She strained to listen, as she sensed he would naturally say something. She could hear the wind rushing beneath the bridge behind her. But he said nothing, at least nothing she heard. He simply removed his coat and covered her with it. And then he walked away.

Peyton propped herself up on one elbow, watching. She called to him, begged him, *Don't go! Please, come back!* But he kept walking, never looking back.

She leaned back, nearly fell into the snowbank. It was red, she noticed, where the white snow had conformed to the shape of her head. The sight of her own blood didn't faze her. Her own injuries were of secondary concern. She stared into the night sky, into the swirling snow, and one fear consumed her.

"Jamie," she said weakly, then gave in to the darkness.

4

KEVIN STOKES WOKE AT 4:17 A.M. AND PEERED ACROSS THE HOTEL
room. His eyes adjusted to the darkness to reveal the evidence
before him. An assortment of empty liquor bottles stood on the
nightstand, all from the minibar. His clothes lay beside the bed in a
heap, right beside hers, right where they had hastily undressed one
another some six hours ago. He prayed to God that he was dream-
ing, but he knew that he wasn't. Too many regrets for one dream.

Sandra had insisted on keeping the bedroom cool—"frisky,"
she called it—but he was warm now beneath the fluffy down
comforter, beside the slender naked body beside him. She slept
on her left side, her back to him. His arm was pinned beneath the
curve of her waist, and his fingers tingled with a thousand needles
from the cutoff circulation. Gently, so as not to wake her, he slid
his hand out from under her, his nearly numb fingers gliding across
the firmness of her bottom. The contrast was remarkable, such soft
skin in such a hard place. Hot, quite literally. It wasn't the kind of
body he'd expected to find beneath those boring gray lawyer suits
she wore to the office. Nothing last night had been what he'd
expected. Now that he was sober, one thought consumed him.

I gotta get out of here.

He pulled his hand free. Her elbow jerked like a catapult and
caught him in the chin. His head snapped back and slammed
against the headboard.

"Ow, shit!"

Suddenly awake, she was half-sitting up, propped up on that wicked elbow. "What's wrong?" she asked with alarm.

The confused look told him she wasn't even aware she'd whacked him. He stretched his jaw, popping it back into place. "You sleep like a Navy SEAL on the ready."

"What are you talking about?"

"Nothing. Go back to sleep."

She shook her head as if he were insane, but she was too drowsy to debate it. Her cheek sank deep into the pillow as she almost instantly returned to sleep.

Kevin sat up against the headboard, eyes wide open. Cold air poured in from the window. It was open just a crack, enough to cool down the room the way Sandra liked it. But it was too cold. The weather had been horrendous all day, and from the sounds of the wind whistling outside, it must have only gotten worse.

I hate Boston.

He suddenly remembered that he wasn't in Boston. He was in Providence, Rhode Island, but to Kevin it was all the same icebox. Cold was something he couldn't get used to. Kevin was a native of the Conch Republic, better known as Key West, Florida. He had grown up in T-shirts and shorts on a balmy island, lived his first eighteen years in a veritable paradise, where it was front-page news if either the air or surf dipped below seventy-two degrees. Winter had been unbearable for him even in Tallahassee, where he'd gone to college and then law school at Florida State University. It was during his second year of law school that he'd fallen for a beautiful and downright brilliant undergraduate whose heart was set more on a career than marriage. She'd married him only on the condition that they move to Boston after graduation so she could attend Harvard Medical School. At the time he would have taken an igloo on the Yukon to complete the nuptials. He was top-ten percent and law review at FSU, credentials good enough to have landed him with the finest law firms in Miami or Atlanta. He sent résumés to all the blue-chip firms in Boston but soon discovered that the big northeastern firms weren't overly impressed by southern law schools, at least not the ones that didn't count Thomas Jefferson among their alumni. Not a single job offer. He could have lowered his sights and landed with some fine smaller firms, but with Peyton's success that would have seemed like failure.

It was autumn, five years ago, when he and his new wife had first come up to look for an apartment, Kevin still without a job. For kicks, they attended a Harvard football game, some pathetic matchup between two Ivy League teams that would have lost to the FSU Seminoles' second-string cheerleaders. Harvard got pounded 42–0, a score he remembered for reasons that any right-minded sports fan might think ridiculous. Forty-two points meant six touchdowns and six extra points. A dozen scores by the opposing team, and with each one the Harvard student section responded in unison with the same loud cheer, an arrogant celebration that, for Kevin, summed up his job-hunting difficulties.

That's all right, that's okay,
you're gonna work for US someday!

It hadn't helped matters that, by the fifth touchdown, his own wife was caught up in the excitement and joining in the chant.

With the help of one of his Harvard-educated law professors, he did finally land an interview with a prestigious two-hundred-lawyer firm, Marston & Wheeler. He impressed them enough to earn the chance to bill more than 3,000 hours a year in pursuit of the elusive brass ring, though he realized that making partner without the Ivy League pedigree would be an uphill battle. Kevin figured that if he worked hard and showed them what he could do, he'd get a fair shot. But the last five years had only proven that the firm's caste system was based almost entirely on sheepskin. Clients hired Marston & Wheeler and paid the big bucks to be represented by Ivy League lawyers—end of story. It didn't matter how good he was; Kevin was not on partnership track.

God, I hate Boston.

The bedroom chill was getting unbearable. The one-inch crack Sandra had raised the window at bedtime was now an Arctic pipeline. He slid from beneath the covers, taking care not to disturb the kick boxer beside him. The tile floor beneath his feet felt like a hockey rink. He tiptoed quickly toward the open window and, in the darkness, promptly smashed his toes into a chair leg. He grunted but didn't shout, hopping on one foot, doing his best not to wake Sandra. The phone rang. Not the phone on the nightstand. It was a higher-pitched ring, barely audible, seemingly muffled. It was coming from the pocket of his suit coat, the coat that was draped over that chair—that *damn* chair.

He fumbled for the phone, hurried to the far side of the room away from Sandra, and answered as quietly as he could. "Hello."

"Is this Kevin Stokes?" the woman asked.

He whispered through clenched teeth, still in pain. "Yes. Who is this?"

"I'm calling from Brigham and Women's Hospital. You're married to Dr. Peyton Shields?"

He glanced across the room at the curves beneath the covers, then looked away. "Yeah. But she works out of Children's Hospital. What's this about?"

"Your wife's been in a car accident."

He was suddenly frozen, though oblivious to the cold. "Is she—"

"She's in the intensive care unit."

"Is she going to be all right?"

"That's all the information I have right now, sir. You're welcome to come down to the hospital and speak to the doctor."

"Yes, I will. You're next to Children's, right?"

"Yes. Check in with the receptionist on the first floor."

"Thank you. I'll be there as soon as I can." He switched off the phone and noticed Sandra sitting up in bed.

"What's wrong?" she asked.

He ignored her, went to the chair, and slipped on his pants and shoes.

"Kevin," she said sternly, "what's wrong?"

"I have to go."

"Why?"

"Emergency. I have to get back to Boston." He hastily buttoned his shirt, got the holes wrong, and started over.

"What kind of emergency?"

He felt a chill against his back. The window was still open. He reached over and slammed it shut. "It's Peyton. I have to go right now."

"You're being paranoid."

He had neither the time nor the stomach for a debate. He grabbed the car keys from atop the dresser. "I need to take the rental car, okay?"

"What?"

"You'll have to cover today's meetings alone. I'll explain later."

He hurried out the door and ran down the hall to his own room. If only he had just stayed there after dinner and told Sandra that he was too tired to go back to her room and "prepare for tomorrow's meeting." He felt like kicking himself, but instead he grabbed his briefcase and travel bag and headed for the elevator. Naturally, it was out of service. He flew down the stairwell, taking two or three steps at a time. He was nearly running, driven as much by the need to reach Peyton at the hospital as the desire to flee from Sandra and this terrible mistake. How the hell his marriage had ended up here he wasn't quite sure. He could have blamed Peyton for making it so easy. When he told her about the trip, she hadn't even bothered to write down where he'd be staying or ask when he'd return. He simply got the same old " 'Bye, hon, see you when you get back." Peyton had no time to talk, no time to listen, no time for sex, no time for anything that didn't involve pediatric medicine. Was it his fault that he couldn't stand the loneliness?

He gave the exit door a shove at the bottom of the stairwell, then needed to shove again, harder. The wind was that strong. It nearly blew him over as he stepped outside, chilling him instantly. The street was a sheet of ice beneath a foot of fresh snow, and the snow was still falling. Cars were indiscernible white mounds. He tried one, then another, unable to tell which of the generic American sedans was the one he and Sandra had rented. On the third try he dropped the key ring into the snow. He kicked around in the cold blanket of white but couldn't find a thing. He got down on his knees and searched frantically till his bare fingers were numb. He found the keys, finally, and tried the door. The lock was iced over. With the key he chiseled at it, then forced the lock and gave the frozen door a yank. As it creaked open, snow fell from the roof like an avalanche, covering his head and slipping inside his shirt collar and down his back. The mountain on the windshield was too heavy for the wipers, so he grabbed the brush and cleared it away. Beneath the powder was a solid crust of ice. With a little plastic hand scraper he hacked away, so fast and furious his knuckles started to bleed. The clear patch was barely big enough for him to see out, but his fingers could stand no more. He jumped inside and fired the ignition. From under the hood came a lethargic murmur, then a click, then silence. He tried again. Nothing.

He stared out the icy windshield, through the tiny hole he had managed to scrape clean. Even inside the car, his breath crystallized. His hands were shaking. He sat shivering in the darkness, thinking of Peyton lying in the hospital barely clinging to life while he lay snug and warm in another woman's hotel room clinging to . . .

His eyes closed in shame and anger.

God, how I hate Boston.

He left the keys in the ignition, slammed the door, and trudged through the snow in search of a bus, a taxi, or maybe a damn dogsled.

5

KEVIN REACHED THE HOSPITAL JUST BEFORE 6:30 A.M. FOR THREE hundred bucks the hotel's night manager proved willing to risk his life and drive Kevin all the way to Boston. What was normally an hour's drive from Providence took nearly two and a half, and that was only because they'd lucked out and followed a snowplow most of the way. Not until he was trudging across the snowy sidewalk toward the windswept entrance did he fully appreciate what a total idiot he'd been. The one night on which he'd finally given in to Sandra's advances was the one night on which Peyton needed him most.

A blast of heat from the vents washed over him as he hurried into the lobby. In less than a minute he was dripping wet. Just in the short walk to the hospital entrance he'd accumulated enough snow and ice on his body to pass for Sasquatch.

"Kevin?"

It was Peyton's mother, Valerie, talking on the pay phone. She hung up and hurried toward him.

She looked beat, unlike the attractive woman she was. She and Peyton had the same exquisite face, the same expressive eyes. Kevin had seen all of the old photos of Peyton and Valerie dressed in matching holiday dresses, matching riding gear, matching bathing suits. It seemed to Kevin that the older Peyton got, the younger her mother tried to look, as if the ultimate goal were to become sisters.

"Where the heck have you been?"

Now there was an interesting question. "I came running as soon as the hospital called. How's Peyton?"

"She's pretty banged up, but she's going to be fine, thank goodness. Poor girl was so confused she couldn't even remember the name of your hotel in Providence. She wasn't even sure you told her before you left."

"I told her," said Kevin. "But she knows I can always be reached by cell. I leave it on even when the battery is charging."

"I've been dialing that number all night."

"I must have slept through the earlier calls."

Valerie seemed a tad suspicious. Perhaps Peyton had told him how they'd been growing apart lately. Or maybe she was just one heck of a rat-sniffer.

"Where's Hank?" he asked, meaning Peyton's father.

"Upstairs. I decided to get away from all that ICU stuff for a couple minutes. Makes me nervous."

"What are the doctors saying?"

"No broken bones, miraculously. Bad sprain to her ankle and a big gash in her leg. Twenty-six stitches in her right calf. That's where she had most of the blood loss. Leg wounds can be real bleeders, they tell me."

"She's going to be okay though?"

"Physically, yeah. Emotionally, we'll have to wait and see. She could have some scarring."

"Her leg, you mean?"

"Yes," she said, then looked off to the middle distance. "And the face."

Kevin nearly rocked on his heels. *That beautiful face.* "What happened?"

"Shattered glass," she said, her voice tightening. "On the left side. Don't really know how bad it is yet. They've got her bandaged up."

Kevin lowered his head, saying nothing.

"She's going to need lots of support from all of us," she

said. "I'm optimistic. Peyton's a tough kid. She's just never been through this kind of emotional trauma. What with the blood loss and everything."

"Why would blood loss be emotional?"

She just looked at him. Kevin asked, "Is there something you aren't telling me?"

"Well. It's like the doctor told me. When a woman loses a lot of blood real fast like that, it . . . you know."

"What?"

"Can cause a miscarriage."

"Miscarriage?"

"I'm sorry," she said. "She did lose the baby."

"Baby?"

Their eyes met. Her confusion slowly turned to anger as she said, "Peyton was in her eleventh week. You didn't know?"

"She didn't tell me."

She stepped closer, glaring. "Listen to me. Peyton didn't know the name of your hotel in Providence. I called you in the middle of the night and you didn't answer your cell phone. Now I find out you didn't even know your own wife was pregnant. I don't like what I'm sensing, so you'd better give me a straight answer. What in the devil is going on with you kids?"

He paused, searching for the right response. "We aren't kids anymore. Maybe that's what's going on."

Jamie. That was going to be the baby's name. It worked well for a boy or a girl, like her own name. Jamie Stokes. Or Jamie Shields. Depending on whether . . . well, that wasn't an issue anymore.

Peyton had been alert enough in the emergency room to tell them she was pregnant. She seemed to drift in and out of consciousness as they tended to her injuries, but she heard one of the doctors mention the need for a D & C—dilation and curettage. She knew she'd miscarried.

"Peyton?"

She tried to open her eyes, but one remained in darkness. Her good eye followed the plastic IV tubes from the bag to her arm, and slowly she started to realize where she was. She felt woozy but strong enough to check her bandage. It seemed huge, covering one eye and half of her forehead. A wave of panic washed over her at the thought of a serious facial injury.

"Kevin?" she said softly. She felt him squeeze her hand, then saw his face. She tried to smile, but her face was numb. At least half of it. The injured half. The God-only-knows-what-it-looks-like half. "What happened?"

"You were in a car accident."

She raised her head slightly from the pillow, as close as she could come to sitting up. "I know. What I meant was, what are they saying about my injuries?"

"The doctor can explain better than me. But she says you're gonna be just fine."

"Do I look fine?"

He didn't answer right away. "You look like the luckiest woman alive."

"Now you sound like my dad."

"Would you rather I sound like your mother?"

"Only if we double the painkillers." They shared a faint smile. Then slowly she scanned the room to gain her bearings. The equipment, the monitors, the sounds she knew from her training. "I'm still in intensive care."

"Only until your vital signs stabilize. You took a pretty good whack to the head, so they're not taking any chances."

"What time is it?"

"A little after nine."

"I feel like Rip Van Winkle."

"You're wiped out, I'm sure. You lost a lot of blood."

His words hung in the air, both of them aware of the bleeding's consequences. Bandages or not, she knew she wasn't doing a very good job of hiding the hurt expression on her face.

"I'm sorry about—"

"Let's not talk about that, okay?"

"I just don't understand. Why didn't you tell me you were pregnant?"

"I'm sorry. I was waiting for the right time to tell you."

"So why did the right time never seem to come along?"

"That's . . . complicated."

"I know there's been some distance between us lately. But things weren't really so bad that you couldn't tell me we were having a baby. Were they?"

"Do you love me?"

He showed some surprise in response to the question, but it didn't strike Peyton as all that genuine. She couldn't put her finger on it, but Kevin didn't seem to be acting like himself.

"You know I do," he said.

"No, I don't. The last few months, you don't even seem to like me anymore, let alone love me."

"Maybe things would have been different if I'd known you were pregnant."

"That's exactly the point. I didn't want you to stay because I was pregnant. Not if there was someplace else you'd rather be."

"How could you even think that?" he said. "Do you honestly think I could ever leave you?"

"A year ago I would have said no. But the further I get in my career, the less you seem to care about me."

"That's so not true."

"Are you tired of me?"

He fell silent for a moment, then brushed her cheek with the back of his hand. "I can't believe we're even having this conversation. You're worrying over nothing."

"Will you be here for me?"

"I will always be here for you."

She tried to smile, but it was a sad one. "I'm sorry. I guess I'm not thinking clearly."

"I understand. I know this must seem like the end of the

world. But you were really very lucky. If that Good Samaritan hadn't come along, you could have frozen to death."

Mention of the rescue set her mind awhirl. In a flash the image came back to her. The man pulling her from the car, laying her in the snow, covering her with his coat. "He just left me there."

"What?"

"He pulled me out of the car and then just left."

"I guess he didn't want to get involved. At least he had the sense to call nine-one-one."

She touched his hand, trying to stop her own from shaking. "I need to talk to the police."

The nurse appeared in the open doorway. "Okay, time to rest."

"Just one more minute, please," said Peyton. She squeezed Kevin's hand harder, refusing to let him go. "I really want to talk to the police."

"Surely the accident report can wait."

"That's just it. I don't think this was an accident. I was run off the road."

"You mean like by a drunk driver or something?"

"No," she said, her tone deadly serious. "I think it was deliberate."

"Why in the world would anyone want to hurt you?"

"I told you about that young mother's creepy boyfriend at the Haverhill clinic. I was afraid he might retaliate. Maybe that's what this is all about."

"Okay," he said. "I'll look into it. But I want you to focus on getting well. I'm sure there's nothing to it, just like the time you thought you heard someone picking at the lock on our front door a couple months ago."

"There was *definitely*—" she started to say, then stopped. Kevin had been out of town when Peyton heard the picking noise at their front door, and when she told him about it, he was gung ho to pack up and move. She didn't want her own paranoia to push him back up on the let's-get-the-heck-out-of-Boston bandwagon.

The nurse reentered the room. "Time to check that bandage. Visitors will have a chance to come back later."

He leaned across the bed and kissed Peyton on the forehead. She kept his hand and pulled him close, speaking softly so the nurse would not overhear. "Maybe it wouldn't hurt to have a guard posted outside the door. Please. I'm a little scared."

"Okay. I'll take care of it."

"Promise?" Her eyebrow was up. It was the look that had never failed her.

"Yes. Promise."

"Thank you."

He left without another word. Peyton looked away, toward the window, and noticed for the first time her faint reflection in the glass. The bandages startled her. Way too big for just a few scratches.

"Now," said the nurse, "let's have a look-see at that eye."

She drew a deep breath, bracing herself. "Okay," she said quietly. "Let's."

6

PEYTON TRIED TO SLEEP, BUT THE SOUNDS OF THE INTENSIVE CARE unit wouldn't go away. She lay with her eyes shut, thankful to be alive but angry that it had happened at all. The eye itself wasn't damaged, though she had quite a gash across the eyebrow. She worried about scarring, which only made her feel guilty, as if every ounce of grieving should have been for the real loss, not the cosmetic ones.

She heard talking but feigned sleep, in no mood for visitors. The voices grew louder as she became more lucid. There was no telling how long her mother and father had been sitting in the room with her, talking to each other as Peyton drifted in and out of consciousness.

"I'm right about this, Hank," her mother said, but Peyton was only half listening.

Funny, there was a time in her life when ignoring her mother would have been a capital offense. She remembered the familiar old drill of, "*Peyton, are you listening to me?*" followed by the inevitable, "*Then tell me what I just said.*" As far back as Peyton could remember, her mother was always trying to educate her. A simple question like "What did you do in school today?" could evolve into a pop quiz in mathematics during the car ride home. When it was finally time for college, Peyton couldn't wait to get away—to FSU, which was contrary to everything her mother had wanted for herself and her daughter. A younger Valerie Stanton had been a pretty, fair-skinned blonde living the life of old Boston Brahmins, complete with summers in Maine and a house in Brookline that was supposedly built by Charles Bulfinch before his commission to design the Capitol in Washington, D.C. She'd gone to Princeton and had been working on her master's in English at Harvard when she'd fallen in love with a handsome jock who was on the six-year plan toward a B.A. from Boston College. He was fun and funny and absolutely nothing like the man she'd thought she would marry. Hank Shields never did get his degree. Valerie never got her master's. She'd gotten pregnant. She spent the rest of her life making sure that Peyton would build a better life. Over and over Peyton had heard the same advice, till she heard it one last time the night before she left for Tallahassee. "Whatever you do," her mother had said, "don't make the same mistake I did."

It amazed Peyton that such an incredibly smart woman could be so oblivious to the real message she had been sending her daughter all these years: *she* was the "mistake."

"What are you doing?" It was her mother again, speaking to her father. Peyton listened with eyes closed.

"Praying," he answered.

Peyton sensed the uneasy silence in the room. She knew her mother didn't talk to God anymore.

"Do me a favor," said Valerie. "Ask Him why this happened."

"I'm not asking Him anything. I'm thanking Him."

The sigh was audible even across the room. "That's my Hank," she said softly, as if talking to herself. "An asteroid could slam into the earth, and we should all thank God for leaving us the moon."

"I heard that," he said.

Peyton sensed a fight coming on. It was eerily reminiscent of her childhood, the way her mother would pick fights with her father right in front of Peyton, as if their child weren't even there. She was about to reveal herself and break it up when she heard her mother ask, "Are you praying for the baby?"

Peyton withdrew and listened. Her father said, "Do you want me to?"

"Only if you think Peyton would want you to."

His voice dropped. "Of course she would."

"You honestly believe that?"

"Yes."

Peyton felt her eyelid quiver, as if yearning to open, but she continued her false sleep.

"Do you think . . ." Her mother started to ask something, then stopped.

"Do I think what?"

"Do you think Peyton wanted this baby?"

It was like a punch in the chest, but Peyton didn't flinch. She just listened. "Absolutely," her father said.

"You answered too quickly," she said. "Think before you speak, for a change."

"I don't need to think about it. I know how torn up she must be."

"Just because she's sad about losing it doesn't mean she was excited about having it. She didn't tell anyone she was pregnant. Not even Kevin."

"That's between her and Kevin."

"The heck it is. Can't you see they're in trouble?"

"Do you have to stick your nose into everything?" he said.

"If her marriage is falling apart, she'll need emotional support from us. We can't help her if we don't know what's going on in her life."

Peyton didn't need to open her eyes to see her father weakening. That was the way her mother had always gotten to him. Put it in terms of Peyton's well-being.

"What do you want to do?" he asked.

"I think we should ask her about the baby."

"Ask her what, if she really wanted it? That's pointless."

"If we can help her realize that she really didn't want it, we can help her get over the fact that she lost it. She'll recognize it was all for the best."

"Let her grieve, will you, please? For once in your life, stop trying to tell your daughter how she should feel."

"Are you going to do it or not?"

"No," he said firmly.

"If you don't, I will."

"I'm not doing it. And if you're half as smart as you think you are, you won't either."

"What do you know about smart, Henry Shields?"

Peyton lay still, eyes shut, hoping just this once to hear a stinging comeback from her father. But she knew he was too big of a person to trade insults with his wife in front of their daughter, even if he did think she was unconscious.

She heard only the shuffle of her father's footsteps and the firm closing of the door.

7

IT WAS ALMOST LUNCHTIME WHEN SHE HEARD KEVIN'S VOICE IN THE hallway. He'd kept his promise. With him was a detective from Boston PD.

"John Bolton," he said in a voice that was just right for a police station, a little loud for the ICU.

Peyton shook hands, careful not to yank out an IV tube. "Thanks for coming."

"No problem." He said "no" like a cow, a long moo with an "n." The closer Peyton looked, the more apt the bovine analogy seemed. He was a large man, undoubtedly muscle-bound in his younger years, simply thick in middle age. The face was round and full. He wore a necktie with the top button of his shirt unbuttoned, not to be casual but because the jowls made it impossible to button it. As he removed his coat, Peyton noticed the burly folds of skin on the back of his neck, little steps that led to his crew-cut head. He had a set of matching steps on his forehead.

"Some water?" Peyton offered, with a nod toward the pitcher on her bed tray.

"Nah, I'm fine," said Bolton. "I know you're not feeling a hundred percent, so I'll make this quick. I read the accident report, so I know just about everything there is to know, except what you can add."

"Did you find out who pulled me out of the car, who called nine-one-one?"

"The call came from a pay phone. The guy did tell the operator he was the one who pulled you from the water, but he didn't want to give his name."

"Isn't that a little odd?"

"Not really. In this day and age, a guy dials nine-one-one and leaves his name, next thing he knows a hotshot lawyer is suing him for smearing some woman's makeup as he pulled her from a burning building. You can't blame people for not wanting to get that involved."

"I guess not," she said, thinking of Felicia's lawsuit against her and the hospital.

"Anyway," said Bolton, as he removed a pen and small pad from inside his coat pocket. "The nurse is going to kick me out in five minutes, so as best you can remember, tell me what happened."

Peyton glanced at Kevin for reassurance, then began. "It was around three A.M. I remember it was snowing hard. Harder by the minute. I stopped at a red light and dialed in for messages on my cell phone."

"At three in the morning?" asked Bolton.

"It's about the only free time I get, but that's not important. The light changed. I turned down Riverway and right before it becomes Jamaicaway, a car flew past me."

"Were you still on the phone?"

"No. I had just hung up."

"Was that the only call you made, the one for messages?"

"Actually I returned one of the calls, but I don't see what difference that makes."

"Details are always important. Who did you call?"

"Dr. Simons. He runs the clinic in Haverhill where I work four days a month. Where I used to work, I guess I should say."

"Why do you *guess* you should say that?"

"Say what?"

"That you used to work there."

She hesitated. "What does that matter?"

"I'm just trying to get the whole picture. You're stopped at a red light and dial in for messages. Something so important comes up that you call Dr. Simons at three o'clock in the morning. If it was a medical emergency, it could have distracted you. If it was a personal matter, it could have upset you. Any of these things impair one's driving ability."

"If you're implying that this accident is somehow attributable to the fact that I was on the phone, you're wrong."

"Maybe. But what was the nature of the call?"

Peyton thought for a moment, choosing her words. "Personal."

"Did it upset you in any way?"

Kevin said, "I don't see how her phone calls have anything to do with this investigation."

"I think you know where I'm going with this," said Bolton. "Can you answer the question, Doctor?"

"All right. I was upset."

"I see." He jotted something on his pad. "So we have you turning through an intersection. Continue."

"Then a car flew past me driving way too fast for the conditions."

"You mean the same conditions under which you were driving with one hand and talking on the phone."

"I told you, I had already hung up the phone."

"How much earlier?"

"Maybe a few seconds."

"So you were still upset?"

"A little."

Kevin said, "Why are you making her defend herself?"

"I'm sorry," said Bolton. "I have to confess, cell phones are one of my pet peeves. Personally, I think they cause more accidents than drunk drivers."

"It didn't cause *this* accident," said Peyton.

"Okay. You tell me what happened."

She collected herself and said, "I hung up the phone. If you must know the details, let's just say that the call was kind of awkward."

"How do you mean?"

She definitely didn't want to get into that. "I spoke to Dr. Simons's answering service, but my message was—inartful, you might say. I was debating whether to call back again to clarify. That's when I noticed a car coming toward me driving very fast. Maybe a hundred yards away."

"And you were still thinking about the previous call?"

"Maybe."

"Okay. So this car is coming toward you while you're sort of preoccupied."

"I wasn't preoccupied."

"Whatever. What happened?"

Peyton paused, the image coming back. "It was strange. The oncoming driver had his bright lights on, so I flashed him. He flashed back. Then he disappeared."

"What do you mean?"

"I couldn't see him anymore."

He looked at her strangely. "Just vanished into thin air?"

"Then he reappeared."

"I see. Kind of like David Copperfield."

"Not at all. He had just switched off his lights. And I guess my own headlights were so covered with snow that I couldn't see very far. I lost him. And then when he reappeared, there was this sudden blast of light. Pointed right at me. He was in *my* lane."

Her voice was trembling. Kevin took her hand. Peyton continued, "And he just kept coming, as if he were some kind of missile locked onto me. He was determined to either run me off the road or slam into me head-on."

Bolton scratched his head. "And you swerved out of the way, I take it."

"Yes. That's when I lost control. I wasn't on the phone. I wasn't distracted. I had to do something, or he would have flattened me."

"You're sure he was in your lane?"

"Yes. He was right in front of me."

"I understand. But as you just pointed out, you had been on the phone, you were upset. It was dark and snowing hard, and the roads were covered with snow and ice. Is it possible you were in *his* lane?"

Peyton paused, as if she hadn't ever considered the possibility. "I don't see how."

"You don't?" he said, sounding as if he did.

"Why would he have turned off his lights and then flashed me like an incoming jet."

"Maybe it wasn't even the same car. You said yourself the conditions were getting worse by the minute. Maybe you didn't see what you thought you were seeing. The car you were watching at first could have pulled into a driveway—disappears, as you put it. Then another car pulls out from a different driveway or maybe a side street. You're driving in his lane. He flashes every light on his vehicle to make you move out of his way. You overreact and end up in the pond."

"I didn't overreact."

"I'm not saying you're a bad driver. In these conditions, the slightest error can have disastrous consequences."

"Tell me this," said Peyton. "Why wouldn't that car have stopped after running me off the road?"

"He might not have even known you lost control."

"I think he was trying to hit me."

"Dr. Shields, if that were the case, we're talking about a suicide mission. My gut doesn't tell me that somebody's out there looking to trade his life for yours in an intentional head-on collision. Now, I might be more concerned if you were Jennifer Aniston or Shania Twain. Not that you weren't pretty. Aren't pretty, I mean."

Peyton caught the slip but let it go. Nothing pretty about bandages. "What about that man I got arrested at the Haverhill clinic? Didn't Kevin tell you about him?"

"He did. Took two minutes to check that one out. That

boy's still in jail. Didn't make bail. No way he could have run anyone off the road."

Kevin asked, "Isn't there something the police can do to put us at ease?"

Bolton asked her, "Did you get a license plate number?"

"No."

"Make and model of the car?"

"No. Could have been a Ford. Maybe."

"I see."

His "I sees" were getting on her nerves. "You think I'm paranoid," said Peyton.

Bolton softened his tone. "I think you've been through hell. The best thing for you to do is rest and get well. Stop worrying about whether someone is out there trying to get you."

She sought out Kevin's eyes, but he seemed to agree with the detective. He laid his hand atop hers and said, "You're going to be fine."

Bolton left his card on the tray beside the bed. "If there's anything you're concerned about, you call me. Good luck to you, Doc."

Peyton watched quietly as the two men shook hands and stepped into the hall. She took his card and read it. Maybe he was right. Maybe it was best to stop worrying. She took another look at his card, however, and committed his phone number to memory.

Just in case.

8

THE SHRILL RINGING OF AN ALARM CLOCK PIERCED THE DARKNESS. A long, languid arm swung from beneath the covers and silenced it. For a moment, he lay motionless beneath the bulky blankets. He had slept for several hours, but it hadn't been restful. This was not his normal bedtime, and he'd fallen asleep chiefly from exhaustion. Three straight days was a long time to go without sleep, even for him.

Rather than switch on the lamp, he simply allowed his eyes to adjust to the dimly lit room. Half-opened venetian blinds cut the moonlight into slats on the opposite wall. Across the room, another slat of light streamed from beneath the closed closet door. On the nightstand beside the bed, the alarm clock's glowing green numbers announced the time: 10:55 P.M.

He slid out of bed and walked sleepily, but dutifully, to the closet. The tile floor was cold beneath his bare feet. As he reached for the handle, the light from beneath the closet door stretched all the way to his toes, giving them a reddish pink hue. From the other side of the door emerged the faint but familiar humming noise, trapped inside. He opened the door and was suddenly bathed in red light.

The sight of his computer brought a thin smile to his face, as if he were seeing an old friend. The closet had been completely remodeled into a computer workstation. Speakers rested on the shelf overhead, like bookends for a neat row of CDs. On the floor was a subwoofer, next to his tower and external zip drive. The twenty-one-inch monitor was in the screen-saver mode, which accounted for the colored lighting. The screen was aglow with one of those strange hues that only a computer could generate, somewhere between the pitch red of roses and the brownish red of blood.

He pulled up his computer chair and by merely touching the keyboard made the red disappear. An array of icons dotted the screen. The clock in the corner said 10:58. Just two minutes to spare. Just a mouse-click on his browser brought up his high-speed Internet connection. He skipped past the advertisements, news broadcasts, and other images that cluttered his home page. He clicked the icon marked "Instant Chat."

He was a regular visitor to chat rooms on the Internet. The concept had long fascinated him, these so-called rooms in cyberspace that Web surfers could enter or leave as they wished. Once inside they could exchange typewritten messages with people they'd never met before or just read the messages others were sending to each other, like reading a transcript of a telephone conversation. The real beauty, of course, was the anonymity. People hid behind screen names like Cowgirl or Bad Ass. It reminded him of the CB-radio craze in the 1970s, when, from the backseat of his family's station wagon he would listen to his dad chatting with other motorists who were on the lookout for smokies. They all had their own "handle," and it seemed every other jerk was a Burt Reynolds wannabe named Bandit, no one really knowing who the dolt really was on the other end.

That was the lure of the modern-day chat room.

It was exactly 11:00 P.M. Rudy entered a chat room where, each night, a dozen or more fans of old movies gathered to chat online. Tonight they were debating whether it was the Americans who had pioneered moviemaking or the French Lumière brothers. Rudy had no interest. For him, this nightly chat room was just a meeting place, like hanging out at the corner of Fifth and Vine because you knew the woman of your dreams passed by this very spot at the same time each night. The small box on the right of his screen indicated that twenty-two people were in the room with him. He didn't recognize her usual screen name among the list of participants, but that wasn't conclusive. She could have created a new one—an alias traveling under an alias. He typed his message in typical chat-room style, all lowercase, letters or numbers substituting for words.

"r u there?"

The message appeared in the dialogue box, right after his screen name, RG. He waited for a response, but deep down he wasn't all that hopeful. It was a one in a million chance that she would visit tonight, right after the accident. Strangely, not so long ago he would have bet his whole computer on her being there at precisely eleven o'clock. She was that dependable. But that was before their whole world had changed.

"is who there?"

The reply was from someone called Windjammer. Maybe that was her new name. Or maybe it was just a stranger eager to strike up a conversation. The problem with such large groups was that your message could be read by everyone in the chat room. Only after you linked up with the person you wanted could you break off into a private chat room, just the two of you.

"is that u, ladydoc?" That had been her screen name up until the accident.

A minute passed. The online debate over the Lumière brothers continued. Line after line of transcribed text appeared on the screen below his query. The diehards were ignoring him as irrelevant. He stared at the screen as if willing a reply, but as the film aficionados rambled on, it became ever more clear that she wasn't there.

That wouldn't stop him from trying again tomorrow night. Nor would it stop him from telling her how he felt—tonight.

"i'm so sorry," he typed, then paused for several seconds. Rudy's apology was a total non sequitur in the film debate, but if she was out there waiting in silence, she would know what he was talking about. She knew his screen name. She would know he was apologizing to her. And she would know what he was sorry about.

It was breaking protocol to use anything but a screen name, but invoking a real name might help convey the depth of his feelings.

"it's from the heart, peyton," he added, then clicked his mouse and exited the chat room.

9

HOME. AFTER THREE NIGHTS IN THE HOSPITAL, IT FELT GOOD TO BE there—for Kevin almost as much as Peyton.

Home was on Magnolia Street, two blocks north of famed Newbury Street, where magnificent old Victorian residences blended with new galleries, smart shops, and outdoor cafés that, especially in warmer weather, lent the area a certain continental élan. Even though it was pricey, Peyton had insisted on taking the apartment. Kevin knew her angle. He wasn't happy about staying in Boston after she'd finished med school, so she dropped him right in the heart of what was considered *the* place for the young and chic to see and be seen.

Ironically, the accident afforded them their first real opportunity to share the place together, alone. Missing work to nurse his wife back to health had also helped Kevin keep his mind off his mistakes; it kept Sandra at bay.

Kevin didn't fully understand the thing with Sandra, having never intended anything sexual between them. She was just good company and a good friend at Marston & Wheeler, a breath of fresh air at a law firm, where most associates competed like gladiators. Sandra had an unusual wisdom and maturity about her. Although she was just a second-year associate, she was ten years older than Kevin. After graduating from Columbia Law School, she'd given up a career to marry a widower and raise three stepchildren. They were driving home from Dartmouth, having just dropped off the youngest child for the fall semester, when her husband of twelve years told her about the lover he'd kept for the past eleven. To her credit, Sandra picked herself up and landed a job at Boston's top law firm, starting at the bottom, determined to make up for the thirteen years she'd lost.

Kevin knew it was stupid to go to bed with a coworker, but that was actually what had made it so easy. When Kevin volunteered to work on the big bank-fraud investigation in Providence because "there was no one to go home to back in Boston anyway," Sandra quickly convinced the senior partner to make her the junior associate on the case. She and Kevin worked long hours, just the two of them. After two months of traveling back and forth from Providence together, conversations inevitably had less and less to do with work. It was on trips that required hotel stays that Sandra, usually over dinner, probed more deeply, more personally. Kevin didn't even realize how much he was revealing about himself and his marriage until, one night, Sandra ordered a bottle of wine with dinner and told him all about her creep of an ex-husband. She probably hadn't intended to plant seeds of doubt about his own marriage, but the fact that someone as smart as Sandra could be fooled by a cheating spouse for eleven years caused Kevin to think, if only for a minute or two, that if his own wife wasn't putting any of her energy into their relationship, maybe there was something—or someone—he should know about. A few weeks later, he foolishly took up Sandra on an invitation to come back to her room to prepare for the next day's meetings. They actually did work for a while, but after watching him check his cell phone at least a dozen times for missed calls, Sandra uttered those fateful words, the proverbial straw that broke the camel's back, which opened up the minibar and turned down the bedsheets: "*Peyton didn't call you back to say good night this time either, did she?*"

It seemed fitting that it happened on a night that culminated in Peyton's accident. A painful ending to the biggest mistake in his life.

"I wish you didn't have to go to work today," said Peyton. She was sitting up in bed against the headboard, her injured leg propped up on a pillow.

"Is that because you'll miss me or because you dread the thought of your mother coming over?"

"I plead the Fifth."

"I thought so." He handed her a cup of coffee.

"You know, this breakfast-in-bed routine reminds me of the first time you ever cooked for me. Remember?"

"Yeah, I remember."

It was back when they were dating in college. He'd baked her brownies, following the directions meticulously, adding the ingredients in the exact order listed on the box. First the packaged mix. Exactly a half-cup of milk. One egg. Then he'd astonished Peyton by diving in with bare hands, chocolate mess up to his elbows. Only when she'd handed him a big wooden spoon did he realize he'd taken the recipe a little too literally: mix for sixty seconds *by hand.* "Proof positive you're destined to be a lawyer," Peyton had quipped. Thirty seconds later they were two students naked on the kitchen floor and covered in chocolate, doing things to each other that not even the threat of raw egg and salmonella poisoning could deter.

It was a fond memory just between them. But he hated when Peyton told that story to others. Made him look like an idiot.

"Maybe you can make us some brownies when you get home," she said, smiling.

"Sure. Whatever you want." He'd sounded more grumpy than intended.

She tasted her coffee, then asked, "Are you okay?"

"Yeah. I just wish I could wiggle out of this trip."

"Then cancel. I love having you here with me."

"I can't. But New York isn't that far away. Just call if there's an emergency."

"You mean if Mother and I finally kill each other?"

"You know what I mean."

"I'm not scared anymore, if that's what you're getting at."

"Good." He went to the dresser and popped open his briefcase. "While I'm gone, why don't you look these over?" He dropped a stack of papers beside her on the bed, then sat next to her. "I was on the Internet last night and pulled up a list of houses for sale. How do you feel about moving?"

"You know I can't leave Boston."

"I don't mean move away. Just give up the apartment. For the same money or even less we could lease a place with an option to purchase when my job situation sorts itself out. Someplace close to the hospital but with a little yard. Something more familylike."

He could see her surprise. Planting roots in Boston was something he'd always resisted.

"I think that's a fantastic idea," she said, her eyes brightening. "It's what I've wanted all along. But you don't have to do this . . . you know, out of pity."

"That's not it." *Guilt, maybe, but never pity.*

"But you hate it here. Why the change of heart?"

"The time we've spent together, just you and me, since the accident. It's made me realize that Boston is where you need to be for your career. Mine's going nowhere anyway."

"You're as good as any lawyer in this town."

"That's not what the firm thinks. None of the partners have told me anything specific, but I can read the writing on the wall. They're finally pushing me out."

"I'm sorry."

"Oh well. I was a fool to have thought I could break into an old Boston firm. A wasted five years. It's not your fault, but I know I've been taking it out on you. That's the reason I've been so distant lately."

"If that's really what was bothering you, I wish you would have talked to me about it."

"You're right. That's why I promise never to make you feel so far away from me again."

"Do you mean that?"

"Absolutely. I'm back. You can count on me."

"Good. But something tells me I'm still stuck with my mother for the next two days."

"I said I'm back. I didn't say I was perfect."

That got a smile. He kissed her as he rose, then grabbed his coat and briefcase. "My plane doesn't leave till two, so call me on my cell if you need me."

"I will."

He started out, but she stopped him.

"Love you," she said.

He turned slowly, then said, "Me too."

He put on his coat and headed down the hall. It was still dark in the living room, but he didn't flip on the light. For a moment, he stood in the archway and stared, suddenly hit by the gravity of what had almost happened. Had Peyton spent just a few more minutes in the icy pond, these last four days they'd enjoyed each other's company might have been spent alone, scrambling to make funeral arrangements. Someone—himself, he presumed—would have selected her burial outfit, her jewelry, the keepsakes that would have followed her to the grave. He wondered what words he would have uttered publicly, what lasting tribute he might have etched in the granite marker, what secrets he might have whispered to his sleeping wife after everyone else had left, when only she could hear, if she could hear.

I'm sorry, Peyton. I'm sorry beyond belief.

The old clock chimed on the mantel. Time to leave. He grabbed his keys and headed out. The front door closed behind him, and the wind slapped his face with a burst of chilly white powder. The sidewalks were still shin-deep in some spots, icy beaten paths in others. Above, a fuzzy sun was trying to break through gray winter clouds. He took one step and stopped. He noticed something at his feet.

A single, long-stemmed red rose.

He picked it up. His hand shook, and not from the cold. What the hell was this about? Someone wishing Peyton a speedy recovery, perhaps. Maybe her parents, a friend, coworkers at the hospital. Flowers would make sense. A nice mixed arrangement. Maybe some fruit.

Not a single red rose.

He knelt to search for a card or note that might have fallen off. He brushed the snow away from the doorstep, gently at first, then more quickly, then feverishly as he checked the top step, the second step, the next one, all the way down from the porch onto the sidewalk. Nothing. He sat on the bottom step and faced the street, exhausted from the little flash of wasted energy. His breath steamed in bull-like bursts as he mulled over the possibilities. Of course there was no note. No card. No signature. There was no need to send any explanation with a single red rose. The message was unmistakable.

Had Peyton found someone else?

He didn't feel any less shame for his own indiscretion. Now, however, he felt sickened by the whole situation, wondering if he was as blind as Sandra had been in her own disastrous marriage.

He snapped the stem in two, pitched the red rose into the street, and headed for the subway.

10

IT WASN'T EXACTLY A LIE. KEVIN WOULD HAVE THROWN A FIT IF HE'D known she was planning on going into work today. So she just didn't tell.

"You're back already?" asked a surprised NICU nurse.

Peyton smiled and kept going, no time to talk. She looked worse than she felt, walking on crutches, a shaved eyebrow full of stitches, her left eye surrounded by tiny but inflamed lacerations from the shattered glass and a bruise as big as a purple doughnut. The mild concussion had passed with no lingering nausea or headaches. Her main problem was the sutured gash in her lower leg, which would require periodic elevation to prevent bleeding.

Sensibly, she planned on staying only two hours today, long enough to make an appearance and attend the daily noon lecture for pediatric residents. She had missed only four days so far, not counting the weekend. The program director had promised that sick time wouldn't be held against her, but the implied understanding was that eventually she'd more than make up the lost time. For any resident, securing free time was like dealing with a loan shark: borrow an hour now, but payback's a bitch.

With her passkey Peyton entered the restricted neonatal intensive care unit. Peyton had no official rounds here, but it had been a week since she'd visited her favorite premie. Little Jacob Gordon had spent the first three months of his life in the NICU, a full trimester that should have been spent in his mother's womb. Each day his mother came to feed him, hold him, rock him. Peyton had assisted the neonatalogist during Jacob's first few hours on the planet and had cared for him daily till her NICU rotation ended two months ago. Each day thereafter she'd made a point of visiting him and his mother. Not because she had to. Because she wanted to.

She scrubbed at the sink and opened the door. As many times as she'd done it, entering NICU still gave her an ominous sensation. The lighting was dim for the benefit of sleeping newborns. Around the unit were more than a dozen separate stations, tiny babies encased in clear plastic isolettes, many of them seriously premature and living on IVs, some jaundiced and sleeping under lamps, all of them connected to heart and respiratory monitors. She cut directly toward Jacob's corner. The monitors were silent. His isolette and crib were empty. Her heart pounded as she feared the worst.

"He's gone home," said the nurse.

"When?"

"Two days ago."

Peyton smiled, heartened to think of Jacob finally at home. Every day his mother used to talk about how she couldn't wait to take him to the park and show him off. Peyton had been careful to remind her that, as with any child, it would be a while before it was safe for him to venture outside. Like twenty or thirty years.

"That's great news," she said, though she was suddenly saddened. Seeing children come and go was part of the job, but not getting to say goodbye to one like Jacob was tougher than usual. Especially on the heels of her own loss.

"You don't look happy," said the nurse.

"I'm very happy." She checked the clock and said, "Guess I'd better get back to work."

The nurse helped her with the door as Peyton passed on crutches. She was halfway down the hall by the time she realized that, at this pace, her bladder simply didn't have the patience for her to hobble across the building to the ladies' room. She did a quick about-face and entered the ladies' room across from the NICU, then stopped short upon hearing her name in conversation.

"Did you see Dr. Shields is back?" It was a woman's voice coming from behind the closed door of a bathroom stall.

"Yeah," came the reply from another stall.

Peyton recognized the voices echoing against the tiled walls and floors. It was two NICU nurses.

"She looks like hell, don't you think?"

"Poor girl. She was so pretty."

Peyton didn't move. They were obviously unaware she had returned to use the NICU bathroom.

"I hear she miscarried."

"I didn't even know she was pregnant."

"My sister works in the ER at Brigham and Women's. She saw the chart."

"What a shame. She would have been a good mother."

"You really think so? How well do you know her?"

"Not well. But she sure seems to love children. She *is* a pediatrician."

"If you ask me, she doesn't really love kids."

Peyton blinked hard, as if trying to comprehend. It was the worst blow since her mother had questioned whether she'd wanted her baby.

"How can you say that?" asked the other nurse. "Little Jacob wasn't even her patient anymore, and she still came to visit him every day."

"That's my point. She loves sick kids. They're like a science project for her. Put her in a room with a healthy baby and she wouldn't have a clue."

Peyton cringed at their laughter, making not a sound. Part of her wanted to announce her presence and set them straight in angry tones, but she couldn't move. Finally, a toilet flushed. Peyton nearly jumped, prompted by an overwhelming need to just get out. Quickly, she opened the door and headed for the exit, leaving them behind with their mean jokes and misconceptions.

She was moving faster than ever before on crutches, even faster than the busy doctors and nurses she passed in the corridor. Moisture gathered in her eyes. Nurse gossip was a silly thing to cry over. She'd left herself vulnerable, however, by not having cried the miscarriage out of her system when she'd had the chance at home. Now she was fighting back tears, refusing to unravel at work.

Her beeper vibrated against her waist, signaling a page. She checked it. There was no number, just a digital message.

I Love You, it read.

She drew a deep breath and nearly managed to smile. She felt so much better. The timing was impeccable. She couldn't confirm the sender, but who else could it have been?

"Thank you, Kevin," she said softly, then continued toward the elevator.

11

IT WAS MONDAY AND IT WAS ALMOST LUNCHTIME. KEVIN WAS SEATED alone in a booth in the back of Murphy's Pub, waiting and burning up stress as he chomped on the ice from his soda.

Only one other booth was occupied as yet, a man and woman holding hands and eyeing each other. They were too well dressed and the food here was too lousy for them to be lunching at Murphy's for any reason other than a secret affair. The chances of anyone in their circle happening upon them here were nil, which of course was the whole point. Cheaters always thought they were so clever.

"Hi," said Sandra.

He managed a strained smile as she slid into the booth. "Hey."

When Sandra had sent the e-mail asking him to meet her for lunch at Murphy's, Kevin's entire focus had been on whether he should go and what he should say to her if he did. He didn't give the venue much thought. But now that he'd arrived and could see what the place was like, he just felt like a dirty cheater.

"I'm surprised you showed up," she said.

"I thought we should talk."

"How is Peyton?"

It was the decent thing to ask, but under the circumstances it struck Kevin as awkward at best. "Pretty good, actually."

"How are you?"

"I'm hanging in there."

Sandra touched her hair, a little sign of nervousness. "Did you tell her where you were when the call came?"

"No," he said firmly.

"Are you going to?"

Kevin drew a breath, then let it out. "Sandra, that's what I came to talk about."

"You're not going to tell her, are you?"

"I want to be honest with you. Peyton and I—"

"You've reconciled," she said, her eyes closing momentarily, as if to absorb the blow. "I knew it."

"She's my wife, Sandra."

"And what about us?"

"That's what I'm trying to tell you. There can't be an 'us.'"

"You should have told me that before you took me to bed."

She wasn't yelling, but she had been loud enough for the waitress to overhear. This wasn't the time to debate who had taken whom to bed. "Sandra, come on, please."

"What did you expect from me? You want me to be happy to hear that all the time and effort I've put into you has just ended with one night of drunken sex?"

"What time and effort? We're friends, and on that one night things just got out of hand."

"I have feelings for you. Isn't that obvious?"

He paused, his well-rehearsed words suddenly not flowing as easily as he had hoped. "Like I said, I want to be honest with you. My original plan was to come here today and tell you that Peyton and I will be patching things up. But I don't think that's the case anymore."

"Are you trying to make me crazy? You can't keep changing your mind."

"It's not a matter of me changing my mind. It's just . . . something happened on the way over here that makes me think that I may have already lost Peyton."

"You mean she figured us out on her own?"

"No. Someone left a red rose for Peyton on our doorstep this morning. No card, no note."

"Did you ask her about it?"

"No."

"Why not?"

"If I had, she could have turned the tables on me and I would have ended up telling her about us."

She made a face. "There always has to be a winner and loser with you, doesn't there? You're so competitive with Peyton it's crazy."

"What are you talking about?"

"Every time you talk about her, it comes out. She has a more rewarding job than you, she went to a better school than you, she has more successful friends than you. You have one of those marriages that should come with a scorecard."

"That's ridiculous."

"Is it? Maybe it actually explains your interest in me. You went out looking for something you were dead sure she didn't have—a lover on the side. You'd finally have the edge. Or so you thought. Now this mysterious rose shows up, and you can't stand to admit she beat you at your own game."

"Look, I understand that you're angry."

"I'm not angry. I'm hurt. I'm disappointed. Because I know what you're thinking: If Sandra were ten years younger, maybe things would be different."

"That's not what I'm thinking."

"I know you," she said. "I just wish you could see that if I *were* Peyton's age, I'd probably be playing the same stupid games that the two of you waste so much energy playing. That night in Providence, I thought maybe you finally understood that. But I was wrong. And I'm tired of this. So go back home and go the full sixteen rounds with Peyton. You two can compete and compete till you're tired of competing anymore. And when one of you is left standing, call me. Maybe we can see where we are."

"Please don't be like this. The two of us still have to work together."

"Like you said, there is no 'us.' At least not until you're ready to leave Peyton behind. Really ready."

"I'm sorry that's the way you see it. Because you're dead wrong about me and Peyton."

"Am I?"

"I don't compete with her."

She smiled flatly and shook her head. "Funny. I thought you were going to say you don't love her."

Their eyes met, but he suddenly realized just how far apart he and Sandra were.

"I'm sorry."

"Could you please just leave," she said.

He wanted to say something to make her feel better, but things were too confused with Peyton to be controlled by Sandra's sensibilities. He slid out of the booth in silence, grabbed his coat, and started toward the door.

On his way out he passed that couple in the booth—the other cheaters—and suddenly thought of Peyton and Mr. Rose trading glances at some bar, caressing each other's hands, moving on to his apartment, kissing and groping all the way upstairs, ripping their clothes off and grabbing for hot flesh like . . . like his one night with Sandra.

He felt another pang of guilt but refused to let this be about him. Sandra was a symptom of their problems, but Peyton was the root. It seemed silly, but it had really all started with that pathetic Ivy League football game they'd attended on their first visit to Harvard and that obnoxious cheer she'd chanted at the top of her lungs with all the other snobs, even though she knew that her husband couldn't find a decent job. *That's all right, that's okay, you're gonna work for US someday!* Sure, Peyton had apologized later, and maybe it wasn't fair to fault someone for getting caught up in the stadium hoopla after too much rum from the flask. But lately, the people she'd counted as friends didn't need liquor to cop an air of superiority.

It was bitter cold outside, and he struggled to button his coat as he left Murphy's. A gust of wind whipped up the snow and knocked him off balance. He slipped on the frozen sidewalk and fell on his ass. He cursed the bar, cursed Boston, cursed himself for ever having set foot in a city so crazy that people actually waxed nostalgic over the fabled hundred-hour blizzard of 1969 and grumbled over the fact that with global warming Boston didn't get *real* snowstorms anymore. He missed his friends in Florida, the balmy winters, the scuba diving trips in warm waters on beautiful coral reefs. He'd given up so much, and for what? A big, prestigious law firm that worked him seventy hours a week with the elusive lure of partnership. A wife who had driven him to cheat. A wife who had cheated on him.

No way. No way in hell would Peyton cheat. Not that he deserved such loyalty. It was just something Peyton would never do.

He kept telling himself that as he plodded through the snow and headed back to the office.

12

PEYTON REACHED THE LECTURE HALL A FEW MINUTES BEFORE NOON. she'd managed to keep the war-wound talks to a minimum, but a friend caught her in the hallway just before she could disappear inside.

"Hey, Peyton," said Gary Varne.

Gary was a nurse and, of all things, an old high school boyfriend. Their first date had been a disaster at one of those busy casual restaurants at Faneuil Hall Marketplace. A hostess was keeping a waiting list and calling out names on a loudspeaker as tables opened. Gary had left the phony name "Itsmy," causing the hostess to announce unwittingly "Itsmy party," upon which Gary cut across the room singing "*It's my party and our table is ready*" to the tune of that sixties pop hit. This, of course, was sidesplitting fun to a fourteen-year-old boy and unforgivable geekiness to his fourteen-year-old date. They didn't have another date until they were seniors, by which time Gary had turned into a hottie and Peyton was more than willing to give him a second chance. Things had gotten fairly serious, until Peyton went away to Tallahassee for college. She met Kevin and knew it was right, and never looked back.

The next time she saw Gary, she was a doctor and he was a nurse studying for the MCATs. He was definitely smart enough. Discipline was his problem. Every now and then, Peyton dropped a polite reminder that you actually had to crack the books if your sights were set on something other than the Caribbean Correspondence College of Last Resort.

"I can't believe you're back at work already," he said.

"Just for lectures. I'm taking it easy till the leg heals."

"Good idea. They'll probably want you to march in the parade when you get back."

"Stop."

"I'm serious. From what I hear, you're a hero among your peers."

"Really?"

"Oh, yeah. The hospital dumps more tasks on its residents all the time. You've pretty much cinched it that they'll never be asked to drive the hospitality bus."

"Very funny."

He winked and started away, but Peyton stopped him. "Hey, I never did get to thank you for that surprise birthday party. That was really sweet of you."

"No need to thank me."

"It was very thoughtful."

"I mean there really is no need to thank me. I had nothing to do with it."

For a moment, she thought he was just being mindful of Kevin's jealous side, denying any involvement in the party so that Peyton wouldn't have to explain anything to her husband about a handsome ex-boyfriend doing something nice for her. Kevin was not one of those people who believed that romance could dissolve into mere friendship—a philosophy that he had made abundantly clear to Gary back in college, which was the last time Gary had called to wish Peyton a happy birthday. But Peyton could see from Gary's expression that he truly had not organized the celebration.

"Then who hired the mime I danced the tango with?"

"I don't know. I got a note telling me to be in the lounge at nine A.M. All I did was show up, like everyone else."

Peyton felt a sudden chill, thinking once again of the way the mime had stared at her on the way out.

"You okay?" he asked.

"I'm fine. I just thought it was you who had arranged the party, that's all."

"Sorry to disappoint."

"So who could it have been?"

"I don't know. It came off the same haphazard way everything happens around here. Everyone got the same message to meet in the lounge for the surprise party, but no one really seemed to be in charge. After standing around a few minutes we finally we came up with the ruse to lure you to the party."

"My supposed meeting with Landau and Sheffield?"

"Right. But that was spur of the moment. No one planned that. If you're really curious, I could check around to see who the mastermind was."

"No," she said, a little too sharply.

Gary looked at her with concern. "You sure you're okay?"

She feared she was coming across as neurotic. "I'm just a little jittery today."

"Maybe you should sit down."

"Yeah. Lecture's about to start. I'll see you around."

She only pretended to watch as he headed down the hall, her mind buzzing. She couldn't shake the thought of that mime staring her down as she'd rushed from the party to the ER. It had scared her a little at the time and in light of everything that had happened since, it scared her even more now. Other than Gary, she couldn't think of another friend who would have gone to all the trouble of arranging a party. If he hadn't done it, who had?

She stepped into the lecture hall, her focus a long way from medicine.

Sandra's words still haunted him. Kevin hadn't thought of his marriage that way—a competition. But maybe Sandra had a point. As with everything else, Peyton had beaten him at his own game.

To be sure, a certain prestige came with being a lawyer at one of the oldest and largest law firms in Boston. Just walking down the halls, you might bump into a former governor or United States senator, a past president of the American Bar Association, or a future federal judge. Kevin himself had been hired in a class of young associates that included a former judicial clerk to the Chief Justice of the U.S. Supreme Court and a winner of the Sears Prize, an honor bestowed on the top two graduates of Harvard Law School. Of course, Kevin's pedigree required that he work even harder to prove he was partnership material. He gave it his all, and a few partners even led him to believe that he was on track. Only after they'd milked him for all he was worth did they begin to make it clear that, for him, the pot was empty at the end of the rainbow.

His in-box was bulging, but he didn't bother with it. He sank into his desk chair, switched on the computer, and opened his favorite file. It wasn't exactly firm business, but it was definitely firm related. Two years' worth of work on the sly. This was one project he would enjoy to no end.

The office door opened. Startled, Kevin looked up and saw his boss, the frenetic Ira Kaufman, standing in the open doorway. On impulse, he hit the kill switch on his computer. The motor whined. The screen went black.

Kaufman shot him a suspicious look. "Surfing the porn sites, Stokes?"

Kevin tried to act normal, but he couldn't hide his fluster. "Uh, no. I was just, uh—"

"Forget it. We just got hit with a slew of interrogatories in the EnviroMedix class action. I need you to work up responses and objections, probably a motion for protective order. Then let's get on the offensive here. Fire some interrogatories right back at those losers and send out notices on the first wave of depositions. Churn some fees and maybe they'll go away."

"When do you need it?"

"Yesterday."

13

THE LUNCHTIME LECTURE WAS ON RECENT ADVANCES IN TREATMENT of childhood asthma but, as always, the real draw was the free lunch. On salaries that computed to something less than two dollars per hour, interns flocked to freebies.

Afterward, in the hallway, Peyton stopped to chat with friends and assure them that she was recovering nicely, which took all of two minutes. That was all the time they had before getting back to work, and it was about as long as Peyton cared to dwell on the injuries.

Peyton found it invigorating to be back in the hospital, even if it was only for a few hours and on crutches. In some ways it was more like being home than actually being home. The hospital was her comfort zone. Back at the apartment, she hadn't the slightest idea of what to do with herself. Here, she had a routine. The morning rounds. The noon lectures. Even the mundane paperwork of patient discharges. It was as familiar as the bitter coffee in the lounge, the lumpy mattress in the on-call suite, the frenetic pace in the ER—and the mime standing at the other end of the long corridor.

He was looking right at her. Then he was gone.

Peyton stopped short, her heart skipping a beat. It had been quite a distance between them, but she could have sworn it was the same clown who had danced the tango with her on the day before her car accident.

She snaked through the crowded hallway as fast as she could on crutches, stopping at the T-shaped intersection at the end of the hall. The cafeteria was to the right. The lobby was to the left. She stood in the middle, unsure of which way to go. A group of nurses passed her. A gurney rested unattended against the wall. But there was no sign of the mime.

Peyton felt a chill. The way he'd stared into her eyes after the dance had troubled her from the beginning. It was all the more disturbing to learn that no one really knew who had hired him for the surprise party. This latest stare and quick departure hadn't exactly put her at ease.

It was time to voice her concerns.

Peyton waited almost forty-five minutes for the residency program director to return from a meeting, but finally Miles Landau was able to see her.

Though Landau was a physician, his long-term service as program director had all but transformed him into a full-fledged administrator. He even dressed each day in a business suit rather than a traditional physician's coat. Part of his job was to make sure each intern and resident was on track to meet the program and certification requirements. Part of it was smoothing the daily bumps in the road.

Seeing that he had two other visitors waiting in the reception area and three other calls on hold, Peyton quickly summarized. He listened carefully, then asked, "Are you saying you're being stalked?"

"I'd be lying if I said he didn't scare me at that party. Then, less than twenty-four hours later, someone ran me off the road. Maybe it was all an accident, and maybe this is just a coincidence. But after what just happened in the hall this afternoon, I don't know what to think."

He scratched his head, thinking. "Didn't you raise this stalking theory with the police?"

"Yes, but they weren't very helpful."

"It was my understanding that they checked into it and ruled it out. You thought the young man you subdued at the Haverhill clinic might have run you off the road. Turns out he was in jail at the time of the accident, which is a pretty tight alibi."

"That's true. How did you know about that?"

"His lawyer keeps us informed."

"What lawyer?"

"This upstanding young man is represented by the same ambulance chaser who sued us over the bullet you fired into Nurse Felicia's hindquarters. Now we also have to answer to this jerk, who claims he had an adverse reaction to the secobarbital injection that knocked him out. His lawyer says you falsely accused him of stalking as an intimidation tactic, so he wouldn't sue."

"That's frivolous."

"Tell that to our underwriters. They estimate our legal fees will be at least fifty grand."

She wasn't sure if it was intentional on his part, but she was beginning to feel like a troublemaker. "I'm sure it will be resolved in our favor once the facts come out."

"Let's hope so. But anyway, back to you. Your concern is what, exactly?"

"I'd simply like to find out who the mime was at my surprise party. Maybe we can check his background, ask him a few questions."

"Because he gave you a funny look?"

"It's more than that." She paused, debating whether to say more, already concerned that she was coming across as paranoid. "From the clinic, it's obvious I know how to shoot a gun. My father was a cop and taught me as a teenager. But I never owned one till a few months ago. I used to jog at night during the summer. That's when I first got the feeling someone was following me, and then one night last December I could have sworn I heard someone picking at the lock on my front door."

"So you believe this stalking has been going on for months?"

"That was the first creepy sensation I had about it. As much as my husband travels on business, I didn't feel safe. I feel the same way now. Maybe I'm crazy on all counts. But just maybe it all ties together."

"No one is calling you crazy. But—"

"I'm not asking you to hit the panic button. Just a little follow-up, that's all."

He glanced at his phone, the lines blinking on hold. "All right," he said, sounding as if he'd run out of time to debate. "I'll have security check into it."

His sudden acquiescence unleashed the butterflies in her stomach. She hoped her fears were unfounded; then again, she didn't want to be the intern who cried wolf. "Hopefully it will all turn out to be a big nothing."

"You don't have to backpedal. The fact is, even if this guy doesn't turn out to be a stalker, he's in trouble. This is a children's hospital. And I freely admit, a very image-conscious children's hospital. We can't have our clowns blowing up balloons one minute and ogling female doctors the next. You did the right thing by bringing this to my attention."

"I'm glad you feel that way."

"Now, if you'll excuse me," he said with a glance toward the blinking lights on his phone.

She was going to shake his hand, but before she could rise on her crutches, he grabbed the phone and turned one hundred and eighty degrees in his swivel chair until he faced the window. She could almost see her own forlorn expression in the shiny bald spot on the back of his head. Between lawsuits and now the suspected paranoia, she apparently wasn't his favorite intern.

"Thanks for your time," she said as she saw her own way out of his office.

Kevin's flight arrived at La Guardia in the late afternoon. He did have a seminar in New York and it did start tomorrow, just as he'd told Peyton. But first he had other business.

A taxi took him to the hotel on Eighth Avenue, a fringe area of midtown Manhattan. Directly across the street were some boarded-up buildings, former adult bookstores that had been shut down in the city's crackdown on petty crime. Just up the street was a modern office tower that housed New York's most prestigious law firm, a veritable institution that was regarded as the most powerful in the world by everyone but its closest rivals across town and a few dreamers in Washington. The hotel was the other nice building on the block, not exactly a palace but still a far cry from the ratty surroundings.

Since leaving Boston, he realized just how glad he was to have made the clean break with Sandra. Before they had ended up in bed together, she had been a good friend and an excellent source of information about the firm. Luckily, he hadn't slipped and shared his secret with her. No one, not even Peyton, knew anything yet. Everyone was better off that way.

For two years he'd been working furtively and feverishly, mostly on nights and weekends. Occasionally he'd get behind schedule and have to catch up in midday, like this afternoon when his supervising partner had caught him at his computer in the office. Despite those intermittent near misses, he had managed to keep his mission to himself. Secrecy was paramount. His status was already shaky at the firm, and he didn't need to fan the flames by giving Ira Kaufman and the associate review committee reason to believe that he was padding his time sheets to make up for the hundreds of hours he had diverted from billable projects to his personal agenda.

"Keep the change," said Kevin as he exited the taxi. He stepped through the revolving door at the hotel's main entrance and walked straight to the registration desk. The cheery attendant checked him in.

"Could you tell me if Percy Gates has arrived yet?"

He spelled the name for her, and she brought it up on the computer. "I don't see a reservation for a Mr. Gates."

Kevin shrugged it off. The meeting wasn't until nine o'clock tomorrow morning. Gates would probably come in for the day. Kevin could have done the same on tomorrow morning's Boston–New York shuttle, barring snow or some mechanical problem. For the price of a hotel room, he wasn't about to risk missing the meeting that could change his life.

He rode the elevator alone, having waved off the concierge. His garment bag was light enough for him to carry it himself, and no way was he going to hand over his briefcase and notebook computer to some stranger. Especially not today.

His room was on the twenty-fifth floor, which put him at eye level with the hotshot lawyers in the fancy building up the street. Six years ago, he would have wanted to be one of them. Six months from now, they would all want to be him. He sat on the bed and switched on the television, but his mind was elsewhere. He wasn't exactly sure what to expect tomorrow morning, even though Percy had explained the entire deal to him by telephone. The whole field was new to Kevin, but he felt confident enough. He knew that in a very short while he'd for once evoke a sweet measure of jealousy from those snotty bastards at Marston & Wheeler. Peyton would sure be proud. Or envious, Sandra might say. Him and his competitive wife.

Nonsense, he thought.

He leaned back against the headboard, kicked off his shoes, and called room service. Without batting an eye, he ordered a thirty-four-dollar cheeseburger and a six-dollar Coke. "And a jumbo shrimp cocktail," he said just before hanging up, completely on a whim.

The irony, he realized, was that he was too excited to eat. He was about to dial and cancel the order, then stopped himself. What the heck? Let it come.

Suddenly, he felt like splurging.

14

A TAXI DROPPED PEYTON OFF OUTSIDE HER APARTMENT. IT WAS EARLY evening and turning very cold. Yet even in the darkness there was something instantly soothing about the quaint street she lived on, where iron picket fences adorned one well-preserved Queen Anne–style residence after another.

Despite a lively student contingent, Magnolia Street was quiet after midnight, especially in winter. The spring would bring it to life, when the trees—it really was *magnolia* street—would come into full bloom. In warmer weather Peyton loved to put on her running shoes and jog on nearby Commonwealth Avenue. The wide French-inspired boulevard epitomized the nineteenth-century spirit of self-indulgence that had driven the upper class from thrifty old Boston into the Back Bay. Running was one of the few ways Peyton could find time to take it all in. She'd pace herself through the Public Garden and around the willow trees that encircled the showcase lagoon, continue at a brisk clip along Newbury and her favorite sidewalk cafés, and finally cut over two blocks and kick it toward home past the old Romanesque-style church whose chiseled trumpeting angels had earned it the sobriquet of "Church of the Holy Bean Blowers."

That was where she'd first noticed him. Some guy who always seemed to be there. She'd thought nothing of it till last December, when Kevin was out of town yet again and she was home alone.

Late one night, she'd thought she'd heard someone picking at the lock on the front door. That's when she'd decided to buy a gun.

A gust of wind swept a wisp of light snow past her feet. It whistled down the sidewalk like a ghostly flying carpet, the tiny icy crystals glistening in the dim glow of old street lamps. Their two-bedroom flat had an outside entrance. She climbed the steps and unlocked the front door. A toasty warmth greeted her in the foyer, which told her she had most assuredly forgotten to turn down the thermostat before leaving this morning. Kevin was always on her back about leaving the heat blasting and the lights on when she left the house. The glowing light from the kitchen marked her failure on that count as well.

She hung her scarf and hat behind the door, then brushed the snow from her coat and tucked it in the closet. Too tired to eat, she headed for the bedroom and stopped halfway down the hall. She could have sworn she smelled paella from the kitchen, one of her all-time favorite dinners. She headed to the kitchen.

"Mother?"

The older woman screamed, then brought a hand to her heart, as if on the verge of cardiac arrest. "My word, child. You scared me half to death."

"I didn't expect to see you either. Didn't you get my message?"

"Yes. But there's no need for you to be a martyr. I don't mind looking after you while Kevin's out of town."

"This isn't really necessary."

"Too late. Paella's in the oven. Extra mussels, just the way you like it. Why don't you help me with the salad?"

Peyton went to the sink and started washing the lettuce. Her mother was being unusually sweet. It made Peyton suspicious, but she decided to give her the benefit of the doubt. "This is very nice of you. Thanks."

"I thought you could use some cheering up."

"I'm pretty cheery these days, considering."

"That's the part that concerns me. The 'considering.'"

Peyton didn't answer. There it was, the reason for the sweet-ness. Another fishing expedition into what was going on in her daughter's life.

"Oh, I almost forgot," her mother said. "A man came by while you were out."

"A man?"

"A process server. He left you a summons and something called a civil complaint. It's on the table."

Peyton dried her hands and glanced at the summons.

"You and the hospital are being sued," said her mother.

"Did you read this?"

"Of course. I thought it might be urgent."

Peyton kept reading. "I knew they'd sued the hospital. I guess now they're going after me individually as well."

"You want to tell me about it?"

"Someone's just looking for a deep pocket to extort some settlement money. It's all a bunch of baloney."

"So you didn't shoot that nurse?"

"It's a long story."

"Is that why you were fired from the clinic?"

"I wasn't fired."

"The complaint says you were fired. Paragraph eleven."

"What, did you memorize it? I didn't get fired. I'm being reas-signed."

"You don't have to hide anything from me. I'm your mother."

"There's no need to be concerned. My work is just fine."

Peyton started away, but her mother gently took her arm to stop her. "It's not your work that I'm concerned about."

"I really wish you and everyone else would stop treating me as if this stupid car accident has turned me into a basket case."

"I don't think the accident caused the problem, dear. I think it's a symptom of a deeper problem. One for which I'm partially to blame."

Peyton blinked hard, not comprehending. "I've blamed you

for a lot of things in my lifetime, but this car accident is not one of them."

"Your whole life I pushed you to be better than everyone else, to do better than I ever did. Sometimes I set goals that were totally unrealistic, just so that when you fell short, you'd still land in a good place. But damned if you didn't exceed even the unrealistic goals. And now that you're a grown woman, you push yourself even harder. Your father and I are proud of all that you've accomplished. I don't think you've ever failed at anything. But everyone eventually fails at something. Getting fired from a stupid clinic in Haverhill isn't worth, you know . . ."

"Worth what?"

"Driving a car into Jamaica Pond."

"You think I tried to kill myself?" she said, incredulous.

Her mother's eyes glistened, moist. "I totally understand how you must have felt. Embarrassed, angry. No one likes to fail. You'd been working insane hours and then there was this fiasco at the clinic. And to top it all off, you were pregnant but so ambivalent that you hadn't even told your husband about it."

"You're getting it all wrong."

"I know things aren't good between you and Kevin."

"Our marriage will be fine."

"Have you asked him where he was on the night of your accident?"

"He was in Providence on business."

"Did you know he had lunch today at an obscure little restaurant with a very attractive woman?"

She was troubled for a moment, as he'd told her that he was just stopping by the office briefly before heading to the airport. Then shock kicked in. "Have you been following him?"

"Your father and I are concerned."

"Don't put this on Daddy. Spying isn't the kind of thing he would do."

"Okay, *I'm* concerned. What's wrong with that? I know what you're going through. You work hard, you're talented, you feel like you should be on the fast track to success. And then, bam, some-body takes away your dreams."

"Not this again. Daddy didn't take anything away from you. And neither did I."

"I know you didn't mean to. But the mind can do funny things to a person. Just like you, I've hit the lowest of the low points. That's why I understand this so well. You find yourself driving down a dark road one night and realize that with one quick jerk of the wheel . . ."

"Are you mad? I'm not suicidal."

"You can't deny that you've been depressed."

"Yes, I've experienced some depression. *After* the accident."

"The accident was a catharsis. You were unhappy before and didn't even know it."

"It was no catharsis. I'm sad because I miscarried."

"And you shouldn't feel guilty for that. Blame me. By pushing you all your life, I've only pushed you away. Believe it or not, there was a time when you wanted to be just like your mommy. And now you're twenty-eight years old and we're practically strangers. That depresses me. Somewhere inside, it has to depress you."

"My feelings toward you have nothing to do with the way you pushed me to succeed. And for the record, I'm not depressed about anything except the fact that I lost the baby. If that doesn't meet the rational, unemotional standard you set when I was a teenager, I'm sorry."

"That's a low blow."

Peyton suddenly regretted her words, but her mother had a way of knocking her off the high road. "You're right. I'm sorry. But for crying out loud, Mother, if you would just stop hitting me over the head with the fact that I was the pregnancy you didn't want, maybe I wouldn't come back at you with the pregnancy you didn't seem to care about losing."

"You're talking about your sister, my own flesh and blood. I was traumatized for months."

"You sure didn't act like it."

"Maybe the only way for me to deal with it was to tell myself that it was the best thing for everyone."

"No, Mom. You mean the best thing for *you*. That's always been the test in our family." Peyton turned away, silencing herself before it was too late. "I'm going to bed."

On crutches she hurried down the hall to the bathroom and shut the door. The accident was no catharsis, but she felt one now. She hadn't yelled at her mother that way since she'd been a teenager, having vowed long ago never to stir up the old, destructive anger. The loss of a child was all but guaranteed to take Peyton and her mother back to those dark days.

She leaned forward with both hands on the sink, staring into the basin, breathing deeply. Slowly, she raised her eyes and took a good look at herself in the mirror. Her eyes were red and she was on the verge of tears. For almost a week she'd toughed out the accident, the miscarriage. Somehow, she'd managed to contain her feelings and remain stoic. She'd canceled the appointment for Jamie's first ultrasound, given one of her patients the prenatal vitamins she no longer needed, even donated to charity the maternity clothes she'd never gotten big enough to wear. All that, without having faltered in the least. Now, however, she felt deprived of the emotional release she'd obviously needed.

Her left eye started to twitch. It hadn't given her much trouble since the injury, but it was suddenly painful. She squinted and leaned toward the mirror. A stabbing sensation emerged just below the lower lid. She blinked twice and noticed a minuscule drop of blood at the outside corner of her eye. She dabbed it with a tissue and realized what it was. A shard of shattered glass had worked its way out from somewhere beneath her skin. Clear and rigid, like a tiny frozen teardrop that had hardened deep inside her. She was suddenly cold, overwhelmed with sadness.

With that, the tears melted and finally began to flow.

15

"BREAKFAST IS READY," HER MOTHER CALLED FROM THE KITCHEN.

Hearing those words was like a time warp for Peyton. So many times they had gone to bed angry at each other. They'd wake the next morning and try to pretend it had never happened. Neither of them was a very good actor.

"Just a sec," said Peyton. She was in the bathroom, checking her eye in the mirror. It hadn't bothered her further since expelling the tiny shard of glass last night. But, cosmetically, the skin around the eye wasn't healing quite as smoothly as she had hoped. She tried not to dwell on it, but it *was* her face. The image came to mind of those ugly ducks along the Prado with all that bumpy extra skin around their eyes and beaks that resembled oozing lava. She knew she was only torment-ing herself, but she leaned over the sink and pressed the injured side of her face flat against the mirror on the medicine cabinet. She angled it perfectly so that half her face—the good half—reflected from the medicine cabinet to the mirror on the wall, to the full-length mirror on the back of the bathroom door, and then back to the other half of the medicine cabinet. In the reflection of the reflections, she was able to create a whole face from the unscarred half, smooth and beautiful. It wasn't exactly the way she used to look (on any face, the right and left sides were always different), but the little game made her wonder if she would ever be pretty again. Every day Kevin told her she was still breathtaking, but did he really mean it?

As much as she tried not to think about it, she wondered, too, if she was prettier than the woman Kevin had lunched with yesterday.

"Toast is getting cold," her mother called again.

Peyton mounted her crutches and headed for the kitchen. Her mother was sitting at the counter, reading the morning paper and sipping coffee. Peyton took the seat across from her, where toast and juice were waiting on the table.

Her mother never looked up from the paper. Peyton didn't want to pick another fight, but she had lain awake last night thinking, juxtaposing the things she and her mother had said against the remarks the NICU nurses had made in the bathroom yesterday. It was bothering her too much to let it go.

"Do you think I would make a good mother?" asked Peyton.

Finally, Valerie lowered the newspaper. "I think you'll make a fine mother."

Peyton took a bite of her toast, which was indeed cold. "Have you ever wondered why I went into pediatrics?"

"I assume you love children. Which is all the more reason you'll make a great mother."

"Have you ever wondered if it had something to do with us? Subconsciously."

Her mother sighed and said, "I don't want to rehash last night. I came here to help you, not to argue. All I want is to be here for you when you need me. I just wish you would let me."

She turned her attention back to the newspaper, but Peyton didn't look away. She wondered if her mother appreciated the irony of her complaining about being shut out. Stoicism in the face of personal tragedy was a family tradition she had learned from her mother. The first hard lesson for Peyton had come at age fifteen. The family had just moved to Florida. It was a temporary relocation that lasted only one school year, just long enough for her mother to carry the baby to term. The pregnancy had been unexpected, and the reasons for the sudden move to Florida weren't fully explained to Peyton at the time, except for vague allusions to the medical benefits of a warmer climate. Peyton wasn't happy about leaving her high school friends behind, but the excitement of having a sibling soon eased that loss. She was fascinated by the changes in her mother's body, the growth of the fetus, and the eventual prospect of her mother actually giving birth. She read books about the subject and researched it. She even accompanied her mother to the obstetrician for her office visits, until the sixth month, when her mother apparently decided that Peyton was becoming a pest. During the third trimester, her mother visited the doctor alone. As the delivery date neared, Peyton lobbied hard for a spot in the delivery room, but her mother refused an audience. Not even her father would be allowed to watch. As it turned out, when the actual day came, Peyton wasn't even allowed in the hospital. Her mother made her stay home. It finally came clear that Peyton was much more excited about this baby than her mother was.

Throughout the day, her father called with periodic updates from the hospital. He had no specifics for her. Finally, more than twenty-four hours after her parents had left the house, Peyton got a phone call from her mother.

"I have some bad news," she said.

"What?"

"The baby didn't live."

Peyton could hardly speak. "What went wrong?"

"There's no one to blame. These things happen."

Peyton wanted details but got none. She, too, was grief stricken and wanted to plan a memorial service. She wanted to select the grave site. She wanted to take care of those heartrending things so that her mother wouldn't have to. The more supportive she tried to be, the more furious her mother became.

"But I want to help," said Peyton.

"You can't. This isn't about you. It's between me and your father."

That was twelve years ago, but the memory was vivid. It was horrible, the way her mother had made her feel like an outsider. Under normal circumstances, Peyton probably would have for-

16

KEVIN ARRIVED AT NINE O'CLOCK. THE MEETING WAS SCHEDULED IN Turlington Hall, which was a fancy name for one of the hotel's mezzanine-level conference rooms. Percy Gates wasn't there, but his assistant greeted him at the door. A crowd had gathered inside, standing in clusters of four or five around the room and conversing. Most were dressed in business attire, except for two balding guys with ponytails who wore blue jeans and tweed jackets. Kevin made an effort to introduce himself to a few people who were mingling around the breakfast bar, hoping to network. His luck, he met only others like him. Aspiring writers.

The Percy Gates fiction writers' conference came with an impressive guarantee: find a literary agent or your money back. After two years of writing and rewriting his novel, Kevin had received enough rejection letters from publishers to know that Percy's premise was correct: The big houses didn't buy a novel unless it was presented by an agent. Percy liked to relate the story of the clever journalist who, as a test, retyped *The Yearling* verbatim and submitted it in manuscript form directly to every publisher in New York. One or two recognized it as the 1939 Pulitzer Prize–winner, but most rejected it out of hand on the assumption that if it wasn't represented by an agent it wasn't any good.

Not that Kevin was shooting for a Pulitzer. Mostly he just wanted to hear that his stuff was entertaining. At times, he'd even been tempted to let Peyton read a few chapters. It would have been a bit like asking his mother if she thought he was handsome, but every writer had to start somewhere. That was where Percy Gates had come in. He claimed to handpick aspiring writers whose sample chapters exhibited "serious talent." That, plus a thousand-dollar registration fee paid in advance, got best-selling wannabes five minutes each at the podium to present their work to a roomful of agents in an informal setting.

By nine-thirty, Kevin counted roughly sixty bodies in the room. With just a dozen authors—Percy had promised there would be no more than twelve—that meant an agent-to-author ratio of four-to-one. If he couldn't score in this room, he didn't deserve to be published.

"Do you have your speaker's card, Mr. Stokes?" It was Percy's ever helpful assistant.

"Yes, thank you," said Kevin.

The young woman stepped up to the microphone and made brief introductory remarks that emphasized the informality of the occasion. Each writer had been given a numbered card and would speak in that order, for three minutes tops. There would be no introductions, and strict silence was not required. Guests were free to continue to mingle and enjoy themselves, listening or not as they wished, as if the authors' cries of *Please represent me!* were no more than Muzak.

Kevin figured his placement—sixth—was perfect, far enough down on the speaker list for things to get rolling but not so far down that people would leave before he got his shot. He watched the initial speakers with an eye toward gauging what type of comments piqued the interest of the audience. The first guy was nervous, sweaty, and horrible. The next three were just flat. Interestingly, they were all lawyers, like him. The fifth had obviously mastered the art of billing by the hour. He droned on well beyond the time limit.

"I see my book as a kind of big-screen, literary thriller," he said. "Sort of Jackie Chan meets *Moby Dick*."

Finally, number five was finished. No one applauded, but no one had acknowledged the previous speakers, either. Less than half the crowd was even listening at all and, of those, half were listening only to be polite. Kevin felt a knot in his stomach. The confidence and energy he'd felt earlier were slowly giving way to embarrassment and desperation. He glanced toward the door and considered making a run for it. What was once opportunity seemed like nothing more than an expensive form of humiliation. But he had waited months for this, and it was his turn. The microphone was waiting.

What have I got to lose? He reached the lectern just as another man did.

"Excuse me," said Kevin. "I'm number six."

"No, I'm number six."

Kevin removed his number from his coat pocket and showed him. "I'm quite certain, I'm number six."

The guy showed him an identical little card bearing the same number. "Looks like we're both number six."

A woman approached. "I'm number six too."

"Me too," said another.

Kevin quickly canvassed the room for Percy's assistant, but she was gone. A wave of concern washed over him. He stepped up to the microphone and asked, "Excuse me, but is there any other author who has the number six?"

Two men to the side raised their hands. At that, Kevin's voice started to quake. "How about number seven?"

"I'm number seven," said four people in unison.

"Seven here," said another.

A murmur of concern passed through the crowd. Kevin said, "Show of hands, please. Who's number eight?"

Six people raised their hands.

"Number nine?"

Another dozen hands went up.

His face flushed red. He was ready to explode, filled with anger and humiliation.

The guy behind him said, "I'm gonna sue this bastard."

"Me too," said another, and another, and so the sentiment passed throughout the room until suddenly it was painfully plain to Kevin what had happened.

He gripped the podium and asked, "Is there *anyone* in this room who is *not* a lawyer aspiring to be a writer?"

Silence, till a short guy in the back finally volunteered, "I'm a dentist."

"I was told there would be agents here," a woman said angrily.

"So was I!"

"Me too!"

"Hey, get this," said another number six, cell phone in hand. "I just dialed Percy's office number. It's disconnected."

The room was abuzz with panic. A bitterness rose in Kevin's throat. He scanned the crowd, believing but not quite willing to accept that so many smart people had been so easily scammed. Dreams could make anyone stupid, and busy professionals with money to throw after their dreams were stupidest of all. Sixty suckers at a thousand bucks a pop. *Not a bad day's work, Percy.*

"Son of a bitch," he said into the microphone without even realizing it, his amplified voice resonating above the angry clamor.

A horn blasted outside Peyton's apartment, and she headed out to the taxi. Boston was generally regarded as a walking city—"Should we walk or do we have time to take a cab?" the old joke has it—but the rules were different on crutches in the dead of winter. With their only car now totaled, cabs would be Peyton's only real option until she was walking normally and ready to fend for herself on the subway.

"Children's Hospital," she said, climbing into the backseat. Her cell phone rang as the car pulled away from the curb. It was Dr. Sheffield from the hospital.

"Dr. Landau asked me to call you with the good news," he said.

"We tracked down that mime you were so concerned about. His name's Andy Johnson."

"I don't recognize the name."

"He's relatively new to Children's, but he works at several other local hospitals in pediatric wards."

"What was his story?"

"Don't be alarmed, but it appears that he may have a little thing for you."

"What kind of 'thing'?" she asked with trepidation.

"Let me say up front that security took your concerns very seriously. Several years ago, we had a resident stalked by a relative of one of our patients, so we know how to handle these situations."

"I can't believe this. I am being stalked."

"No. All I'm saying is that security did everything by the book. They interviewed Johnson thoroughly. At first he denied acting inappropriately toward you in any way. But things started to unravel when security asked him who arranged for the surprise party and who hired him to dance with you. He said that one of the clowns at Mass General told him he had been hired for this job at Children's and was unable to cover it. Supposedly he paid Johnson seventy-five bucks to fill in for him. He told us the guy's name was Rudy, but when security called Mass General, it turned out they don't have any entertainers named Rudy."

"Which means what? Johnson organized the surprise party himself just to dance with me? I don't even know him."

"That would appear to be a possibility."

Her heart began to race. "Did you ask him about the car accident?"

"This is the really good news," said Sheffield. "Our security director was able to persuade Johnson to submit to a polygraph examination. They asked him several questions about the accident. Whether he knew anything about it. Whether he was involved in it in any way. He was even asked point blank whether he ran you off the road. He denied any knowledge or involvement, and the examiner concluded that he was telling the truth."

"What happens next?"

"He'll probably be dismissed. The legal department will figure out the exact grounds, but I would imagine it will have something to do with violation of the hospital's sexual harassment policy."

"Will there be any follow-up with the police?"

"In what aspect?"

"Lie detector tests aren't infallible. Isn't anyone going to investigate to see if Johnson really did run me off the road?"

"I'll have to check with security on that."

"I'm on my way into the hospital right now. I'd like to talk with them."

"My advice to you is to concentrate on getting well."

"But this is important."

"Yes, and so is your well-being. Please don't take this the wrong way. But Dr. Landau and I both thought it would be appropriate to remind you that the hospital has two psychiatrists available to counsel residents in times of stress. More people take advantage of that than you would think. There's no stigma. If this accident has you feeling fearful, angry, guilty, paranoid, or whatever, you can talk it out."

That was the reaction she'd feared. "I'll be okay."

"I know you will. I hasten to add that although it's early in your residency, my observations so far tell me that you have true star potential. You will get through this."

"Thank you."

"But do think about that counseling. I know the accident was especially stressful for you. We all respect your privacy, but it has percolated up through the grapevine that you miscarried. I'm sorry."

"Oh," was all she could say. *Was anything private anymore?*

"An accident that results in injury to an innocent or unborn child is bound to generate feelings of guilt. Psychologically, you may need someone to blame. But the blame game is a dangerous road, because you may eventually come to realize that this mysterious other car wasn't at fault. You may then blame yourself for having driven when you were too tired or when the weather was bad, or for not having taken another route home. The reality is, no one is to blame. It was just an accident."

"What are you suggesting? I'm making up stories about another car to shift responsibility for the miscarriage to someone else?"

"No one is judging you. We don't know where this investigation of Andy Johnson will lead, but it may not provide all the answers you're looking for. If you want to talk it out, counselors are available any time."

"I'll keep it in mind. Thank you."

They said goodbye. Peyton switched off her phone, her thoughts a jumbled mess. She had been on the fast track to success throughout med school, and she knew that Dr. Sheffield's compliment about her "star potential" wasn't just fluff. A month ago he'd planted seeds in her mind about pursuing the elite pediatric fellowship program after her residency. The mishap at the Haverhill clinic and the ensuing lawsuits were enough of a setback to her young career. She didn't need remarks like "paranoid delusions" in her evaluation file. Dr. Sheffield only meant well by recommending counseling, but the best thing for her career right now was to knock off all this talk of kamikaze cars and mysterious villains.

"Eight-fifty," said the driver.

She gave him a ten and stepped down to the sidewalk. The main entrance to the hospital was straight ahead. To the right of it, a plate-glass window displayed billboard-size paintings of Scooby-Doo, the Tasmanian Devil, Sylvester the Cat, and other cartoon characters. Above them was an ominous sign that read EMERGENCY. That seeming contradiction summed up her feelings. Try as she might to laugh the whole thing off, underneath it all was a true crisis. She planted her crutches on the wet sidewalk and started for the entrance, having resolved on the spot that her sick leave was over. She didn't care what Sheffield or Landau thought. She didn't need a psychiatrist.

She was going straight to the director of security.

17

KEVIN WAS ON THE VERGE OF NODDING OFF WHEN HIS CELL PHONE vibrated. Percy Gates be damned, he really did have a seminar to attend, and a full afternoon of tedious analysis of recent SEC enforcement actions was having the inevitable effect. His eyes blinked opened, and it took a half second for him to remember that he was seated in a packed auditorium. He'd zoned out ten minutes after the lights had dimmed for the overhead projector. He grabbed his phone and headed for the exit, trying hard not to disturb those lawyers who had managed not to snooze through the guest of honor's speech.

"Hello," he said the instant he reached the hallway.

It was Peyton. She sounded wired, but in two minutes he fully understood why. It took her that long to tell him all about Andy Johnson.

"Unbelievable," was all he could say. "Do they think he's the guy who ran you into Jamaica Pond?"

"No. They gave him a lie detector test. Apparently it showed that he didn't have anything to do with my accident."

"That's not a hundred percent reliable, but it should give you some comfort."

"It doesn't. I just spent the last forty minutes in a meeting with the director of security here at the hospital. If you ask me, the test they gave Johnson is totally unreliable."

"Why do you say that?"

"If I tell you, do you promise not to wig out on me?"

"Yeah, I guess. What are you getting at?"

"One of the questions they asked Johnson was whether he and I had ever been sexually involved."

"Really?" Suddenly, Kevin could think only of the red rose he'd found outside their door. "What was Johnson's answer?"

"Kevin, you promised not to wig out."

"I'm not wigging out."

"I know that tone. It's the same voice you get whenever I mention Gary Varne. It makes me afraid to talk to you about certain things."

"I just want to know what this guy said, that's all."

"He said no, of course. But here's why I think the polygraph was bogus. The examiner concluded that his answer showed signs of deception, which is ridiculous."

The part about it being "ridiculous" didn't even register. Kevin didn't answer, knowing that he would only be giving her "that tone" again.

"Kevin, are you still there?"

"Yeah."

"Then say something."

"I just don't understand why the examiner would even ask if the two of you had been sexually involved."

"Because security wanted to know what kind of stalker personality he might be."

"Stalker personality?"

"The way he explained it to me, law enforcement uses different labels for different kinds of obsession. If a stalker has had a previous relationship with his victim, that's called a simple obsession stalker. But if the stalker is obsessed with someone he never really even met, that's a whole different kind of stalker personality. They call it love obsession."

"Why didn't they just ask *you* if the two of you had ever been involved?"

"Because I'm married. I guess they thought I would lie."

"Would you?"

"Would I what?"

"Lie."

"Please. Now you're making me mad."

"You didn't answer the question."

"I'm not a liar," she said, a little too loud.

His head was spinning. "I'm sorry. I've actually had a terrible couple of days here in New York."

"That doesn't make it okay to effectively accuse me of . . . you know."

"Well, try to put yourself in my shoes. How could any man just ignore a lie detector test that shows his wife was sexually involved with another man?"

"That's not what it showed. Johnson was asked if we were sexually involved, and his denial showed signs of deception. You have to remember how stalkers think. They live in a fantasy world. He may have thought that by dancing the tango with me, he and I were sexually involved. Or maybe he's fantasized about having sex with me so many times that in his mind we have been sexually involved."

"I suppose that's possible."

"It's more than possible. God, Kevin, I hate this. All this mistrust. I mean, it's gotten to the point that even my own mother suspects . . ."

"Suspects what?"

She hesitated, then said, "She thinks she saw you with someone at lunch yesterday."

His heart nearly stopped. "Oh, really?"

"Look, I'm sorry I even said that. I don't want us to be pointing fingers. I was so happy the way we seemed to be reconnecting."

"Me too. Let's just kind of move forward."

"That's exactly what I wanted to hear. When are you coming home?"

"Seminar ends tomorrow afternoon."

"I wish you could come sooner."

"Ditto," he said with a nervous chuckle. "I gotta go, okay? I'll call you later."

As they hung up, he nearly fell against the wall, drained. The lunch reference was just a whisker away from a direct question about Sandra. But why had Peyton backed off?

Maybe she wasn't ready to confront him, just as he wasn't ready to press for answers about the rose he'd found outside their door. Surely she would have said it was just another unwelcome expression of love by her stalker. Perhaps that was the truth, in which case telling her about it would only scare her. If it was a symbol of something else, however, and if Kevin was going to make an issue out of it, he wanted to look her in the eye when she explained that rose away. Peyton probably wanted the same face-to-face advantage, if she was going to take him to task about the lunch.

He suddenly recalled Sandra's parting words to him: He and Peyton were competitors, and she'd beaten him at his own game. He'd dismissed that as crazy at the time. Peyton's middle name was monogamy. But with he and Sandra traveling so much together, Peyton could well have suspected something long before her husband had crossed the line. It seemed unlike Peyton to take a lover out of spite. But maybe she did find another man. Not a man. A clown. A damn *clown*!

He shoved his phone in his pocket and headed for the cloakroom. To hell with the seminar. To hell with everything.

It was time to check out.

18

ANDY JOHNSON WAS MAD AS HELL. AFTER FIFTEEN YEARS OF PART–TIME work at a half-dozen different hospitals in Boston, his career was over. Children's had been the first to advise him that his services were no longer required. The other hospitals quickly followed suit. One suggestive look at a young female doctor and he was suddenly blacklisted all over town. He knew that image-conscious hospitals like Children's were understandably sensitive about the misconduct of personnel who came in direct contact with pediat-ric patients. But from the way the administration had overreacted, it was as if he'd cornered Peyton in a restroom and exposed him-self. The whole politically correct world was going crazy.

"Buy you a beer, pal?"

He'd heard the same offer every ten minutes for the past hour. Some lonely old stranger had planted his ass next to him at the bar and seemed determined to become his drinking buddy. After a few minutes of reluctant small talk, Andy loosened up. Two or three shots later, Andy found himself nearly boring the old geezer to death with the whole stinking story.

"They put a damn memo in my in-box," said Andy. "Can you believe that? Didn't even have the guts to tell me to my face."

"That's pretty low," the old man said. "Maybe you should sue them."

"For what? Clown discrimination?"

"They can't just fire you for giving some woman the eye."

"There's more to it than that. They must think I'm after her."

"Are you?"

Andy shot a look. "What do you mean by that?"

"Just a question. Are you after her or not?"

Andy examined the foamy head on his beer, then smiled thinly. "You ever just look at a woman and know it would be great?"

"Know what would be great?"

"What's wrong with you, old man, out of Viagra? I'm talking about sex."

"So, you are after her."

"I'm not *after* her. I was just, you know, fishin'."

The old man nodded in silence. Andy said, "Whole thing started when I got hired to dance the tango with her at a surprise party. It was all pretend, but when a good-looking woman like that can step into a role in front of a crowd of people and have that much fun acting all sexy and everything, it makes you stop and think. Here's a woman with no hang-ups. She has got to be a firecracker in the bedroom."

"So you just want to nail her."

"Well—yeah."

"You're sick."

"What?"

"You're a sick son of a bitch," he said, a little louder this time.

Andy sat up straight. "Listen, pal, I don't care how old you are. You watch your mouth."

"We're all sick. Every last one of us." A smile crept to his lips as he raised his glass to toast. "Here's to us sickos, and to the women who made us that way."

Andy was beginning to wonder if the old guy was all there, but he seemed harmless. "I'll drink to that," he said. They finished their beers together and set the empty glasses on the bar.

"Buy you another, fella?"

"Nah, thanks," said Andy. "I gotta make a pit stop and head home."

Andy slid off the stool and started toward the bathroom. Halfway there, he felt dizzy. It was a good buzz at first, but it quickly intensified to something discomforting and then disorienting. He stopped to get his bearings. The television behind the bar had been playing in the background all night, but he could suddenly hear it clearly, as if the volume had raised itself. Then it faded. His attention shifted to two guys shooting pool in the back who seemed to be laughing at him. That faded too. The kitchen was behind a set of swinging double doors in the back, yet the clanging sounds of pots and pans rattled in his brain. He shook that off and turned his gaze toward a fat woman at the pay phone. Or maybe it was a man. He couldn't tell. It was impossible to focus. His hands felt numb. His knees were weak. A flash of hot then cold ran from the base of his spine to the top of his head, and he suddenly felt himself falling. He reached for the nearest chair, which happened to be occupied.

"Hey, watch it!"

A big guy pushed him, and Andy fell to the floor. He tried to stand but could only rise on one knee. He tried to prop himself up, but he was groping someone's thigh.

"Get your hands off my girl!"

The big guy shoved him again. Andy tumbled backward and sprawled on the floor, his limbs tangled in the upright legs of overturned chairs. He tried to get up but could barely lift his head. It took all of his strength just to hear the conversation above him.

"What's the problem here?" asked the bartender.

"This drunken slob is falling all over us."

"I'll get him home. Everybody just calm down, okay?"

Andy recognized the shaky third voice. The old man lifted him to his feet and showed Andy his wallet. "You're so wasted you left it sitting right on the bar," he said, tucking it back into Andy's coat pocket. "Come on, let me help you out of here."

He could barely walk, but somehow he got his arm around his new buddy. They squeezed through the doorway side by side, his feet dragging with each step. The blast of cold night air helped him sober up a little and triggered a few coherent thoughts. The whole experience was strange. Five beers were well within his limit. The old man had talked him into two shots of tequila, but that shouldn't have put him under the table. Or had it been six beers and three shots? Maybe that was the problem. He'd lost count.

"Juss call me a cab," said Andy, his words slurred. "I'll be okay."

"No way a cabby is gonna risk you puking all over his car."

"Can't walk. It's too far."

"How about the subway?"

"Yeah," Andy mumbled. "Red line to Quincy. Lass train's at twelve-thirty."

"I'll take you."

Andy leaned on his friend as they headed down the sidewalk. The extra burden had the old man huffing and puffing, his breath steaming in the cold air. Andy hardly noticed the chill.

The nearest station was Downtown Crossing, a maze of long underground tunnels and platforms where the red and orange lines intersected. During business hours, it was like a busy ant mound. At midnight with temperatures near zero, it was deserted. The old man fed the fare into the slot and pushed Andy through the turnstile. Andy was about to turn and thank him, but he was right on Andy's heels.

"I'll see you to the train," he said. "Don't want you falling on your face."

"Thanks, old man."

They followed the signs to the platform. Dim overhead lighting did little to brighten the dank cement surroundings. Graffiti covered the advertisements on the walls. A half-frozen puddle of urine glistened in the corner. The old man led him to the far end of the platform where the red line fed into the station through a narrow tunnel. They stopped at the thick yellow line that marked the edge of the platform. Beyond was a several foot drop to two rows of tracks. Andy was suddenly aware of how alone they were, just him and the old man. They'd left the street noises somewhere behind in the underground tunnels, and the silence was palpable. Andy's numbness from the drinking and the cold was dissipating, and he was starting to feel his toes again. He took a long look down the track but saw only darkness. He wondered if they'd already missed the last train. Slowly, his eyes were drawn to the humming noise below the platform.

"Third rail," said the old man, having noticed it too. "Six hundred volts of electricity. Watch your balance."

The mere suggestion had Andy feeling wobbly. "I wanna sid-down."

"Not now. Train's coming."

Down the track, a pair of headlamps was indeed drawing closer to the station. Andy tried to take a step back from the yellow line, but the old man was standing right behind and holding firm. *Strong for such an old guy.*

"Let's back up," said Andy.

"I got you. Don't start squirming around on me."

Andy could hear the train now, feel its vibration under his feet. It was fast approaching. He was close enough to the edge to actually see the conductor in the lead car. The old man was still behind him, standing just outside the tunnel's opening and out of the conductor's line of sight. Again Andy tried to back away from the line, but the old man's grip only tightened. Andy was feeling flushed, the way he had back at the bar.

"I really gotta sit."

He thought he heard the guy tell him to shut up, but the noise from the rails had drowned it out. The speeding train was just twenty yards away and closing in quickly. Suddenly, the old man grabbed him by the jacket collar, whirled him around, and shouted into his face.

"You can't have Peyton!"

Their eyes locked just long enough for the crazed look to cut to Andy's core, long enough for Andy to realize that this close, chin to chin, the old man no longer seemed old. With that, Andy felt the power of the other man's rage squarely in the chest, both hands hitting him with the force of a much younger man. Andy flew back across the yellow line. He reached for the assassin's hand, his coat, anything he might grab to stop from falling, but he garnered only fistfuls of cold air. He heard himself scream, which sent his mind racing. For a split second, it was as if he were outside his body and witnessing his own peril. Arms flailing as he tumbled off the platform. The speeding train screeching into the station. An explosion of hot, red blood at the moment of impact. His vital organs crushed and splattered across the windshield. His severed limbs scattered across the tracks, landing with a sizzle on the electrified third line.

"No!" he shouted. He reached for the old man one last time but came up empty, then met the train head-on as his vision became reality.

19

HE HAD A JELLY BEAN UP HIS NOSE. THAT WAS THE IMMEDIATE PROB-
lem facing Peyton and her patient on what was turning out to be
a quirky first full day back in the ER. There were seven other boys
with the same condition, all from the same birthday party. The kids
would be fine, but with the angry mob of relatives in the waiting
room, the same could not be said for the parents who'd hosted
the party.

"Peyton, can you come with me, please?"

She looked up and saw Dr. Sheffield, chief resident, peering
through the open doorway. Peyton had a syringe in one hand and
the seven-year-old boy's trembling hand in the other. She gave
Sheffield a little shrug, as if asking whether it could wait.

"It's important," he said.

From the expression on his face, she knew it truly was important. She reassured the boy and his mother, excused herself, and
stepped out with Sheffield. "What's up?" she asked, pulling off her
latex gloves.

"Police are here. They want to see you."

"Me? What about?"

"I was hoping you could tell me. They're waiting at your
locker, and they don't look happy."

The locker lounge was just down the hall, next to the on-call
suite. Dr. Sheffield opened the door and Peyton followed. Standing

near Peyton's locker were Dr. Landau and two detectives, one of whom she recognized.

"Detective Bolton," she said, somewhat surprised. "What brings you here?"

He shook Peyton's hand, ignoring her question to introduce his colleague. "This is Detective Andrea Stout. She's with the MBTA Police."

"Mass transit has its own police?"

"Yes," she said, all business. "We know how busy you are, so if you could just give us a minute, we'd like to see your house key."

"Why?"

Bolton said, "It's in your best interest, Doctor."

Peyton hesitated but saw no point in protest. She opened her locker, dug the key from her purse, and handed it over. Detective Stout removed a sheet of paper from her bag that bore the outline of another key. She laid it on the bench and placed Peyton's key inside the lines.

"It's a match," she said.

"A match for what?" asked Peyton.

Bolton said, "Andy Johnson—the clown who danced with you here at the hospital—was found dead last night. Hit by a subway train."

"That's awful."

"Before you get all weepy, I should tell you that we found a house key in his coat pocket that didn't belong to him. It now appears to be a key to your house."

Peyton took a half-step back, stunned. "How is that possible?"

"Somehow he made a copy."

"So he was stalking me."

"Evidently. That seems even more likely in light of the additional piece of evidence we found on his person. It's what made us really suspect the key was to your apartment in the first place."

"What is it?"

Bolton looked at the other cop, then back at Peyton. "He had a photo of you in his wallet. A snapshot."

She was suddenly dizzy. "He took my picture?"

"It's a close-up, so it was either taken by someone who knows you and Johnson stole it or he took it himself with a telephoto lens."

"I don't know what to say."

"It shouldn't be a total shock," said Bolton. "I understand that you complained to administration that Mr. Johnson scared you at a surprise party here in the hospital."

"That's true. I even thought it was possible that it was Johnson who had run me off the road the night of my accident. But it turned out he passed a lie detector test."

"Don't quote me on this," said Bolton, "but those things aren't a hundred percent reliable. A lot depends on the skill of the examiner."

Landau jumped in, true to his role as residency program director. "I should point out that the hospital did the right thing. We did terminate Johnson."

Bolton said, "And so did every other hospital he worked for. Which is why we don't think Johnson's death was accidental."

"You're saying he was killed?"

"Suicide is more like it. We're still investigating. Unfortunately, there were no working security cameras at this station and, so far, no eyewitnesses that we know of. But my gut tells me that Johnson was on the edge. Lonely guy who falls head over heels for a woman he hardly knows, gets rejected by her, then loses his job over it. Toxicology report showed a pretty dangerous combination of alcohol and drugs the night of his death. Who knows what kind of problems this guy was having? Seems to have been pretty far gone if he was walking around with your house key and photograph in his wallet."

"It's creepy, for sure. But I feel terrible that he killed himself. The guy worked in our hospital. We could have helped him."

"That's one way to look at it," said Bolton. "I, on the other hand, prefer the glass-is-half-full perspective."

"Meaning what?"

"You can stop worrying about being stalked. And even better, no one thinks you're paranoid anymore."

She glanced at Dr. Landau, who said impishly, "I suppose that's something."

He blinked as Peyton added, "Yeah, that's something, all right."

20

PEYTON WANTED TO TALK TO KEVIN. HE HADN'T CALLED HER LAST night before going to bed. He hadn't called this morning, either. She assumed he was still fretting about the lie detector test. It was hard to be giddy about anyone getting smashed by a train, but in a weird way she wanted to let Kevin know that whatever threat he might have perceived to their marriage was over. Definitely over. She reached him on his cell phone and got right to the point. "Andy Johnson is dead."

"What? How?"

Her one-minute explanation left him silent. Finally, he asked, "How do you feel?"

"I'm trying to take Detective Bolton's advice and be thankful that it ended in his death and not mine."

"It's the ultimate closure, I suppose. He's gone."

"I just wish there were a way to confirm where he was the night of my car accident. Everyone is now assuming that if someone did run me off the road it was him. But I would have liked the chance to ask him myself. I would have put it right to him: Where *were* you?"

She could hear the strain in her own voice, but she wondered if Kevin realized where it was really directed.

"Unfortunately it's too late to ask that question now."

"Yeah. Too late."

"You sound upset," he said. "Are you still mad about the way I treated you on the phone yesterday?"

"I'm not mad."

"If you are, let me say it again. I'm sorry."

"Kevin?"

"What?"

"Where were you the night of my accident?"

He chuckled nervously. "What do you mean?"

"It's not a trick question."

"You know where I was. I had that business trip to Providence."

She didn't say anything. Kevin broke the silence and asked, "What makes you raise this now?"

"Your lunch date with that woman before you left for New York."

"I thought we agreed to drop that."

"I think· I deserve an explanation. When you left the house, you told me you were going to the office and then straight to the airport."

His reply was slow in coming. "That's true."

"So, you lied?"

Again, he paused. "Okay. You got me."

Her voice shook. "What are you telling me?"

"I was keeping this as a surprise, but I may as well tell you now. You know I haven't been happy at the firm. I'm exploring another career. The woman your mother saw me with is someone who I thought could help me."

"Help you what?"

"Look, I won't deny she's attractive. But she's only a friend at work. I don't question you about your friends. Gary, for instance."

"Are you kidding me? When I told you I was going to help Gary study for the MCATs, you acted like I was going to try out his new water bed. But let's not make this about me and Gary. It's about you and your friend. Exactly how is she going to help you?"

"This is something I've kept secret from everyone, especially the firm. I'll tell you all about it tonight."

"I don't understand."

"You will. In fact, I think you'll be proud of me. Let me surprise you."

"What is going on?"

"Nothing is going on."

She didn't say it was her mother ragging at her. And she couldn't stop herself from asking, "Are you seeing another woman or aren't you?"

"I swear, I'm not."

"*Were* you seeing someone?"

"Peyton, maybe it was the accident, maybe it was those days afterward that we spent together at home. But I'm more sure of my feelings for you than ever before. Why do you think I got so upset when I heard about Andy Johnson and the lie detector test?"

"I don't know."

"Because I couldn't stand the thought of you with someone else. Come home right now. I can't wait to see you."

"You're at home?" Since she'd called him on his cell phone, she'd assumed he was still in New York.

"Seminar was worthless. I cut out early and came home."

She paused, then said, "I can't come home yet. Today's my first full day back."

"Then let's have a nice dinner. I'll tell you all about my new career. Or at least my hopes for a new career. How about that? Is it a date?"

"I guess so. But it'll have to be around ten."

"Ten it is," he said.

"Okay. See you."

As she hung up, a fleeting thought gave her pause. It had to do with yesterday's telephone conversation and his angry reaction to the lie detector test and her supposed "sexual involvement" with Andy Johnson. Kevin had always been a jealous partner. In college, after they'd gotten engaged, he'd nearly broken a guy's nose for coming on to her at Bullwinkle's bar. Kevin was no killer, but outbursts like those could have made a more suspicious mind wonder whether Kevin had returned from New York before or after Andy Johnson ended up dead on the third rail.

She shook it off in an instant. Just a passing thought. It had barely crossed her mind. But it had still crossed it.

She collected herself and headed back to the ER.

21

ANOTHER FRIDAY NIGHT, ANOTHER NIGHT ALONE IN BED. ALONE WITH thoughts of Peyton.

Rudy's room was dark, save for the faint glow of a street lamp outside his window. Noise from the busy L Street Tavern one floor below seeped through the floorboards, the usual weekend revelry. The music was loud enough for him to pick up the tune. He hummed a few bars, fudging a lyric here and there until he was finally able to place the song: "L.A. Woman" by the Doors. An oldie but goodie.

The glowing crystals on his alarm clock said 10:57 P.M. It pleased him to realize that he'd managed to sleep for a few hours. He hadn't been sleeping well lately. The emergence of Andy Johnson on the scene had been reason for concern.

News of Johnson's firing had reached him quickly. Gossip what it was, it took only minutes for the entire hospital to know Andy had been canned for ogling Peyton Shields. Rudy had even heard rumors that they'd been "sexually involved." He'd watched Peyton closely enough over the past few months to know that couldn't possibly have been true. But the prospect that perhaps Johnson had wanted her was distressing enough. The last thing he needed was to be stabbed in the back by the very clown he'd hired to stand in for him and dance with her at the surprise birthday party. He didn't need more competition. Kevin Stokes was competition enough, even if the idiot didn't appreciate the gem that was his wife, sleeping with his little whore.

You deserve better, Peyton.

Ever since he'd run her off the road, Rudy had been scrambling for ways to convey that simple message. Leaving the rose on her door-step. Sending the "I love you" message to her digital pager. Not that she would have necessarily linked those gestures to him. The rule in their Internet chats had been never to disclose their true identities, a common way for married people to cheat on the Internet and protect their consciences as much as their privacy. He knew her as Ladydoc. She knew him as RG or Rudy. Unless she'd been in the chat room last week and seen his personalized apology to "Peyton"—and he was sure she hadn't—she had no idea that Rudy knew her real name. She couldn't possibly have known that he'd snagged her address and pager number. Those details were part of the vast store of information in his dog-eared daily journal that included virtually every number that had even the most remote connection to the daily life of Peyton Shields. Home phone number, cellular number, pager number, street number, driver's license number, social security number, bank account number, locker number at the hospital lounge, number of steps from her front door to the subway station, number of times she used the restroom on an average twelve-hour shift, number of bites it took her to consume half a turkey sandwich on a twelve-minute lunch break. Twelve, if it was on her regular whole wheat bread with just lettuce, no tomato, and a small swipe of mayo. Sixteen, if on a kaiser roll. He even knew her bra and panty size. He wondered if she'd ever complained to Victoria's Secret for failing to fill a mail order that, unbeknownst to her, had disappeared from her box.

None of the numbers—or even the undergarments—were as important to him as the one gnawing at his gut lately: Four. For four straight days after the accident, she and her husband had been together at home while Peyton convalesced. They had surely reconnected, and it made him sick to think about it. The whole "accident" was not what he had imagined it would be. Driving Peyton off the road just so that he could be the one to save her—

to decide whether she should live or die—was probably not one of his better-conceived fantasies. It was now more important than ever that he express his feelings, but by sending no card with the rose and dialing her pager from a pay phone he'd made it impossible for her to know that he was the one saying "I love you." The problem was, he wasn't ready to reveal himself that clearly. If he put too much on the line, she could reject him.

He couldn't take that. Not again.

He slid out from beneath the blanket and placed his bare feet on the floor. Wearing only jockey shorts, he crossed the dimly lit room, allowing his eyes to adjust before turning on a light. He stopped at the bathroom sink and flipped the switch. He washed up quickly, then went to the dresser and put on a pair of sweatpants and a T-shirt. It was almost 11:00 P.M., the magical hour that night after night drew him to his computer and the chat rooms. One more evening of trolling for Ladydoc. Even when they used to chat regularly, rarely if ever did they team up on a weekend. Tonight, he hoped, might be different. The death of Andy Johnson had changed everything.

He smiled to himself, wondering if they'd ever catch the guy who did it.

He logged on and found their usual site, one frequented by old motion-picture buffs. The chatting usually started at eleven, but it was a few minutes after and he was still alone in the chat room. Not even the woman who had created the site and usually kept the conversation going had bothered to show up tonight. Part of him had expected a no-show. Another part, however, was growing angry at the snub.

Staring at the blank screen, he typed a short query in his usual chat format.

"r u there?"

He waited, then tried again.

"*HEY!* i said, r u there?"

He knew that he was alone, that his typewritten words were falling on the cyberspace equivalent of deaf ears. Yet he felt compelled to continue, as if he wanted to record his own loneliness and see it spelled out on the screen before his own eyes.

"y r u not here?"

Getting angry wasn't productive, but he couldn't help it. Running her off the road was something he had instantly regretted. He'd said he was sorry. He'd told her it was from the heart. He'd even pulled her from the icy pond. He'd saved her life, damn it.

Just three lines stared back at him from the screen, all typed by him. No response from anyone. Not so much as a hello, let alone a thank-you. He banged out a final message on the keyboard, not even aware that he'd abandoned the cutesy chat-typing format.

"You owe me. Big time."

With a click of his mouse he exited the chat room. He took a deep breath to quell his rising rage, but it wasn't working. He was tired of sucking up and tired of being snubbed. He'd been nothing but sweet to her for long enough.

With another click, the screen displayed a list of Web sites marked "Favorites." His hand shook. Entering would be a huge regression. He was furious with Peyton for the way she was treating him, for dragging him back to this place. No woman could ever like this side of him. But it was all Peyton's fault. She had made him angry. Anger made him go there. Sometimes he went for hours at a time, day after day, till his rage subsided. Maybe that was what he needed. A little time away. With all that had happened in the last two weeks, it would be risky to make another direct run at Peyton. Things needed to blow over.

Then they could really get serious.

He clicked on one of the files and waited anxiously as the image came into focus from top to bottom. It was a digital photograph. He could see the top of a woman's head at first, her blond hair. Then her face came into view, eyes wide with fright. Then her long, slender neck wrapped in a leather collar. She was down on both knees, hands and feet bound, naked except for the collar and some kind of spiked harness that was strapped so tightly below her breasts that she was bruised and bleeding at the ribs. The photograph was slightly grainy, clearly taken by an amateur. Amateur *photographer*, that is. From the looks of things, this guy was a real pro. This wasn't that silly stuff posted on the Web by fat old men who hired young hookers, got their buddy to snap some pictures before the Viagra wore off, and voilà! they were porn studs. This was the work of a true master who'd earned the right to showcase his work to the world. Some pervs got off on the kiddie-porn Web sites, turned on by young girls having sex for the first time. Others—guys like Rudy—got off on women having sex for the very *last* time.

He scrolled down to the bottom of the page, to a message that was superimposed on the photograph, written in bold, blood-red letters: HAVE YOU FED YOUR SLAVE TODAY?

From the length of this blond's dark brown roots, she'd obviously been captive for quite some time. Yet she still looked hot. And her master still had his sense of humor.

My creative side, thought Rudy.

With a gleam in his eye he adjusted his chair and switched on the stereo, preparing himself for another visit to those pretty, familiar faces. Every one of them had shown such attitude at one time, a lot like that Little Miss Excuse Me who had teased him into following her off the subway and then disappeared, snubbing him. He hated teases. Photographs didn't come close to capturing the excitement of the conquest, but they were all the spark he needed. They were his photographs, his slaves, gone but never to be forgotten.

It would be another dark night down memory lane.

Part II

SUMMER

22

VENDORS OF ITALIAN ICES WERE SMILING IN THE NORTH END. KIDS IN South Boston literally danced in the streets, frolicking in the cool fountain of relief from opened fire hydrants. Hospital emergency rooms were nearly overrun with cases of heat exhaustion. It was the third week of July, and the question on the tip of everyone's parched tongue was the same: When would daytime highs finally fall short of the recommended cooking temperature for grilled pork tenderloin?

Peyton was better suited for the heat than most New Englanders, having spent her freshman year at FSU in a dorm room with no air-conditioning. Boston in July—even this July—was no match for Tallahassee in late August and early September. Even so, the heat wave was taking its toll on her, emotionally more than physically. Time and again she found herself wondering what it might have been like to be this hot, this sticky, and thirty-six weeks pregnant.

The miscarriage was behind her, but occasional thoughts of "what might have been" lived on. The first real setback had been a pop-up reminder on her computer for her week-sixteen ultrasound appointment. Today the blazing heat was the unexpected trigger, probably because a scorching summer had been her biggest fear from the moment she'd calculated an August due date.

Fortunately, the last six months had brought more positive life changes. Minor plastic surgery had taken care of the scars around her eye. The death of Andy Johnson was officially ruled a suicide, and she'd seen no signs of a stalker since. That left her free to focus on getting her career back on track—and her marriage.

For her and Kevin, the cornerstone of reconciliation turned out to be his novel. Peyton was so impressed that he had written something that good while billing fifty-plus hours a week at the law firm. A book was something for them to be passionate about together. Peyton did some line editing and was especially helpful with the dialogue of female characters, striking things that she knew a woman would never say. At spring's end they pitched the new and improved manuscript to a legitimate literary agent, who snatched it up in a weekend. It sold to a major publisher in less than three weeks.

Almost overnight, Kevin was a changed man. Selling the book had restored his lost confidence and knocked the Florida-sized chip off his shoulder. It helped their marriage, their sex life, their everyday interaction. It had even boosted Kevin's precarious status at Marston & Wheeler. His success had caught the attention of the Boston media. Kevin didn't care how the firm might feel about him once his book was actually released and in the bookstores, but until then, he was not quite ready to quit his day job, and he was savvy enough to say only nice things about his employer. In turn, the firm was image conscious enough to appreciate the kind words and paranoid enough to fear the dreadful tales he might tell some reporter if his colleagues didn't treat him with a new level of respect. It had struck Peyton as an unseemly foundation for an ongoing professional relationship, akin to honor among thieves, but Kevin assured her that this sort of mutual admiration inspired by fear was the glue that held together every major law firm in America. At bottom, so long as he was happy, she was glad to have him acting more like the man she'd fallen in love with years ago.

"Hot enough for you?" asked the driver.

The taxi driver in Boston had asked her the same silly question on the way to the airport. A short plane ride later, here it was again from his counterpart in Manhattan. What did they expect her to say, *No, I'm from Uganda?*

She met his eyes in the rearview mirror and smiled politely. "Plenty hot, thank you."

The trip to New York had been spur of the moment. Kevin had been gone all week taking depositions at a Park Avenue law firm in a big trademark infringement lawsuit. This morning, out of the blue, she'd realized that today was the tenth anniversary of their first date. It made her smile to think that things were going so well between them that, in the middle of reviewing the results of an abdominal CT scan with contrast, she remembered a personal milestone that might have been overlooked in less happy times. She'd decided to jump on a plane and surprise him.

The cab stopped at the curb. Peyton paid the fare, grabbed her overnight bag, and stepped out. The humidity hit her instantly. It was still hot, even at eight o'clock at night.

"Welcome to the Waldorf," said the doorman.

A bellboy hurried across the lobby to take her bag, but at all of eight pounds it was hardly a burden. She carried it herself to the elevator and rode to the fourteenth floor. Her heart pounded as the doors opened. This trip was so spontaneous, so unlike her. She couldn't contain the silly grin on her face. It was the kind that marked mischief.

There was a spring in her step as she walked down the long hall to Room 1426. Kevin had phoned her with the room number the day he'd checked in. She knocked twice, dying to see the look on his face.

No one answered.

She pressed her ear to the door but heard nothing inside. He was probably having a late dinner with a colleague or client. The thought of cooling her heels till they finished coffee and dessert wiped the smile from her face.

Across the hallway, a chambermaid was entering another room for turndown service, which gave Peyton an idea. She could be in his bed when he returned, maybe with one of those little bedtime chocolates resting on her belly beneath a black lace teddy. An even better surprise.

"Can you help me?" she called to the maid. "I locked my key in my room."

"I'm sorry. You'll have to check with the front desk."

"Please, don't make me go all the way back down there. The line's a mile long."

The maid seemed sympathetic. Or maybe an honest face had a way of opening doors, literally. She opened the room for Peyton with her master key.

"Thank you."

Peyton was quickly inside, but the maid came with her. "You'll have to find your key and show it to me," she said. "It's just a matter of security."

"Oh," said Peyton as she switched on the light. The room was a mess. The bed was unmade. Wet bath towels were on the floor. A room-service tray was resting on the nightstand, the meal gone. She noticed another tray on the desk, also empty.

Why two?

She moved in for a closer look. One had a few cold french fries remaining on the plate. The other bore the remnants of a grilled chicken Caesar. That gave her pause. Even if he'd been hungry enough to order two meals, Kevin was not a salad kind of guy. She hoped it had been business, maybe Kevin and a witness preparing for tomorrow's deposition over dinner.

"Miss," said the maid. "Your key, please?"

A tightness gripped Peyton's chest as she backed away from the dinner trays and peered into the dark bathroom. In the shadows, something was hanging from the shower rod. She turned on the light, and her worst fears were realized.

It was panty hose.

On the counter was a makeup bag, a tube of lipstick, and a bottle of shampoo and conditioner for treated hair. She turned away quickly and opened the sliding closet door. The entire left side was filled with women's clothing.

In a panic, she hurried to the door and double-checked the number—1426. The right room, she was sure of it. Hanging on the back of the door was all the added confirmation she needed. It was a plastic dry-cleaning bag from the hotel laundry service. Inside were two shirts. The monogrammed initials on the sleeves were proof enough, but she checked the receipt stapled to the bag anyway: K. Stokes, 1426.

"I really must see your key," said the maid.

For a moment, Peyton could barely stand on her own feet. "I'm sorry. This was all a mistake. Just a terrible mistake." Her bag in hand, she hurried out the door and ran to the elevator, hurt and angry.

Over the past six months she'd fooled herself, she realized. She'd let Kevin off the hook too easily, having felt sorry for him with his troubles at work. On some level, she'd managed to convince herself that he hadn't strayed. On another, she'd forgiven him even if he had, blaming herself for spending so much time at the hospital and not being there for him. Ironically, his novel had helped draw them back together by diverting their attention from the real problems, when all along it should have been her final clue.

He *was* a good storyteller.

Damn you, she thought as the elevator doors closed. *I'm not your fool.*

It was almost midnight when her plane landed back in Boston. The last place Peyton felt like going was home to their bed, their sheets, their pillows, their memories. Dropping by her parents' was not an option. Her father might have been helpful, but she didn't need her mother's big *I told you so.*

Funny, and perhaps it was because tonight marked the tenth anniversary of their first date in college, but she was suddenly thinking of her first big blowup with Kevin in Tallahassee. Kevin didn't like the fact that she still wore a necklace her old boyfriend Gary Varne had given her as a high school graduation present, and from there the argument escalated to an even stupider display of jealousy. Peyton had not made many friends at FSU, focusing all her energy on Kevin and her studies, so she called Gary back in Boston. It was their first conversation since Peyton had told him that their long-distance relationship was not working and that she'd met someone new. They talked for hours, and Gary ended up bucking his own self-interest and convincing her to give Kevin another chance. Kevin never would have believed that in a million years, but Peyton saw it as proof positive that old lovers could become good friends. She thought about calling Gary again tonight, but instead opted for the one place she was always welcome, day or night. Work.

"What are you doing here?"

The sound of Gary's voice startled her. He was working the late shift at Children's until med school started in the fall. He'd surprised himself (but not Peyton) by how well he'd scored on the MCATs.

"Working," said Peyton. She continued down the hall toward her locker. Gary followed.

"I thought you went to New York."

"I went," she said, as she fiddled with the combination. "I'm back."

"Oh." It was an ominous "oh," as if it were painfully obvious that things hadn't gone well. "You want to talk about it?"

"Thanks. But it's nothing you can fix."

The locker popped open. Gary came closer and sat on the bench beside her. "I wouldn't be so sure about that."

"About what?"

"That I can't fix it. I actually have a theory about that."

"You have a theory about everything," she said, half smiling, half groaning.

"True. But you haven't heard this one. It's about you and me."

She stopped in the middle of tying her shoe. "You and me?"

"Yeah. Nurses and doctors."

"Oh."

"We are the last repairmen on earth."

She managed a weak smile, sensing another Gary-ism coming on, hopefully something a cut above the "Itsmy party" stunt on their first date in high school. "Okay. This I want to hear."

"No one in modern society knows how to fix anything any-

more. It's getting to the point where the only thing worth repair-
ing is your own body. Anything else breaks, you're better off just
throwing it away and buying a new one."

"Like TVs and CD players."

"Especially TVs and CD players."

"What about cars? You gotta get your car fixed."

"They already make cars that go a hundred thousand miles
without a tune-up. Mechanics are on the bubble, baby."

"How about things around the house, like garbage disposals?"

"Total scam. There's actually no such thing as a garbage disposal. You flip that switch, it just makes noise."

"You know, you have an uncanny ability to say totally absurd
things with a totally straight face."

"That's because I believe it. Before you know it, everything
but the human body will be disposable. Doctors and nurses will
be the last repairmen on earth."

"Does that mean every time I squat in my kitchen half my ass
is going to hang out of my blue jeans?"

He started to laugh, then coughed.

"Come on, Gary, it's not *that* frightful an image."

She'd made him blush. He recovered and said, "So, you want
to tell me what happened tonight?"

"No."

"All right. Then let's say we don't talk about it and go get a
milk shake?"

"Can't. I gotta work."

"Forget work. You're supposed to be in New York. Come on."

She thought for a second. "I don't know. It would probably do
me some good to get out, but the last thing I need is to feel fat
on top of depressed."

"Bag the milk shake," he said. "How about a vodka tonic?"

"Let's do coffee."

"Party pooper."

"Yeah," she said, wondering what Kevin was up to now. "Every
party has one."

23

A RAY OF SUNLIGHT WAS STABBING HER IN THE EYE. LIKE A LASER beam, it shined though a narrow slit in the bedroom curtains. Her brain urged her to turn her head to one side, but she lacked even that minimal strength. It was one of those mornings when it actually hurt to blink. She hadn't felt this lousy since the morning after her first drunk, back in high school, when she'd developed a permanent aversion to bourbon.

If memory served her, Gary Varne had masterminded that disaster too.

They'd started at Chauncy's, closed it down at 2:00 A.M., then proceeded to some nightclub that Gary claimed was all the rage. They met up with some friends of Gary's who were hard-core clubbers. Somewhere between shots of tequila and dancing to insufferably loud music, she'd told him about Kevin. It wasn't one of those sappy crying-on-the-sleeve episodes. Peyton had just gotten to the point.

"It's over," she'd said, the music pounding in the background.

"What's over?"

"Kevin and me. He cheated."

"I'm sorry."

"It's okay. It's not the first time. I'm pretty sure he was up to no good about six months ago too."

"I'm really sorry."

"Don't be. What's that old saying? Fool me once, shame on you. Fool me twice, shame on me."

"Only one thing to do."

He gave her a long, ambiguous look that made her uncomfortable. He seemed to be hinting at something, but she didn't want to go there, not with him or anyone else, at least not till she'd confronted Kevin.

"Have another drink?" she said, sort of changing the subject.

"Yeah, sure. Let's have another drink."

That was the last thing she really remembered.

And now her head was pounding. She lay with her head beneath the sheets, but there was still enough light for her to notice that the linens were totally unfamiliar.

She nearly jackknifed in the bed. The room was spinning, but it revolved slowly enough for her to know it wasn't *her* room. She peeled away the covers and then pulled them right back, seeing she was wearing only her panties and a man's T-shirt.

Her heart raced with panic, but she drew a deep breath, trying to get her bearings. She couldn't possibly have *slept* with Gary. There had to be some other explanation.

The adrenaline was flowing, and she suddenly heard the shower running in the bathroom. A man was singing. The voice was Gary's.

She jumped out of bed, then paused to get her balance, still too hungover to get vertical that fast. She rummaged through the bed, even checked under it. Her clothes were nowhere to be found.

What in the world happened last night?

She found her wristwatch on the nightstand. She checked the time and nearly fell over. It was after two o'clock in the *afternoon*. Even if her surprise visit to New York had gone as planned and she'd spent the night with Kevin at the Waldorf, she would have been required to report back to the hospital more than an hour ago. She needed her beeper; she found it in her shoe across the room, and checked it. No messages, thank God. Just to be sure no one was searching for her, she grabbed Gary's phone and dialed her home answering machine.

"You have no new messages," said the digital voice. "You have one saved message."

She checked the saved message. Kevin was notorious for listening to her messages and then saving them.

The saved message was from 4:13 P.M. yesterday. It was Kevin.

"Peyton, hey, it's me. Ira Kaufman shipped me off to L.A. on another one of his emergencies. I'm headed for JFK now and should be gone at least two days. I'll call you tomorrow and let you know where I'm staying."

Los Angeles? A wave of panic washed over her. She'd checked the answering machine yesterday before leaving for New York. Except she hadn't checked the *saved* messages. That idiot Kevin. He'd left her a message, dialed in later to check for messages, listened to the one he'd left for her, and then sent it to the never-never land of "saved."

Peyton hung up quickly and had directory assistance connect her to the Waldorf.

"Room fourteen twenty-six, please."

It rang three times before a man answered. It wasn't Kevin.

"Who's this?" she asked.

"Steve Beasley."

She knew Steve, one of the associates who worked in Kevin's litigation group. "This is Peyton Shields. I was trying to reach Kevin."

"He left yesterday afternoon for L.A."

That jibed with the message. "I see. But why are you in his room?"

"Ira sent me at the last minute to pinch-hit so he and Kevin could go to L.A. I didn't even have time to go to the hotel and check in, so Kevin just left the room under his name and credit card. It's worked out great. My fiancée is here with me, so we've run up about a ten-thousand-dollar bill on his AMEX."

"What?"

"Just kidding. About the bill, I mean. My fiancée really is here with me. She goes to law school at Columbia, so we're making a little weekend of it here at the Waldorf."

"Oh my God."

"You okay?"

"I will be. I think."

"By the way, Kevin had to take off before his shirts came back from the laundry. Just tell him that they delivered them here to the room. I'll bring them to work on Monday."

Peyton felt numb. She couldn't even speak.

"Hello?" he said.

"Monday, sure. That's fine."

Gary shouted from the bathroom, "You finally up, Peyton?"

She freaked, fearing Steve would hear the voice of another man. "No."

"Shower's all yours."

"I'm on the phone," she said with urgency, thinking that would shut him up. She uncovered the mouthpiece and said, "Hi, Steve, I'm back."

Gary shouted, "Don't be shy, I've already seen you naked."

She nearly died. She was sure Steve had overheard. "I'm sorry, Steve," she said into the phone, "did you say something? That darn TV was so loud I couldn't hear you."

"No," he said nervously. "I didn't hear anything. I mean, say anything I'll let you go."

The line clicked before she could even say goodbye.

Gary switched on the blow-dryer. She sat alone in the bed, wearing nothing but panties beneath Gary's T-shirt, holding the phone in her hand and not quite believing where she was.

What the hell did I do?

24

THE TRIP TO LOS ANGELES COULD HAVE LASTED WEEKS. KEVIN'S
assignment was the one thing he hated most about big commercial
litigation: the production of corporate records.

For five days and nights, his team of unlucky paralegals and
staff sifted page by page through thousands of roach-laden boxes
of business records that had been archived and scattered over eight
different rat-infested warehouses with no air-conditioning. By the
sixth day it had become unbearable. His only escape was the lawyer's version of hara-kiri. He pointed out to a senior VP that the
company would save a ton of money in legal fees if the company's
in-house counsel were to supervise the project herself. Kevin was
on a flight home that afternoon.

The timing on his part was no accident. Kevin had stayed as
long as he could, but he had to return by Thursday night. At 8:00
P.M., he had his first appearance as an author at Booklovers' in
Boston.

Booklovers' was not the biggest or best-known bookstore in
Boston, but for over five years it had been Kevin's favorite. It was a
little place that had nurtured his very big dreams. The store usually
held two or three events every week. Authors—some well known,
some completely unknown—would stand at the lectern in the
reading room and talk about their books and their careers to anyone who cared to stop and listen. Booklovers' catered to dreamers

like Kevin, who used to attend two or three events a month and wonder if, someday, someone would come listen to him.

The day after Kevin signed his book deal he called the owner. He wanted Booklovers' to be his first appearance. The news wasn't good. His novel was slated for publication the following winter. By then, Booklovers' would be history. Like so many other independent booksellers, Booklovers' had come down with a terminal case of megastore-itis.

His publicist told him that it was a waste of time to make any appearances before his book was even published. For years he'd dreamed about making his debut at Booklovers', and that was exactly what he intended to do. He just wished Peyton were there to share the moment with him. Her beeper had sounded just as they were headed out the door. Another emergency at work. Not everything had changed in their relationship.

"Good evening," he said to a crowd of about a half-dozen loyalists. "I'm Kevin Stokes, and I have to say I'm more saddened than honored to be the last author to speak at Booklovers'."

"Excuse me," said a woman in the first row. "What's the name of your book?"

"That's kind of up in the air. My editor hates the title, so we're working on a new one."

"So the book's not out yet?"

"Not yet. But I left a few copies of the manuscript here last week for anyone who wanted to check it out and read it. I see two of them are missing, so I guess somebody might have read it."

"I did." It was an old man, leaning against the bookshelves in the back. "Excellent book."

Kevin smiled. "Thank you. You read it?"

"Yes, and it's a strange twist of fate that I did. Last Wednesday I got off the bus at the wrong stop. It was raining, so I came into the bookstore. Resting right on the counter was this manuscript. I started reading it and couldn't put it down."

"That's great. It's supposed to be a thriller."

"Your wife's a doctor, right?"

Kevin blinked. That was out of the blue. "Yeah."

"Pediatrics?"

"That's right."

"I would guess she's about twenty-eight years old?"

He smiled nervously. It was getting a little personal. "This really isn't about my wife."

"But it is. What do you think, you have to pen an autobiography to reveal yourself though your writing?"

"I understand what you're saying. But there's no one like my wife in this book."

"She's all over this book. You just don't know it."

The tone was a little accusatory, the old man's stare not exactly friendly. Kevin averted his eyes and checked his notes just to break away. "Anyway, the rest of the crowd is probably wondering what we're talking about, so let me tell you something about the book."

"It's about a beautiful and successful woman who is forced to make a life-or-death decision," the old man said.

"Well, there's more to it than that. It's about trust, betrayal, and—"

"A kidnapping. That's the most important thing."

Kevin said, "I think the characters are most important."

"Hah! You've preordained a tragedy. That's what's most important."

"This is a novel. I haven't preordained anything."

"Is that what you think? Just write the story and wash your hands of it? Fourteen years before the *Titanic* went to the bottom of the ocean, there was a novel written about the exact same thing, *The Wreck of the Titan, or Futility* by Morgan Robertson. Some called it prophetic, but prophecy merely foretells the future. I believe Mr. Robertson's book actually shaped it. It's in the Bible, mister. Nothing new under the sun. By writing this story, you've sealed someone's fate."

"It's a story. It's all made up."

"Where do you live?"

"I don't think I want to answer that."

"I *know* where you live."

He was glaring with contempt from the back of the room. No one in the crowd moved. Finally, the owner approached the angry old man.

"Excuse me, sir. But I'm going to have to ask you to leave."

The old man was frozen, his eyes locked on Kevin.

"Sir, don't make me call the police."

He scowled and said, "I was leaving anyway."

They watched uneasily as he stormed toward the exit. He slammed the door on his way out, nearly rattling the little entrance bells right off the frame. A brief silence lingered, but a sudden pounding on the window startled them again. The old man was standing on the sidewalk, knocking on the plate glass and peering inside. He pointed to Kevin, then pulled the manuscript from his bag. He whirled crazily and pitched it into the air, laughing as five hundred loose pages whipped in the wind and fluttered onto the city street. With two hands he flipped everyone a double bird, then turned and ran.

The owner went to the window and closed the blinds. "I'm sorry about that, Kevin."

"Yeah," he said, his voice cracking slightly. "Me too."

25

PEYTON DIDN'T DARE TELL HER HUSBAND.

All week long, she managed to avoid Gary at the hospital. Wisely, he seemed willing to let her chill after explaining what had happened.

She'd gotten sick. Too much tequila and she'd thrown up on her clothes. Not exactly a class act, but it wasn't adultery either. Gary had taken her back to his apartment, which was just around the corner. He'd removed the smelly garments, thrown them in the wash, and let her sleep it off alone in his bed. He took the couch. Just a trained nurse putting a dead-drunk doctor to bed in her panties and a borrowed T-shirt. "No monkey business," had been Gary's words on that morning after. Totally innocent.

Kevin, however, wasn't the type to believe that "nothing had happened." He'd nearly gone into orbit last winter over Andy Johnson's lie detector test, all because the stupid polygraph examiner had thought he'd seen signs of deception in Johnson's denial of "sexual involvement" with Peyton. True, Kevin was more self-assured now than he'd been last winter—more than ever before, really. But no matter how successful Kevin became, the fact that his mother had walked out on his father and him would always be a part of his psyche. He'd told Peyton the story only once, but she would never forget the fire in his eyes. "Nothing but white trash," his mother had shouted on her way out, slamming the door of their two-bedroom trailer. Kevin was eight years old, and he would never see his mother again. She'd left Key West to be with "some suit," as Kevin had put it, a tourist she'd met as a cocktail waitress.

Some lawyer from Boston.

Under the circumstances, silence seemed like Peyton's wisest course. She loved Kevin. She would never have let coffee with Gary turn into drinks with Gary and his night-owl friends if she hadn't thought Kevin had been unfaithful to her. And she would never have stooped to "retaliation sex" no matter how many women she'd thought Kevin had slept with. She had more respect for herself than that.

Silence was definitely the way to go. She had impressed that on Gary before leaving his apartment, speaking through the fog in her brain that she assumed was the lingering effects of way too much to drink.

"This is just between us, you understand. Not a word to any-one."

"Peyton, I am the one man in this world you can always count on."

He'd flashed that look again, the one she'd seen just before sharing that last round of drinks that had seemed to erase all memory of everything that had occurred thereafter.

Funny, but now that some time had passed, even with all that had happened, his brief look was the one thing that played most vividly in her mind.

Her pager buzzed right in the middle of a respiratory check on a nine-year-old asthma patient. She excused herself and headed directly to the second-floor conference room. It was the call she'd been dreading for weeks. It was from her lawyer.

Massachussetts civil action number 05-1132, *Kersip v. Children's Hospital, Brookline, and Peyton Shields, M.D.*, was now almost six months old and well into the discovery phase. Today was Peyton's deposition.

The original suit filed by Nurse Felicia had settled weeks

earlier. On principle, however, the hospital refused to succumb to the related suit filed by the creep who had jabbed his girlfriend and son with a needle on a stick and then barged into the clinic, causing the whole disaster. Since Peyton was sued individually, she needed her own lawyer separate from the hospital. Vince Edwards was waiting for her outside the conference room.

"Ready?" he asked.

"Sure. I just want to get this over with."

The stenographer was waiting inside, seated at the head of the table. On the other side was Peter Jenkins, the plaintiff's lawyer. He was a stout man in his fifties. His body had that scrunched and stocky effect, like someone who'd done a ten-story free fall in an elevator and lived to tell about it. His nose was buried in his notes. He didn't rise to greet them, didn't even look up to make eye contact.

Peyton and her lawyer seated themselves in the chairs near the door. Jenkins removed his reading glasses, then cleared his throat and nodded toward the stenographer to indicate his readiness.

"Good morning," he said as the stenographer's fingers danced on the keys. "Let me begin by stating for the record that my client is not attending this deposition. As the plaintiff, of course, he has every right to be here and observe, but because of the way Dr. Shields has assaulted and intimidated him in the past, as alleged in this lawsuit, he is quite naturally afraid to be in the same room with her."

"Knock it off," said Vince, groaning.

"Knock what off?"

"The grandstanding. One more idiotic statement like that and we're leaving."

"Are you trying to intimidate me?"

"Just making a point. A statement like that is no more appropriate than my stating for the record that your client isn't here today because this is a frivolous lawsuit fueled by a lawyer who's working on a contingency fee for a deadbeat client who couldn't care less."

"Swear the witness," Jenkins told the stenographer.

Peyton gave the familiar oath. The lawyers glared at one another. She was ready for the usual opening of "Please state your name for the record," but Jenkins clearly had no intention of easing into things.

"Dr. Shields, how many people have you shot in your lifetime?"

"Objection."

"Noted. Answer the question please."

"Just one," she said.

"*Just* one? Let me get an understanding what you mean by *just* one. In your view, would that be A, more than; B, less than; or C, equal to the number of people shot by the average living and breathing human being?"

"Objection."

"If you're objecting to this, we're going to have big problems."

"Oh we're going to have huge problems, I'm sure of it."

"Fine. So long as I get my answers. Which is it, Doctor? A, B, or C?"

She answered coolly. "I would say it's more than the average person."

"Very good. A. Or perhaps it's more like D: equal to the average gang member."

"Objection. I told you to knock it off, and I meant it."

"Do you own a gun, Doctor?"

"Yes."

"What kind?"

"Smith and Wesson, thirty-eight-caliber."

"Did you have it with you on the day my client was shot?"

"Of course not. That was Dr. Simons's gun. Mine is kept at home."

"Do you consider yourself a careful gun owner?"

"Yes, very."

"Do you keep your gun properly stored?"

"Yes. It's in a locked metal box, on the top shelf of my bedroom closet."

"Do you know how to use it?"

"Yes."

"Do you have the courage to use it?"

"Objection. Vague. When, where, what circumstances?"

"Let's be specific. On the day of the incident in question at the Haverhill clinic, were you prepared to shoot my client if you had to?"

Peyton shifted uneasily. "I don't know how to answer that."

"You pulled a gun, didn't you?"

"Yes."

"You fired it."

"I fired a warning shot. I was aiming at the jar on the counter, just to show him that I knew how to use it."

"We've already established that you know how to use it. My question was, were you prepared to use it? Were you ready to point the gun at my client and shoot him dead if, in your judgment, you needed to?"

"I object to this. It's just harassing."

"It's the heart of the lawsuit. Please answer the question."

Peyton wrung her hands nervously. "I suppose, if the circumstances required it, I probably would have shot him."

"Perfect. So let's go back to that day in Haverhill. My client was facedown on the floor."

"Yes, after I fired the warning shot, he got down."

"He was unarmed?"

"As far as I knew, yes."

"You had a gun pointed at him?"

"Yes."

"And by your own testimony here today, you were prepared to shoot him if the circumstances required it."

Her mouth was going dry. "That's what I said."

"And at this juncture, you decided to inject him with secobarbital sodium."

"Correct. To sedate him."

"Where did you think he was going?"

"I didn't know what was going to happen."

"Nor did you know that he was allergic to secobarbital sodium."

"No, I didn't know."

"Because you didn't bother to ask if he had any allergies."

Peyton hesitated, a bit at a loss. "This was not a normal patient consultation."

"ER doctors ask that question every day, don't they?"

"Yes. They do, but—"

"I'm sure you've even asked that question yourself in an emergency situation before, haven't you?"

"Sure, many times. But—"

"But you didn't ask my client."

"No."

"Because you didn't care."

"Objection."

"I want an answer. You didn't ask because you didn't care. Isn't that right, Doctor?"

"That's not true."

"I see. Let me put it another way, then. You didn't ask because you *did* care?"

"I didn't ask because . . ." She glanced at her lawyer, then back at Jenkins. "I just didn't ask."

"Good answer, Doctor."

"Objection."

"A little late, Counselor." He closed his notebook and rose from the table. "That's all I need. I'm done here. Call me when you want to talk settlement."

He gathered his notes, grabbed his briefcase, and walked out the door. Peyton looked at her lawyer, confused. "Five minutes. That's it?"

Vince led her into the hall, outside the earshot of the stenographer. "Brevity is a good sign. If he was serious about this lawsuit he would have deposed you all day. He just wanted to rattle your cage, hoping to push the insurance company into coughing up some nuisance money."

Peyton shook her head, still unsettled. "Those questions he asked about having the courage to use a gun. I felt so cold saying that I could kill another human being."

"Don't worry about that."

"I don't want you or anyone else to think that just because I own a gun I relish the idea of having to use it."

"You don't have to explain."

"I got one only because there was a time when I truly did fear for my safety."

"Peyton, really. I know all about the stalking incident. I understand."

"It just pained me to have to listen to my own answers. I must have sounded like I have ice water in my veins."

"It might come across that way on the black-and-white transcript. But don't worry. This case will never go to trial."

That wasn't exactly the consolation she was looking for.

"You okay?" he asked.

She looked away, then back, her expression serious. "I don't think I could have shot him."

"What?"

"That's what has me so upset. The answers I just gave under oath didn't ring true to me when I gave them, and they don't ring true now. That's why I tried to sedate him. That's why I was so scattered that I didn't even think to ask if he was allergic. I didn't want to shoot him."

"That's normal."

"I'm not sure I *could* have shot him. Not even if he'd come at me."

"I don't think you ever know the answer to that question until it's time to pull the trigger. Thankfully, you didn't have to face that."

Peyton glanced at her hands and said, "Look at me. I'm shaking."

"Depositions can be upsetting."

"No. I'm just now realizing how much danger I was in. It scares me to think what might have happened if that clown who was stalking me hadn't killed himself. What if he had confronted me? All along, I was fooling myself into feeling safer because I owned a gun. I probably would have ended up like one of those people who pull the gun and freeze up, afraid to fire even in self-defense."

"That's behind you now. Don't let this lawsuit and showboat lawyer dredge up those old nightmares."

"I guess it's all closer to the surface than I thought. I still think about it a lot. Especially the car crash."

"I wish I could help you with that, but—"

"I know. You're my lawyer, not my shrink. I shouldn't be hitting you with all this."

"It'll get better with time."

"I know. Keep me posted on the case, okay?"

"Sure thing." They shook hands, and he headed for the exit.

Peyton suddenly needed an antacid. She made a quick run to the locker room, then stopped just a few feet short of her own locker. Taped below the lock was a cardboard tube from a used roll of paper towels. Carefully, she checked inside and found a flower.

A single red rose.

A card was attached to the stem. It was unsigned. The message was handwritten, just two words: "Let's talk."

Her stomach churned as she opened her locker. This was exactly what she'd feared most—not that Gary would blab all over the hospital that she'd gotten drunk and ended up sick in his apartment, but that he'd try to take things between them to another level. All along she'd known that simply avoiding Gary wasn't the answer. She'd have to deal with it.

She grabbed the entire roll of antacids and closed the locker, pitching the tube with the rose in the trash as she headed back to work.

26

KEVIN WORKED THROUGH LUNCH, SEATED AT HIS COMPUTER, WRIT-
ing. it wasn't fiction this time. He had a brief due tomorrow. In
twenty pages he had to convince the court that even though his
client, a major car-rental company, had been hitting customers
with phony gasoline charges for almost three years, management
had been completely unaware of the scam. The goons pumping
gas for minimum wage were the real masterminds.

In a way, this *was* a work of fiction.

This latest assignment was one of several he'd received in the
last month from partners who had never before offered him work.
Now that he'd sold his novel, he was becoming the go-to associate for quality briefs. Just this morning, a young partner who had
never so much as said hello to Kevin had stopped by with a short
motion he'd drafted, asking for Kevin's thoughts. The director of
recruiting wanted Kevin to conduct a writing workshop for the
second-year law students who were spending their summer with
the firm. He even had a new office—one with a view. He'd never
thought the day would come, but he was actually starting to enjoy
working at Marston & Wheeler.

A knock on his door broke his concentration, but only slightly. He was still staring at the computer screen when he said,
"Come in."

"I need a minute." It was Ira Kaufman, his expression sullen.

He closed the door but didn't sit. Kevin turned in his desk chair to face him.

"What's up?"

He dropped a copy of Kevin's manuscript on the desk. "This," he said as it landed with a thud.

"My book. Don't tell me you were actually one of the people who went down to Booklovers' and grabbed an advance copy."

"No. One of our secretaries did. She brought it to me last night. In fact, she felt compelled to bring it, having worked here for twenty-two years and maintaining a sense of loyalty to the firm that you obviously lack."

Kevin shrank slightly in his chair. "Did you read it?"

"Yes. I was up all night, and not because it was thrilling. I find it disgusting."

Kevin tried not to flinch. "These things are very subjective."

"This isn't a matter of taste. What you've written is downright dishonest."

"I see it quite the opposite way."

"You've used this book as a way to attack completely innocent people."

"This is a work of fiction. There are no real people."

"That's a crock. You've just changed the names. I'm in there, and so are other lawyers from this firm. Every one of us is portrayed as an asshole."

"I think you're overreacting. The story is about a woman who happens to be a powerful attorney, but the stuff about her law firm is all just atmosphere."

"Atmosphere my ass. You've written the *Primary Colors* of Marston and Wheeler."

"Even if that were true, it says right in the front of the book that all characters are entirely imaginary and that any resemblance to persons living or dead is coincidental."

"Maybe that shit floats when you launch a veiled attack on public figures. But I'm not a public figure, and I'm not about to lie back and let anyone soil my good name and reputation in the name of entertainment. I assure you, no one else in this firm is going to stand for it either."

Ira's eyes were actually bulging. Kevin had seem him angry before, but never like this. "What are you asking me to do?" said Kevin.

"I'm *telling* you that you have two options. Pull the book. Or clean out your desk—and prepare for war. I want a decision by next week." He opened the door and slammed it on the way out.

Kevin turned his swivel chair to face the window. He wasn't naive. He'd written the book knowing full well that a stuffy Boston law firm probably wouldn't have a sense of humor about the parallels between fiction and reality, even if it was, as he'd told Ira, just "atmosphere." The short-lived honeymoon between the budding young author and the high-powered law firm had been fun, but the answer to Ira's ultimatum was obvious.

War it would be.

"Can I listen to your heart, darling?"

Peyton was trying her best at sweet talk. Her uncooperative three-year-old patient was seated on the examination table, arms crossed tightly, her lower lip protruding beyond her turned up little nose. Each time Peyton extended her stethoscope toward her skinny bare chest, the child brushed it aside angrily.

"You want me to pin her down?" the mother asked. "That's the way I used to do it with my boys."

Peyton shook her head, then placed the stethoscope on the girl's knee. "Hmmm. I can't hear a thing in there."

The girl fought back a smile. "Dat's not my heart."

She placed it on top of her head. "Nothing there, either. You sure you have a ticker?"

"Yeah," she said, giggling. "It's right here!"

Peyton smiled. The job had many rewards, and there was

none bigger than connecting with one of the kids. That was especially true on a day like today, where it was a struggle just to stay focused.

Confiding in Gary had been the initial mistake. Funny, but the entire time she'd worked at Children's, she'd thought that the two of them had successfully made the leap from past romance to simple friendship. She'd enjoyed reconnecting on a new level, reuniting as friends ten years after they'd fumbled their way through losing their virginity together.

Gary's unique place in her life had made a complicated situation even more complicated.

She procrastinated away most of the day, but finally she forced herself to track Gary down in the hospital cafeteria. He often ate dinner there while on the evening shift. It was a bustling and noisy place, the ideal setting to hold an awkward and obligatory conversation and still avoid a scene.

"You wanted to talk?" she asked, almost having snuck up on him.

"Whatever." He folded up his newspaper to make room for her at the small table for two.

She took a seat and rested her typical dinner of raspberry yogurt and one fresh banana on the table. Staying hungry had a way of keeping her from falling asleep on longer shifts, though nodding off was the least of her concerns at the moment.

"How've you been?" he asked.

"Okay. You?"

"About as you might expect."

She avoided eye contact and started on her yogurt. "I got your message."

"Message?"

"On my locker."

"I haven't gone near your locker."

"Are you telling me that it wasn't you who taped a rose to my locker with a little message that said 'Let's talk'?"

"Why would I send you a flower?"

She sensed he was being coy. She put her yogurt aside and said,

"Gary, let me just start by saying that I'm glad we've been able to become friends again."

"I feel the same way."

"I really respect you for that. I know it was probably harder for you than for me to put the past behind us."

"Why? You think I was still carrying a torch for you since high school or something?"

"No, it's just that I'm married now. Married to the guy I met when I went away to college and left you here in Boston."

"Are you forgetting that I was the guy who talked you into giving him a second chance nine years ago, when you called me all broken up over your first fight down in Tallahassee? I don't mean to sound like a jerk, but rest assured: I got over you."

"That's good to hear. Because this past week I was starting to fear that maybe you were hoping for something that just isn't going to happen. Which was my fault. I told you that Kevin had been unfaithful, which probably made you think I was soon to be available. But as it turns out, I was totally mistaken. Things are fine between me and Kevin, and I want it to stay that way."

"I see."

She thought she saw disappointment in his eyes. "So when you sent me the rose—"

"I told you I didn't send you any stupid flower."

She didn't believe him, but she didn't want to antagonize. "Okay, you didn't send it. But just to finish my thought—"

"No, it's my turn to talk," he said, his tone suddenly harsh. "Do you have any idea how pissed off I am at you?"

"For what?"

"For what?" he said, incredulous. "Who do you think I am, some girlfriend you can seek out every time you have man troubles?"

"No. But I thought we were friends."

"We are. Kind of." He grimaced, as if sorting out his emotions. "It's complicated. I've tried to be your friend, but it's really hard to do that when, frankly, you're such a manipulative bitch."

"Gary, please."

"No, you need to hear this. You came to me all torn up inside because your husband had cheated on you. You wanted to go out and get drunk."

"I merely suggested we get coffee."

"Yeah, and we all know what that's code for."

"Coffee means coffee."

"Whatever. All I did was suggest we extend the coffee buzz and meet some friends of mine, and the next thing I know you're belting back tequila."

"You ordered the tequila."

"But you drank it. And after you did, it was your idea to go back to my place."

"That's not true."

"It is. You just don't remember."

"I admit, I don't remember much at all about that night. But you said yourself that I got sick. You were too drunk to drive me home, so we walked the block and a half to your place."

"And I was kind enough to clean the vomit off your clothes. And trust me, had it been up to you, you wouldn't have woken up with your panties on."

"That's ridiculous."

"You begged me to take you home with me. You ended up half-naked because you practically ripped off your own clothes. If you hadn't passed out, those panties would have come off, and we definitely would have had sex."

"Don't make stuff up."

"Why would I make it up?"

She paused, trying not to let things escalate into a full-blown argument right in the busy cafeteria. "Because you're mad, and I suppose I can understand that. You thought Kevin and I were splitting up, you sent me a rose, and now I've just thrown a big bucket of cold water all over your intentions."

"I told you I didn't send any damn flower."

"Fine. Forget about the flower. But we have to straighten this out."

"You're just a user, you know that?"

"Nobody used anybody."

"But you tried. I was being a friend to you because you told me your husband was a creep. You turned around and tried to use me to validate your own self-worth or make your cheating husband jealous."

"That is so outrageous. The only accurate statement you've made in the last five minutes is that I told you I thought Kevin had cheated."

"And the reason you thought that is because you *wanted* it to be true. You wanted your husband to be unfaithful so that you could feel free to cut loose and be with whoever you wanted to be with."

"For your information, Kevin is the third man I've been with in my life. And so long as he wants me, there won't be another. I don't go around looking for it."

"Then why did you fly from New York and come straight to the hospital searching me out."

"I was coming back to work."

"Right," he said snidely.

"Gary, I was trying to be nice about this. But you're making it really difficult."

"Then let me make it simple. I am not your girlfriend, your boyfriend, or any other type of friend. I had no intention of fucking you that night or any other night. So go fuck yourself."

Their eyes locked in an icy stare. She wanted to defend herself, but a spat in the middle of the hospital cafeteria seemed pointless. "If you have any lingering hopes of us ever speaking to one another again, you had better say you're sorry."

"Sorry?" he said, scoffing. "You think *I* should be sorry?" He leaned closer and spoke barely above a whisper in a voice so deep it didn't even sound like him. "Maybe someday you'll know what sorry is."

She watched in silence as he gathered his tray, rose from the table, and walked away.

27

THE HEADBOARD SLAMMED HARD AGAINST THE WALL. IT WAS JUST after midnight when the antique bed finally stopped rocking and Kevin collapsed between her thighs. His arms shook as he propped himself up on his elbows. Peyton lay naked beneath him, her cheeks flushed red in the dim glow of a scented candle on the nightstand. An errant wisp of hair was pasted to her chin, as her face, neck, and breasts glistened with a thin layer of his sweat and hers. His body shivered as he pulled away. She kissed him lightly, then slid out of bed and walked quietly to the bathroom.

This one had been a marathon. Not that he was in an especially studlike mood. He'd simply had too much weighing on his mind to reach orgasm any sooner.

He still hadn't told Peyton about that heckler at Booklovers'. He didn't want to scare her, especially after what she'd gone through last winter with Andy Johnson. What if the book was a smash and he really became famous? Crazies galore.

Ira Kaufman was another matter. He felt like he did have to tell her that his day job was in jeopardy sooner than expected. He kept the candle burning as she crawled back into bed beside him.

"That was great, honey," she said softly.

"I aim to please."

"Bull's-eye," she said as she snuggled at his side.

He was lying on his back, staring at the ceiling. Her arm felt heavy on his chest. She'd be sound asleep soon.

"Peyton?" he said.

"Hmmm."

"I think I may have gone too far with the book."

She raised her head from the pillow. "What do you mean?"

"Ira Kaufman read it. He thinks some of the characters are too much like real lawyers in the firm."

"Who cares what he thinks?"

"He wants me to pull the book from the publisher. Or he says he'll fire me."

"You can't pull the book."

"I can't afford to lose my job, either."

"Honey, let's be real. You knew that if you set your story in a law firm people would think you were drawing parallels to Marston and Wheeler. You had to realize that there was at least some risk of losing your job."

"I know. But I was hoping to hang around long enough to see if the book did well enough to let me quit the practice."

"You'll find another job."

"What firm will hire me after Marston and Wheeler fires me for supposedly making them look like idiots in my novel?"

She rested her chin on his chest, thinking. "Start your own firm."

"There aren't enough hours in the day to start up a law firm while trying to launch my writing career."

"Try telling that to the director of my residency program."

"You know what I'm saying."

"I know. You're right."

"It's funny," he said. "The worst part about this is that it has me thinking that maybe I'm not as good a writer as I thought I was."

"Don't say that."

"It's true. When I was writing the book, I guess I deluded myself into thinking that the real-life inspiration for some of the characters wasn't quite so transparent. But obviously I was wrong."

"Don't let Ira make you second-guess your writing."

"It's not just him. It really started with something that happened at Booklovers' the other night."

"What?"

He paused, still not ready to tell her how scary the heckler had been. "One of the people in the audience suggested that I had revealed myself through my writing."

"Meaning what?"

"To be specific, he said my wife was all over the book."

Peyton made a face. "Me?"

"I had the same reaction. But after Ira accused me of defaming him, I started to think. Maybe on a subconscious level I did draw too much from the people around me."

Peyton suddenly felt stiff in his arms.

"What's wrong?" he asked.

"Nothing."

"It's my lead character, isn't it?"

"Well, yes," she said quietly. "You wrote a story about a beautiful, intelligent, successful woman who happens to cheat on her husband."

"And it's just a story."

"Right," she said. "Just a story."

"Except for the beautiful, intelligent, and successful part. That's clearly my wife."

"There you go. Three out of four. I guess technically I am all over your book. And I have no plans to sue or fire you. So just tell Ira Kaufman to go to hell."

He smiled and held her close. "Thanks."

"You're welcome."

He held her for another moment, still feeling guilty for not having told her how crazy that guy at Booklovers' had really been. It was for her own good, he told himself, though he knew that rationalizing was a handy way to justify concealment of just about anything.

Even Sandra Blair.

"Good night, love," he said as he leaned across her body and blew out the scented candle.

Three in the morning, and Peyton lay wide awake. She was thinking about Kevin's book and Gary's accusations. It seemed strange. Two men, one her husband, the other her first love. Both had made up stories about her. Both had cast her as an adulteress.

She checked the clock once more. Time was moving slowly in the dark bedroom.

If confiding in Gary about Kevin had been her first mistake, her second had been not telling Kevin that she'd gotten drunk, become sick, and ended up recuperating at Gary's apartment. Now Gary was twisting the truth, making it impossible for her to come clean. She'd always considered herself honest, which only compounded her problem. She wasn't sure what troubled her more, the fact that she'd concealed the truth from her husband or that she'd been able to rationalize it. Of course, those forced justifications were as old as lying itself. *It was harmless. It would look worse than it really was. He was better off just not knowing.* Those were just excuses, and they rang hollow.

Not even the miscarriage had left her feeling this empty. She knew how lies between loved ones could change things forever. She'd learned that from her own family.

It had been years ago. Peyton had been a teenager at the time. Her family was still living in Florida, just a few weeks away from their move back to Boston. Almost three months had passed since her mother had phoned her from the hospital to tell her that the baby hadn't survived. Virtually not a word had been spoken about it since, at least not in Peyton's presence. For Peyton, the conspiracy of silence had only made it harder to accept the death of a sibling she had never known. She'd needed some closure for herself. Before moving out of the house and returning to Boston, she wanted to visit her sister's grave. On moving day, she'd caught up with her mother in the empty dining room as she was packing the family china into a cardboard box.

"You can't visit," her mother had told her.

"I just want to stop by the grave and say a little prayer."

"There is no grave."

"What?"

"We decided on cremation."

"Isn't there some kind of marker or memorial?"

"No."

"Why not?"

"Because we didn't buy one." Her mother was almost robotic in her responses, never breaking the rhythm of her packing to look Peyton in the eye.

"Aren't you going to buy one?"

"No. The ashes were scattered."

"Where?"

She stopped and glared. "What does it matter?"

"She was my sister. It matters."

"Fine. The ocean."

Peyton watched carefully. Her mother seemed flustered, almost angry as she wrapped the sugar bowl in newsprint and stuffed it into the box. Peyton moved closer and stepped on the stack of papers on the floor, preventing her mother from pulling out another sheet. Her mother looked up, and finally their eyes met.

"I think you're lying about something," said Peyton.

That was well over a decade ago, but the memory was very much alive for Peyton. The same feeling was twisting her into knots now. Granted, the situation then had been reversed. She had felt deceived rather than deceptive. But there was a strange commonality between lying and being lied to: they both seemed to drain the soul.

Still wide awake, Peyton stared at the ceiling, wondering what had made her think of that ugly confrontation with her mother. She covered her eyes with the pillow, remembering what her father used to say to her when she was a girl—how things were always worse at night, that it wouldn't be so bad in the morning.

This time, she wasn't so optimistic. Maybe that was the reason she resolved right then and there to call her father for lunch. He could make her feel better, even if she was too embarrassed to tell him exactly what was wrong.

Or maybe she finally wanted to make sense of an old family lie that she'd never fully sorted out.

28

THEY MET FOR A SATURDAY LUNCH AT FUGAKYU, A POPULAR JAPANESE restaurant in Brookline whose peculiar name usually elicited an indignant "Excuse me?" from anyone unfamiliar with it. They shared the house specialty, salmon- and tuna-filled maki rolls. It was a small place where patrons at other tables could have easily overheard, so Peyton kept the lunch conversation light. Her father, however, had apparently sensed that something was gnawing at her. He was the one who suggested they go for a walk after eating. They strolled side by side up the wide and tree-lined sidewalk on Brookline.

"Everything okay with you?" he asked.

"No, actually."

"You want to talk about it?"

She kept walking, saying nothing for a few steps. "You mind if I ask you something personal?"

"Why would I mind?"

"Did you and Mom ever name the baby who died?"

He almost tripped on the sidewalk. "No. Where did that question come from?"

She stopped at a bench near the entrance to the park. "Sit for a minute?"

He took a seat on the bench, but Peyton remained standing. "You don't have to answer this, but there's something I've wanted to know for a long time. And right now, where I am in my life, I need to know more than ever."

"What?"

"Do you ever wish Mom had never told you the baby wasn't yours?"

His mouth opened, but no words came for several long moments. "How did you know it wasn't?" he asked, barely audible.

"I just knew. The way we moved out of Boston as soon as Mom started showing. The lack of joy in the house before the baby was born. Mom never did set up a nursery. It seemed there was always a cloud over the pregnancy. Then after the baby died, everything was just as hush-hush. Am I right?"

He looked past her. "Yes. You're right."

"Like I said, you don't have to answer. But do you ever wish Mom had just never told you?"

"I hate to admit it. But I guess knowing made it easier for me to deal with the way things turned out."

"Put that aside if you can. Just look at it from the standpoint of her infidelity. Would that be something you wish you had simply never found out about?"

"Is this about me? Or is it about you and Kevin?"

She tried to look him in the eye but couldn't.

"Did Kevin cheat on you?"

"Dad, please. This is really hard for me."

He nearly growled. "Don't tell me your mother was right about him."

"Nobody cheated on anyone. It's more of a perception problem."

"What does that mean?"

"It's too complicated. I just want to know how you dealt with it. In hindsight, are you glad Mom told you?"

"All I can tell you is that I've forgiven her. That's all that matters."

"Because she told you. Is that why you forgave her?"

"No. That's why we stayed married, but that's not why I forgave her."

"I don't understand."

"Her contrition made it possible for my ego to get out of the way. But that has nothing to do with forgiveness. I forgave her because I loved her."

They exchanged a long, soulful look. Peyton took a seat on the bench beside him. She couldn't help but think of all the times in her life she'd heard people say she'd inherited the brains from her mother.

"You're a very wise man."

He let out a mirthless chuckle. "Or just an old fool."

"Not in my book," she said as she laid her head on his shoulder. "Not ever."

The summer's longest heat wave was over. Sunday joggers were everywhere. Kevin and Steve Beasley had just finished a pickup game of basketball in the park and were cooling down, one shooting jump shots till he missed while the other rebounded. Steve was a second-year associate at Marston & Wheeler, a member of Ira Kaufman's litigation team, like Kevin, but a few years his junior. They'd worked together on various cases throughout the year and had become friends to the extent of sharing lunch twice a week and shooting hoops every other weekend.

Kevin took aim from the free-throw line. "No time on the clock. Tie ball game. Make this shot, and the Celtics win the world championship."

"Miss it and you buy me and my fiancée dinner at our favorite restaurant."

"Hope you're not hungry." Kevin let it fly. Off the rim. "Damn."

"Will that be cash or charge, sir?"

"Depends on whether you and Jeannie want fries with your Happy Meal."

They exchanged a smile as Kevin took a seat in the grass just off the court. Steve toweled the sweat off his face and plopped down beside him. They watched in silence as a mother duck and five ducklings waddled across the court.

"You want to get some lunch?"

"Sure."

"I'll give Jeannie a call if you want to invite Peyton."

"Nah, Peyton's at the library. Some research paper she's working on with the chief resident."

"She puts in a lot of hours, huh?"

"Comes with the job."

Steve opened his jug of Gatorade and took a sip. "Do you ever wonder—ah, forget it."

"What?"

"It's not my place to say."

"Say what?"

"I've debated whether I should say anything. But if it were me, I'd want to know."

"Well, now you've done it. Either you're going to tell me what you were about to say, or I'm going to have to beat it out of you."

He took another sip. "All right. Remember a couple of weeks ago when Ira called you at the Waldorf and shipped you off to Los Angeles?"

"Yeah. You filled in for me."

"Right. In fact, I just took your room, remember? We didn't even bother with guest registration."

"So what are you trying to tell me? There's going to be a room charge for a three-thousand-dollar hooker on my next AMEX statement?"

"Actually this is pretty serious."

Kevin's smile faded. "What is it?"

"The morning after you left, Peyton called. She was looking for you. It was a strange conversation."

"In what way?"

"I told her you were in Los Angeles and how I'd taken your room. I kept getting these long periods of silence after everything I said. She seemed distracted. And then toward the end of the conversation, I heard a man's voice in the background."

"A man?"

"Yeah. I don't know who it was."

"Did you hear what he said?"

Steve paused and nodded. "That's what makes this so difficult."

"Just tell me what he said, damn it."

"He said, 'Don't be shy, I've already seen you naked.'"

Kevin went numb. "Then what happened?"

"She got flustered and tried to blame it on the TV."

"Maybe it was the TV."

He shot a knowing look. "It wasn't the TV."

"How can you be so sure?"

"I can tell the difference in the sound."

Kevin looked away, unable to speak. It was as if some huge hand had reached up from his stomach, pierced his heart, and grabbed him by the throat. Then he had another thought and was immediately suspicious. "Why are you telling me this?"

"Like I said, if it were me I'd want to know."

"Did you discuss this with Ira?"

"Of course not. It's personal."

Kevin narrowed his eyes. "Did Ira put you up to this?"

"What are you talking about? Ira has nothing to do with this."

"Two days ago Ira came into my office and threatened to fire me because he thought there were too many unflattering parallels between Marston and Wheeler and the fictional law firm in my novel. He told me to cancel the book or prepare for war. Two days later, his favorite young associate informs me that my wife is cheating on me."

"Do you think I'm making this up?"

"My book is about a woman who cheats on her husband. Funny coincidence, isn't it?"

"Look, I'm sorry I said anything. Just forget it."

Kevin rose and quickly packed his gym bag. "Forget it? Not for a long time."

"Come on. You're falling off the deep end."

"I just can't believe you did this."

"All I did was tell you something as a friend."

"A friend wouldn't have waited two weeks to tell me, at least not if it had really happened. I know what this is about. Ira declares war, his soldiers go to battle."

"Now hold on."

"Nice to know whose side you're on." He threw his bag over his shoulder and headed for his car.

29

SUNDAY WAS SUPPOSED TO BE HER DAY OFF, BUT SHE HAD VOLUN-
teered to help the chief resident with an article on the increas-
ing incidence of adult-onset diabetes in children. Everything she
needed was accessible from her computer. Articles, reports, studies,
patient histories. Just a click of the button and they'd appear on
her screen via the Internet or from a CD. For Peyton, however, it
didn't feel like research if, at least at some point during the project,
she didn't find herself in the silence of a library surrounded by real
books.

The hospital library was deserted, typical for a Sunday in summer. She was at an isolated carrel reviewing the online version
of an article from the *Journal of the American Medical Association
Journal* article on her notebook computer when an instant message popped up. She hated when that happened. Invariably she'd
be in the middle of something important whenever one of those
unwanted boxes would take over her screen with some silly message from a friend who just wanted to chat. The Internet may
well have revolutionized communication, but in some ways it
was a throwback to the old days of party lines, a time when you
could just pick up the telephone, find out who was talking, and
jump right in. Except that on the Internet, people could travel
under any screen name they wanted.

The instant message read, "hi. u there?"

She didn't recognize the sender, but people could change their screen names at will or even get more than one. Whoever it was, he was an experienced chat-room typist, all lowercase, letters and numbers substituting for words. Peyton was too much of a perfectionist for that. She typed, "Who is this?"

"u wouldn't come 2 me, so i came 2 u."

"Still don't recognize the name."

"it's new, like yours."

That only confused her further. On the advice of the hospital security director, she'd changed her screen name after the Johnson stalking episode, just as she'd changed her phone number, pager number, and the lock on her apartment. But that was months ago.

"thought we could use a fresh start," the message continued.

That answered it for her. She wished he would go away, but it was clearly not going to be an easy break. "It's not possible."

"y not?"

"That's just the way it has to be."

"how can u still feel that way after all this time?"

"It's hardly been any time at all."

"been forever. i been trying 2 win you back 2 long."

"Stop it. We're not in high school anymore."

There was a long delay. Peyton wondered if he'd signed off. Finally, the response built on her screen, one letter at a time. "Who do you think you're talking to?"

Her fingers froze on the keys. No more cutesy chat-room typing. This was getting weird. "I know it's you, Gary."

"It's not Gary."

That chilled her. "Who is this?"

"You got my rose, my message on your locker. You must know."

"Sure. I know it's Gary."

"It's *NOT* Gary!"

"I don't believe you."

"I'll prove it. Look out the window."

"Will you please just leave me alone?"

"Just do as I say. Keep your computer online. Go to the window overlooking the garden and look outside."

Instinct told her to log off. She was tired of being manipulated. But the way this was escalating, she might someday need proof that Gary was harassing her.

"Okay. I'm going." Slowly, she rose and walked to a reading area by the wall of windows that overlooked the garden. It was a small, urban-style green space surrounded on all sides by buildings in the hospital compound. Trees, birds, and flowers turned it into a little oasis. Two teenagers were throwing a Frisbee on the lawn. A cancer patient with an IV pole was taking a slow walk alongside her parents toward the sculptured otters that reclined in the center fountain. Peyton saw nothing out of the ordinary.

Her anger rose as she realized he was playing games. Quickly she retraced her steps through the reading area, past the bookshelves. She stopped just a few feet away from her carrel and nearly gasped. Her computer was gone—and all her work with it.

On impulse, she ran to the main entrance and peered down the hall toward the cafeteria but saw nothing. She ran back inside and checked the library's rear exit, which led to the alley. She saw only parked cars and Dumpsters. A block away, traffic was moving steadily on Longwood Avenue, an easy escape route.

Her heart sank at the realization: She'd been distracted and scammed. It was the common thief's oldest game. But she knew this was no common thief.

"Gary, you son of a bitch."

Peyton reported her computer as "missing" to the hospital, on the off chance that a janitor or someone else might find it lying around. She didn't bother with a formal police report. The cops rarely did anything to recover stolen items of insured personal property, and she preferred to keep her troubles with Gary under wraps anyway, at least until she confronted him and confirmed he was the thief.

Gary lived within walking distance of the med school library. In ten minutes she reached his apartment and knocked firmly on the door. She heard footsteps approaching. He was home, but that didn't rule him out as the culprit. He could have raced home with her computer, switched on the television, and jumped in the easy chair.

"Peyton?" he said. "What a surprise."

She glared. "Where's my computer?"

"What?"

"Somebody just played a little game with me at the library and stole my computer."

"Are you accusing me?"

"You knew I was working on this study. You knew I've been going to the library every Sunday for the past month."

"So did a lot of other people."

"Nobody else is petty enough to engage in sabotage."

"Gee, you say the nicest things."

"This is getting way out of hand," she said. "Just give me back my computer, and we'll forget this ever happened. But if you keep standing there like a jerk pretending you don't know anything about it, I'll report it stolen. I'll tell the police and I'll tell the hospital who I think took it."

He chuckled. "Yeah, right."

"Don't test me."

"I didn't take your stupid computer. But if you want to accuse me, fine. Dig your own grave. In six months you've dropped from being the superstar resident to the resident troublemaker. You shot the clinic nurse in the butt and got the hospital sued. Andy Johnson ended up killing himself over you, and rumors are still flying about whether you two were sexually involved. And now you want to drag the hospital into a spat between you and a nurse who very recently carried you dead drunk back to his apartment."

"You're enjoying this, aren't you?"

"A little. Too bad about your computer. But I think you put it best ten years ago, the first time you dumped me: Goodbye and good luck." He closed the door in her face.

On one level, Peyton was angry enough to beat down the door. But mostly she was shocked by the depth of Gary's resentment toward her. His past gestures toward friendship obviously belied deeper, unresolved emotions. Her efforts to remain his friend had apparently been interpreted as nothing more than teasing by a "manipulative bitch" who just wanted to keep him around in case, someday, she decided to climb into bed with him. It hurt and confused her, and it underscored the fact that she had much bigger problems than a stolen computer. Gary was right in one respect. She was down to her last strike—with the hospital and her husband.

Quietly she walked away, fearful that the man she'd once considered her best friend at the hospital was now determined to see that she got everything he thought she deserved.

And he seemed to have her exactly where he wanted her.

30

ON MONDAY EVENING, KEVIN LEFT THE OFFICE AT SIX–THIRTY, A LITTLE earlier than usual. Peyton had strong-armed him into attending a cocktail party at Harvard with her. He normally hated those events, the lone lawyer amid a roomful of Ivy League doctors. He knew he'd end up standing around munching baby corn on the cob hors d'oeuvres as Peyton networked as usual. For this, he'd turned down a friend's offer of seats behind home plate for tonight's Red Sox game.

The things we do for love.

He had yet to say anything to Peyton about the story Steve Beasley had told him on Sunday. He didn't want to think Steve was a liar, but he didn't think Peyton was a cheater, either. That left a dilemma: How could he put Peyton on the spot about something that was little more than a rumor without opening the door to questions about his own past indiscretion? He saw no point in bringing it up, at least not until he knew more.

He took the elevator to the fourth floor of the parking garage and walked toward his car. Footsteps echoed off walls, floors, and ceilings of unfinished concrete. With the press of a button on his key chain, the alarm chirped and led him to his vehicle near the end of a long line of cars. He removed his pinstriped jacket and placed it in the backseat with his briefcase. Just as he opened the driver's door, something on the windshield caught his eye. It was a single white sheet of standard-size paper, blank on the side facing up. He slid it from under the wiper and checked the other side.

It was a typed page from his manuscript, presumably from one of the copies he'd left at Booklovers'—the dedication page. "To Peyton" was what Kevin had written. That message was crossed out with broad, angry strokes of red ink. Beneath it was a hand-written note.

"She's spoken for, asshole."

The paper began to shake in his hand. On impulse, he crunched it into a tight ball and hurled it across the garage. *Ira fights dirty,* he reminded himself.

But he was less than convinced.

The reception was held at the Fogg Art Museum, a worthy affair to mark the generous decision of a wealthy Harvard Medical School alumnus to drop a proverbial bundle in honor of his deceased older brother. While not on the university's famed Tercentenary Quadrangle, the museum's atrium-style courtyard was an attractive setting for everything from wedding receptions to fund-raisers. The guest of honor had wanted the party in Cambridge, even though the medical school was in Brookline, well away from the main campus. It was a fitting tribute, as the museum was near Memorial Church, where his brother's name was forever etched in marble beside those of other Harvard men killed while serving their country since World War I.

Kevin arrived late. The courtyard was filled with about a hundred and fifty well-dressed friends and alumni, most of them from the medical school. The donor, a distinguished gray-haired gentleman, was speaking from a lectern to an attentive gathering. Kevin spotted Peyton across the room. He snaked his way through the crowd, reaching her side just as the speaker reached the tail end of his speech.

"In closing, I refer you to our school motto engraved on the

Harvard crest. *Veritas*, it reads. Latin for 'truth'. For me, that word sums up my brother. He was true to himself. True to his family. True to his friends. And true to the beliefs he died defending on the battlefield. He stood for the truth. Let us all stand for the truth."

After what seemed like a dozen utterances of the word "truth," Kevin took a side glance at Peyton. She looked back nervously without making eye contact.

"I'm proud to make this grant to the medical school in the name of Douglas Hester, the truest man I ever knew. But the real truth is, I'm thirsty. So in Doug's honor, the bar is officially open. Please join me."

A proper level of applause filled the courtyard, followed by the murmur of emerging conversation. Kevin and Peyton still hadn't looked at one another.

"Nice speech," he said.

"Yes. Very nice."

Kevin had resolved to say something to her about the note on his car, but he was losing his nerve. All this talk about "truth" had him feeling hypocritical. Mere mention of the note would trigger talk about what Steve Beasley had told him, about the rose he had found outside their front door last winter and never mentioned to Peyton, about the heckler at Booklovers' that he'd kept to himself, and on and on. So many secrets, all of which circled back to his own deception, the series of lies and ongoing cover-up that now seemed even worse than his single act of stupidity on that cold night in Providence.

Maybe it was time for the truth. "Peyton—"

"There's Dr. Sheffield," she said. "Do you mind if I mingle?"

It took the breath out of him, or at least the wind out of his sails. "You go right ahead. I'll get us drinks."

"Nothing for me, thanks."

"Okay. I'll get myself one." *I could use it,* he thought. He watched as she disappeared into a crowd that was gradually breaking into small, conversant groups.

"You look bored."

He recognized the voice from behind. He turned and tried not to panic. "Sandra?"

"Are you going to say hello, or just stand there and gawk?"

"What are you doing here?"

"Same as you. My date's right over there." She pointed with a nod toward a handsome but older man who somehow made Sandra seem older, too. He was engaged in conversation in a group near Peyton.

"Well, it was good to see you again, Sandra," he said, trying to break away.

"I was sorry to hear about you and Peyton."

He stopped cold. "Hear what?"

"It is rather ironic, don't you think?"

"What are you talking about?"

"You write a story about a successful woman who gets tangled up in a kidnapping after cheating on her husband. Then Peyton ends up cheating on you."

"Where did you hear that?"

"Steve Beasley told me. Right after he read your manuscript. He also told me that one of the more incidental characters is a tramp who tries to sleep her way up to partnership in a Boston law firm. There's a nasty rumor floating around the firm that you based that character on me."

That one hurt on several levels, not the least of which being that it wasn't true. "None of the characters is based on anyone."

"Good answer."

"Please listen to me. I'm sorry about the way things went with us, but it's important for me to know that you believe me on this. The entire time I was writing this book, I thought of you as a friend. A good friend. Even if I had intended to put you into the story, it would never have been like that."

"Thanks for being so concerned about my feelings," she said coolly. "But if Ira has anything to say about your writing career, you've got much bigger things to worry about."

"What have you heard?"

"Just that he's determined to show you that nobody takes on Marston and Wheeler and wins."

Kevin did a quick shoulder check to see if anyone else from his firm happened to be at this event. "Sandra, if you know anything specific, I would really appreciate it if—"

"I'm sorry about you and Peyton," she said, nipping that one in the bud. "That's all I wanted to say to you. Goodbye, Kevin." She turned and walked away.

Kevin retreated to the hors d'oeuvres table. He staked out a spot nearest the exit, sampling the smoked salmon on little square toasts as his eyes darted across the courtyard in search of Peyton.

Of all the people to show up—Sandra. Peyton still didn't know a thing about her. He regretted it, for sure. But it had happened at a time when his marriage was faltering so badly that Peyton hadn't even told him she was pregnant. Who could say which was the greater deception? There could be no betrayal unless both people were being true to each other. Or so he had nearly convinced himself. This much he was sure of: It certainly would have been a betrayal of the highest order if he had strayed during happier times, when things had been going strong between him and Peyton, say as recently as two weeks ago—precisely when his friend Steve claimed to have overheard Peyton's lover on the telephone.

He was popping clumps of salmon as if they were peanuts, his mix of emotions suddenly so stirred up that he wasn't even aware of how overstuffed his mouth was. He kept an eye on Peyton, then finally got her attention. After dozens of events like this one, they had that nonverbal-communication-from-across-the-room routine down pat. He signaled and started toward the exit. She followed.

He headed down a lonely marble corridor and found himself at a set of locked doors at the entrance to a lecture room. He would have preferred to go inside the hall, but it seemed private enough at the end of the long corridor.

Peyton caught up to him and said, "We can't leave yet. We just got here."

"I'm sorry. I have something to say that just can't wait."

"What's the matter?"

This wasn't the ideal place to tell her, but they were alone—and it was time. "Three times in the last two days I've been told that my wife is seeing another man. *That's* the matter."

She froze, speechless. Kevin continued. "Supposedly it happened when I was in Los Angeles."

All color seemed to drain from her face. His pace quickened, as he sensed he was on to something. "Steve Beasley said you called him at the Waldorf looking for me. He overheard a man in the background. I've been trying to convince myself that it can't be true, that maybe Ira Kaufman was putting Steve up to playing a dirty trick on me. Is that all it is? Or am I fooling myself?"

"Kevin—" She started to say something, then stopped. "Do we have to talk about this here?"

"Don't tell me it's true."

"I just want a chance to explain. In private."

"I can't *believe* this." He turned away, then glanced back and asked sharply, "Was it somebody I know?"

"I didn't sleep with anyone. I . . . I had too much to drink and got sick. I ended up spending the night at Gary's apartment. I wasn't unfaithful to you, I swear."

"Oh, spare me. The guy said he saw you naked! Steve heard him!"

"Kevin—"

He walked away before his anger could make him say something stupid. Peyton hurried to keep up. "Don't make me chase you."

"No one asked you to come along."

With that, she stopped. Kevin continued down the empty hall, turned the corner, and nearly slammed into another woman. He was about to excuse himself, until he realized who it was. Sandra. It was either one heck of a coincidence, or she had strategically positioned herself just around the corner at the entrance to the ladies' room. Neither one said a word, but from the look on her face he knew that she had managed to hear it all.

"Kevin, nothing happened!" Peyton was still out of sight, trailing behind him.

He shot Sandra a look and headed briskly for the exit, wondering which of the two might follow him out.

31

PEYTON WAS HOME BY TEN O'CLOCK. SHE HADN'T CHASED AFTER Kevin, but she hadn't expected him to leave her stranded at the cocktail party either. She waited long after most guests had already left, hoping he would return. No such luck.

A taxi dropped her at the curb outside her apartment. She climbed the front steps and unlocked the door. Before going inside, she took a long look up Magnolia Street, then down, as far as the old glowing street lamps would allow her to see. Their car wasn't there. Kevin hadn't come home.

She opened the door and stepped inside. Today's mail was at her feet in the foyer. She gathered it up and went to the bedroom, where she dropped it on the bed with her purse. She checked the answering machine, but he hadn't called. She tried his office and his cell. No answer.

Wherever he was, he clearly didn't want to talk to her.

She let her bathwater run as she removed her makeup and got undressed, then eased herself into the tub. A long soak would do her good.

The phone rang just as she'd gotten comfortable. She was tempted to let it go, but maybe it was Kevin. She jumped out and wrapped herself in a towel, then ran to the phone and answered it.

The dial tone hummed in her ear. She hesitated just a moment, then dialed *69, the call return service that automatically dialed back the last number that had called. For all Peyton knew, she was calling back some obnoxious telemarketer. After nine unanswered rings, she resigned herself to the fact that she would never know if it had been Kevin. She hung up and went back to the bathroom.

She had one foot in the tub when the phone rang again. Startled, she slipped and went down on one knee on the hard tile floor. She gathered herself up, pulled on her robe, and hobbled back to the phone.

"Hello," she said, but again she was too late. There was only a dial tone. Immediately she dialed ★69. After three rings, she got an answer.

"Yeah." It was the gruff voice of a man.

"Who's this?"

"Lenny. Who's asking?"

"Did you call me a minute ago from this number?"

"No."

"Did somebody just call me from your phone?"

"Only if they got your number off the bathroom wall. This is the pay phone at Sylvester's."

Peyton could hear noise in the background, like a crowded bar. "Okay, thanks."

She hung up, unsure of what to do. She'd never heard of Sylvester's, but it was more than conceivable that Kevin had left the party and gone straight to a bar. Maybe he'd had a couple of drinks, called her from the pay phone, and then chickened out.

She cinched up her bathrobe, went to the kitchen, and pulled out the yellow pages. Sylvester's was in South Boston, relatively easy to reach by taxi at this time of night. But what was the point? She wasn't even sure it was Kevin who had called. Better to stay put and wait for him to call again.

She was suddenly hungry. Kevin had managed to rob her of an appetite for hors d'oeuvres at the cocktail party. The last she'd eaten was at the hospital's noon lecture. She grabbed a boil-in-the-bag dinner from the freezer and dropped it in a pot of water on the stove. In twelve minutes it was done, in another eight she'd finished eating. After cleanup, it was almost 11:00 P.M. Still no word from Kevin.

She stretched out on the living room couch and switched on the late news. It was the usual smattering of daily violence, but she was hardly watching. In her mind, she was already rehearsing her speech to Kevin for when he walked through the front door—which would be soon, hopefully. She'd tell him the truth, of course. It was about time for that.

The question was, would he believe the truth?

She grabbed the remote and channel surfed for something that might at least distract her, if not ease her mind.

The phone rang. Peyton's eyes opened to the sight of a test pattern on the television screen. She checked the clock on the mantel. It was 4:11 A.M.

She'd fallen asleep on the couch, waiting up for Kevin. Obviously for nought. She rubbed the sleep from her eyes and answered the phone. There was no dial tone but no reply, either. She sensed someone was on the line. "Hello," she said, a little louder this time. Still, there was no response. She hung up and sat bolt upright on the couch. If that had been Kevin, she didn't like the game he was playing.

Seconds later, the phone rang again. She answered, "Who is this?"

There was silence on the line. Again, she sensed the caller was still there. After several seconds, she detected the sound of someone breathing.

"Who's there?"

The breathing became louder, and she quickly hung up. No way was that Kevin. He'd lost his temper at times, but never had he been that mean to her. Then again, he'd never had reason to believe she'd cheated on him before, either.

Moments later, the phone rang again. She let it ring nine times before she finally answered. "I know who this is. Stop it, or I'm calling the police."

"Check your mail."

"What?"

The line clicked. The caller was gone. She laid the phone in the cradle and paused, confused. *Check the mail?*

Instinct told her to dial the police, but her curiosity said otherwise. She was sure it wasn't Kevin, which meant it had to be the same joker who had stolen her computer—Gary. With any luck, he had been foolish enough to send her something in the mail that would help her prove he was harassing her. She rose from the couch and started toward the bedroom, where she'd left the mail unopened beside her purse. As she crossed the hallway, something caught her eye on the floor in the foyer. It was an envelope.

She knew it hadn't been there earlier. She'd picked up all the mail on her way in. Someone had evidently delivered it in the middle of the night as she lay sleeping on the couch. Slowly she approached and picked it up. It was a standard business-size envelope with no postage and nothing written on it at all. She opened it carefully. There was no letter inside. Just an inch-long lock of sandy brown hair. Human hair.

Chills raced up her spine, as she was not sure what to make of it. She hurried back into the living room to dial the police, but just as she reached the phone the lights went out.

She continued dialing, but the phone was dead. It was a cordless model that didn't work without electricity. Through the front window she could see porch lights burning across the street. It was clear that someone had cut off her power, probably through the master circuit outside the building. That realization sent her heart racing.

Her first impulse was to run out the door screaming her head off till she found a neighbor. But maybe that was exactly what he wanted her to do. Perhaps he was out there waiting. She needed another plan. Her gun was locked in a strong box on a shelf in the pitch-dark closet. Useless. She had another thought: the cell phone. It was buried at the bottom of her purse on the bed, where she'd left it.

A dim glow from the street lamp streamed into the apartment, just enough to feel her way down the hall now that her eyes had adjusted. It was progressively darker as she neared the bedroom, and her steps became more tentative. She only assumed the power had been cut off from the outside. She'd never really fiddled with the circuit breakers. That was Kevin's realm. What if they were inside? What if *he* was inside?

A ringing noise pierced the darkness. It was from the bedroom. She was about to scream, then realized what it was. It was coming from her purse.

Someone was calling *her* on her cell phone.

Peyton didn't move. It kept ringing. She entered the bedroom slowly, then approached one step at a time, feeling her way along the edge of the bed until she could reach across the mattress and grab the purse. She dug inside and answered in a shaky voice.

"Hello."

"Got your lover." The voice was garbled, disguised by a mechanical device. It had a low, almost underwater creepiness to it.

"Who is this?"

"I said, I have your lover."

"I don't know what you're talking about."

"His name's Gary Varne."

"Who is this?"

"I have pictures. Drinks at Chauncy's. Dancing at Colombo's. You lying on his bed while he undressed you."

Peyton froze. He knew the exact bars she and Gary had visited that night. "What do you want?"

"Ten thousand dollars. Cash. Or your husband sees the pictures."

Her throat tightened. She realized that the pictures wouldn't show that she'd been sick and was unconscious while Gary had removed her soiled clothing. "I won't be blackmailed."

"Then don't pay me. Or better yet, go to the police. You do either of those things and Gary Varne lands on your doorstep. Dead."

"You mean, you've kidnapped him?"

"Bingo. If you're smart, you pay. If you're dumb, he dies. Do you understand me?"

She now realized the hair in the envelope was Gary's. It was his exact color. She could barely speak. "Yes. I understand."

"In two days I'll call again. Have the cash in order. And don't even think about calling the cops."

She clutched the phone till she heard the dial tone. Unable to move, she simply stared into the darkness. It had all been a horrible mistake. And now Gary Varne had been kidnapped. By some guy with pictures.

Now what do I tell Kevin?

32

THE DEAD BOLT CLICKED AT DAWN. PEYTON RACED TO THE FRONT door AS it opened. In walked Kevin.

"Thank God you're back."

He looked awful, eyes puffy. He was wearing the same suit he'd worn to last night's cocktail party. "I've been up all night."

"Where?"

"My office."

"I called your office."

"I know. I just didn't pick up. What you said last night set me off in a bad way, but ultimately that's not what bothers me." He lowered his eyes, then looked straight at her. "There's something I should have told you a long time ago."

"No," she said in her most serious tone. "There's something I need to tell *you*."

For fifteen minutes Peyton laid it all out, from her mistaken assumption that Kevin had cheated, to her latest suspicions that Gary was harassing her, and finally to the call from the kidnapper. He listened to every word, she was sure of it, barely moving in the chair opposite hers at the kitchen table.

Finally, he spoke. "We're not going to pay."

"He said he'd kill Gary if we went to the police."

"Not to worry. We're not going to the police."

"You can't just ignore it."

"Do you have feelings for him?"

"No. I told you, we went out drinking, I got sick and—"

"Do you really expect me to believe that?"

"Yes. It's the truth."

"Would you believe it, if you were me?"

She didn't answer immediately. He seized on her hesitation. "You shouldn't have to think about that one."

"Kevin, let's not make this about the two of us and every problem we've ever had. Gary is in danger. Let's focus on that."

"He was harassing you, for crying out loud. Two minutes ago you said he stole your computer."

"I said I thought he'd stolen it. In light of this, I'm not so sure it was him. I'm not even sure the rose on my locker was from him either. He denied all of it each time I confronted him. It's possible he basically left me alone after I walked out of his apartment. In a way, I've been the one harassing him with false accusations."

"Sounds to me like you do have feelings for him."

"I just want to do the right thing."

"Which would be what, in your view?"

"We should call the police."

"Let's not be knee-jerk. We need to think this through."

"We can't pretend this didn't happen. What if this threat is for real? Gary could get killed."

"He's not going to get killed."

"How do you know that?"

"Because I think it's him."

"What?"

"The kidnapper is Gary. Who else would have pictures of you undressed? Was there anyone else in the room?"

She stopped and thought for a second. "That's a good point."

"Don't you see? He staged it."

"But why would he do that?"

"Because he's a scumbag and he's pissed. You told him I had cheated, you went out partying with him, and you spent the night at his place. Then you told him that you were wrong, I hadn't cheated, and that you and I had patched this up. You said yourself he was obviously ticked off about that and nearly blew a gasket right there in the hospital cafeteria. He had a thing for you, and you jerked him around and then dumped him. For the *second time* in his life you've dumped him, and both times it was for *me*. So now he's going to make us pay the only way he can. He's going to squeeze some money out of us."

"Why a staged kidnapping? Why wouldn't he just blackmail me?"

"It's a clever ploy on his part. If he were to come to you and say 'Give me ten thousand dollars or I'll tell your husband we had sex,' he could go to jail for extortion. But the kidnapping ruse gives him a layer of protection. If you pay the phony ransom, he pockets the money. If you call the police, he pretends he really was kidnapped. This way, he doesn't have to make any explicit demands that you could tape-record and hand over to the district attorney for a slam-dunk conviction on charges of extortion."

"That sounds like something a lawyer would concoct. Not Gary."

"Maybe he's smarter than you think."

"I just don't want to be wrong about this."

"How did you leave it with the caller?"

"He wants me to have the money ready in two days. He said he'd call back."

"Perfect. When he calls back, tell him you already confessed to your husband. Tell him I'm cool with it."

"Stop it, Kevin. There's nothing to be cool with. I didn't cheat on you."

"That's really irrelevant."

"How can you say that?"

"Because if you didn't cheat on me, I'm happy. If you did, I love you, and I forgive you. It's as simple as that."

She wished he would believe her, but it heartened her to think that he really loved her enough to forgive her. *Or was he just saying that?*

"This is such a mess," she said.

"Nothing we can't handle. When that kidnapper calls again for the ransom, I want you to tell him that we decided Gary Varne isn't worth ten cents, let alone ten grand."

"I just want to go to the police."

"Will you forget the police, please?"

"I'm afraid someone is going to get hurt."

"No one is going to get hurt. I'm telling you, there is no kid-napping. It's Varne."

Their eyes met, then Peyton blinked and let go of his hand. Only a few times before had she seen that look on Kevin's face. She knew his mind was made up.

"You're angry," she said.

"Yes, I am. But I'm not speaking out of anger."

Her gaze drifted toward the phone. She dreaded the thought of another call from the kidnapper in two days, the thought of what she was going to tell him.

"I hope you're right about this," she said quietly. "God, do I hope you're right."

33

KEVIN FELT USELESS. EVEN IF HE HADN'T BEEN PHYSICALLY EXHAUST-ed from lack of sleep, he was way too preoccupied to practice law.

He faked his way through some easy billable hours in a morning conference call among eleven different lawyers who represented four different defendants in a nationwide consumer class action. Thankfully, two lawyers from New York did most of the talking, plotting clever ways to delay the trial until well after the thirty-six-year-old judge who'd been kicking their collective asses died of old age.

For lunch he ordered a sandwich and ate alone in his office. It was tasteless, neither bad nor good, like old gum. Don's Deli strikes again. Or maybe it was him. This was part of the overall numbing of the senses. First to go was the subconscious sense of guilt. Next were the physical senses. By morning, he'd be a zombie with no remorse. Such were the effects of habitual lying.

It did seem to be habit forming. He'd sat at the kitchen table and listened to Peyton's painful explanation about Gary Varne, never uttering a peep about him and Sandra. It hadn't seemed like the right time. It never seemed like the right time.

The door opened. Ira Kaufman entered and closed the door behind him. "I need a decision," he said.

Kevin set his cardboard sandwich aside. "On what?"

"Your book. I wasn't kidding. I'm not going to let you publish it as written."

"Then fire me if you want. I'm not going to change a word."

"Don't be a fool. I'm giving you a chance to keep your job. If you spit in my eye, you'll lose your job and the lawsuit."

"What lawsuit?"

He pitched a file onto Kevin's desk. "This one."

"You actually sued me?"

"Not yet. As a courtesy, I'm giving you a chance to read it over before we file. Hopefully, you'll come to your senses. If you don't, we'll file by Friday and have an injunction by Monday."

"You can't get an injunction against the publication of my book. First Amendment. Freedom of speech. Any of that ring a bell?"

"Read it. I think you'll be surprised. *Un*pleasantly." He smiled thinly as he opened the door and left.

Kevin glanced at the file on his desk but didn't reach for it. He was more intrigued by the timing than the content. Sandra must have reported back to Ira about their encounter at the cocktail party last night. Maybe she'd even told him about the argument she'd undoubtedly overheard, he and Peyton wrestling over infidelity. Ira was a master of timing. Hitting 'em while they were down was his patented punch, and this was the kind of low blow that Ira would especially covet. The sense of poetic justice would have enormous appeal, the way Kevin's life was imitating his own fiction. A successful woman cheats on her husband. Her lover is kidnapped.

Just like in his book.

Of course, Ira couldn't possibly know that the second half of Kevin's story had played out in real life—the kidnapping. The only people who knew that were Peyton, himself, and the kidnapper. Just the three of them.

He leaned back in his chair, concerned, wondering if the thought had yet crossed Peyton's mind that perhaps it was just the two of them—Peyton and himself.

....*

Peyton worked a typical thirteen-hour shift at the hospital on both Tuesday and Wednesday. Thursday started with morning rounds, followed by a chance to observe one of her six-month-old male patients undergo surgery for a stomach disorder that she had correctly diagnosed as pyloric stenosis. She thanked God she wasn't the surgeon. Her mind was a million miles away.

The deadline had technically passed at 4:00 A.M., if by "two days" the kidnapper had meant exactly forty-eight hours. Peyton was glad for the extra time.

Gary hadn't been to work since Monday evening. Yesterday she'd discreetly asked so many people whether they'd seen Gary that her mission was becoming not so discreet. Only this morning was she able to nail down that he had called in sick early Tuesday morning, just a few hours after she'd gotten the kidnapper's call. At first she'd taken that to mean that Kevin was right. Gary had staged his own kidnapping. On reflection, however, it seemed just as plausible that the kidnapper had forced him to call in sick so that his sudden disappearance wouldn't be cause for alarm.

The stomach surgery was a success. Peyton was due back in the ER after watching it, but she stopped at the lounge to use the phone. Just to see what would happen, she dialed Gary's home number. The machine picked up. His usual greeting played, followed by at least a dozen beeps, one for each message already on it. The machine switched off without giving her a chance to talk. It was too full to take any more messages. If he was staging a kidnapping, he was at least doing a convincing job with respect to unanswered phone messages.

Dr. Sheffield entered the lounge just as she was checking her mailbox.

"How's our article coming?" he asked as he poured a cup of coffee.

"Fine," she said. "Little computer mishap on Sunday but nothing major."

"I'm sure you'll sort it out." He started for the door, then stopped. "By the way, if this phase of your research turns out half as good as the last one, I was planning to credit you as a coauthor."

"That would be an honor. Thanks."

He left as quickly as he'd come. She was about to head out herself when the lounge phone rang, startling her. She answered on the third ring, only to hear that mechanically disguised voice again.

"Where's my money?"

Peyton shuddered, not sure that she could pull off Kevin's plan. "How did you know I was at this phone?"

"Same way I got pictures of Gary Varne undressing you."

That strengthened her resolve. Like Kevin had said, who but Gary himself would have those pictures?

"Do you have the money?" he said.

She stretched the cord as far as it would go to check the entire lounge to make sure that no one else was in the room, such as an exhausted resident flopped on the couch or passed out by the computers. All clear. "I was hoping we could talk about this."

"Nothing to talk about."

"My husband knows about . . . the incident. I told him."

There was silence on the line. "That must have been grand. What did you tell him? It was all a mistake. That you don't have any feelings for Gary?"

"I don't."

"Then it doesn't look good for poor Gary Varne, does it? My price is the same. Ten thousand."

"I don't think I can pay."

"You'll pay. Or I'll kill him."

He sounded like he meant it. Peyton felt herself wavering, but she tried to be firm. "Please—"

"Please *what*? If Gary doesn't mean anything to you, you got nothing to worry about. You don't care if he dies, you don't care if he lives. You don't care what happens to him."

Her voice shook. "What is going on?"

"You tell me. Who are you lying to, bitch? Me? Your husband. Or yourself? Have the money by midnight. And cut the crap. This is what you get for lying with strangers. You didn't know you cared."

The line clicked, and the caller was gone.

34

PRIVACY WAS HARD TO COME BY IN THE HOSPITAL, BUT THE ON-CALL suites worked in a pinch. They were windowless rooms (hardly suites) for residents who might somehow manage twenty or thirty minutes of sleep on their on-call night, complete with bunk beds, a small shower that always seemed to have plenty of ice-cold water, and a telephone. Peyton ducked inside, closed the door, and dialed Kevin at the firm. He answered his own line, which startled her a little. She'd expected his secretary.

"It's me," she said. "He called again."

"When?"

"Just now. Somehow he knew I was standing right next to the phone in the hospital lounge. It rang, and I answered. It's creepy the way he tracked me down."

"Don't let him scare you."

"How can I not be scared? He's obviously watching me."

"He's just playing games with you. Did you tell him that I know everything?"

"Yes. He doesn't care. He still wants ten thousand in ransom."

"What a crock. I hope you were firm with him."

"I was."

"What did he say?"

"Have the money by midnight or he's going to kill Gary."

"If that's the way he wants it, let the fool kill himself."

"Kevin," she said reprovingly.

"I'm not serious. And neither is he. He's not going to kill himself."

"That's the part I don't understand. How can you be so sure it's him?"

"It's obvious. If you're objective."

"How can *you* be objective? You're the one . . ."

"Who was cheated on?" he said, finishing the thought for her.

"Who *thinks* he was cheated on. Damn it, the fact that you won't accept my innocence only confirms what I'm saying. Neither one of us can possibly be objective about this. We shouldn't be making decisions that could literally be a matter of life and death."

"It's a charade. Gary Varne is jerking us both around."

"All right, assume he is. That doesn't mean he's not dangerous."

"He's just a loser. Period."

"Death row is full of losers, and that doesn't make the victims any less dead."

"All he wants is money."

"I'm not sure he knows what he wants. This last phone call, he said something that makes me wonder if he's even all there. He said, 'This is what you get for lying with strangers.' Obviously he thinks that I slept with Gary, just like you do."

"What's your point?" he said, a little defensive.

"I'm not sure it makes sense. Gary wasn't a stranger."

"He is, in the sense that he isn't your husband."

"I don't think that's what he meant."

"What else could it mean?"

"That I was with someone I only thought I knew. But I really don't know him."

"Well, that's probably true. How well do we really know the people we work with? Gary could have a dark side. Maybe he even has some kind of split-personality disorder. Schizophrenia."

"Schizophrenia and multiple personalities are two different things. And true cases of multiples are extremely rare. Even more rare in men than women."

"Which only proves my point. Gary is no Sybil, or whoever that woman was with the sixteen personalities. He's a lowlife blackmailer who has decided that if he can't have my wife he'll destroy her. We're *not* paying him."

"I'm not saying we should. But I wish you'd reconsider going to the police."

"No. I still say this is a private matter, and we should keep it private. Your friend Gary doesn't have the nerve to see this through, especially now that he knows we're standing together on this."

"I'm still scared."

"Don't be. If he calls back and keeps pushing for the money, we'll call the police. Trust me on this. My bet is that he's just going to drop it."

"And if he does drop it, what then? We just drop it, too?"

"Absolutely. With your own string of bad luck at the hospital, you should be just as eager as I am to keep this quiet."

Interesting. Gary had told her the same thing after her computer had disappeared. "All right, we'll wait," she said. "But if I so much as get a call and a hang-up, even if I just *think* it's him, we call the police."

"I can live with that," said Kevin.

Hope I can, too, she thought, but she didn't say it. She just said goodbye, hung up, and checked the clock. Almost 2:00 P.M. Ten more hours until he called back—or not.

Either way, it was going to be a long day.

35

IRA KAUFMAN WAS TRUE TO FORM. HE'D GIVEN KEVIN A DEADLINE OF Friday to make a decision about his novel. By Thursday afternoon he'd already filed the complaint and hauled Kevin into court for an emergency hearing. Typical Ira.

The hearing was scheduled for 4:00 P.M., less than an hour after Kevin was served with his subpoena. With it came his official notice of termination. Kevin hadn't even notified his agent or publisher of the threatened litigation. He hadn't hired a lawyer himself to defend himself. By default he would have to be his own lawyer.

Kevin was still reading the complaint and motion as he rode the elevator and hurried down the busy hall to Judge Cosgrove's chambers. He was the last to arrive. Ira was seated on the battered Naugahyde couch in the waiting room, the lone representative of Marston & Wheeler. Ira was a client for a change. Beside him was the gray-haired and distinguished Irving Beckle, the retired chairman of the firm's litigation department. No longer formally associated with the firm, he was its lawyer today. When it came to defending the firm's honor, there could have been no better choice than bringing Beckle out of retirement. He was of the old school of lawyering, a throwback to the days when a handshake had meaning and advertising was for department stores. It didn't hurt, either, that his daughter and Judge Cosgrove were once sorority sisters at Cornell.

"Mr. Beckle," Judge Cosgrove said with a warm smile as she greeted him at the door. "What a pleasure to see you again. Please do come in."

That surely wasn't the norm, the judge rising to meet a lawyer. Usually it was a secretary leading a trail of obsequious lawyers before Her Honor. "Kevin Stokes," said Kevin, introducing himself.

Her smile faded. "Have a seat, Mr. Stokes."

The hearing would be held in chambers, rather than the courtroom, which wasn't unusual when a judge intended to hear only argument from counsel with no live testimony from witnesses. There was no stone-faced bailiff, no high mahogany bench from which the judge presided. The intimacy of a proceeding in chambers, however, did not connote informality. The judge wore the same black robe, and lawyers were just as respectful as in open court. Her carved antique desk was at the far end of the chambers, positioned so that her back was to the tall, arched window. A table extended from the front of her desk to create a T-shaped seating arrangement. The lawyers sat on opposite sides of the table, the plaintiff to the judge's left, the defendant to the right. The court reporter was off to the side near the floor-to-ceiling bookshelves.

"Good afternoon, gentlemen," the judge said. "We're here for an emergency hearing in the case of Marston and Wheeler LLP versus Kevin Stokes. The plaintiff seeks a temporary restraining order that will prevent the defendant from disseminating any further copies of his unpublished manuscript."

"That's correct," said Beckle. "At this point in time, we have sued only Mr. Stokes, since he has distributed unpublished copies of his script to a local bookstore called Booklovers'. On Monday we intend to file suit in New York to prevent his publisher from printing and disseminating the published work."

"All right," said the judge. "At the plaintiff's request, this hearing is being conducted *in camera*, out of the public eye, because Mr. Stokes's novel allegedly discloses confidential information about clients of the law firm of Marston and Wheeler. It therefore violates the attorney-client privilege. An interesting theory. Mr. Beckle, proceed."

"Thank you, Your Honor. This is not your typical First Amendment freedom of speech case. As an associate attorney at Marston and Wheeler, Mr. Stokes had access to confidential information that was protected by the attorney-client privilege. No client of our law firm has agreed to waive the privilege so that Mr. Stokes can include information about them in his novel."

The judge asked, "But doesn't every novel contain the printed disclaimer that it's a work of fiction?"

"That doesn't work in this case," said Beckle. "By way of example, suppose that Marston and Wheeler represented Coca-Cola. Suppose further that in the course of that representation Mr. Stokes became privy to the secret formula for Coca-Cola. Would he then be free to write a novel about the largest soft drink manufacturer in the world, disclose the secret formula, and protect himself from liability simply by changing the name of the company? No one could seriously contend he has the right to do that."

"That would be an easy case," the judge agreed.

"This case is just as easy. Although Mr. Stokes's novel is not technically about a law firm, he has chosen to set his story in a major Boston law firm that resembles Marston and Wheeler in every way but the name. Through his novel Mr. Stokes reveals intricate details about our clients that should not be disclosed in this malicious and thinly veiled work of fiction."

The judge leaned back in her chair, thinking. "What do you have to say for yourself, Mr. Stokes?"

"First, let me say that this entire hearing is unfair. Mr. Kaufman told me that I would have until tomorrow to make a decision about the book before filing his complaint."

"Did you intend to burn your book if he gave you until tomorrow?"

"Honestly, no."

"Then stop bellyaching and get to the argument."

He glanced at Ira, who seemed awfully smug. It was time to drop the gloves. "Judge, all this talk about breach of attorney–client privilege is nonsense. I wrote a work of fiction about a married woman who is the managing partner of a major Boston law firm. She also happens to be sleeping with one of her associates. Her secret lover is kidnapped, which leaves her three alternatives. She can go public with her infidelity and call the police, which would ruin her marriage and probably get her fired. She can pay the ransom and hope the press and her husband never find out about it. Or she can simply deny the guy was ever her lover, tell the kidnapper to pound sand, and let him fend for himself."

"Intriguing," said the judge. "Can't wait for the movie."

"Your Honor," said Beckle, groaning.

"Sorry. Continue, Mr. Stokes."

"Let's face it. What Mr. Beckle—Check that, what Mr. Kaufman doesn't like is the fact that the head of the law firm in my novel is married and slept with a young lawyer who was hoping to make partner. That is what's driving this motion."

"What is that supposed to mean?" barked Kaufman.

"Judge, let the book go to print. If Mr. Kaufman really thinks that certain plot points running through my novel are not fiction and all I did was change the sex of the managing partner, he has a remedy. He can sue me for portraying him as the kind of lawyer who would sleep with ambitious young associates. And then I'll assert the best defense available in any defamation lawsuit. Truth."

"Oh, that's outrageous!" Beckle shouted, rising.

"Mr. Stokes, please," said the judge. "I realize that this hearing is being held in private and that lawyers enjoy immunity for things they say in a judicial proceeding, but let's be discreet about levying accusations like these."

"I stand by everything I just said," said Kevin.

Beckle said, "And that's exactly why we need this court's assistance. This young man has no self-restraint."

Kevin locked eyes with the judge, speaking without words.

Beckle slipped a sheet of paper before the judge. "For the

court's convenience, I've taken the liberty of preparing an order to reflect Your Honor's ruling. If you would sign right here."

"I haven't ruled." She was still looking at Kevin as she spoke. He sensed a breakthrough.

Beckle said, "Of course you haven't. Please take a minute to read it over."

"I'll be honest, Mr. Beckle. I read a good chunk of Mr. Stokes's book over the lunch break. I also read your motion and affidavit setting forth all of the alleged breaches of the attorney-client privilege, which frankly proved to be a lot less engrossing than Mr. Stokes's writing. You may say and even believe that his novel is about your law firm, its clients, and its lawyers, but I just don't see it. He set the story in a law firm because he's a lawyer and he's following the old adage of 'write what you know.' But he could have put it in a bank, a university, or even a hospital. This novel is about a beautiful, successful woman who cheats on her husband and then ends up having to deal with her lover's kidnapper. Period."

"Judge, if you'd like us to brief these issues further, we're more than happy to do so."

"I don't need more to read. I'll think more about this over the weekend, but that's my leaning at this point."

Ira spoke up. "Your Honor, we were hoping to have your ruling in hand when we went into court against the publisher in New York on Monday morning."

"Really? Well, you just might be glad you *don't* have my ruling by Monday morning." She flashed a foreboding look, then rose and shook Mr. Beckle's hand. "Sir, as always, a pleasure."

"Likewise," he said with a wan smile. He looked as if he'd bet the farm on the fallen Goliath—and lost.

"Now, if you will all excuse me, I have a pretrial conference in two minutes." She started toward the side door that led to her courtroom, then stopped and looked at Kevin. "Good luck with your writing career," she said in a pleasant tone, then left her chambers.

The lawyers stood mute on opposite sides of the table. Kevin leaned forward, palms flat on the table, and spoke in a tone suitable for a funeral. "I believe this is traditionally the moment when the plaintiff wants to talk settlement. Unfortunately for you, this defendant's not listening."

He restrained himself on the way out of the judge's chambers, but the instant he reached the hallway he let out a hoot that echoed all the way to the lobby. He hoped with all his heart that Ira and old man Beckle had heard it.

36

IT WAS HALF–PAST MIDNIGHT, AND THE PHONE WAS STILL SILENT. PEYTON was seated on the living room couch; Kevin, in the easy chair. The television screen was black. A brass lamp glowed on the end table. They hadn't moved, hadn't spoken since the clock on the mantel chimed a dozen times. All they could do was wait.

"I told you he wouldn't call back," said Kevin.

"He didn't say he would call at midnight. He just told me to have the money by then."

"He's a scumbag."

"You don't even know him."

"No, *you* don't."

"You're right. I really don't. Which is why I'm so scared."

Kevin gulped down some coffee, then winced at the bitterness. "You did the right thing by telling him you wouldn't pay. He won't be back."

"Or maybe he will be back, angrier than before. Maybe even violent. I know we agreed not to call the police if he didn't call back, but maybe we should anyway."

"That's exactly the wrong reaction."

"Why?"

"It's like the stories you see on the news, where the woman goes into court and gets a restraining order against her ex-lover. Two hours later, the guy shows up at her house, kills her, and kills himself."

"Why are you so sure that ignoring this is the right thing to do?"

"I just don't believe the police are very good at handling love-sick puppies like Gary Varne. We're handling it fine on our own."

She glanced out the window, then back at Kevin. "Do you think he read your manuscript?"

"I don't see how."

"You left free copies at Booklovers'. Who knows who walked out with them?"

"I suppose it's possible," he said with a shrug.

"Do you think that's where he got the idea for the kidnapping?"

"I don't know. Maybe."

"You wrote a book about a married woman whose lover was kidnapped. Two weeks after you gave away copies, Gary Varne was kidnapped. All you can say is *maybe*?"

Kevin gave her a chilling look. "Are you admitting that you slept with Gary?"

"No. He wants you to think I did, so he's playing out his own kidnapping the way it played out in your book."

"What difference does it make where he got the idea?"

"None, I suppose."

"Then why dwell on it?"

"Because the whole thing is creepy," she said. "Especially the way the husband in your book reacted when he found out his wife had cheated."

"You know, I have to say that I'm getting sick and tired of having to explain to people that these characters and their stupid problems are all made up."

"Are they really?"

"Yes, damn it."

"So not one ounce of your wife is in the character you created?"

"No."

"That can't be."

"Fine, Dr. Freud. You're in it. Every woman I've ever known is in it."

"Every woman's an adulteress and needs to be punished? Is that the way you see it?"

"I didn't say that."

"It's what you think, isn't it?"

"No, you're twisting my words."

"Then stop treating me like the worst adulteress who ever lived. I don't deserve it. I didn't even cheat on you."

"It doesn't matter. Whether you did or didn't, I said I've forgiven you."

"I don't need forgiveness. I didn't *do* anything."

"Then what do you want from me?"

"Stop testing me," she said, her voice rising. "Stop forcing me to prove my love for you by doing everything you say, by letting you handle every joint decision exactly the way you think we should handle it."

"I can do that. Just tell me the truth and stop trying to make me believe that you got drunk and woke up half-naked in your old boyfriend's apartment and that absolutely nothing happened."

"That is the truth."

"I'm sorry, Peyton. I don't believe it."

"I'm *not* an adulterer."

"As my friend Bill Shakespeare might say, methinks the lady doth protest too much."

"Damn it, I am not a bad wife! I'm not like your mother!"

She couldn't believe her own ears. It was the taboo subject in their marriage, his runaway mother, the cocktail waitress.

"Go to hell," he said in a voice that chilled her.

"I'm sorry. I didn't mean that."

"Then you shouldn't have said it." He grabbed his jacket from the closet, then headed for the door.

"Where are you going?"

"Out."

"Don't leave me here by myself."

"You'll be fine. Call the police, if you want. Call the FBI. The National Guard. Alert the media while you're at it. Pay Gary Varne his money. Pay him twice his money plus interest. Do whatever you want. I don't care anymore."

The door opened. She hurried after him. "Where do you think you're going?"

"Hell if I know. I don't even have an office to go to anymore."

She stood in silence as he slammed the door.

37

KEVIN FOUND AN OPEN BAR ON NEWBURY STREET. IT WAS MORE tony than he'd wanted, offering expensive French wines by the glass and burgers without meat, just a big ol' portobello mushroom on a rosemary-bread bun. He sat at the end of the bar, ordered a draft, and ate peanuts from the shell to create that hole-in-the-wall feeling he desired. Halfway through his Budweiser, his cell phone rang. The illusion faded. Back to reality.

"Weaver here," said the caller.

It had been ten years since Walter Weaver had retired from the FBI to form his own private detective agency, but he still had the bureau habit of using last names only. Over the years Kevin had used him countless times for investigative work on behalf of clients. This time, he'd only said it was for "a client." It was a background check on Gary Varne.

"Do you know it's after midnight?"

"Did I wake you, Stokes?"

"No."

"Then don't bitch. You told me to call as soon as I got anything, and boy did I get it. I want you to know in advance that this is going to be double my normal charge."

"What do you have?"

"No criminal convictions. Of course, your normal background

search would have stopped right there. But I went the extra mile and found the real goods."

"I'm listening."

"Stokes, my old friend. I think you've hit the jackpot."

The alarm woke her at 5:00 A.M.

Peyton rolled over and killed the buzzer, nearly knocking the clock off the nightstand in the darkness. She hadn't fallen asleep until sometime after 4:18 A.M., the last time she'd checked the glowing numbers. She'd lain awake thinking, reacting to every sound in the night. The hum of the refrigerator. The air conditioner clicking on and off. In the stillest moments, her mind had even taken her outside the apartment to investigate curious little noises. Magnolia Street was generally quiet, especially on weeknights after bedtime. Cars would usually pass by unnoticed. Last night, however, Peyton had heard every one of them. She'd probably even imagined a few.

She stayed in bed longer than she should have. She barely had time to shower and get dressed. There was definitely no time to eat. She had to be at the hospital by six o'clock. She grabbed her purse and car keys and headed out the door.

Outside it was still dark but showing signs of brightening. The faint glow from the street lamps waned in anticipation of dawn. The car was still parked across the street, where she'd left it last night. Kevin had obviously walked or taken a cab to wherever he'd gone. This was getting to be a habit, his not coming home at night.

She crossed the street with only a casual check for traffic, no cars in sight. She unlocked the door, opened it, and slid into the driver's seat. She pitched her purse onto the passenger seat and turned the ignition. She put the car in reverse and checked in the rearview mirror.

Her eyes met a stranger's. A man in a black ski mask.

She was about to scream, but his hand covered her mouth, and a knife was at her throat.

"Don't move," he said.

She froze on command, her eyes wide with fear, her heart racing.

"Listen carefully. I have some questions for you. I'm going to take my hand off your mouth so you can answer. If you scream, I'll slit your throat. Nod if you understand."

She nodded once, feeling the blade against her jugular as she did. Slowly his hand slid away from her mouth. The knife remained.

"Do you have the money?" he asked.

"I can get it. Don't hurt me. Whatever you want."

"I don't want you to get it. I asked if you got it."

"No. But, please, I can get it."

"Just calm down and answer my question. Did you get my money by midnight?"

"I can get—"

"Hush!" he said, pressing the knife more firmly against her neck. Peyton went rigid.

His voice developed an edge, a sign of agitation. "Keep this very simple. Just answer my questions. No pleading, no explanations. Do you understand?"

She nodded.

"You remember our phone call, right?"

"Yes."

"You heard me say your deadline was midnight, didn't you?"

"Yes."

"You heard me say that I'd kill Gary Varne if you didn't get the money. Yes or no."

"Yes."

"Did you get the money?"

Her lips quivered. He grabbed her by the chin, as if to force a response. "Yes or no," he said firmly. "Did you get the money?"

"No."

She could hear her own erratic breathing, short panicky breaths. Slowly the tight grasp on her chin released as he said, "Good for you, Peyton. You made the right call."

Suddenly a rag was over her mouth, a pungent smell. She couldn't breathe. She struggled to get free and even pounded her fists on the horn, which didn't blast and had obviously been disconnected—her last coherent thought. She met his eyes once more in the rearview mirror, but her resistance was at an end.

Then something clicked in her brain, a memory—a recognition. The sound of his voice, the look in his eyes. On some level of semiconsciousness, it seemed to register that she'd seen this man before.

With one last whiff from the rag over her mouth, she felt a rush through her body and dizziness in her head. Then everything turned black.

38

FOR KEVIN IT WAS DÉJÀ VU, RUSHING TO THE HOSPITAL AT SUNRISE, his wife's fate in the hands of modern medicine. This time it was Massachusetts General Hospital, thankfully not the intensive care unit. She was in one of the ER's small, curtained-off recovery areas when Kevin arrived. The slow drip of IV fluids fed into her veins. A nurse was helping her sit up in the bed as a young ER physician checked her heart and breathing with a stethoscope. To Kevin, she looked barely conscious.

He stood frozen for a moment, overcome with concern. He'd never told her that he was checking into Gary's past, and he hadn't had the chance to tell her what his investigator had uncovered. It hardly seemed to matter at this point. "I'm so sorry," he said, as he went to her side.

Peyton almost seemed to recognize him but didn't really respond. The doctor said, "She's still pretty out of it."

"I'm her husband. Is she okay?"

She plucked the stethoscope from her ears and let it hang around her neck. "Your wife was unconscious but breathing when she was presented to the ER. She lost a lot of fluids from the vomiting. Her stomach's been pumped. She had—"

"I know. I talked to the police outside."

"Okay, then you know. We'll keep her here for observation for a little while. Once she's lucid, a psych counselor will pay her a visit. Then if everything remains stabilized, she can go home."

"Are you doing anything to treat her?"

"Right now, just the IV to replace fluids. The nurses have been walking her for the past twenty minutes. They'll continue to do that every five minutes or so, till she fully regains consciousness."

"I can do that."

"Great. Ring the nurse if you need anything."

The doctor was gone before Kevin could even thank her. The nurse was holding Peyton up in a seated position on the edge of the bed. Kevin took her place, then pulled Peyton close to his side as the nurse disappeared on the other side of the curtain. Peyton buried her head into his shoulder languidly, as if she were drunk. After a minute or so, her body jerked several times in his arms. She was sobbing.

"Peyton. Are you okay?"

"I'm so glad you're here." Her voice was weak, her eyes mere slits.

"Me too. I called your folks. They're cutting their vacation short and will be here just as soon as they can catch a flight."

"This is awful. The whole thing."

"I know." He stroked her head, trying to console. "Why would you do such a thing?"

"Do what?"

"You don't have to be ashamed. This is my fault more than yours. I'm sorry for the way I treated you last night. I should have realized how much stress you've been under, how close you were to the edge."

Slowly, she became more coherent, as if forcing herself to regain control. "What in the world are you talking about?"

"We all know. The police found the pills."

"What pills?"

"They found your car parked down by the wharf. You were slumped over the wheel with half a bottle of sleeping pills spilled onto the floor. They assumed you'd taken the rest of them. That's why they brought you here and pumped your stomach."

"They think I tried to kill myself?"

"Don't worry, we're going to get you help."

"I don't need help," she said, frustrated. "I was abducted. A guy in a ski mask was hiding in the backseat of my car. He put a knife to my throat."

He tried not to look skeptical. "A ski mask?"

"*Yes.* Yes!"

The curtain was suddenly pulled back. Kevin looked up and saw a police officer standing before them. It was the same tall, African-American guy he'd talked to in the lobby. Another officer was behind him, one he didn't recognize.

"Sorry to bother you, Mr. Stokes."

"What is it?"

"I was wondering if you or your wife knows a man named Gary Varne."

Kevin went cold. "Yes. My wife knows him."

The officer nodded slowly, exceedingly polite. "I hate to have to ask you this under these circumstances and all. But do you think you and your wife might be up to answering a few questions for me?"

"What kind of questions?"

"Actually, it's more like one question."

"Sure."

His eyes narrowed. "Do you mind telling me what Mr. Varne's dead body was doing in the trunk of your wife's vehicle?"

Kevin nearly fell over. His instincts as a lawyer told him not to say a word, but that didn't matter.

At that moment, he simply couldn't speak.

39

PEYTON WAS RELEASED FROM THE MASS GENERAL EMERGENCY ROOM after the lunch hour. It was standard procedure in any case of attempted suicide for the patient to be referred to counseling, so it took some string-pulling to be discharged without it.

With their car impounded indefinitely by the police, she and Kevin took a cab home. It was a comfortable summer afternoon, shorts and shirtsleeves weather. As the cab headed up Magnolia Street, Peyton noticed several of her neighbors out enjoying the sunshine. Strangely, they were all headed in the same direction—toward Peyton's apartment.

Then she noticed the squad cars. Two from the Boston Police Department and a third unmarked vehicle were parked in front of her apartment. Their front door was wide open and two uniformed officers were posted on the front porch. A handful of rubbernecking neighbors had wandered by to see what was going on.

The cab stopped directly across the street. "Have we been robbed?" asked Peyton.

"I have no idea," said Kevin as he paid the fare. Together they slid out of the backseat, crossed the street, and climbed the front stairs. The two police officers didn't move from their post. Their landlord came out to meet them at the threshold.

"What's going on?" asked Peyton.

The landlord didn't have a chance to answer. A large man

dressed in a short-sleeved white dress shirt and a loosely knot-ted necktie emerged from the foyer and said, "We're executing a search warrant."

Peyton did a double take. It was Detective Bolton, whom she hadn't seen since Andy Johnson's death last winter. A pair of thin latex gloves covered his pudgy hands, and he was holding a clear plastic bag that contained a gray metal strongbox that Peyton rec-ognized as hers.

"I'd like to see the warrant," said Kevin.

"Your landlord has your copy."

"It really wasn't necessary to make a neighborhood spectacle out of this. If you had just called, we would have let you in."

"Sure," said Bolton. "And we would have found what we were looking for in a Dumpster eight blocks from your apartment rather than your bedroom closet."

"Peyton and I have nothing to hide."

"No, not anymore you don't." With a thin smile he thanked the landlord and headed down the steps. As if on cue, the stoic officers in uniform followed him to the curb. Peyton watched as they got into their cars and pulled away.

The landlord handed Kevin a copy of the warrant. "This better not be about drugs or you'll be looking for a new apartment faster than you can say eviction." She glowered, then climbed down the stairs, leaving them alone in the foyer. Kevin closed the door and quickly read the warrant.

"That box he carried out is where I keep my gun," said Peyton. "Is that what they were searching for?"

"That's what the warrant says."

"So what happens now?"

"I presume they'll run ballistics tests to see if there's a match on the bullet that killed Gary Varne."

"That's good. Because it won't match."

"Let's hope not."

"What do you mean, hope? You don't think I shot him, do you?"

"This is just moving so fast. And it keeps getting weirder. Even this warrant is strange. Warrants are required by law to be specific, but this one seems to have been prepared by someone who's omniscient. Obviously the cops would know what kind of gun you own from registration records, but it's beyond me how they were able to identify the metal box you kept it in."

She thought for a moment, then it clicked. "My civil deposition. The lawyer for that jerk who sued me over that disaster at the Haverhill clinic questioned me about my gun. I said I kept it locked in a strongbox on the top shelf of my bedroom closet. The whole deposition turned out to be four transcribed pages. It would have taken the police about thirty seconds to read it."

"It's still weird that they would even have known about your deposition, let alone have a copy of it. Unless someone's feeding them information."

"You mean an informant?"

"That's a very neutral term. I was thinking more along the lines of whoever the son of bitch is who killed Gary Varne and is trying to make it look like you did it."

They exchanged anxious glances, then Peyton asked, "What do you think we should we do now?"

"You want my advice as a husband or a lawyer?"

"Both."

"Hire a lawyer. A good one."

"Got any suggestions?"

"Just one," he said in a serious tone, then walked to the kitchen and picked up the telephone.

Thirty minutes later they were downtown in the law offices of Falcone & Associates. Tony Falcone was a savvy trial lawyer who'd done only criminal defense his entire twenty-year career, the first five years at the public defender's office in Boston and the balance in private practice. Peyton had seen his name in the newspaper a

few times on some high-profile cases but had never met him. It
had been Kevin's idea to call him, though the recommendation
came with a small caveat: Tony was immensely talented but full of
surprises.

His secretary brought them coffee and told them that Tony
would be with them just as soon as he got off the phone. They
waited in silence in the reception area outside his personal office,
seated side by side on the silk-covered couch. Kevin kept glancing
sideways every few seconds, as if checking to see if Peyton had any
questions. She didn't feel like talking.

The waiting area was decorated tastefully, an eclectic mix of
modern furniture with some antiques for accent. The oil paintings
and watercolors were all originals and lit perfectly, which suggested they were admired by their owner and probably of some
value. It felt more like a cozy gallery than a law office. No plaques,
diplomas, or other badges of honor cluttered the cherry-paneled
walls. Peyton took that as a good sign. In her experience, the true
leaders in any profession didn't substitute résumés for wallpaper.

"Sorry to keep you waiting," said Tony, emerging from his
office.

The introductions were quick. As Peyton rose to shake his
hand, she realized that she had seen him interviewed a few
months ago on the evening news, where he'd come across as hard
and serious. In person he exuded more of a relaxed confidence,
casual but stylish, dressed in an Armani jacket, dark blue shirt, and
slightly darker blue tie, very unlike the pinstripes, white shirts,
and berry ties that seemed to be the required uniform at Kevin's
firm. He was taller than expected and more handsome than she
remembered from television. Peyton would have guessed he'd just
returned from vacation, the way his perfect white teeth played
off the suntan. She returned his smile, though under the circumstances hers was forced.

"How's the novel coming?" asked Tony.

"That's a whole 'nother story," said Kevin.

He glanced at Peyton and said, "Kevin was good enough to

buy me a few lunches in exchange for some insights into criminal lawyering while he was writing his book."

"I know. He told me what a great help you were."

"All I did was tell war stories."

"So I guess that means Kevin knows all your tricks."

Tony was still smiling, but the ego was showing. "Not by a long shot."

He stepped aside to let them enter first. Peyton noticed an old brass plaque posted on the office door that read CONFESSIONS DAILY 7–9.

"Cute," said Peyton.

"Oh, that. I took my little niece down to St. Anthony's for confession a few months ago and saw it in the vestibule. I had to have it."

"You stole from a church?"

He shrugged impishly, as if that were a gray area. "I said two Hail Marys and dropped a hundred bucks in the poor box. It all comes out in the wash."

"Not where I do my laundry," she said, only half kidding.

"Peyton," said Kevin, groaning.

"It's okay. Your wife's not a wallflower. I like that. Especially in such an attractive woman."

The remark seemed innocent but still was out of place. She and Kevin seated themselves in two chrome and leather director's chairs that faced the lawyer's desk with an impressive view of Boston harbor in the distance. The desk was an unusual piece, an ultramodern design that consisted only of a kidney-shaped sheet of beveled glass resting on three narrow columns of polished granite. It looked as though it might fall over at the slightest touch, so Peyton didn't dare get too close or even breathe too heavily.

His secretary appeared in the open doorway. "Excuse me, Mr. Falcone. There's a reporter on line two."

All three of them shot a look, as if to ask, *Already?*

"It's about the police kickback case," she clarified.

Tony reached for the phone on his desk, then apparently

thought better of talking to the press about a client in front of new ones. "I'll just be a minute," he said, then stepped out.

As they waited, Peyton watched a ship pass in the harbor, a tiny toy boat from this high up. Kevin was fiddling with a creepy little thing he'd found on Tony's desk. It looked like a dried apple with a long wisp of hair, then Peyton realized it was a shrunken head—phony, she hoped. Probably a memento from some exotic vacation. Or his last jury trial.

"Do you really think this guy's the best?" she asked quietly.

"No."

"Then why are we here?"

"Because he's the best we can afford."

"What are you saying, he's the trial lawyer equivalent of an HMO?"

"Only if your HMO charges a hundred grand up front, satisfaction not guaranteed."

"You're kidding."

"Welcome to the real world, Doctor. Criminal law is as real as it gets."

Tony returned and closed the door. "Okay, let's get started," he said as he took his place behind the desk. "I want you two to tell me everything. Start at the beginning of the world if you have to."

"It's interesting you say that," said Peyton. "After watching all those courtroom dramas on television, I was under the impression that criminal defense lawyers didn't want to know everything."

"Depends on the lawyer. Some do, some don't."

Kevin said, "I think there's a larger, legitimate concern that Peyton is trying to articulate."

"I understand," said Tony, speaking more to Peyton now. "Too much knowledge about the facts might make some lawyers feel constrained as to the type of defense they can present at trial. For example, if the client says she was home alone sleeping in her own bed the night of the crime, the lawyer might be nervous about calling an alibi witness to the stand who wants to testify that the defendant was out all night dancing with her at the clubs."

"Exactly," said Kevin. "It creates an ethical dilemma."

"Yes, but only for the lawyer who actually remembers everything his client tells him."

There was silence, then Tony cracked a smile. "I'm kidding. Lighten up, you two."

Peyton forced a nervous smile.

"Look," said Tony. "I'm a straight shooter, totally. It's my job to put the best spin on the facts if and when we present them to a jury. It's not your job to filter the information that flows between us in the privacy of my office. So tell me exactly what happened. Whatever it is, we'll deal with it. Peyton, why don't you start?"

"I think I'll let Kevin tell it. I'll fill in what he leaves out."

"Fine with me," said Tony.

"It really all began last winter," she heard Kevin say, though she wasn't fully listening. Tony was taking notes on his legal pad, seeming to get every word. She hoped he had spoken the truth about being a straight shooter, but that earlier crack about his convenient memory was gnawing at her. Maybe it was humorous between lawyers, but for her it was less than reassuring. And what kind of guy steals from a church?

She forced herself to stay focused on Kevin's narrative, not quite sure what to make of the esteemed Tony Falcone.

40

KEVIN WAS JUST MINUTES INTO THE STORY, AND ALREADY PEYTON had filled more holes than a road-repair crew. Her first thought was that he was awfully forgetful of the important details, followed by her rising suspicions that he was intentionally holding things back from their lawyer, culminating in her unsettling realization that there were plenty of things that for one reason or another she simply hadn't told her husband. Likewise, there were things he had never told her, including the single red rose he'd found outside their doorstep after her car accident, the heckler at the bookstore, and the dedication page in his manuscript on which someone had scrawled the threatening message, She's spoken for, asshole.

After about the tenth time one of them looked at the other and said, "You never told me that," Tony laid his notepad on the desktop and offered an assessing look.

"Do you two know each other?" he asked facetiously. "Kevin, meet Peyton Shields. Peyton, Kevin Stokes."

It took a solid hour to get through the entire history, followed by another fifteen minutes of follow-up questions by their lawyer. At the end of it all, Tony leaned back in his chair, thinking for a solid minute in silence. Finally, he said, "You know what I think?"

"We're crazy?" said Peyton.

He shrugged, as if that went without saying. "Let's cogitate like the district attorney for a minute. Let's assume he has both of you in his crosshairs. A pretty safe assumption, given the fact that the body was found in the trunk of your car and the police showed up today at your apartment with a warrant for your gun. Here's one possible theory. First, Peyton cheated on Kevin and slept with Gary Varne. Agreed?"

"Not agreed," said Peyton. "I didn't sleep with the guy."

"I'm not talking about reality," said Tony. "I'm trying to figure out how the prosecutor will shape the facts at hand into a story with real jury appeal."

"Maybe he won't be quite as focused on adultery as you think," said Kevin.

"Are you kidding me? I'm being gentle here, using all the nice euphemisms like affair and cheating. Wait till the prosecutor gets into the act and, even worse, the press. It'll be reduced to its basest element. A hot, young stud thrusting himself into the loins of another man's wife, a stranger ejaculating into the very canal through which the children of this once happy union should have entered the world. I'm not trying to be crude, I just want you to be ready."

"We'll be ready," said Peyton. "So long as our own lawyer is careful to distinguish between perception and reality."

"For some prosecutors perception is reality. So point one of the government's case is this: Peyton and Gary do the deed. After that, pretty much everything is a matter of conjecture, but if I'm a prosecutor I see it this way. Peyton tries to break off the relationship. Varne starts harassing her. He pesters her at work, steals her computer from the library. When it's finally clear that Peyton is done with him, he threatens to tell Kevin about the affair and blackmails her. Faced with the blackmail, Peyton confesses all to her husband. Are you with me so far?"

They nodded. Tony continued, "The blackmail backfires on Varne. After the confession, Kevin wants him dead. Peyton wants her husband back, so she goes along with the plan. The end result is that either Peyton or Kevin shoots Varne with Peyton's gun. One or both of you put the body in the trunk for disposal. Peyton is driving to the wharf to dump it when she's finally overcome with guilt over what she's done. She parks the car and swallows sleeping pills to kill herself. Fortunately for her, the police find her in time and take her to the hospital."

"What about the kidnapping?" asked Peyton.

"Never happened," said Tony. "Later, with the help of their attorney, the defendants concoct a sensational story that Gary Varne was kidnapped and that some mysterious man in a ski mask abducted Peyton and framed her for Gary's murder."

"He'll say we just made it up?" asked Peyton.

"Plagiarized yourselves is an even better way to put it. The blackmail, the kidnapping, the whole implausible defense mirrors the plot in Kevin's novel, a work of fiction. It is a curious coincidence, don't you think?"

Kevin asked, "Are you playing devil's advocate, or does Tony Falcone think it's a curious coincidence too?"

"Too early to pass judgment."

"What about the guy in the ski mask who was hiding in Peyton's car? That's not in my novel. Doesn't that sway you?"

"Did you tell the police about that?"

"No. Peyton told me about it when she regained consciousness in the emergency room. Two seconds later the cops were telling us about a body in the trunk of her car. My instincts told me we should see a lawyer before we start talking."

"Good instincts."

"Shouldn't we tell them now?" asked Peyton.

"I'll help you with that. You shouldn't be talking directly to the police at this point. They'll eat you for lunch."

"Are you going to tell them about the kidnapping—Gary Varne's kidnapping, I mean."

"Problem is, if we tell them about that kidnapping, we also have to tell them you were being blackmailed. That's dicey."

"It's a frame-up. Why not scream it at the top of our lungs?"

"Because in my opinion the prosecutor will believe only half of what you say. He won't accept that Gary Varne was kidnapped. It's too much like Kevin's book. But he will believe that you were being blackmailed, and then he'll twist your words into a theory that Gary Varne was the blackmailer. Once Varne is cast as a blackmailer, that gives you a serious motive to kill him in a planned and deliberate fashion. Without that element, the case has more of an aura of jealous rage than premeditation, more suitable for the lesser charge of manslaughter than first-degree murder."

"So you want us to keep our defense to ourselves?"

"For now. Let's wait and see if the prosecutor knows anything about blackmail before we tell him."

Kevin shook his head, grimacing. "I respect your judgment, but I don't see how putting the prosecutor to the test benefits us."

"It doesn't," said Peyton, her eyes narrowing. "I think the test is for our lawyer's benefit. He wants to know if we're lying to him."

"That's an interesting theory," said Tony.

"I'm not sure I follow it," said Kevin.

"If I was being blackmailed by an old boyfriend, only three people on the planet knew anything about it. Two of them are in this room. The other one is now dead."

"That's a certainty."

"But if Gary Varne really was kidnapped, there was obviously a fourth person involved—the kidnapper. So if Kevin and I keep our mouths shut and still the prosecutor starts talking about blackmail, we know he must have a source. It's probably anonymous, and by process of elimination it has to be the kidnapper. That would satisfy our lawyer that there was a kidnapping and that we're being framed."

Tony was silent, then smiled thinly. "You're a very suspicious person, Doctor."

"And you're more transparent than you think," she replied.

Her tone wasn't hostile, but Kevin was visibly uncomfortable with the way she was challenging Tony. "I don't know if Peyton is right or not," he said. "But how soon till we find out if the prosecutor has any information about blackmail?"

"If he isn't explicit about it from the get-go, he'll tip his hand soon enough. For example, he could subpoena your bank records to check for large cash withdrawals in the few days before the murder. I assume that would turn up nothing, since you two agreed not to pay the ransom."

"That's right," said Peyton.

Kevin coughed. "Well, uh, that's not exactly right."

"What do you mean?"

"I—" he paused, struggling. "I withdrew money from our brokerage account."

"What?"

He was speaking to Peyton but looking at the floor. "I refused to pay because I thought Varne was blackmailing us. By the second day, part of me started to worry that maybe he really was kidnapped and maybe the kidnapper would turn violent against us if we stonewalled him. So just in case, I withdrew the money."

Peyton glared. "For two days you let me agonize over the possible consequences of refusing to pay the ransom. And now you're telling me that you had the money in hand and were ready to pay it."

"Only if I thought you were in danger."

"Damn it, why didn't you tell me?"

"I couldn't. Not until I knew . . ."

He stopped, but she finished it for him. "Knew that I was willing to let Gary die?"

He didn't answer.

Peyton said, "Is that how you intended to satisfy yourself that I didn't sleep with Gary Varne, that I didn't have feelings for him?"

He lowered his head and said, "I don't know what I was thinking."

Peyton looked away, not quite believing him. It was suddenly quiet enough to hear the breeze from the air-conditioning vents.

Tony broke the silence. "Well, that was enlightening. Why don't we all take a break. Get some coffee, get some air, maybe one of us get a new lawyer."

"What?" the clients said in unison.

"I've seen enough to know I can't represent you both, not even at this preliminary stage. Eventually you would need separate counsel, so you might as well do it now. Kevin, you've seen it enough in civil practice. We'll mount a joint defense, cooperate at every stage of the case. But each of you needs your own lawyer looking out for your own interest. Before you kill each other."

She glanced at Kevin, then at Tony. "Who do you recommend I retain?"

"Me," said Tony.

"What?" said Kevin.

"You're a perfect match for my wife. She's a tough former prosecutor who can handle a lawyer as a client. You'll love her."

Kevin seemed deflated, like the kid not picked in a round of playground basketball. "Well, if that's your recommendation."

"It is."

"When can I meet her?"

"Her office is across the hall. I'll walk you over."

"You want to me go right now?"

"No time like the present."

"Okay, I guess. There were just some things I was planning to talk out with Peyton and you at this meeting. Things I learned through this investigator I hired, and some other things."

Said Tony, "My advice is that from here on out you consult your own lawyer before you talk to me or my client about anything that relates to the case."

His client, thought Peyton. *Client first, wife second.* Their world was surely turning upside down.

Kevin glanced at Peyton, as if to ask if the new arrangement was okay with her. She didn't respond. He rose slowly and said, "I'm not sure how long this will take. I guess I'll meet you back at home."

Peyton didn't answer. Tony said, "That's best. Peyton and I have a lot of work to do."

Kevin waited for her to look up at him, but she didn't. "Well, good luck," he said with a shrug.

"You too," she said, and finally she did look at him. "I think I'm going to have dinner with my parents tonight. They're concerned about me, and I haven't had much of a chance to talk to them since they rushed back from their vacation. You're welcome to join us, but . . ."

"No, that's all right. You be the good daughter. I'm fine on my own."

She nodded. Tony directed him out the door, then stopped in the doorway for some parting advice to his remaining client. "Don't look at this as divisive, Peyton. Think of it as the only sane way to protect your common interest."

"Sure," she said, watching him lead her husband away. "I'm all for the common interest."

Whatever's left of it.

41

PEYTON'S PICTURE WAS IN THE NEWSPAPER. NOT A VERY GOOD LIKE-ness. Rudy had much prettier ones. Dozens of them, all taken from a distance with a telephoto lens, all without her even knowing it.

He was lying on the bed, the newspaper spread across his pillow. He'd read the story at least a dozen times, but he kept going back to the printed photograph of her walking into her apartment, a profile shot with Kevin in the background. Rudy stared at her face so hard that he could actually count the grainy dots in the ink. If only the picture had been taken head-on with her staring directly into the lens. He needed to see right into her eyes to get inside her head. One good look into those eyes and he could always tell what was on her mind.

He tossed the newspaper on the floor and rolled onto his back, thinking. He knew Peyton had to be suffering. Things weren't looking good. The body in the trunk. The sleeping pills in the car. The salacious hints of some kind of "relationship" between her and Gary Varne. Anyone who read today's paper would have pegged her for an emotional wreck. But not Rudy. Even in that cloudy photograph, he didn't see a murderer and adulteress, and certainly not a woman on the brink of suicide. He saw a woman in need. Just like that woman in her car after the accident, the woman he'd pulled from the icy waters of Jamaica Pond.

I've always helped you, Peyton. I can help you again.

All she had to do was send him a sign. He'd be there in a minute.

He sat up in bed, suddenly inspired. It was five minutes past eleven. He thought it worth a try. Maybe tonight was the night. She had to be feeling lower than ever before. Maybe she'd reach out to him, her friend from the past.

He slipped out of bed and walked over to his computer workstation. The screen saver was glowing. He went online, straight to where they'd met, that chat room on old Hollywood movies.

Eleven people were in the room. On the screen, right before his eyes, meaningless conversations were unfolding in various colors and fonts. He jumped right in and typed his own message in chat room-ese.

"r u there?"

He'd used his familiar old screen name, "RG." If she was in the chat room, the initials before the message would tell her that it was him. He waited, then typed another message.

"please b there."

A few moments passed, then he couldn't believe his eyes. One joyous letter at a time, the response emerged on screen.

"i'm back."

The screen name before the response nearly stopped his heart: "Ladydoc." His hands shook as he typed the follow-up.

"is it really u?"

"yes."

"prove it."

He held his breath and waited. Finally, Ladydoc typed, "Rodolfo Guglielmi."

Rudy smiled. She remembered. He'd told her months ago in a private chat room, just the two of them. She was the only person on the planet who knew what the "RG" in his screen name stood for. "Rodolfo Guglielmi." Rudolph Valentino's real name.

"i'm so happy it's u."

"private chat?"

His skin actually tingled. He'd been waiting months for that invitation. He used to love it when they'd break away from the group, the things she'd say in the privacy of their own chat room. He couldn't believe they were going back.

"can't wait," he wrote.

Together they exited the crowded public chat, just the two of them.

42

IT WAS THE LONGEST WALK OF HER LIFE. PEYTON HAD BEEN DETER-
mined to go back to work at the hospital and restore some sense
of normalcy to her life. Her plan didn't work. She was almost
immediately summoned to administration.

The director of the residency program was housed in the old
wing of Children's Hospital. Getting there was a hike through a
twisted path of hallways that connected the old wing to the newer
buildings, and then a lonely climb up three flights of a grand
nineteenth-century stairwell. It was a cavernous atrium-style
building, suitable for administrative offices. Peyton could hear her
own footsteps reverberating off the walls as she climbed one
step at a time. On the third tier, lining the hallway that led
to the director's office, were portraits of some of the people
who had made Children's Hospital the best in the world. The
first surgeon to perform a pediatric heart transplant. The first
woman chief of staff. Not likely that Peyton's mug would be there
anytime soon: First pediatric resident to be plucked from Jamaica
Pond, stalked by a clown, blackmailed by a lovesick old boyfriend,
and—her most recent achievement—targeted as a murder suspect.
Too many firsts for her blood, though she was well aware that this
wasn't the first time she'd been called on the carpet. It was almost
déjà vu, eerily reminiscent of the fallout from the Andy Johnson
stalking incident.

There were two people in line to see the director, but the secretary didn't make Peyton wait. Paradoxically, that wasn't a good sign.

Miles Landau rose as she entered, though it was hardly a greeting. Craig Sheffield, the chief resident, was the only other person in the room. He didn't make eye contact with Peyton. Another bad sign.

"Please sit down, Peyton."

She took the chair facing Dr. Landau. He addressed her in his most serious voice, though his words seemed rehearsed. "As director of the residency program, I have a keen interest in the well-being of all our residents."

So far so good, she thought.

"But there comes a point at which the interest of the hospital is paramount."

Her heart sank. "I see."

Dr. Sheffield jumped in. "We're not prejudging your guilt or innocence."

"But you read the newspapers," said Peyton, "and you don't like the bad publicity."

"This is not about publicity," said Landau. "It's a patient care issue."

"Patient care?" she said.

"We've discussed your situation with our legal counsel. From the hospital's standpoint, there are basically two possible explanations for your predicament, neither of them good. One, you were somehow connected to the death of Gary Varne, you drove his body to the wharf, and you tried to kill yourself by eating a bottle of sleeping pills. If that's the case, you shouldn't be seeing patients."

"That's not the case," she said, nearly bursting. "My lawyer won't let me go into details, but I'm being framed."

"That's the second possible explanation," said Dr. Sheffield. "Believe me, we haven't ruled that out."

Dr. Landau said, "But the truth is, if you are being framed, you should be devoting your every waking hour toward figuring out who's behind it. You can't lead the life of a junior resident at this hospital."

The words cut to her very core. "Am I being kicked out of the program?"

Landau lowered his eyes. "We would prefer it if you would just defer a year. Come back next year, once this is all cleared up."

She sat for a moment, stunned. It wasn't that they'd surprised her. She was simply less prepared than she'd thought. Once upon a time, she'd dreamed of the day when she'd be sitting in this room with these two men, smiles all around, Dr. Landau congratulating her on being selected as chief resident at Children's Hospital, the best of the best. Today, there were no smiles.

"I'll do what I have to do," she said.

They seemed relieved to avoid a fight. They shook hands, and the men wished her well.

She left in silence, alone completely.

Her beeper rang as she was cleaning out her locker. She recognized the number as Tony Falcone's. She used the phone in the on-call suite for privacy.

"What's up?" she said.

"Got a little tip from one of my sources over at the police station."

"Good or bad?"

"A little of both. Detective Bolton's search warrant turned up an interesting twist."

"A twist? All he took was my metal box with the gun in it."

"Right. Except there was no gun in it."

She lowered herself into the chair. "That's not possible. I don't even use that gun. I bought it when I thought I was being stalked. It stays locked in the box on the top shelf of my bedroom closet."

"The box was there, but the gun wasn't."

"Then somebody stole it."

"I suppose that will be our story."

"It's not a story. It makes sense that it would be stolen. It proves I was framed. If they'd found my gun, they could have done a ballistics test, right?"

"Definitely."

"Well, a ballistics test would have proved that it wasn't my Smith and Wesson thirty-eight-caliber that killed Gary Varne."

"That's true. But how would this person who framed you know that you kept a gun in a metal box on the top shelf?"

"The same way the police knew. I testified about it in that lawsuit I was involved in from Haverhill clinic."

"I suppose that's possible. Or maybe you told someone about the gun."

"The only other person who knew about it was Kevin."

"That's kind of my point."

Peyton gripped the phone. "I think you're barking up the wrong tree."

"Really? I was reviewing my notes from our joint conversation. Let me double-check some facts with you. Where was Kevin on the night Varne was kidnapped?"

She thought for a minute. "We had a fight. He was out."

"How about the night Varne was killed?"

"Out again."

"You know where?"

"Honestly, I have no idea." There was silence, and she could easily imagine him making a little note on his pad.

"Let's go back in time," he said. "How about the night that guy Andy Johnson fell or jumped and somehow ended up on the tracks in front of the subway? Where was Kevin on that night?"

"He was in New York at a seminar."

"You sure?"

"Actually, no. Now that I think about it, he came home early from his seminar. I'm not exactly sure when he got back to Boston."

Silence again. She sensed he was making yet another note. "What are you thinking?" she asked.

"I'm thinking that it's a good thing you and Kevin retained separate counsel when you did. Your husband may have even bigger problems than I thought."

"Still not as big as mine."

"Why do you say that?"

"Just because I don't know where Kevin was on those nights doesn't mean there isn't someone out there who does."

"You think he has an alibi?"

"I don't know. What I'm really saying is that I don't."

She felt butterflies in her stomach. It wasn't the first time she'd thought that through, but it was the first time she'd said it out loud.

She didn't like the sound of it.

43

AT NINE O'CLOCK FRIDAY MORNING, TWENTY-THREE GRAND JURORS sat in a windowless room in the basement of the old state courthouse, waiting for the show to begin. Expectations were high. They'd seen the flock of reporters perched outside the grand jury room.

By law, grand jury proceedings were secret, with no one allowed in the room but the jurors and the prosecutor. The constitutional theory was that the grand jury would serve as a check on the prosecutor's power. In reality, the prosecutor almost always got the indictment he wanted. Today, Charles Ohn wanted Peyton Shields.

"Good morning," he said, greeting his captive audience.

Ohn was smiling this morning, and it was genuine. This case had stardom written all over it. A beautiful, smart doctor and her lawyer husband as suspects. A former boyfriend and possible lover as victim. This case could be his breakout, his ticket to the talk-show circuit, and he'd been waiting a long time. Ohn was a twenty-year veteran of major crimes who had plenty of ability, hundreds of victories, and not much publicity. He worked for a district attorney who was a veritable media hound. Ohn had brought the office some of its most impressive wins, but at the press conferences he somehow always found himself positioned just far enough away from the D.A. to be offscreen on the evening news. He did the work, the district attorney took the bows. This time, he vowed it would be different.

That wasn't to say that the D.A. had given him free rein. Ohn had his marching orders: full speed ahead. That was fine by him. At 9:05 he had his first witness on the stand, sworn and ready to testify.

"Your name, sir," said Ohn.

"Steven Beasley."

"Where do you work?"

"I'm an associate attorney at the law firm of Marston and Wheeler."

With just a few well-rehearsed questions he led Beasley toward pay dirt, establishing him as a friend of Kevin Stokes, someone the grand jurors could believe. He conveyed just the right amount of reluctance as he described the awkward phone call he received from Peyton Shields and the voice in the background.

"What did you hear?" asked Ohn.

"A man's voice."

"What did he say?"

"He said, 'Don't be shy, I've already seen you naked.'"

Ohn stopped him. That was the beauty of the grand jury. No restrictions on hearsay evidence, and he could stop and explain things at any moment. "At this time," said Ohn, "I bring to the grand jury's attention state's exhibit one. These are copies of long-distance bills from Gary Varne's apartment. I've highlighted the entry which shows that a phone call was made from Gary Varne's apartment to the Waldorf-Astoria in Manhattan, exactly as Mr. Beasley has just testified."

He gave the jurors a moment to review the records. An old woman in the front row raised her hand, and Ohn braced himself. It was legally permissible for grand jurors to ask questions, unlike in a trial, though the prosecutor never knew what was going to come out of their mouths.

"Excuse me," she said. "But is Mr. Beasley saying that Peyton Shields was cheating on her husband with Gary Varne?"

Ohn smiled. Nothing like a friendly question to move things along. "That's for you to decide."

"Well, you convinced me. What else you got?"

The prosecutor struggled to contain his excitement. Too bad there wasn't a way to put this woman on the real jury.

"Maybe we should move right to the photographs of Gary Varne's body stuffed into the trunk of Peyton Shields's car."

He dismissed the witness and moved to his box of exhibits.

Kevin spent most of the day trying to find a quiet place to think. Jennifer had given him the task of coming up with a list of possible witnesses who could build his anticipated defense. All morning, the phone in the apartment had not stopped ringing. Even a few newspapers outside Boston were beginning to take interest in the case. He ended up escaping to the park just to have time to himself.

His lawyer had told him that the case was moving fast. Secrecy was yet another myth about grand juries. Leaks were common. One day into the proceedings and newspapers were already reporting that the prosecutor had presented enough evidence to secure indictments. Kevin wondered what he was waiting for.

At six-thirty he went home. Peyton was out. It wasn't planned, but they seemed to be avoiding each other ever since their meeting with Tony Falcone. Kevin changed into his jogging shorts and headed out for a run. He got only as far as the bottom step of his front porch. A man was standing on the sidewalk, blocking his way.

"How are you, Kevin?"

He figured it was a reporter, then did a double take. He'd never met Charles Ohn, but his face was familiar from the newspapers. "Since when do prosecutors track down suspects at their home?"

"I hear you have your own lawyer," he said, not really responding.

"That's true. And you should be talking to her, not me."

"You're a lawyer. We can talk."

Kevin was tempted to keep right on going, but curiosity grabbed him. "What about?"

"Your future."

"That's pretty vague."

"Grim was what I was thinking," said Ohn. "Unless you do something to change it."

"Spare me the veiled threats. If you have something to say, tell it to my lawyer."

Just as Kevin started away, the prosecutor said, "I'm offering you a deal."

Kevin stopped in his tracks. "What kind of deal?"

"I want you to help me build a case against your wife."

"What makes you think I'd be willing to do that?"

"Because she cheated on you."

Kevin took a half-step back, as if punched in the chest. "Peyton denies that."

"Don't they all?" he scoffed.

His anger was rising, but he kept his cool. "I'm not interested in any deal."

"Just hear me out, pal. Your wife's a pretty easy target, what with the body found in the trunk of her car. We can probably tie you in with the jealous husband angle. It all hinges on my ability to prove that you knew that your wife was sleeping with Varne before he was killed."

Kevin didn't respond. He tried not even to react.

Ohn continued, "I concede that right now I don't have ironclad evidence of your prior knowledge. Your friend Beasley waffled on the witness stand this morning about what he remembers telling you about that phone call from your wife."

That lifted his spirits. Maybe Steve was a friend after all. Or maybe Ohn was bluffing. "If you don't have the goods, why should I deal?"

"Because I will have them by the time we get to trial. I prom-ise you that. By then, it will be way too late for you to cut a deal. So I'll give you a day to think about it. Give me something to cement the case against your wife, and you walk free. Complete immunity. Or you can stand by your woman. Your cheating wife. And go right down with her."

Kevin wanted to tell him to shove it, but the words didn't come. He stood mute as the prosecutor turned and walked away.

44

IT TOOK KEVIN ALL OF FIVE MINUTES TO GET OUT OF HIS JOGGING shorts and into street clothes. It took him only another twenty to be in the law office of Jennifer Dunwoody.

At first blush, Jennifer seemed like the last woman on earth to be married to Tony Falcone, and that wasn't just because she'd kept her maiden name. For all his talents and good taste, Tony still had an element of the slick, career criminal-defense lawyer. By comparison, Jennifer was a model of sophistication, an attractive and smartly dressed former prosecutor who seemed more likely to file a bar grievance against a guy like Tony than marry him.

Kevin was her last appointment of the day, an impromptu one at that. She listened with pen in hand but without taking notes as he recounted the entire meeting with Ohn.

"That is so slimy," she said with all the indignation of a former prosecutor. "I can't believe he approached you directly, knowing that I represent you."

"Let's get past that. What should we do?"

She laid down her pen, then folded her hands atop the desk. "What do you want to do?"

"Who are you, Socrates? What's with this answering a question with a question?"

"I simply want to know your thoughts."

"I have one reaction on an emotional level. But all feelings aside, I think it boils down to one question. Why would any putative defendant take a deal when he doesn't think the prosecutor would ever be able to build a case against him in the first place?"

"That's a powerful argument."

"Rational, right?"

"Absolutely."

"So you agree that I shouldn't try to cut a deal?"

"Would you like me to try to change your mind?" she said.

"Only if you think you can get me past the emotional reason not to."

"Which is what?"

"I can't say that I seriously considered Ohn's offer. Not even for a minute. But I wanted to analyze it logically. By forcing myself to think it through, I thought I might take an honest look at this case—and at me and Peyton. But the more rational I tried to be, the more I realized that I was simply fishing for arguments that would support my own gut feeling. The bottom line is, I love Peyton and would never turn against her. It's important for you to know that, just in case Ohn approaches you about a deal."

"I understand exactly where you're coming from."

"Good." He checked his watch. "Sorry I kept you late. It bothered me that I hadn't said it yesterday when Peyton and I met with Tony, so I felt like I needed to say it to you."

"Don't worry about it."

He rose and started for the door.

"Kevin," she said.

He stopped and turned. "Yeah?"

"I find it interesting that you left out one very important reason not to cut a deal for yourself."

"What's that?"

"That you believe with all your heart that Peyton is innocent, and that you would never do anything to convict an innocent person."

"I think that goes without saying."

"Does it really?" she said.

"Yes, of course."

"People could read an omission like that different ways, both on the conscious and subconscious level."

He paused, measuring his response carefully. "There's no point in reading anything into it. Like I told you: I love her."

His lawyer waited, as if expecting to hear more.

He simply said good night and closed the door on his way out.

Peyton was dressed in her favorite blue-and-white cloud pajamas, standing barefoot before the bathroom mirror, a glob of toothpaste on her toothbrush. It was almost midnight, and she looked beyond tired. She looked defeated.

Her father had told her not to read the newspapers, but how could she not? Juicy tidbits that the police and prosecutor deigned to leak to the press were her only real source of information. She had virtually no one to talk to, not even Kevin. Least of all Kevin. Things had been awkward between them since the meeting with Tony Falcone. Kevin had apologized, but that didn't restore the battered trust. She hated having doubts about him, and she sensed that he was doubting her. She'd talked to Tony about her concerns that afternoon, and he'd made a suggestion. It fit with his overall strategy of the case, and he saw no faster way to bridge the gap between Peyton and Kevin.

"Tony wants us to take lie-detector tests."

Kevin dropped his toothbrush into the sink. He picked it up, collected himself. "Why?"

"Obviously because he thinks we would pass."

"Of course we would pass," he said with a nervous chuckle. "But polygraph results aren't admissible into evidence. And examiners can make mistakes. Why take the risk of mistake if we can't use it at trial anyway?"

"If we pass, Tony says he can ask the prosecutor to present the results to the grand jury. The grand jury can consider it even if the results wouldn't be admissible at trial."

"Just because we ask the prosecutor to pass along the test results doesn't mean he will."

"Tony says that it would be a real PR blunder if he didn't. The D.A.'s office would appear to be hiding the truth."

Kevin rinsed his mouth and put the toothbrush back in the cup. "What happens if we don't pass?"

Their eyes met in the mirror. "You mean, what if the examiner makes a mistake and thinks we're lying?"

"Uh, yeah. That's what I'm saying."

"Tony says that we'll just keep the results to ourselves. No one will ever have to know we even took the test."

He took a deep breath. "Have you decided to do it?"

"It has to be a joint decision. Since we're preparing a joint defense, Tony thinks it would look really bad if one of us took a lie detector test and the other one didn't."

"Do you want me to take it?"

"Only if you want to."

He looked her in the eye for what seemed like forever. "All right. I'll do it."

"Thank you," she said as she turned out the light.

45

PEYTON SAT STIFFLY IN AN OLD WOOD CHAIR WITH AN INFLATABLE rubber bladder beneath her and another tucked behind her back. A blood pressure cuff squeezed her right arm. Two fingers on her left hand were wired with electrodes. Pneumograph tubes wrapped her chest and abdomen.

Seated across the table was Ike Sommers, a former FBI agent who, in the estimation of Tony Falcone, was now one of the finest private polygraph examiners in the business. He was watching his cardio-amplifier and galvanic skin monitor atop the table. The paper scroll was rolling as the needle inked out a warbling line.

"All set," said Ike.

Peyton felt queasy. She'd been too nervous to eat breakfast, and now she'd wished that she'd gone first and Kevin second. Waiting in the lobby until the conclusion of his test had only made her more anxious.

"Should we leave?" asked Tony. He was off to one side of the conference room, seated beside his wife, Jennifer.

"This whole examination is covered by the joint defense privilege," said Jennifer. "We watched Kevin's, so I don't see why the lawyers can't watch Peyton's. Unless we're making her too nervous."

"I'm okay," said Peyton. Still, she was glad that they'd made Kevin wait outside.

"Let's go then," said Ike.

Tony had explained the basic process to Peyton in advance, so she knew that the examiner's first task was to put her at ease. He started with questions that would make her feel comfortable with him as an interrogator. Do you like flowers? Did you ever have a dog? Is your hair purple? They seemed innocuous, but she knew that with each answer he was monitoring her physiological response to establish the lower parameters of her blood pressure, respiration, and perspiration. It was almost a game of cat and mouse. The examiner needed to quiet her down, then catch her in a small lie that would serve as a baseline reading for a falsehood. The standard technique was to ask something even a truthful person might lie about.

"Have you ever thought about sex in church?"

"Mmm, no."

Peyton gnawed her lip. What a giveaway. Didn't need a polygraph to know that she'd lied about that one.

The room fell silent as the examiner focused on his readings. He appeared satisfied. Peyton knew that she'd been caught, and now he knew what it looked like on the polygraph when she lied. Now he could test her truth-telling on the questions that really mattered.

"Is your name Peyton?"

"Yes."

"Do you like ice cream?"

"Yes."

"Are you a medical doctor?"

"Yes."

"Did you have sex with Gary Varne?"

"Yes."

One glance at the lawyers and Peyton knew that they hadn't expected that answer. She felt compelled to explain. "The summer before I left for college. We were going steady."

"Just answer yes or no," said the examiner.

Kevin's lawyer didn't seemed satisfied. Peyton had a sick feeling that her response would somehow be misconstrued, but the examiner pushed on.

"Is today Sunday?"

"No?"

"Have you ever climbed Mount Everest?"

"No."

"Did you kill Gary Varne?"

"No."

"Are you sitting down now?"

"Yes."

"Are you a woman?"

"Yes."

"Do you know who put Gary Varne's body in the trunk of your car?"

"No."

"Are you deaf?"

"No."

"Are you fluent in Chinese?"

"No."

"Did you hide your handgun from the police?"

"No."

"Are you glad this test is over?"

"Yes," she said with a cathartic smile.

The examiner turned off the machine.

Tony rose and gave her a little pat on the back. Jennifer headed for the door, saying nothing.

"What's with her?" asked Peyton.

"Ah, she'll be all right."

"She didn't like my answer about having sex with Gary Varne, did she?"

"Don't worry about that," said Tony.

"I told you yesterday that Gary was my first. We lost our virginity together the summer before I left for college. It was before I even met Kevin."

"I understand."

"The examiner just framed a bad question. There was nothing wrong with my answer."

"You're absolutely right."

"Somebody needs to explain that to Jennifer. I saw it on her face. She thinks I've been lying all along about not having an affair."

"Relax. She'll be fine."

Peyton let it go, but inside she felt a growing sick feeling that Kevin's lawyer was no longer in her camp.

Peyton decided to wait at her lawyer's office for the official results. When she went back to the reception area, it surprised her to see that Kevin had already left. She wondered if he feared what the test might reveal. She wondered if he'd stormed out in anger after Jennifer had misrepresented his wife's response to the question about sex with Gary Varne.

It would take a little while for the examiner to interpret the examinations. At Tony's suggestion, Peyton went out to lunch and came back in ninety minutes. The receptionist sent her straight back to Tony's office. She stepped in, uttering not a word, the question written all over her face.

"You passed," said Tony.

She nearly fell over, she was so relieved. She took a seat on the couch.

"What about Kevin?"

"You both passed."

She tried not to look surprised. "That's great."

"Yes. It's fantastic."

"But we need to straighten out that question about my having sex with Gary Varne. I don't want anyone to interpret my answer to mean that I was cheating on Kevin."

"I've already cleared that up with the examiner. Any polygraph examination is good for only three or four test questions. He'll confine his final written report to three substantive questions. Did you kill Varne? Do you know who dumped his body? Did you hide your gun? No one will ever know that you were even asked about having sex with Gary Varne."

"Kevin's lawyer knows."

"She heard your explanation."

"I don't think she believed it."

"Look, you're just going to have to straighten that out with your husband."

His intercom rang. He hit the speaker button and his secretary announced, "Mr. Esposito is here to see you."

"I'll be right there." He switched off the intercom, started for the door and said, "I'll be right back, Peyton. That's my tailor. He just needs a couple measurements."

"I'll be fine," she said.

The door closed, and she was alone. Her eyes started to wander, roaming first over the David Hockney lithographs on the wall, and settling finally on the papers on his desk. She tried to focus from five feet away, then walked over to the desk and took a closer look. It was Tony's copy of the questions that the examiner had asked her. She picked it up. Beneath it was a copy of the questions he'd asked Kevin.

She looked at hers first. It contained some comments in Tony's handwriting. Just as he'd promised, the question about having sex with Gary Varne was crossed out with a little note indicating that it would not appear in the final report.

She put hers back and picked up Kevin's. It looked much like hers, basically the same format. Obviously, Kevin hadn't been asked about sex with Gary Varne. But as she skimmed from top to bottom, she noticed that something else was missing. She flipped to the second page but still couldn't find it. She went back and forth, searching, sure that she was just overlooking it.

It has to be here.

But it wasn't. The examiner had never asked Kevin if he'd killed Gary Varne.

The paper shook gently in her hand as the implications washed over her. Kevin had passed the exam, but he was asked just two substantive questions that related only to his possible role as an accessory after the fact to murder: Did you put Gary Varne's body in the trunk of Peyton's car? Did you hide Peyton's gun?

The door opened, and Peyton quickly put the reports back on Tony's desk.

Tony looked at her, half smiling and half concerned. "You look like you've seen a ghost."

"Really?"

"Is everything okay?"

She struggled to keep her gaze from drifting back toward the list of questions atop the desk. "I hope so," she said in a voice that faded.

46

THE MOMENT SHE HEARD THE TONE IN TONY'S VOICE OVER THE
phone, Peyton knew that the news was bad. She'd thought that
she was prepared, that she'd resigned herself to the inevitable. Over
and over she'd repeated Tony's words like a mantra in her head,
that an indictment was merely a piece of paper and that she'd be
vindicated in the end. Still, she nearly dropped the phone when
her lawyer dropped the bomb.

"It's a two-count indictment," he said.

"Tell me," said Peyton, her hands shaking.

"You and Kevin are charged with the same crimes. Count
one, second-degree murder. Count two, accessory after the fact to
murder."

"Second degree? That's good. I mean, better than first, right?"

"It's still punishable by life in prison."

"Then how is it different from first degree?"

"You're eligible for parole with second degree."

"Great. Maybe the hospital will let me pick up my residency
when I'm sixty-two and a free woman."

"It wouldn't take that long. But that's not really what I'm focused on."

He sounded genuinely befuddled, which didn't comfort
Peyton. "What's eating you, Tony?"

"Honestly, this is a very strange indictment to me."

"How do you mean?"

"The technical legal distinction between first- and second-degree murder boils down to premeditation and deliberation. In this case, the question would be did you have time to reflect before you shot Gary Varne? Did you and Kevin plan the murder? Normally a prosecutor would just charge you with first-degree murder and let second-degree murder be a fall-back position for the jury, just in case the evidence on premeditation and deliberation doesn't play out at trial."

"So he's being kind to us?"

"No. I think he's being clever."

"Explain."

"If he had charged you with first-degree murder, you would have no right to bail. You and Kevin would be locked in jail until trial."

Peyton shook her head, confused. "Again, that sounds like he's being kind to us for some reason."

"Not hardly. Keeping you two together plays right into his strategy."

"I don't understand."

"He doesn't want the two of you sitting in separate jail cells awaiting trial. He wants you in the same apartment together, sharing the same bed at night."

"Why?"

"You've read the newspapers. Grand jury proceedings are supposed to be secret, but it has already leaked out that the foundation of the government's case is that you and Gary Varne were having an affair."

"But that isn't what happened."

"That won't stop him from trying to prove it. If you think it's bad now, wait until the trial begins and he unleashes all of his proof of your alleged infidelity."

The thought jarred her. "I can only imagine what might go through Kevin's mind."

"That's exactly my point. By keeping you two together, Ohn is building a pressure cooker. The more time you spend together, the more opportunities you have to argue over what really happened between you and Gary Varne."

"So he's hoping to make life miserable for us?"

"Not just that. The more you two scrap, the more likely it is that one of you will break ranks and hang the other one."

"I would never. Kevin would never."

"Never say never," said Tony.

Peyton lowered her head, allowing herself to at least consider the possibility that he might be right. She drew a deep breath and asked, "What happens next?"

"I don't want police officers coming to your house and hand-cuffing you on an arrest warrant, so I'll call Ohn and try to set up a time for you and Kevin to turn yourselves in. You'll be arraigned and, like I said, probably released on bail. I'll give you a call as soon as we've ironed out the details."

She was staring at the blank bedroom wall, numbed by the harsh reality that was finally setting in. *I'm being charged with murder.*

"Peyton, are you okay?"

Tony was speaking in his normal tone, yet he sounded far away. "Yeah, sure," she said in a flat, weak voice. "See you at the party."

47

TONY FALCONE MISSED THE EVENING NEWS BROADCAST AT SIX, SO AT 11:00 P.M. he was glued to the television from the comfort of his king-size bed. He wasn't sure what priority the story would receive, and of course he was torn about it. On the one hand, he knew that publicity would pain his client. On the other hand, what the hell? If he weren't getting all the attention, it would simply have fallen on some other less-deserving lawyer.

"Jennifer, come quick," he shouted.

His wife emerged from the bathroom, dressed in an oriental silk robe, a hairbrush in hand.

"Lead story!" he said, then increased the volume by remote.

A smart-looking anchorwoman was on the tube, using her signature sensational delivery. "A major development today in what is already Boston's most-talked-about criminal case."

Behind her on the screen appeared a photograph of Peyton's face. It was extremely flattering, almost sensuous in the way her lips were parted, her hair slightly blown. Obviously the camera crews had snapped enough shots to turn up the alluring, sexy expression that suited the angle of their "news" coverage.

The anchorwoman continued. "A grand jury returned a double indictment for murder against a husband and wife accused of killing the man who ended up on the losing end of a tawdry

love triangle. At a news conference this afternoon, assistant district attorney Charlie Ohn had this to say."

They shifted to footage of Ohn standing at a lectern beside the American flag. "This afternoon . . ."

"Blah, blah, blah," said Tony.

"I want to hear," said Jennifer.

"For heaven's sakes, you're a former prosecutor. You could recite his canned speech in your sleep." He waved his arm and added in a mocking, baritone voice, "With liberty and justice for all."

"Shush," she said, then did a double take. Tony was suddenly on the screen.

"What the hell are you doing on television?"

"I held a little conference of my own."

"You snake. I thought we had agreed to do it jointly, tomorrow."

"Don't you know better than to trust your own husband?"

She slammed him with a pillow. Tony rolled off the bed and positioned himself in front of the set, riveted to his own image.

"Now," said the televised Tony, "these polygraph examinations were conducted for our internal purposes only, so I have no idea how the results leaked to the press. But now that they're public knowledge, so be it. I'm not afraid to tell you that my client, Dr. Peyton Shields, has told me from the very beginning that she is innocent, and I believe her."

The segment was over. The anchorwoman was onto another story of wasteful spending on road construction and the Big Dig. Tony switched off the set.

"What do you think?"

Jennifer grimaced. "I'll be honest. I'm not real comfortable with it. What's this baloney about how you don't have any idea how the polygraphs leaked to the public?"

"Hey, if the prosecutor can keep a straight face and say that he can't account for grand jury leaks, I can play the same game."

"That's exactly what I'm talking about. You view this too much as a game. That's why I didn't want to do this case with you."

"Come on. We've been married ten years. It's about time we tried a case together."

"We have totally different styles. It makes for an interesting marriage. I'm not sure it makes for a very smooth trial."

He smiled mischievously and came to her, placing his arms around her waist. "So who likes smooth?" He kissed her lightly on the lips, then at each corner of her mouth.

"What are you doing?" she said, a little ticklish.

His hands slipped inside her robe. She tossed her long, red hair back and smiled.

"Come on," he said as he led her toward the bed. "I'll show you smooth."

A pressure cooker. Those were the words that somehow stuck in Peyton's mind. More than arrest, arraignment, or even second-degree murder. More than anything Tony had said to her. Pressure was the one thing that felt real to her.

She could feel it already as she lay awake in her bed well past midnight. Kevin was sleeping on his side, though she sensed he wasn't really sleeping either. Who could sleep on a night like this, the night before husband and wife went marching into court to be arraigned on murder charges?

"Kevin?" she said in the darkness.

"What?" He answered without budging, his back to her.

"Why didn't they ask you if you killed Gary Varne?"

He still didn't move, didn't answer right away. Finally, he rolled over and faced her from across the bed. "How did you know that?"

"I saw the questions the polygraph examiner asked you."

He propped himself up on his elbow and moved a little closer. He seemed to be looking her in the eye, though it was almost too dark to tell. "There was a very good reason for that," he said.

"I want to hear it."

"It has to do with the blackmail or the ransom or whatever you want to call it. I was the one who told you not to pay the money, remember?"

"I remember that very well."

"And when we didn't pay, Varne got killed. I talked that over with my lawyer, and she was convinced that, subconsciously, I may harbor strong guilt feelings over that. Jennifer was afraid that my feelings of indirect responsibility for his death might translate into perceived deception on my part if I was asked whether I killed him."

Peyton tried to read his expression, but the dim glow of the nightlight wasn't quite enough.

"Does that make sense to you?" he asked.

She wasn't sure. But for the moment, she knew the right answer. "Yes, of course."

He stroked her hair gently, then rolled over and returned to his side of the bed.

"Good night," she said, her mind racing. Without a doubt, his explanation had made sense. Perfect sense.

Almost too much sense.

She closed her eyes and tried to get some sleep, knowing it wouldn't come.

48

"ALL RISE," ANNOUNCED THE BAILIFF. HE CALLED THE CASE NUMBERS, adding "The Commonwealth of Massachusetts versus Peyton Shields and Kevin Stokes. The Honorable Judge Oscar Gilhorn presiding."

Peyton and her lawyer stood side by side, as did Kevin and Jennifer. To their left, at the table closest to the empty jury box, was Charles Ohn and a young assistant district attorney. The rumbling behind Peyton sounded like a marching band, as several camera crews and at least thirty reporters rose to their feet to acknowledge the arrival of Judge Gilhorn.

"Please be seated," he said from the bench.

The old courtroom filled with a brief shuffling sound as the spectators returned to their seats. Then silence.

Peyton gripped the armrests of her chair tightly. She didn't know what to expect and wasn't sure that her lawyer knew either. All Tony had said beforehand was that their arraignment would not be conducted in the usual perfunctory manner. Ohn had filed an emergency motion of some sort that required legal arguments.

"Let's get the formalities out of the way first," said the judge. "How does defendant Shields plead?"

Peyton started to rise, but Tony was already on his feet and said, "Innocent, Your Honor."

The judge peered out over his glasses, casting a reproving look.

"A simple 'not guilty' will do, Mr. Falcone." He glanced at Jennifer. "And Mr. Stokes?"

"Not guilty," she said.

"Mr. Ohn, would the government like to be heard on the question of bail?"

The prosecutor rose and said, "Release on their own recognizance is acceptable to us."

The judge did a double take. "On a second-degree-murder charge?"

"These are defendants with roots in this community. We don't regard their risk of flight as substantial."

Tony leaned toward Peyton and whispered, "Remember what I told you. He wants you two together."

The judge said, "I assume the government's position is fine with the defense?"

"Fine," the lawyers said in unison.

"Done," said the judge. "Now let's move on to the meat of the matter. I received about an hour ago an emergency motion from the D.A.'s office. At first blush I thought it was a rather transparent effort to overdramatize the arraignment. But as I read it, I realized that it raised an extremely important point that, in all candor, is a bit of a pet peeve of mine. Mr. Ohn, if you would please."

"Gladly," he said. "As the court is aware—and as practically the entire city of Boston is aware—Mr. Falcone held a press conference last night. The subject of that conference was, frankly, the alleged innocence of his client, Peyton Shields. He discussed polygraphs that have been leaked to the press, disclaiming all responsibility for the leak."

The judge interrupted. "That's not the point of your motion, as I read it."

"No, Your Honor. That just sets the context. The basis for our motion is the parting comment he gave in the news spot. Mr. Falcone's exact words were, and I quote: 'I'm not afraid to tell you that my client, Dr. Peyton Shields, has told me from the very beginning that she is innocent, and I believe her.' End quote."

Tony looked at Peyton, as if to say *So what?*

"Now, if you analyze that statement closely, you realize that Mr. Falcone has done two things. One, he has revealed in a public setting something that his client told him in a privileged and confidential conversation. Two, he has stated in a public setting that he believes what she told him. It is our position that by doing that, he has waived the attorney-client privilege."

"What!" Tony shouted.

The judge gaveled him down. "Mr. Falcone, please."

The prosecutor continued, "The law on the attorney-client privilege is very clear on this point. If any portion of a privileged conversation is voluntarily revealed to the public, the entire communication must be exposed. A lawyer cannot selectively reveal the favorable portions of a conversation and conceal the unfavorable portions that relate to the same subject matter."

The judge nodded, seeming to agree. "And the remedy you seek is what?"

"A complete waiver of the privilege. Our motion seeks copies of all notes of conversations Mr. Falcone had with his client. If he believes that his client is innocent, and he chooses to blab about it in public, then the government is entitled to discover the basis for his belief."

"This is preposterous!" said Tony. "It's pure grandstanding."

"*Sit down*," the judge said.

Tony retreated to his seat.

Peyton tried not to look horrified, but she was certain she was failing. She could almost feel the camera lenses tightening in on her from the press gallery.

The old judge leaned back, as if to pontificate. "Some people say I'm old-fashioned. Some people say I'm just old. But in my day, lawyers had a certain professionalism. I have nothing against lawyers who put on a vigorous defense in the courtroom. What I hate, quite frankly, are the flamboyant showmen who have a penchant for turning every criminal trial into a media circus."

He leaned forward, glaring at Tony. Peyton still felt as if the words were directed at her.

"I am sick of watching criminal defense attorneys on the news every night vouching for the innocence of their clients. In my view, a lawyer should never vouch for his client. He should only represent and defend him."

Peyton glanced behind her. The press corps was eating it up.

The judge said, "I realize that Mr. Ohn's motion is a bit aggressive. I don't think it's fair to prejudice Dr. Shields because of some boneheaded ploy her lawyer pulled. The court will deny the motion. But, Mr. Falcone, consider yourself gagged."

"But, Your Honor—"

"Gagged," he said, making a zipped-lip motion across his mouth. His gaze shifted toward Kevin's lawyer. "And as for you, Jennifer. I've known you since you were a law student interning at the district attorney's office. I'm surprised you would condone this kind of nonsense."

She shrank for a moment, then her face turned red with anger—at Tony. "It won't happen again, Judge."

"I certainly hope not. Now, enough said about that." He raised his gavel, ready to adjourn. "If we can all agree to act like adults from this point forward, then we are—"

"Judge," said the prosecutor, just in time to stop the gavel from falling. "There is one more point I'd like to raise with the court at this time."

"What is it?"

"It has to do with the evidence we obtained through the execution of the search warrant."

"Is that something we have to address now?"

"I would just like to alert the court to the potential problem we've discovered."

"Problem?" said the judge.

"The search warrant that was issued identified two items. A metal box and the gun that it normally contained, both of which belonged to Dr. Shields. We retrieved the box, but the gun wasn't in it."

The judge just shrugged. "Win some, lose some."

"That's really my point, Your Honor. We really hit pay dirt. The gun wasn't in there, but something else was."

Tony jumped to his feet, "No way, Judge. No way can they use a search warrant to obtain evidence that is not listed in the warrant. The warrant listed the gun and the box. That's it. Anything else they took out of that house is inadmissible."

"You don't even know what the evidence is," said the judge.

"It doesn't matter," said Tony. "If it wasn't a gun or a metal box, the government can't use it."

The judge asked, "What did you get, Mr. Ohn?"

Ohn seemed to swell right before Peyton's eyes. He glanced at the judge, next at the press. Finally, his gaze rested right on Peyton. "Communications between Dr. Shields and the victim, Gary Varne."

Her heart raced. She had no idea what he was talking about.

"You might call them love letters."

Tony jumped in. "This is totally out of order, Judge. We haven't seen the letters, we don't know what letters he's talking about."

Peyton wanted to grab him, tackle him, and tell him there were no letters. There couldn't *possibly* be love letters.

Kevin had yet to even look her way, but she could see the shock registering on his normally stoic profile.

"Well," the judge grumbled. "I have to agree to some extent with Mr. Falcone. This does appear to be an issue that should be fully briefed before the court makes any kind of decision about the admissibility of the letters. Of course, assuming they're relevant."

"Oh, they're relevant, all right. The government intends to prove that Mr. Varne and Dr. Shields were having an affair, which led to Mr. Varne's murder. These letters are rather convincing evidence of that. They are a yearlong trail of communication. And they are, shall we say, sexually explicit."

That got a reaction from the press. The judge banged his gavel, "Order, please."

Tony said, "We need to see these letters."

"That only seems fair," says the judge. "Mr. Ohn, can you please provide copies to the defense?"

"I have two sets of copies right here," he said. He crossed the courtroom and dropped two large envelopes at the defense table. It seemed strategic to Peyton, the way he dropped both sets right in front of Kevin. Peyton tried to catch her husband's eye. She'd been trying since the words "love letters" were first uttered. But Kevin wouldn't even look at her.

The prosecutor said, "I should point out that these are not handwritten letters in the conventional sense of the word. They are printed transcripts of chat-room conversations that were conducted by computer over the Internet. Some would call it cybersex."

The judge rolled his eyes. "Now you're really over this old man's head."

"The technical computer stuff isn't all that important, Your Honor. The point is that Dr. Shields collected printed copies of these communications with the victim and hid them in a secret place, much the way lovers have been hiding their love letters for centuries."

"Well, submit these letters or transcripts with an appropriate motion, and the court will make its decision. Anything else?"

"Nothing here," said Ohn.

"No," said Tony.

"We're adjourned." He banged his gavel and headed out a side exit to his chambers. The rumble from behind signaled the charge of a hungry media. They stopped at the rail, twenty feet away from the defense lawyers and their clients. Peyton didn't even want to turn around, though she was already being pelted with questions from the other side of the rail. *What about the letters? What did you write?*

At Tony's insistence, the four of them huddled at their table. He spoke in a coarse whisper. "We'll be mobbed on our way out. I want us single file, close together. Jennifer first, followed by Kevin, Peyton, and then me. And, Kevin, you are going to hold Peyton's hand as you lead her out of here. Understood?"

He seemed ready to protest, but Jennifer answered, "Understood."

"Don't answer a single question from the media, and don't

look worried. But the minute we get back to my office, I want a full explanation of those letters."

"So do I," said Kevin.

Peyton felt harpooned.

Jennifer started walking. Peyton extended her hand. Kevin took it, though his touch conveyed no warmth.

Single file, the four of them collided with a loud and overheated press. Most of the cameras were aimed at Peyton. It was difficult to hear any single question above the shouting and commotion, but the loudest ones dealt with the alleged affair.

"Is it true?"

"Did you love him?"

"Did your husband know about it?"

Keeping her head up, she struggled to look past the frenzy and show no reaction. Still, it was impossible not to make eye contact with the really aggressive ones who got right in her face. Each time her eyes locked onto one of those excited expressions—even if only for an instant—it only confirmed her sinking realization that the prosecutor had delivered to the wolves exactly what they'd wanted.

Her.

49

NO ONE SAID A WORD DURING THE CAR RIDE FROM THE COURT-
house. Peyton and Kevin sat in the back of Tony's Jaguar. Tony and
Jennifer were up front. They agreed to meet back at Tony's office
in two hours, after they'd all had a chance to review the "material,"
as Tony called it.

As soon as the clients were out of the car, Jennifer unloaded on
her husband. "I have never been so humiliated in my life."

"You? The judge slapped a gag order on me. Every reporter in
Boston is now poring over these so-called love letters that Peyton
supposedly wrote. And *you* were humiliated?"

"Have you already forgotten the way he singled me out right
in open court? He even called me by my first name: 'As for you,
Jennifer, I'm surprised you would condone this kind of nonsense.'"

Tony stopped the car at the traffic light. "He's just an old
coot."

"He's a respected jurist. And judges talk to each other. I have
a reputation."

"Oh, and I don't?"

"It's different. I'm a former prosecutor. I spent nine years on
the other side, and I still have friends in the D.A.'s office who
respect my credibility. You've spent your entire career doing
criminal defense. You're expected to . . ."

"To be sleazy?"

"That's not what I said."

"It's what you were thinking."

A horn blasted behind them. Tony grumbled and accelerated through the green light. Jennifer looked out the passenger window and said, "I just wish you would tone down the ego and respect my wishes."

"Honey, if you want out of the case, now's the time."

She didn't answer immediately. Finally, she gave him a little smile to defuse things. "You're not going to get rid of me that easy, you turkey."

That softened him a bit. "Actually, I think your exact words were, 'For better or for worse.'"

"My word is my bond."

He steered into the entrance of their office building's garage. "Does that mean you're in for the long haul?"

"You mean the marriage or the case?"

"The case, smart-ass."

"I'm in. Unless, of course, the prosecutor drops the charges against Kevin."

"Fat chance."

She couldn't tell him about the deal Ohn had offered her client. She could only guess how the love letters might change Kevin's thinking.

"Stranger things have happened," she said, leaving it at that.

Peyton returned to Tony's office at five-thirty. Kevin was with her, but only in the sense that he was physically accompanying her. He'd hardly spoken since leaving the courthouse.

They'd read the chat-room transcripts at home. Tony had kept one copy, so she and Kevin had only one set between them. Sitting down and going over them together had been out of the question. Kevin insisted on reading them first, which had proved to be a mistake. If he had let her go first, she could have at least given her side of the story before he got the shock of his life. As it was, he spent twenty minutes reading them and then another fifteen stewing alone in the living room as Peyton took her turn. By the time she was ready to talk, Kevin was anything but ready to listen. That was precisely the reason she opened the meeting in Tony's office with the same refrain that at home had fallen on deaf ears.

"I didn't write a word of this," she said.

The team of four was seated at a round table in the conference room. The transcripts rested in the center of the smoked-glass tabletop.

"Then what were they doing in a metal box in your closet?" asked Jennifer.

"I don't know. Somebody planted them there."

Jennifer looked skeptical. Tony said, "Let's not prejudge here. First of all, it's not at all obvious from the face of the transcripts that these chats were between Peyton and Gary Varne. The materials," as he liked to call them, "have been doctored."

"I don't know much about chat rooms," said Jennifer. "How can you tell they've been altered?"

"The best way is to show you." He pulled his chair up to the computer on the credenza and logged onto the Internet. "I'll enter any chat room randomly," he said. With a few clicks of the mouse, the screen blipped twice, and he was in.

"Here's one on sports. Now, as we sit here and watch this online chat unfold, you see two things. First, each person's screen name is spelled out in the left margin. Second, his or her typed message is to the right of the screen name. That's how you know who is saying what."

Jennifer looked at one of the printed transcripts. "There're no screen names here. Just the text of the message."

"Exactly," said Tony. "Now let me show you what happens when you print a transcript of this chat." He clicked the print button, and the printer churned out a single-page transcript. He laid it on the table beside the alleged Peyton chat.

"Look at the top of the one I just printed."

Peyton said, "Today's time and date."

"And, it gives the name of the chat room I was in. Significantly, none of that information is on these transcripts produced by Ohn."

Kevin asked, "So what's going on?"

"Somebody altered these transcripts," said Tony. "Without the screen names or the tagline, it's impossible to contact the Internet carrier and find out the true identities behind the screen names. The prosecutor will never be able to prove who was in these chats."

"Why would someone remove that information?"

"Because it was somebody else in the chat," said Peyton. "Whoever altered these transcripts is the same person who planted them in my strongbox. Which means that he's the same person who stole the gun that I ordinarily keep in the box, which also means that he is probably the same person who used my gun to shoot Gary Varne. I'm being framed! Doesn't anybody get that?"

She stopped, giving her theory time to sink in. Only Tony seemed impressed.

"One other possibility," said Jennifer. "Like the prosecutor argued, let's say the wife keeps the transcripts locked and hidden in her strongbox, just as people have done for centuries with letters from secret lovers. It might be the wife who would remove the screen names and the tagline. That way, if anyone ever finds the transcripts, her husband wouldn't be able to track down her lover."

"That's not what happened here. I never had a lover."

"We're really missing the obvious point," said Kevin. The pain was all over his face. "I've tried to read these transcripts objectively, though it's not easy when some guy is talking about how hot he is for your wife's body. The more important material isn't the racy, sexy stuff. It's in the boring details. The woman in these chats never comes right out and says 'My name is Peyton.' But she might as well have. She talks about her pediatric residency at Children's Hospital, the neighborhood she lives in, where she went to medical school. She even talks about her husband the lawyer. She talks about things that only Peyton would talk about."

"*But it doesn't sound like me,*" said Peyton. "Yes, one of the speakers mentions a few details that match my personal situation. But everything in there could easily be discovered by anyone who's willing to do a little background search. The more important point is the voice—the word choice, the phraseology. All that cutesy chat room-ese, the lowercase letters and numbers substituting for words. It isn't me. As my husband, you should know that."

"I'm not sure what I know about you anymore," he said.

An uncomfortable silence fell over the group.

Tony said, "Clearly we're not going to resolve this here. As Peyton's lawyer, however, let me make this observation. These letters will never get into evidence at trial. For the reasons we just talked about, the prosecutor can't possibly establish that they truly are transcripts of chats between Peyton and Gary Varne. We'll object on a million grounds, and the judge will sustain it."

"Then why did Ohn wave them in front of the judge this morning?" asked Peyton.

"He got the press going wild, and he dropped a bombshell on us. The two of you are behaving exactly as he'd hoped. I told you this earlier, Peyton. That's the reason he charged you with second-degree murder and then didn't even insist on bail. His strategy is for the two of you to slit each other's throats. With the delivery of these transcripts this afternoon, he placed the knives right in your hands. I'm sorry to say, the knives are already bloody."

"What the hell do you expect from me?" said Kevin. "These letters may not have any dates on them, but in one of them they wish each other a Happy Halloween. How do think it makes me feel to know that I've been a fool for almost a year?"

"You haven't been a fool," said Peyton, pleading. "I know this sounds crazy, but somebody was pretending to be me. Somebody is framing me."

"I'd love to believe you. I want to believe you. But who would go to all that trouble?"

All four exchanged glances, as if the same thought had come simultaneously to each of them.

"Now there's the question of the hour," said Tony.

50

DINNER WAS AT EIGHT. THE TABLE WAS SET FOR FOUR: PEYTON, HER husband, and her parents.

Valerie and Hank Shields had stopped by the apartment in a joint show of support for their wounded daughter. Peyton's mother insisted on cooking Kevin and her daughter a nice dinner. Technically speaking, she'd insisted only on cooking Peyton a nice dinner. It was her father who'd invited Kevin to the table. Valerie had never liked Kevin, not even during the happiest times of their marriage. She was never openly hostile toward her son-in-law, but she had a way of getting under his skin like no one he'd ever known.

"So what do you think of all this, Kevin?"

It was as if Valerie had whacked him in the head with her wooden spoon. Kevin finished his mouthful of spinach salad, and said, "All what?"

"Oh, come now. We're all adults. I'm talking about all this nonsense that Peyton was supposedly having cybersex on the Internet."

"Mother, please."

"I'm on your side, dear."

"Can't we just have a nice dinner?" asked Hank.

"We're all family," said Valerie. "I think it's important for everyone to know where everyone else stands. Now, here's the way I see it. In the first place, my daughter would never do something like this. But Kevin, as her husband, may not have the same level of confidence in her as I do. So I wish to point out this fact."

"You don't have to do this," said Kevin.

"I want to," said Valerie. "Because one thing that these seedy reporters don't seem to mention is that my daughter is one of the busiest people on earth. She is a pediatric resident at the premier children's hospital in the world. Her father and I have hardly seen her since she started medical school, and we live in the same city. She works anywhere from thirteen to twenty hours a day, six days a week. Does anyone at this table think for one minute that our Peyton has the time to sit in front of a computer and chat with this Gary Varne about the size of his penis?"

"I'd really rather not discuss this," said Kevin.

"I just want to know, have you thought about that?" Hearing no response from Kevin, Valerie looked at her daughter. "Haven't you explained that to him, Peyton?"

Peyton took some wine, struggling with what she was about to say. "I guess I was hoping that it wouldn't come down to proving myself by pointing out that there wasn't enough time in my day to cheat on my husband. I was hoping for a little show of trust."

She was looking at Kevin. He was looking down into his plate. Finally, he looked up and spoke to Peyton's mother. "I'm sure you mean well. But this is really a conversation that Peyton and I should have later, just the two of us."

"I agree," said Hank. "Can we move on to something a little lighter? How about some lasagne?" he said. Conversation ceased, and it was just the clang of the serving spoon on dishes as Hank served the others and then himself.

Valerie flattened her napkin in her lap and said, "You know, your father and I had a nice little lunch the other day."

"Where was that, sweetie?" said Hank, seeming not to have a clue.

"You remember. It was a little hole-in-the-wall downtown. It's called Murphy's Pub."

Her father shot a quizzical look. "I don't recall eating—"

"Kevin," she said, cutting off her husband. "It's not far from your old office. Have you ever been there?"

Kevin shifted nervously in his chair. Murphy's Pub was where he had met Sandra for lunch last winter, when he was supposed to have been on his way to the airport for a seminar in New York. He wasn't sure how Valerie knew about it, but it was clear she did. "Yeah," said Kevin. "I've been there."

"You should take Peyton there sometime," she said.

"I will."

"Good. You do that."

Just like that, she'd swooped in like the Luftwaffe and dropped it—the five-hundred-pound bomb with Sandra's name on it. Part of Kevin hated Valerie for doing it, but he also knew she was right. If he was going to be such a jerk toward Peyton about the cyber-sex letters, it was time he'd come clean about his own secrets.

"More wine?" said Valerie.

"Yes," he said. "I'd really love some."

After dinner, Kevin walked for an hour, no particular destination in mind, though he did drift in the general direction of Copley Square. In front of the reflecting pool at the Christian Science cathedral was where he had told Sandra to meet him at 10:00 P.M.

Her text message had come earlier that evening. *Let's talk*, it said. He presumed that she'd seen the news about the love letters between Peyton and her dead lover. His first instinct was to ignore Sandra, figuring that she wanted to rub salt in his wounds. After that uncomfortable moment at tonight's family dinner, however, Kevin was beginning to suspect that she had his mother-in-law's ear. If he was truly resolved to tell Peyton everything, he had to know what Sandra had been telling Peyton's mother.

The Christian Science complex was a monumental campus in a busy urban setting. The 670-foot-long reflecting pool in front of the huge basilica and smaller original church was reminiscent of the mall in Washington, D.C. At night, however, it was closed to the public. Sandra was waiting on a bus-stop bench on the sidewalk outside the locked iron entrance gate.

"You came," she said with surprise.

"Let's keep walking," he said. Side by side, they continued up the sidewalk. Said Kevin, "I suppose you heard about what happened in court today."

"That's why I'm not at home on my computer. Chat rooms are buzzing with 'be careful what you type' warnings."

"That's not funny."

"I'm sorry."

"Why did you text-message me?"

"Hopefully for the same reason you text-messaged back and ask me to meet you here tonight." She shot a sideways glance that made him uncomfortable.

"That seems unlikely, Sandra."

She didn't react. "Have you been thinking about us at all?"

"Honestly—and I'm not saying this to be mean—I've tried not to."

"And have you been successful?"

"Yes, pretty much. Until tonight."

"What happened?"

"Peyton and I had dinner with her parents. Her mother made it crystal clear that she knows something about you and me. At the very least she knows about our lunch at Murphy's Pub last winter."

"Aye, Kevin. After all you two have been through, you still haven't told Peyton about us?"

Her tone made him feel even worse than Valerie's little stunt had. "No. I haven't told her." He paused, then said, "Have you?"

"Me? Of course not."

"Did you say something to Peyton's mother?"

She stopped walking and looked him in the eye. "Are you accusing me?"

"I'm just trying to find out how my mother-in-law knows about us."

"Well, it wasn't from me," she said. "I told you before—at Murphy's Pub, in fact—that I don't play the kind of games that Peyton plays with you. When I'm in a relationship, it's not about outsmarting the other person. It's about trust. Complete and unconditional trust. That got me burned in my first marriage, but I can't let that change who I am because . . . well, to put it in terms that you and Peyton can understand, because that would mean my ex-husband wins."

Kevin looked away, the traffic noises whirring in the background. Then he allowed his gaze to shift back to Sandra, and her expression surprised him. He had prepared himself for anger or disappointment, even bitterness. He had also braced himself for smugness and gloating, her savoring the sweet satisfaction of seeing an ex-lover get his due. But her eyes showed just a hint of something that he hadn't expected in the least.

She seemed a little desperate.

"I should go," he said, then started away.

"Kevin," she called.

He stopped and faced her.

She stepped toward him, then leaned closer than she'd been since the one and only night that had changed everything. Her voice was barely above a whisper. "If you need an alibi for the night Gary Varne was killed, I could be it."

The look in her eyes cut to his core. He took a step back, saying nothing.

"You don't have to say anything now," she said. "Just think about it."

A bus rumbled past them on Huntington Avenue. "Good night," he replied. Then he just started walking, alone, not even sure he was headed in the right direction.

51

PEYTON'S PARENTS LEFT AROUND TEN-THIRTY. HER MOTHER LEFT BEHIND a stack of newspaper clippings. She'd been saving them all, as if Peyton wanted to keep the smear campaign for her scrapbook.

What on earth goes through that woman's mind sometimes?

Peyton walked to the front window and checked outside. No sign of Kevin. Earlier she'd dialed his cell phone but got no answer. She seemed to be losing the adultery issue on all fronts. Kevin didn't believe in her innocence, at least not completely. And the prosecutor's release of the bogus chat-room conversations had certainly killed her sympathetic image as a young doctor who was devoting her life and talents to the treatment of sick children. Reality aside, she was now cast as an adulteress who had quite a naughty way with words in the Internet chat rooms. Surely they'd already been posted verbatim on the Internet, tonight's cheap titillation for lonely old losers from Boston to Budapest.

She resisted the impulse to watch the eleven o'clock news. It would only depress her. By ten after eleven, however, her curiosity compelled her to see how the coverage was playing out. The set switched on in time for her to catch one of the many legal analysts talking about the prosecutor's motion to pierce the attorney-client privilege, a substantive issue that had been lost in all the hoopla over cybersex. He was a law professor, a distinguished-looking fellow with a gray beard and spectacles, who seemed to be enjoying his moment in the sun at Peyton's expense, pontificating about various hypotheticals.

"Of course, if you were to talk to anyone at the district attorney's office, they would probably tell you that if Dr. Shields was truly innocent, she wouldn't object to turning over the privileged files."

Peyton switched off the set. She'd heard enough.

How does a girl win this fight?

She tossed the remote onto the couch and headed for the bedroom. Television was no option tonight. Maybe a good book instead. She flipped on the light in their home office and went to the storage closet. It was filled with books, mostly from a bygone era when she'd had time to read for pleasure. There was nothing new on her side, so she scanned Kevin's shelf. From the looks of things, the only books he'd read lately were titles like *How to Get Happily Published, How to Write the Perfect Query and Synopsis, How to Get Rich Telling Other People How to Get Published.*

She continued through another row of nonfiction, then froze. She knew that in the name of research Kevin had purchased some unusual reference books about things like autopsies and knife wounds, even one about hanging yourself. It seemed a strange coincidence that this particular book was right at the top of his stack. It was as if he'd consulted it recently.

How to Beat a Polygraph was the title.

Her impulse was to confront him as soon as he got home, but she knew what he'd say—research. He was a crime novelist now and needed to know such things. She was willing to concede that perhaps at some point in his writing he truly had needed to know about polygraph exams. A deep concern, however, was buzzing in her mind.

What suddenly had made him think he needed a refresher?

She returned the book and shut off the light.

It was almost eleven-thirty, and Rudy was worried. He'd been waiting in their private chat room for almost thirty minutes, and Ladydoc was nowhere to be found.

He'd thought surely she'd come tonight, with all the buzz over their past chats. Perhaps she'd felt betrayed by the transcripts he'd left in the strongbox. She might even have jumped to the conclusion that he'd stolen her gun and killed Gary Varne. He needed a chance to explain himself. All he'd wanted was her attention. He'd put the letters in the box long before she'd come back to their chat room the other night, and by then the police had already taken the box. That "reunion" chat had been too brief anyway. She'd seemed tentative, afraid to open up to him, afraid to commit to another chat. He just wanted things to be the way they used to be.

Where are you, Ladydoc?

The computer screen was blank. He felt drained. She had no right to be mad. He had hundreds of other transcripts of their late-night chats, scores of them more sexually explicit than the ones he'd planted in the box. His goal hadn't been to embarrass her. He had no intention of letting strangers intrude on their private place in cyberspace. That was the reason he'd removed the screen names and taglines from the transcripts. He didn't want scores of imposters contacting him, scores of other suitors contacting her.

He was growing tired. The bright light from the LCD in his dark little apartment was rough on the eyes. Finally there was a hint of activity, then a message at the top of his screen.

"Ladydoc has entered the room."

He was suddenly wide awake.

"sorry i'm late," she wrote. "wuz up watching the news."

"u r famous," he replied.

"thanks 2 u."

"thanks 2 gary Varne."

The screen was still. He feared that he'd offended her. "i didn't mean that. r u ok?

"i want 2 see u."

He paused. Chatting with her was one thing. He had so many stolen passwords that no one would ever be able to trace a conversation back to him. Seeing her in person was a whole different level of risk. And her track record wasn't good.

"last time u stood me up."

"i got scared."

"and i got burned. we picked the perfect spot. we had the time all set."

He grew angrier as he typed, not even realizing that he was switching out of cute chat room–ese. "I went there and waited for hours. HOURS! You could have told me you were scared. You just didn't show up."

"i wuz busy."

"LIAR!!!!!!! I went back to our chat room for a week. YOU NEVER CAME!!!!!"

"i did come back."

He could have punched the screen. "You came back to dump me."

"u don't know what was going on in my life then. i had 2 end it."

"So did I. Which is how you ended up in Jamaica Pond."

She didn't answer immediately. He'd always assumed that she knew who'd run her off the road, but the delayed reaction had him fearing that he'd said too much.

"Still there?" he typed.

"u r scaring me."

He closed his eyes, brought his anger under control. "Sorry. I didn't let you drown last time. I won't let you drown this time either. So long as you do as you're told."

"what do u want me 2 do?"

"Prove that you're worth saving a second time."

"how do i do that?"

"You know how."

There was another pause. His heart pounded with anticipation.

"i wish i could see u."

"What do you want to see?"

"u kneeling over me, huge, towering over me."

A thin smile crept to his lips. He reached inside his shorts and typed with the other hand. "keep talking, baby. you know what i like."

Part III

AUTUMN

52

AUTUMN BROUGHT BUTTERFLIES. PEYTON COULD FEEL THEM FLUT-
tering in her stomach, as the end of summer meant the beginning
of her trial. At first, the six weeks between indictment and trial had
seemed like plenty of time to grow accustomed to the notion that
she would stand before a jury. But no amount of time could lessen
the blow of having to answer for a murder she hadn't committed.

It almost didn't seem real, she and Kevin finally seated at
the mahogany table beside the husband-and-wife team hired to
represent them. Jury selection had taken all of Monday and part
of Tuesday, with lawyers for both sides employing what appeared
to be some combination of voodoo and pop psychology to pick
the perfect group of so-called peers. By 3:00 P.M. Tuesday they
had a jury. Eight women and four men, including an elementary
school teacher, a janitor, two housewives, a bus driver, a grad student from MIT, a self-proclaimed artist, two folks between jobs,
and three retirees. Tony and Jennifer had seemed satisfied. By the
same token, so had Charles Ohn.

After a short break, they returned to the courtroom for opening statements. Peyton's parents sat in the front row of public seating, directly behind their daughter. Kevin's father was deceased,
and he hadn't seen his runaway mother since childhood, so he had
no family in attendance. The press gallery was filled to capacity,
well beyond the handful that had watched voir dire. Likewise, the

general audience had nearly doubled in size since the break. It was as if the scouts had phoned their friends to tell them that things were about to get interesting. Peyton had the sickening sense that they were.

"Mr. Ohn," the judge said, "please proceed."

The prosecutor rose and stepped to the well of the courtroom, that stagelike opening before the bench where lawyers could seemingly step away from the action and speak directly to the jury, as if delivering a Shakespearean soliloquy.

Ohn buttoned his suit coat, bid the jurors a good afternoon, and dived right into his theme, no notes, no mincing words.

"A wife cheats on her husband. The husband finds out about it, and he's furious. The wife tries to break off the affair, but her lover won't let go. The lover ends up dead."

The courtroom was utterly silent. For a moment, it seemed as if he might return to his seat, having said enough.

"Who did it?" he asked in hushed urgency. "Who killed Gary Varne?"

"Was it the husband acting out of jealousy?" Ohn said, his voice rising. "Or was it the wife trying to bring an end to the affair forever?"

Across the courtroom, Peyton shrank inside. The prosecutor was glowering at her.

He continued, his tone matter-of-fact. "Gary Varne was shot in the back of the head at close range. The murder weapon was a thirty-eight-caliber firearm. The gun was never found, but Peyton Shields owned a thirty-eight-caliber Smith and Wesson handgun that mysteriously disappeared from her apartment after the murder. The victim's body was found in the trunk of the defendants' car with Peyton Shields passed out in the driver's seat. A spilled bottle of sleeping pills lay on the seat beside her.

"I ask you again: Who killed Gary Varne?"

He paused, and for Peyton the silence was insufferable. Half the jurors were looking at her, the other half at the prosecutor.

Ohn opened his arms, palms up. "The answer will be Peytonly

obvious," he said, a wordplay on "patently." He gave the jurors a long, satisfied look, as if to assure them that the government had charged the right defendants. Then quietly he returned to his seat.

Peyton and her lawyer exchanged glances. For seven weeks the defense had been waiting for some signal from the prosecutor as to which of the two defendants would be tagged as the trigger person and which would be tagged as the accomplice after the fact. Ohn hadn't completely precluded the possibility that he'd go after Kevin for murder too. But his "Peytonly" pun was the most significant signal they'd received so far.

"Mr. Falcone, your opening statement?" said the judge.

As Tony rose, Peyton saw the ambivalence in his eyes. She was fully aware of the joint defense team's advance strategy on opening statements, but with Peyton now the apparent focus of the murder charge, Tony seemed to have the same reservations that she was having.

"Defendant Shields will defer her opening to the start of her case," he announced, sticking to the plan.

"Very well. Ladies and gentlemen of the jury, defendant Shields has elected to save her opening statement until after the state has presented its case. That's her right to do so, and if any defense is necessary, you will be hearing from her lawyer at that time. Ms. Dunwoody, you may proceed."

Kevin's lawyer rose and stepped to the lectern. Behind Peyton was a quick shuffle of reporters jockeying for position, then silence. Jennifer began, serious yet cordial in her delivery.

"A cheating spouse, a dead lover. If it were really all that simple, this jury would have the easiest job on the planet.

"But it isn't easy. Your job is to make the prosecutor prove his case against Kevin Stokes and Peyton Shields beyond a reasonable doubt. That standard applies to each of them. They are husband and wife, but the charges against them are separate. Each has been charged with second-degree murder. Each has been charged as an accessory after the fact. It's as if the prosecutor wants you to tack a scarlet letter on each of their foreheads and simply conclude that they did it. *They did it."*

She shook her head, saying, "He's got it all wrong, folks. There is no *they*. To convict my client, the government must prove beyond a reasonable doubt that *he* did it. To convict Dr. Shields, the government must prove beyond a reasonable doubt that *she* did it. It isn't enough that one of them might have done it. Two weak cases do not add up to a conviction.

"I submit that after all the evidence is in, you will conclude that neither one of them killed Gary Varne. But bear in mind, if your conclusion is that one or the other might possibly have done it, your verdict must be the same. Not guilty."

She allowed her message to sink in, then returned to her seat.

Peyton tried not to stare, but she was gauging the jurors, taking their pulse. It was a stoic bunch. Either that, or they'd already condemned her.

Judge Gilhorn broke the silence. "It's almost five o'clock, so let's reconvene tomorrow at nine. Jurors are reminded of their oaths. We're adjourned," he said with the bang of a gavel.

All rose, and as the judge exited the courtroom Tony was quietly congratulating his wife on a job well done. Peyton caught Kevin's eye. Though she could only guess what he was thinking, she would have bet that she was right.

All this talk about reasonable doubt was nice. But it would have been even nicer to hear someone say a little louder and a lot clearer that neither one of them had done it.

53

WEDNESDAY MORNING TECHNICALLY MARKED THE THIRD DAY OF THE trial, but for Peyton it felt like the real beginning. It was time for live human beings to flesh out the accusations that the prosecutor had hurled at Peyton and her husband. It started with Steve Beasley.

The last time she'd heard Steve's voice was her infamous phone call to the Waldorf-Astoria from Gary's apartment. It would have suited her just fine never to have heard it again.

The witness walked straight to the stand with little expression on his face. He didn't look at Peyton, which wasn't remarkable. She'd never been his friend, having known him only through her husband. But his failure even to glance in Kevin's direction struck her as bad news indeed.

He swore the oath and looked only at the jurors, with an occasional glance at the prosecutor. He seemed to keep the entire left half of the courtroom out of his line of sight, as if the whole thing was made easier by pretending that she and Kevin weren't even there.

"State your name, please."

The questions kept coming, and his answers flowed like lines from a script. Peyton had seen the transcript of his grand jury testimony, so nothing came as a surprise. Still, reading it on a printed page had been one thing. It pained her to hear the most sordid part aloud in a packed courtroom.

"What, exactly, were the words you overheard while speaking on the telephone to defendant Shields?"

The witness looked at the jurors, as if to make sure they were listening. "I heard a man say, 'Don't be shy, Peyton, I've already seen you naked.'"

The schoolteacher on the jury raised an eyebrow. The artist smirked.

Peyton had known it was coming—the hearsay objections had all been overruled in pretrial motions—yet it was still impossible not to react. She could almost hear the pencils scratching on reporters' notepads. Now everyone in the courtroom knew what Peyton Shields supposedly did when her husband was out of town. Soon, with the power of the media, the whole blessed world would be in on the dirty little secret.

"Did you ever tell Mr. Stokes about this?" Ohn asked the witness.

"Yes. We were playing basketball one Sunday. I told him exactly what had happened."

"What was his reaction?"

"He pretty much blew his stack."

"He got angry?"

"Livid, I'd say."

"Thank you. No further questions." Ohn seemed pleased as he returned to his seat.

Jennifer rose for cross-examination, but Tony gave a hand signal, as if to say *I'll take this turkey.* He grabbed the grand jury transcript and moved to within ten feet of the witness, feet planted firmly.

"Mr. Beasley, you testified before the grand jury in this case, did you not?'

"Yes."

"Mr. Ohn asked you about the phone call from Peyton Shields. Specifically, about the man's voice in the background."

"That's right."

"You told the grand jury what the man said."

"Yes."

"At that time you gave the following answer." He opened the transcript to the clipped page and read. "He said, 'Don't be shy, I've already seen you naked.'"

"Right. And that was also my testimony today."

"No, it wasn't." Tony went back for his legal pad, checking his notes. "According to your testimony today, the man in the background supposedly said, 'Don't be shy, *Peyton*, I've already seen you naked.'"

He blinked twice. "That's what he said. He mentioned her name."

"That's the way you remember now?"

"Yes. He mentioned her name. I'm sure."

"I'm sure too," said Tony, indignant. "I'm sure it makes it easier for the prosecutor to prove he was actually talking to Peyton."

"Objection."

"Sustained."

"Let's move on," said Tony, hands in his pockets. "Sir, are you aware that Mr. Varne dated Dr. Shields before she married Kevin Stokes?"

He shrugged and said, "I wouldn't know about that."

"So, assuming that this man in the background was actually Gary Varne, and assuming that he was talking to Peyton, and further assuming that he actually uttered the words 'I've already seen you naked,' you don't know if he was referring to the previous night or ten years ago."

He thought for a moment, then answered reluctantly. "No, I couldn't say."

"Now, let's talk about how Mr. Stokes got so mad on the basketball court. 'Livid,' I think was your word."

"That's right."

"Just to elaborate, is it fair to say that he accused you of making the whole thing up?"

"That's exactly what he did."

"He told you he didn't believe that Peyton had been unfaithful."

"That's right."

"He didn't say that he was mad at Peyton, did he?"

"Well, no. I guess not."

"He didn't even say he was mad at Gary Varne, did he?"

"Not that I recall."

"The only person he was mad at was you."

"That's—yes, as far as I know."

Tony scratched his head, as if confused. "So, what does this boil down to, a case of misdirected anger? Mr. Stokes got so mad at you that he and his wife decided to kill Gary Varne?"

"Objection," said Ohn, groaning.

"I'll withdraw it. That's all the jury needs to hear, Mr. Beasley. Unless there's some other aspect of your grand jury testimony that you'd like to change now."

"Objection."

"Sit down, Mr. Falcone."

"I'm sitting, Judge," he said with a thin smile. "I'm sitting."

I'm dying, thought Peyton, still stung by Beasley's testimony, sharing little of her lawyer's thrill of victory in the courtroom war of words.

Sandra Blair was fighting back tears.

It was cool, but sunny, colored leaves ablaze against magnificent blue skies, the perfect autumn day to cruise in a convertible Mercedes with the top down and the heat on. She wasn't really much of a car person, but her ex-husband had been a collector. This vintage vehicle was one of the spoils of defeat that she'd taken for raising his children and playing his fool.

She was tired of being the fool.

Sandra had told no one about the night in Providence, but it was well known at the firm that she and Kevin had been friends. It was also no secret that she had been speaking to the prosecutor, though no one knew for certain whether she would be a witness and, if so, what she might say. Lawyers at the firm were under strict orders not to discuss the case with her. Nonetheless, as the trial wore on, Marston & Wheeler became an increasingly uncomfortable place for Sandra. Things were especially tense on the day Steve Beasley took the stand, so she decided to get out of town and visit her youngest stepchild at Dartmouth.

Of her three stepchildren, Sandra had always felt closest to Chelsea. She was just six years old when her real mother had passed away and eight years old when Sandra had married her father. Sandra had taken her literally from pigtails to a college dormitory, from SpaghettiOs to Domino's. She had always felt a real bond with Chelsea and thought Chelsea had felt the same. Sandra was perfectly comfortable driving up on a whim to see her at Dartmouth.

So when Chelsea asked her not to do that anymore, Sandra could hear only her ex-husband's voice.

She sucked back one last tear as she headed into Boston, and her thoughts returned to Kevin. With the Peyton-and-Kevin show playing out in the media, Sandra had been thinking a lot about Kevin lately. There was no doubt in Sandra's mind that he was being used. It was beyond dispute, at least in Sandra's mind, that Peyton and Gary Varne had been lovers. Sandra was equally convinced that Kevin was no killer, which left only one obvious explanation for Gary's murder. She hadn't laid it out that clearly the last time she'd spoken to Kevin, but she was still worried about him. If he wasn't careful, he'd end up paying way too much for his loyalty to an undeserving and downright dangerous woman.

She was suddenly angry at herself for even caring what happened to him. The wind in her face made her forget her worries for a moment, though a quick glance in the rearview mirror reminded her that she wasn't twenty-eight anymore. She was just passing the Salt and Pepper Bridge over the Charles River when another Charles rang her on the cell phone.

"I hope you take a lesson from your coworker," said the prosecutor.

Sandra pulled the phone away from her ear; Charles Ohn had one of those pipe-organ voices that carried way too loud over wireless networks. "What are you talking about?"

"Steve Beasley got himself sliced and diced this morning. A little disparity between today's testimony and his grand jury transcript."

"I don't know anything about that."

"I'm not saying that you do. I'm just telling you that if there's someone you Marston and Wheeler lawyers are trying to impress, please knock it off."

"I really don't know what you're talking about, Mr. Ohn."

"I know that certain people at your law firm aren't too happy about the novel Kevin Stokes wrote. Your managing partner even took him to court trying to get an injunction against publication—which I understand was denied just recently. As a postscript, the firm probably wouldn't shed a tear if Stokes went down in this trial. So don't stretch your testimony by pandering to the powers that be."

"Is that what Steve did?"

"All I know is that we had Beasley recounting the 'I've seen you naked' remark, coupled with a long-distance phone bill that shows Peyton Shields was calling from Varne's apartment. Now that evidence is totally discredited, all because he tried to insinuate the name Peyton into the conversation. I don't know why he would do that, other than to please his boss."

"What do you want me to do about it?"

"Just take the stand and tell the truth, damn it. Don't be trying to please me, please your boss, or please anyone. Don't let anyone shape your testimony."

"You don't have to worry about that."

"Good. I'll see you tomorrow."

"See you tomorrow," she said, then hung up the phone. But her mind was still racing. Shaping her testimony. What a concept. No one was shaping Sandra Blair's testimony.

No one but me.

54

KEVIN FELT THE WEIGHT OF THE PROSECUTOR'S STARE AS OHN ROSE to make his announcement.

"The state calls Sandra Blair," he said.

Kevin's heart sank. He'd been on edge since leaving her outside the Christian Science complex, where she'd offered to be his alibi witness. He'd never even considered getting back to her, but it suddenly occurred to him that perhaps that wasn't the end of the matter. Maybe she had her own agenda. Maybe she had even been wearing a wire.

Did she set me up?

Heads turned as she walked down the center aisle of the courtroom. The prosecutor met her at the swinging gate and directed her to the witness stand. She was dressed in a dark business suit, simple jewelry, nothing sexy. Kevin crossed his fingers. Mercifully, she hadn't dressed the part of the femme fatale. He could only hope that she'd limit her self-description to that of "coworker."

Sandra's offer to be his alibi had thrown Kevin. Before going to see her that night, Kevin had resolved to tell Peyton about Sandra. But by the time he'd returned home, he had completely changed his mind. He'd actually convinced himself that she probably wouldn't testify at trial, particularly since he had no intention of taking her up on her alibi offer. If Sandra wasn't going to be a witness at trial, Kevin's reasoning had gone, telling Peyton about her at this juncture would only put more needless strain on their marriage and their joint defense. Kevin would tell his wife everything in due time, after the trial. Clearly that kind of cowardly thinking had bordered on delusional.

Peyton glanced his way as Sandra swore the oath. Kevin could appreciate his wife's confusion, as Sandra hadn't testified before the grand jury. He should have told Peyton about her last night, last week, last month, last winter. Now, here she was in the flesh, with no grand jury transcript to tip off the defense as to her possible testimony. Just about anything could pop out of her mouth. "Anything," however, wasn't what he was worried about.

Just please don't let it be everything.

"Ms. Blair, where do you work?" asked Ohn.

She leaned toward the microphone and told him.

"Did you know Kevin Stokes when he worked at Marston and Wheeler?"

For the first time since entering the courtroom, she made eye contact with Kevin. "Yeah. We know each other."

"Know him well?"

Kevin was starting to sweat. She glanced his way, then back at the prosecutor. "Fairly well, yes."

Ohn stopped. Or at least it seemed as if he'd stopped, as Kevin braced himself for the next question.

"How about his wife? Do you know her?"

Kevin could breathe again. Miraculously, he was moving on.

Sandra said, "I wouldn't say I know her. I've seen her before."

"When was the last time you saw Mr. Stokes?"

The tightness was back in Kevin's chest. Again, he wondered: *Did she set me up?*

Sandra said, "I believe the last time I saw Kevin was at a dedication and fund-raising event at Harvard University. He was with his wife."

Kevin was only partially relieved. No mention of the night at the Christian Science complex. But the fund-raiser had its own pitfalls.

The prosecutor asked, "When was that event?"

"Last summer."

"In relation to the day Gary Varne's body was found in the trunk of Dr. Shields's car, when was it?"

"Three days before."

"Three days," he said, underscoring the importance for the jury. "Did you speak to Mr. Stokes?"

"Briefly."

"Did you happen to have the opportunity to hear Mr. Stokes speaking with his wife?"

"Yes, I did."

"How did that come about?"

"I was on my way to use a pay phone. I overheard them shouting at each other at the end of the hall."

"Were they alone?"

"Yes."

"Did you make your presence known?"

"No. I was actually quite embarrassed for them."

"Come now, Ms. Blair. Let's just be upfront about this. You were eavesdropping, weren't you?"

She blushed, and Kevin prayed that this wouldn't lead to a discussion of why she was so interested in their marital disagreement. "I really did go to use the phone," she said. "But yes, once I heard the shouting I did what anyone would probably do. I listened."

"We're not here to pass judgment. At least not on you. Can you tell us what you heard, please?"

Tony rose. "Objection. Hearsay."

Ohn replied, "These are admissions by the defendants themselves. That's not hearsay."

"Overruled."

Sandra said, "Kevin was very angry and quite loud. Apparently someone had said something to upset him."

"Just tell us what he said, please."

"He accused Peyton of having spent the night at Gary Varne's apartment while he was away on business."

"What was Peyton's response?"

"I believe she said, 'Kevin, do we have to talk about this here?'"

"She didn't deny it?"

"Not that I heard."

Kevin started as Peyton grabbed his hand and squeezed it tightly. He knew it had been purely instinctual, knew that she wanted to jump up and shout to the courtroom, the world. Regardless of whether he'd believed her, he recalled that Peyton had denied any intimacy with Gary at least twice.

"Then what happened?"

"Just a lot of sniping back and forth. At this point my sense of curiosity was giving way to my sense of . . . well, it was just getting ugly. He was screaming at her for getting drunk and sleeping at Gary Varne's apartment, that sort of thing."

"Then what?"

"He stormed away. Flew right past me in the hallway."

"Did you get a look at him?"

"Yes."

"How did he look?"

She looked at Kevin, then at the prosecutor. "I don't really remember."

The prosecutor's expression fell, as if his witness had suddenly turned against him. "You don't remember?"

"Not really."

Ohn went to his assistant, who handed up Sandra's signed statement. "Perhaps this will refresh your recollection. Do you recall giving a statement to me in my office about a month ago?"

"Yes."

"Do you recall my asking you how Mr. Stokes looked as he left the event you just described?"

"Yes, I recall that."

"Do you recall giving the following response: 'Kevin looked like he could kill someone.'"

"Objection," shouted Tony.

"Move to strike," said Jennifer.

"Overruled and denied."

Again, Sandra glanced at Kevin. Then she lowered her eyes, as if embarrassed for having spoken out of anger, particularly to a prosecutor. "Yes. I believe I said that."

Ohn was clearly enjoying it, though careful not to gloat too much in front of the jury. "I may have already asked, but just so we're clear, this happened how many days before Gary Varne's body was found in the trunk of Dr. Shields's car?"

"Three days," she said.

"Thank you. No further questions," he said, returning to his seat.

Peyton finally released Kevin's hand. She was whispering something to Tony, presumably her repeated denials of the affair. Kevin sat in silence, watching Sandra. He didn't see contempt, didn't see resentment. With her eyes, she seemed to be saying that she had just called it as she'd seen it. Then, slowly, in a gesture that only seemed casual, she pushed her long hair back behind her ear. Kevin tightened his focus and saw the message.

She was wearing the earrings she'd worn the night they'd slept together.

It was as if she'd reached across the courtroom and hit him between the eyes. Without words, she was telling him something. At first blush it seemed like a threat: *I have the power to bury you.* But as their eyes met once more, he sensed no ill will. To the contrary, maybe in her own peculiar way, she was hinting at reconciliation. It might have been a tacit renewal of the offer she'd made that night outside the Christian Science complex.

I could be your alibi.

"Ms. Dunwoody, your witness," said the judge.

It was Jennifer's turn for the defense. She started to rise, but Kevin stopped her. He cupped his hand to her ear and whispered, "No cross-examination."

"What?"

"Don't go there."

The judge said, "Ms. Dunwoody, if you please."

She remained locked in debate with Kevin, whispering. "We have to cross-examine. She killed us."

"It can get a lot worse. Just let it go."

Her look was incredulous, but with a touch of concern. "Let's talk about this."

The judge said, "Does the defense have any questions for this witness or not?"

Jennifer rose to address the court. "Your Honor, I'd like to have a brief recess to speak with my client."

"Forget about it. I'm not going to stop the trial every time you want to have a chat. We'll be here all year. Now proceed with cross-examination or the witness will be dismissed."

Tony rose, confusion on his face. "Could I have just thirty seconds with my co-counsel?"

"Thirty seconds," said the judge, growling.

The whole team huddled at the table, whispering so as not to be overheard, trying to show no emotion so that neither the press nor the jury would sense disagreement.

Tony whispered, "You want me to do the cross?"

"No," said Kevin. "No one should do it."

"That's nuts."

"Look, her testimony hurt me a lot more than Peyton. And I'm telling you, it can only get worse if you cross-examine."

Peyton just looked at him, as if looking right through him. "What are you saying?" she said in a hushed but piercing voice.

The judge interrupted. "Thirty seconds are up. What's it going to be, Counsel?"

Kevin and Peyton were locked in silence. The lawyers checked their clients, then looked at each other. Finally, Tony rose and said, "No questions at this time, Your Honor. But it is possible that one of the defendants may recall her as part of our defense."

"Very well. The witness is excused. Ms. Blair, please do not discuss your testimony with anyone, since there is the possibility of your return to the witness stand."

Sandra stepped down and crossed before the bench, her stride a little faster than normal. She was looking right at Peyton, Kevin noted, and as she passed their table she slowed her step. Her eyes shifted toward Kevin, and he looked away awkwardly, only to meet Peyton's glare. He looked the other way but still felt the weight of her smoldering suspicion.

He heard the click of Sandra's heels as she headed up the aisle, heard the heavy door open and shut in the back of the courtroom. Sandra was gone, but it was as if she were still there, sitting right between them, showing Peyton her earrings.

55

THE PHONE RANG ON JENNIFER'S DESK. SHE WAS ALONE IN HER office preparing for tomorrow's witnesses. She pushed aside her plastic takeout container of chicken Caesar and snatched up the receiver. It was Ohn.

She stiffened with surprise. "To what do I owe this honor?"

"Your client passed up a good deal before trial. Testify against his wife, he gets complete immunity. I'm renewing the offer."

"What makes you think he'd be interested now?"

"I saw the way he and Sandra Blair looked at each other in the courtroom today. More important, I saw the way his wife looked at him. My well-honed prosecutorial instincts tell me that it's only a matter of time before Peyton tubes her husband. This is your client's last chance to take a preemptive strike."

"Am I to infer from this conversation that the prosecution's theory is that Peyton Shields pulled the trigger?"

"I'll tell you this much. If your client doesn't take the deal, I can only assume that it's because *he* was the triggerman. In that case, I might just turn around and offer the same deal to his codefendant."

"You're just a model of integrity, aren't you?"

"The offer's good till tomorrow morning."

"I'll let you know," she said, then hung up the phone.

★..★..★

Peyton got home around eight-thirty. At her insistence, there had been no joint defense strategy session at the conclusion of today's testimony. It had been just Peyton and Tony in his office, leaving Jennifer and Kevin to meet or not on their own. Kevin had tried to corner Peyton alone, but she'd avoided it. Somewhere deep inside she'd known all along that Kevin was hiding something. Ironically, had anyone but her mother planted the initial seed of doubt she probably would have confronted Kevin long ago. But that telling little exchange between Sandra Blair and him in the courtroom had finally put a face on her suspicions and fears.

Peyton entered the apartment quickly and hung her coat in the foyer. Out of the corner of her eye she saw Kevin seated in the living room, but she didn't look his way. She continued down the hall to the master bedroom. She pulled a suitcase and garment bag down from the shelf in the closet and threw them on the bed. She started packing slowly, then more furiously, driven by hurt and anger.

"What are you doing?" It was Kevin, standing in the doorway.

She continued sifting through the panty-hose drawer, not even looking up. "What does it look like?"

"Why are you doing this?"

She stopped and glared. "Are you going to look me in the eye and tell me you were never with that woman?"

He shifted nervously, right foot to left foot, then back again. "Peyton, I swear it was only one night."

She chuckled pathetically. "*Only* one night. That's beautiful, Kevin. Why don't we try that defense at our trial. But, Your Honor, we only shot Gary Varne in the head *once*."

"I didn't shoot him in the head any times."

"Neither did I, asshole. I was only making a point."

"I know. You have every right to be furious."

"You're damn right I do," she said, her voice shaking. She ducked into the closet and grabbed a few dresses and shoes for court, then threw them on the bed. "You bastard. How could you do this to me?"

"It was last winter. You were so busy at the hospital, it seemed like I saw you about two hours a week. Things weren't very good between us, remember? You didn't even tell me you were pregnant."

"So it's my fault, is that it? You wouldn't have cheated if I'd told you I was pregnant?"

"No. That's just a symptom of how bad things had gotten between us. I'm the only guilty one here, and I regretted it from the day it happened."

Her eyes narrowed. "You know what I really don't understand? How could you make me feel so horrible over nothing but a complete misunderstanding with Gary Varne, when all the while you were hiding this secret about you and this . . . this *woman*."

"Because I was afraid you loved Gary. And in my whole life, I've only loved one woman. You."

She zipped her suitcase and said, "You have a lousy way of showing it."

"I'm not proud of the way I acted. But for me, the thing with you and Gary was never about one night. I worried about your renewed friendship with him from the day you started at Children's. I blamed him for the way you seemed to stop loving me."

Peyton grabbed her bags and pushed past him. "Don't put this on me."

He followed her down the hall to the foyer. She slowed just enough to throw on her coat. He touched her shoulder as the door flew open. She stopped in the open doorway, but didn't dare turn to look at him. Her emotions were running the gamut from hurt to betrayal, anger to disappointment. She was determined not to lose control in front of him.

His voice quaked behind her. "I wish I knew what to say."

"Don't say anything."

"I wish I could undo it, just go back in time. When I was sitting in the living room waiting for you to come home tonight, I was thinking about our second date back in college. I remember it more clearly than any night in my life. I remember what you wore, what we said. I remember dropping you off at your apart-ment afterward. Most of all, I remember going home and, for the first and only time in my life, literally thanking God for bringing a woman into my life."

She closed her eyes tightly, holding back tears.

"I am sorry, Peyton."

"Me too," she whispered, then rushed down the porch steps, no looking back.

56

RUDY LAY WAITING AND WATCHING, CONCEALED FROM SIGHT BY thick shrubbery and the dark shroud of midnight. He was only following orders.

The night before the trial began, he'd chatted with Ladydoc again. It had been almost two months since they'd reestablished Internet contact, roughly the same time Peyton and Kevin had been indicted. In that first reunion chat, she'd given him exactly what he'd wanted in their private chat room. Ever since then, she'd been playing hardball. A year ago, at the peak of their relationship, she would come to their regular cyber meeting place almost every night at eleven. Since the indictments, she'd come some nights but not others, no schedule whatever, never making a date for another go-around. Rudy had to log on and check the chat room each night at eleven, disappointed more often than not. Even when she did show up, it wasn't like before. She'd leave abruptly, right in the middle of one of their steamy sessions, threatening never to take him all the way again unless he agreed to meet her in person. Each time he'd refused, but this last time she'd given him the ultimatum. "Meet me in the Back Bay Fens, or you will never hear from me again," had been her exact words. Whether she meant it or not he couldn't say. But he knew he couldn't take the teasing anymore, the aggravation of her leaving him swollen and unsatisfied time after time. It was ruining the illusion, the way she'd get him all worked up, take him to the brink, and then—bleep—*Ladydoc has left the room*. It was an empty feeling, like making it with some bitch only to discover that in the middle of the act she'd fallen asleep or passed out, or that the knife had penetrated a little too close to the heart and that she'd bled to death before he could finish.

If she wanted to see him in person, fine. He brought his blade, just in case.

"So where the hell are you?" he muttered, checking his watch.

Ladydoc didn't know what he looked like, so her directions had been detailed and specific. "Meet at the park bench facing the Mud River. Sit on the north end. Cross your right leg over your left, then your left over your right. Then I'll know it's you."

Rudy agreed to it, but he wasn't an idiot. In the back of his mind, he suspected that the minute he sat on the bench a half-dozen FBI agents would come flying out from behind trees to apprehend him. So from his hiding spot in the bushes, he watched from a distance as the homeless guy he'd hired for twenty bucks performed the ritual. He sat on the bench, crossed his right leg over his left and then his left over his right. And he waited.

A minute passed, and nothing happened. Rudy replayed the performance in his mind, making sure that the guy had done it right. He had, he was sure of it.

Two minutes passed, and still there was nothing.

Rudy was getting edgy. This whole idea had been hers, not his. She'd made the rules, and he'd played by them. At least, as far as she'd known, he'd played by them. She had no reason to know that the guy on the bench wasn't the real Rudy.

Going on five minutes, and still no Ladydoc.

The good news was that she hadn't invited him here to lure him into a police trap. The cops would have been all over his homeless stand-in if that had been the case. But that gave him only a moment of calm. The bottom line was she'd stood him up.

Damn her!

He was shaking with anger, trying to keep control of himself. The homeless guy was now prone on the bench, half-asleep. In a fit of rage, Rudy sprang from his hiding spot and sprinted toward the bench. He pounced on the guy from the blind side.

"Hey, what the—"

Rudy pummeled him with both fists, tearing at his coat, ripping the pockets. "Give me back my twenty bucks!"

The man groaned as he rolled off the bench. With his twenty back in hand, Rudy gave the guy a kick in the kidney and headed off into the night.

His hands smelled from having dug in the guy's pockets. Using a stand-in had been a mistake. That had to have been the reason for Ladydoc's no-show. She could have watched from a distance—maybe even used binoculars—seen the homeless guy on the bench, decided that she didn't like what she saw, and gone home. If that was the case, her no-show was his fault. He'd have to go online and confess what he'd done, tell her that he wasn't some drunk who reeked of dried urine and fell asleep on park benches.

Who the hell are you kidding?

She'd stood him up, he knew it. *Again.* Just like last winter, when she'd promised to meet him, chickened out, and then told him it was over. She was a manipulative bitch back then, and he'd let her do the same thing all over again. Five weeks ago he'd warned her and told her that she needed to prove that she was worth saving. This proved only one thing. He shouldn't have pulled her out of Jamaica Pond. She hadn't been worth saving then. She wasn't worth saving now. One thing, however, was for certain.

This would be the last time she'd ever stand him up.

He knifed through the darkness of the park's north end and headed straight for the overpass, clutching his recovered twenty bucks, knowing that, for money like that, the sluts on the street would blow him *without* a condom.

Who needs you, Peyton?

★..★..★

It was 5:26 A.M. and Peyton had slept about an hour all night. Her mind refused to shut off. Anytime she managed to think of something other than her split from Kevin, her mind shifted to the trial. Hardly the stuff of sweet dreams.

Last night, she'd gone from her apartment straight to the logical place: her parents' house. They'd taken her in with open arms and, surprisingly, very few questions—or perhaps not so surprisingly, given their own taste of marital infidelity years ago. In any event, Peyton didn't want to talk about it, and no one forced her. It made for a relatively painless move, but it didn't necessarily add up to a good night's sleep, not even in her old bed. Staring at her from the foot of the bed was old Wilbur the teddy bear, who'd served in a pinch to keep the headboard from banging against the wall the time she'd brought Kevin home from college to announce their engagement. She'd come here tonight to escape the ghosts, but Kevin had been part of her life since she was nineteen years old. Ghosts were just about everywhere.

Her alarm would ring in about a half hour, but she saw little point in waiting. In her robe, she went downstairs to the kitchen and started the coffee. She checked the front step, but the newspaper had yet to arrive. Just as well. She was trying to avoid reading about herself anyway. The coffee aroma lured her back into the kitchen. She poured a cup, then wondered what she was going to do until the rest of the world woke. It wasn't as if she could call anyone at this hour. She sipped her coffee and, like magic, it gave the brain a jump start. She hadn't checked her e-mail since the beginning of the trial.

Her parents had a computer in the den. She logged on to her server as a guest and pulled up her home page. She had countless unanswered e-mail messages. A few good wishes from friends. Some coupons from computer software companies. And one that she didn't recognize.

She opened it, read it once, then read it again. The second time through, she started to tremble.

The sender was identified not by a screen name but a number. The e-mail had been sent to her from one of those twenty-four-hour copy/office centers that rent workstations with computers with e-mail capabilities. She knew that it would be impossible to trace the electronic message back to the true sender, since it would simply lead back to the subscriber, Fast Fred's Copy Center. That was yet another way to retain anonymity in the world of cyberspace. Whoever this anonymous someone was, however, he or she seemed to want to help her.

The message read, "The man you need to meet will be seated on a bench facing the Mud River in the park in Back Bay Fens tonight at midnight. Go there. Bring the cops."

Peyton wasn't sure who "The man you need to meet" was, exactly. But with someone posing as her in cybersex chats and someone else framing her for murder, she would have settled for either one.

She hit the print button to get a copy of the e-mail, not sure who to call first. "Tonight at midnight" didn't leave much time to prepare. A wave of nervous excitement washed over her, and then an even bigger wave of despair. The message, she noticed, bore yesterday's date. "Tonight at midnight," meant *last* night at midnight.

Almost numb, she fell back in her chair, staring at the screen, wondering how huge was the opportunity that had just slipped through her hands.

57

"NEVER," SAID KEVIN.

It was seven-thirty in the morning, and he was seated in his lawyer's office. The fourth day of trial wouldn't begin for another ninety minutes, but Jennifer had called to tell him that there was something they needed to discuss beforehand. In just two minutes, Kevin had heard enough.

"I told you the last time this came up. I would never cut a deal that involves turning against Peyton."

Jennifer leaned back in her leather desk chair, seemingly frustrated. "Circumstances have changed. Your wife has walked out on you. I don't know where that leaves the joint defense arrangement."

"I don't care. We're still married."

"That's honorable, but in the context of a joint murder trial that could go either way, it could also be suicide."

"You're asking me to testify against the woman I love."

"I'm advising you to do what's best for yourself."

"Okay, then let me talk in terms you can understand. Even if I wanted to take the deal, there's nothing I can offer the prosecutor in exchange for immunity. I have absolutely no evidence that Peyton killed Gary Varne."

Jennifer looked doubtful but said nothing.

He said, "Do *you* think she did it?"

Again, she didn't answer.

Kevin shook his head, flabbergasted. "The last time we talked about this, you burned me for not citing Peyton's innocence as one of my reasons for rejecting the prosecutor's deal. Well, this time, let's put Peyton's innocence at the top of the list."

"Your decision," she said in a clipped tone. "Just keep in mind that Charles Ohn may be right. If you turn down the deal, Peyton may start pointing the finger at you."

He lowered his eyes and said quietly, "Maybe I'd deserve it."

She did a double take. "Are you trying to tell me something?"

He realized what he'd said, how it might have sounded. "I meant that I deserved to be betrayed because I cheated on my wife."

"Is that so?"

"I wasn't saying that I deserve to be convicted because I killed Gary Varne."

She gave him a sobering look. "Either way, it's okay with me. Just so we understand each other."

"I didn't kill Gary Varne."

"Fine. We'll leave it at that." She closed her notebook, as if to add finality.

"Fine," said Kevin, not sure he'd convinced her.

Peyton's early-morning meeting with Tony meant watching him sweat. He was in the workout room beside his office, going full tilt on the treadmill, wearing sweatpants and a Boston Bruins T-shirt. A dark triangle of perspiration dipped from his shoulders to his sternum, as if pointing to the paunchy belly he was trying to work off. Peyton sat facing him on the weight bench.

It took her just a few minutes to bring him up to speed on the e-mail she'd opened a day too late. Tony seemed to be listening, though he never broke stride.

"You have no idea who sent it to you?" he said, winded.

"No. It came from a rented computer terminal at some copy center."

"But you're convinced that this person knows who's framing you?"

"The message said that the man I need to meet will be in the park at midnight. Bring the cops. Why else would I need to bring the cops?"

The treadmill kicked up a notch, whining loudly. Tony was struggling to keep up.

"Should we call the police?" asked Peyton.

He punched the control panel and slowed the pace. "No."

"Why not?"

"Because that message could have come from a friend, your husband. Just about anybody who wants to help substantiate your theory that you're being framed."

"Or it could be the legitimate link we need to prove that Gary was kidnapped."

He stopped the machine and leaned on the panel, catching his breath. "That would be pretty convenient at this stage, don't you think?"

"You think I created this e-mail myself to bolster my kidnapping defense?"

"No. But it's possible someone you know did exactly that."

"Meaning Kevin?"

"Meaning who else?"

"That's crazy."

"Is it?"

She shook head, frustrated. "So you're saying we should just forget about it?"

"Yes. I told you at our very first meeting that I don't want to inject the kidnapping claim into this case. The jury won't buy it, and the prosecution will twist it into an argument that Gary Varne was blackmailing you and Kevin, which only strengthens your motive to murder him. So far, Ohn shows no sign of going there. I don't want to be the one who opens the door for him by sharing a mysterious e-mail that probably came from your own husband."

Peyton struggled to contain her anger. "You don't believe any of it, do you?"

"Any of what?"

"That someone's impersonating me on the Internet. That someone kidnapped Gary and demanded a ransom. You think Kevin and I made it all up before our first meeting with you."

He toweled off his sweaty neck. "Let me say this much. I believe I can get you acquitted without going into any of that."

"How are we going to get through this trial if you don't believe me about the kidnapping?"

"I didn't say I don't believe you."

"That's what I'm hearing."

"Then you're not listening closely enough. What I'm saying is, I don't trust your husband."

She lowered her eyes. "A few days ago I might have taken you to task on that. But after yesterday, those aren't exactly fighting words."

Tony took a seat on the bench, facing her eye to eye. "Trust me on this kidnapping argument. And level with me on one point, will you?"

"What?"

"I'm asking this only because I want to understand Kevin's state of mind right now, not as your husband but as your co-defendant. And be honest, please. Did you leave Kevin because of Sandra? Or did he kick you out over Gary Varne?"

With that, she glowered. There were only so many false accusations she could stand, and one more from her own lawyer had her just about over the edge. "I'll trust your instincts on the kidnapping defense, Tony. But don't you dare ever ask me that question again."

She shot a parting glare, then rose and left the room.

58

PEYTON WISHED SHE COULD BE SOMEWHERE ELSE. ANYWHERE ELSE. It was bad enough having to watch the prosecutor parade one witness after another before the jury, each one trying to paint her as a murderer. Having to sit quietly at the defense table beside the man she'd walked out on just last night was a real test of personal fortitude. Their greeting had been cool but not openly hostile, not with the press watching, and definitely not with the eyes of the jurors upon them.

"Morning, Peyton."

"Morning, Kevin."

Those had been the only words exchanged all morning. It might have been painful if there hadn't been so much else to worry about.

Ohn began the day with the first officer on the scene, whose testimony was brief and straightforward. He'd spotted what he thought was an abandoned car by the wharf and stopped to check it out. He found Peyton slumped unconscious in the front seat with an open bottle of sleeping pills spilled on the floor. He radioed for an ambulance, and after Peyton was whisked away, he noticed blood seeping through the backseat, apparently from the trunk. So he popped it open.

"What did you find?"

"A white male. Late twenties. He'd been shot in the head."

"Was he dead?"

"Quite."

At that point, Ohn dragged out the enlarged photographs of the crime scene, including the victim, and Peyton felt numb. It was bloody, but not so bloody that she couldn't plainly see Gary's likeness. Ohn was asking follow-up questions on the position of the body, its condition and so forth, but Peyton couldn't concentrate, not even on her own lawyer's methodical cross-examination. For days, maybe weeks, her only focus had been on the fact that she had *not* killed Gary Varne. Seeing the pictures made her face head-on the chilling fact that someone *had* killed Gary, that it had been terribly violent, that he'd spent his final moments on earth stuffed in a trunk with a loaded gun to his head—an absolute horror that she would have wished on no one.

Mercifully, it was over in short order. The prosecutor quickly transitioned to his next witness.

"Dr. Sidney Gersch," the witness said, introducing himself to the jury. "I'm a forensic pathologist with the medical examiner's office."

He was a gray-haired man with dark, tired eyes that peered out from behind wire-framed spectacles. With rounded shoulders he seemed incapable of sitting up straight even in a courtroom, as if so many years of stooping over dead bodies had given him terrible posture.

"You were called to the crime scene when the victim's body was discovered?"

"That's correct. And I was also the attending pathologist at the autopsy."

Ohn breezed through preliminaries, then asked, "What was the victim's cause of death?"

"Gunshot. A single thirty-eight-caliber bullet that entered at the right temple. Exit wound was at the left temple. We refer to this as a through-and-through wound."

"So the bullet passed completely through his skull?"

"That's correct."

"Did you determine the manner of death?"

"The medical examiner's finding is homicide."

"How did you rule out suicide?"

"For one, no gun was found anywhere near the body."

"Isn't it possible that someone came along and stole it?"

"Theoretically. But the victim's hands were also tied behind his back."

"Not to be a fly in the ointment, Doctor, but isn't it at least theoretically possible that Mr. Varne killed himself, then someone happened by who stole the gun and tied his hands behind his back to make it look like homicide?"

Peyton glanced at her lawyer, wondering where Ohn was headed with what seemed to be undue concern over the possibility of suicide.

"That would be pretty illogical, but I see your point. The third and perhaps conclusive reason that we ruled out suicide was that there was no blood spatter on the victim's hands."

"Explain that for us, please."

"Sure," Dr. Gersch said as he turned to face the jury. "The entrance wound was basically a bullet hole surrounded with soot that was easily wiped away. The presence of soot suggests that the firearm was discharged at fairly close range, perhaps one to three inches."

"Wouldn't that be consistent with suicide?"

"Yes, but with a close-contact entrance wound there would certainly be what's known as blow-back spatter of blood. Essentially, the entrance of the bullet at high velocity causes the blood to break into fine aerosol-like particles. In a near-contact execution-style shooting, these particles are dispersed back toward the barrel of the gun."

"And what's the significance of that in this case?"

"Mr. Varne had no traces of blood on his hands. If it had been a self-inflicted wound, we would have found it."

"So, even though Dr. Shields was found in the front seat with a bottle of spilled sleeping pills, it's clear that this was not a botched attempt at a joint suicide? A so-called lovers' pact?"

"Objection."

"Overruled."

Peyton cringed inside. Even when questioning the medical examiner, Ohn was clever enough to find a way to keep the jury focused on infidelity.

The witness answered, "Someone murdered Mr. Varne. I can't say what happened to Dr. Shields."

Ohn moved on to other areas of questioning, but Peyton's thoughts were stuck on the last exchange. The schoolteacher on the jury was flashing a judgmental look. The young artist in the second row seemed to be shooting Peyton looks, as if hoping to be next in the growing line of men who had seen her naked. Maybe she was imagining it, but maybe not. She glanced at Kevin, wondering if he appreciated the irony of *her* being the one painted as unfaithful.

"Just a couple more questions," said Ohn. "Dr. Gersch, were you present on the scene when the victim's body was removed from the trunk of the car?"

"Yes. I supervised it."

"How big was Gary Varne?"

"We measured him at six foot two. One hundred ninety-eight pounds."

"How many people did it take to physically lift his body out of the trunk?"

"Two."

Ohn turned toward the defense table, his gaze coming to rest first on Kevin and then on Peyton. It was as if he were counting—a-one and a-two—giving the jury just enough time to come to the realization that if it had taken two people to lift his body out of the trunk, it had probably taken these two people to put it in, the murderer and the accessory after the fact.

"Thank you. No further questions."

"Cross-examination?" said the judge.

It was Tony's turn to go first for the defense. He rose and approached the witness, his gait slightly tighter than normal, as if stalking his prey from the weeds. Some might have thought it was a strategic adjustment to his normally strident style, but Peyton knew that he'd simply pushed too hard on the treadmill this morning. Then again, maybe it was choreographed. She was beginning to realize that little happened by accident with Tony.

"The cause of death was gunshot," he said, more a statement than a question. "You determined that from your examination of the wound, correct?"

"Obviously."

"Well, at the risk of stating the obvious, there was no gun at the scene."

"There was a bullet. But frankly, I don't need a gun or a bullet to recognize a gunshot wound."

"My question was, there was no gun, correct?"

"That's right."

"And there was no back spatter of blood on Gary Varne's hands."

"That is correct."

"Is it fair to infer from your testimony that whoever did pull the trigger on this missing gun would have had back spatter of blood on their gun hand?"

He thought for a moment, as if sensing a trap. "With a shot at such close range, yes."

"For example, if Peyton Shields had shot Mr. Varne before losing consciousness in the front seat, she would have had back spatter on her hands, maybe even her clothes."

"One might expect that."

"Would it surprise you to know that neither the paramedics in the ambulance nor the physicians in the emergency room noted any sign of blood on Peyton's hands or clothing?"

"Objection."

"Overruled."

"Washing would remove it. And a change of clothes."

Tony smiled thinly. "So let me get this straight. No gun. No back spatter on my client's hands or clothing. Are you suggesting that Dr. Shields shot the victim at close range, threw away the gun, washed her hands, changed clothes, came back to the car, and swallowed a bunch of sleeping pills to kill herself?"

"Objection. That's way beyond the scope of this witness."

"Your Honor, I'm just trying to understand how much trouble murderers normally go through to cover up their crimes before they kill themselves anyway."

"No speeches, and you're not going there with this witness. Sustained. Move on."

Tony looked toward the jury. "I think we all got the point. Nothing further."

Tony returned to his seat, flashing his client a smug look. Peyton gave him a subtle acknowledgment, though in her mind the score hadn't been as big as Tony seemed to think it was.

Jennifer was on her feet before Tony had fully settled into his chair. She spoke from behind the table, right where she'd been sitting, as if suggesting that she would be even more brief than her co-counsel.

"Dr. Gersch, do you have an opinion as to where Gary Varne was when he was shot?"

"It appears that he was shot while lying in the trunk."

"What do you base that opinion on?"

"As I mentioned, the bullet entered the right side of the head and exited through the left. The blood-spray patterns found in the trunk are consistent with this type of exit wound. And perhaps most important, the bullet was found lodged in the wheel well."

"So he was alive when he was put in the trunk?"

"That would be my opinion."

She nodded, seemingly satisfied. "Your autopsy report notes only one injury, one wound. That's the single gunshot that killed Gary Varne."

"That's true."

"You performed a thorough examination, I'm sure."

"Very thorough."

"You found no signs of blunt trauma to the skull, such as might be found with a blow to the head."

"Just the gunshot."

"You performed a toxicology report?"

"That's standard in a case like this."

"No signs that the victim had been drugged."

"Nothing of that sort."

"So no one clubbed him over the head, then put him in the trunk and shot him?"

"It wouldn't appear that way."

"No signs that anyone had drugged him into an unconscious state, put him in the trunk and then shot him?"

"No."

"By all indications, Gary Varne was alive and conscious when he got into the trunk. And he was shot while he was alive and fully conscious."

"That was probably the case."

"To follow up on Mr. Ohn's question about how many people it took to remove the body from the trunk, let me ask you this. How many men or women holding a gun does it take to order a fully conscious man to step into the trunk?"

"One, I would presume."

"Thank you. That's all I have."

Peyton caught her eye as Jennifer took her seat. Before coming to court today, Tony had told her that they needed to be more careful now that she and Kevin had split, and watch every move of their codefendant with a little more circumspection. It had seemed as though Jennifer had been trying to help both defendants by proving a lone gunman. But now that it was over, Peyton was getting the same ugly vibes that she'd gotten after her polygraph.

She just didn't like the way Jennifer was looking at her.

At the break, the lawyers went straight to the attorneys' lounge in the courthouse, leaving their clients behind. Tony needed a moment with his wife, and he didn't intend to hold back. He closed the door, checked the bathroom to make sure he and Jennifer were alone, then proceeded to unload.

"What the hell are you trying to pull in there?"

"What are you talking about?"

"That last question. How many men or women would it take to order Varne into the trunk at gunpoint?"

"I was just being gender neutral."

"Don't give me that."

"My only point was to debunk the prosecution's theory that it would have taken two people to lift Varne's body into the trunk. Someone made him get in the trunk at gunpoint, then shot him. It's the perfect setup for your theory that Peyton was framed."

"Don't do me any favors."

"I'm not. I'm only trying to prove that my client was not involved."

"Then don't do it at my client's expense."

"I'm sorry if you don't like my approach," said Jennifer. "But it's my duty to watch out for my client. Especially a client who refuses to watch out for himself out of love for a wife who slept with the victim."

"She didn't sleep with Varne."

"Oh, come on, Tony. I know that even you don't believe that."

He stepped closer, looking her in the eye. "You think she killed him, don't you? That's what you're up to. You weren't in that courtroom today trying to prove it was a lone gunman. You're trying to prove it was a lone gun*woman*."

She gave him a serious look, no anger in her tone. Just conviction. "It's the prosecutor's job to prove it, Tony. But, yeah. I think she did it."

Tony watched as his wife headed for the door.

"Jennifer," he said, and she stopped.

"What now?" she said.

"You're not a prosecutor anymore."

"What's that supposed to mean?"

"You don't have to convict my client to acquit yours."

She considered his words and shot back a look that cut right through him. "Funny. I have the exact same worries about you." Then she turned and left the room.

59

PEYTON AND TONY HAD DINNER AT HIS OFFICE. PEYTON WAS IN NO hurry to go home to her parents, and she and Tony had plenty of work to do.

Ohn had introduced the government's final element of proof after the lunch break—a gun registration, showing that Peyton had owned a .38-caliber weapon, coupled with testimony from Detective Bolton that the gun was not found in the search of her apartment. With that, the prosecution rested. The defense argued motions for judgment of acquittal, urging the judge to throw out the case for insufficient proof. The judge listened patiently, then denied the motions. Tony gave the delayed opening statement on Peyton's behalf, and they adjourned at 5:00 P.M. with orders to reconvene at 9:00 A.M. for the start of the case for the defense.

"How deep of a hole am I in?" asked Peyton.

They were seated on opposite sides of the conference table, the city lights of downtown Boston glowing outside the big plate-glass window. Half-empty cartons of Chinese takeout cluttered the polished mahogany between them.

"He kept it simple," said Tony. "Your affair. Your argument with Kevin. The dead body found in your car. Your attempted suicide. The thirty-eight-caliber handgun missing from your apartment, which is exactly the type of weapon that killed Gary Varne. A completely circumstantial case, but it might be enough."

"That schoolteacher already has me convicted, I can tell."

"There's at least a couple others who I think are solid for us. Your schoolteacher might change her mind once she hears what they have to say back in the jury room."

"I don't want to wait that long. Hopefully I'll change her mind once she hears what I have to say."

Tony dropped his egg roll, then laid his chopsticks aside. "That's something we need to talk about."

"My testimony?"

"Whether you testify at all is the first question."

"You just said there's a chance I'll be convicted. I'm not going to let that happen without telling my side of the story."

"I fully understand your impulse. But there are two things I want to talk out with you before you commit to the idea of taking the stand in your own defense."

She drank her soda. "Go ahead."

"First, how are we going to handle the Gary Varne affair?"

"I'm going to say it never happened, of course."

"Well, not exactly. You're going to say that you invited your ex-lover out for a drink, that you went dancing, that you drank so much you don't even remember what happened, and that all you know is that you woke up the next afternoon in his apartment in his bed wearing only panties and his T-shirt."

"But we didn't have sex."

Tony rolled his head back, groaning. "No reasonable juror is ever going to *believe* that you didn't have sex."

"So what do you want me to say?" she said, scoffing. "That I had sex with Gary, even though I didn't?"

He just looked at her, stonefaced.

Peyton said, "You can't be serious."

"In my opinion, you need to look those jurors straight in the eye, admit to that affair, and tell them you regretted it. If you deny it, they won't believe another word out of your mouth."

"You expect me to lie under oath and admit to an affair I never had?"

"Your alternative is to not testify at all."

"My alternative is to take the stand and tell the truth."

"That's a fine option, if your objective is to be convicted and spend twenty-five years in the state penitentiary."

Peyton leaned into the table, pressing her point. "Look, you're my lawyer, but on this point I don't care what you say. I'm going to testify, and never in a million years am I going to admit to something I didn't do."

"I had a feeling that would be your reaction."

"Well, you guessed right. So let's move on to the next problem."

"I'm not sure this one's any easier."

"What?"

"Is your husband going to testify?"

"I don't know. I assume so."

"I ask because it's an important strategy point. If our joint defense were as solid as it once was, we'd be coordinating these decisions more closely. You don't want one defendant to take the stand if another isn't going to testify. Looks bad to the jury."

"I'm sure that if you ask Jennifer, she'll tell you."

"My question wasn't whether or not we can *ask* them. I was getting more to the question of influence."

"What do you mean?"

"If you want to testify, you'd better have him on board."

"What are you saying, exactly?"

"If you're going to testify, he's going to testify. And if he's going to testify, you had better know what he's going to say."

Peyton sighed. "We haven't really even spoken since I moved in with my parents."

"That's my point. If you want to testify, you've got some work to do, lady."

Her gaze drifted toward distant city lights outside the window. "You're telling me."

★..★..★

Kevin and Jennifer worked through the dinner hour without dinner. Kevin hadn't had much of an appetite since Peyton left him, and Jennifer didn't eat much in general. Tough decisions were the only things on the menu.

"Personally, I like things the way they are," said Jennifer.

"How do you mean?"

"The case against you is virtually nonexistent. All they have is Sandra Blair saying that you stormed away from your argument with Peyton looking as if you could kill someone. Honestly, I can't understand why Judge Gilhorn didn't grant our motion for a judgment of acquittal."

"So when you say you're happy with the way things are, you mean the way things are for me?"

"Of course."

"What about for Peyton?"

"I don't represent Peyton."

"I know. I'm just curious to know if you think she's in trouble."

"That's not for me or you to worry about. Peyton's troubles are Tony's problem."

"So you do think she's in trouble?"

"More trouble than you are, that's for sure."

"I want to help her, if I can."

Jennifer massaged the bridge of her nose, as if a migraine were coming on. "That's going to be difficult, Kevin. Because my advice to you is not to take the stand. I'm hoping that I can persuade Tony to give his client the same recommendation."

"Why don't you think I should testify?"

"The case against you is so weak, you can only hurt yourself. Lawyers in general make lousy witnesses. But beyond that, if you testify, we'll have to get into the whole kidnapping issue and possible blackmailing. It will only give Ohn more ammunition."

"But that may be Peyton's only shot. She has to convince the jury she's being framed."

"Granted, that's a tough spot for her. But if you take the stand, you're going to create a tough spot of your own."

"What?"

She looked at him coldly, as if suddenly assuming the role of prosecutor. "Mr. Stokes, where were you the night Gary Varne was killed?"

He lowered his eyes. "You're right. Tough spot." And then he told her.

60

PEYTON WENT HOME FROM TONY'S OFFICE, TO HER REAL HOME, where Kevin slept alone these days. If she was going to testify, Tony wanted it to be first thing tomorrow morning, giving the prosecutor as little time as possible to prepare his cross-examination. That gave her even less time to clear the air with Kevin.

It was a weird feeling, walking tentatively up the front steps and knocking on her own front door. One moment it felt as though she'd never lived there, the next, as if she still did. She almost chickened out, but the door swung open.

"Peyton," Kevin said, standing in the open doorway. It seemed like a reflex, the way he'd uttered her name.

"Tony thinks we should talk."

"So do I." He stepped aside, inviting her to pass.

She hesitated, then entered. Kevin helped her with her coat, almost too eagerly. "Can I get you something?"

She didn't really want anything, but he had such a hopeful look on his face. It would have seemed cruel to say no. "Is there any of that carrot-tangerine juice left?"

"Of course. Nobody drinks it but you and Florida rabbits."

They shared a weak smile as she followed him to the kitchen. He poured the juice and offered her a chair. She stood at the kitchen counter.

"No, thanks. This shouldn't take too long."

"You sure? You hungry? I've got some . . ." He flipped open the refrigerator. "Olives."

"I'm not hungry.

"How about—"

"Kevin, I'm planning to testify tomorrow."

He closed the refrigerator door and walked to the side of the kitchen counter opposite her. "I can't say that surprises me."

"Do you disagree with my decision?"

"It's not my decision to make."

"You know what I'm saying. I'm sure Jennifer gave you the same speech that Tony gave me."

"I have a feeling mine was a little different."

"What do you mean?"

"Nothing. Whatever you decide, I'm completely behind it. In truth, I was undecided as to what I would do. But if you're going to testify, I imagine I will too."

"I just want us to be clear on this. My decision to testify isn't going to create a problem for you that you can't solve, is it?"

He hemmed and hawed, but gave no verbal answer.

"Is that a yes or no?" she asked, concerned.

He looked away, then back. "The night Gary Varne was killed, you and I had a fight. I walked out, remember?"

"Yes, I remember."

"I don't have an alibi."

"Neither do I."

"But you can tell the jury that you stayed home all night. It's going to be a bit more difficult for me to explain where I ended up."

For a moment, she couldn't speak. Her eyes were like lasers. "You told me you were with her only once."

"Who?"

"You swore that you and Sandra were together only that one night last winter."

"We were."

"Don't try to backpedal now."

"You got it all wrong. That's not what I was trying to say."

"You must take me for a fool." She turned and headed for the foyer.

"Peyton, wait."

Angrily, she pulled on her coat. "You know, last night I was thinking that maybe you made a mistake. Maybe you really did regret it. Maybe I could forgive you for just one indiscretion. But the lies just keep coming, don't they? I don't even know why I bothered coming here."

"But I wasn't with Sandra. Not that night."

She wheeled and said, "Then where were you?"

"Jennifer says . . ." He hesitated, seeming to struggle. "It's best that you just not know."

Her anger swelled as she flung open the door. "Damn you!" she shouted, slamming the door on her way out.

At ten-thirty Charles Ohn was relaxing in his La-Z-Boy in front of the television, just himself, a beer, a big bag of pretzels, and ESPN. Tonight was his favorite, the *World Series of Poker*. Ohn was probably the hardest-working prosecutor in Boston, and coming home after ten to unwind in front of the television was pretty much his nightly routine since the divorce six months ago. In fact, it had also been his nightly routine before the divorce, which his wife had pointed out quite loudly before closing the book for good on their twelve years of marriage.

The phone rang. Ohn dug out the portable from between the seat cushions. It was Jennifer Dunwoody. "Congratulations on surviving the motions for acquittal this afternoon," she said.

Ohn lowered the volume on the TV with the remote. "Oh, thanks. But it's hardly something to be congratulated on. If a prosecutor can't build a strong enough case to keep the judge from throwing the case out before the defendants even put on a defense, he's not much of a prosecutor."

He thought he heard a little chuckle in her voice, but perhaps it was just his own insecurity. After all, it was Jennifer's husband who had coined his nickname, the "Ohn-anator." Ohn had actually embraced it at first, thinking it a play on Schwarzenegger's *The Terminator.* Finally, someone told him about Onan, a biblical figure whose name had become synonymous with masturbation.

"To be honest," said Jennifer, "I thought the motion should have been granted as to my client."

"If that's what this call is about, there's a little game of Texas Hold 'Em that I'd like to get back to watching."

"Actually, I'm trying to decide whether to put Stokes on the stand."

She suddenly had his undivided attention.

"Talk to me."

"Well, there are a couple of possibilities."

"There always are," said Ohn. "Either he testifies or he doesn't."

"This one has a little wrinkle to it. If he takes the stand, he could testify as part of his defense. Or he could testify as part of your rebuttal."

"Are you saying that he's willing to testify against his wife?"

"He says he'll never do that. But I say you never know. I just want to be able to advise my client of all his options. So I'm just checking to see if that deal you offered earlier could perhaps be back on the table."

Ohn glanced at the television set. His favorite player had just bet everything on a pair of aces. "Sorry, Jennifer. The offer no longer stands."

"What?"

"No deals. I'm taking them both down."

"All right," said Jennifer. "We'll see about that."

"Yes, we will," said Ohn. "Soon enough."

At 11:00 P.M., Rudy was online, back in the usual chat room, trolling for Ladydoc.

He hated himself for doing it. She didn't deserve another chance, not the way she'd stood him up last night for the second time. It wasn't his nature to be so forgiving, and it made him wonder about the balance of power in their relationship. Not that it was anything to beat himself up about. He had the upper hand: He knew where she lived. She might have thought she could get rid of him just by exiting a chat room, or by changing her screen name, or by being a no-show at their real-life rendezvous. Others had made that same mistake before. The last little bitch who'd tried to blow him off had revealed so much about herself online that Rudy even knew she kept a pitcher of banana smoothies in the refrigerator at work for lunch. Dressed as a deliveryman, he dropped by her office, sneaked his way to the kitchen, locked the door, jerked his load into her smoothie, and put it back in the fridge. Who had the power there? *Drink that banana, baby.*

Disgusting, yes, but it wasn't the smoothie that had killed her.

The computer screen glowed in the darkness, a blank white page with only a blinking cursor to keep him company. He typed nothing, just watched and waited. Two minutes past eleven o'clock, the message he'd hoped for flashed on the screen.

Ladydoc has entered the room.

The anger turned to excitement. It was just the two of them in their private chat room.

"u came," he typed.

"of course."

"don't say of course. u stood me up last night."

"sorry."

He waited for more, but he knew it wouldn't come. She hadn't offered any explanations last winter either. Just a no-show at their agreed-upon meeting, then one final chat where she dumped him, supposedly for good. And then the swim in Jamaica Pond.

Don't even think of dumping me this time.

"is that all you can say, sorry?"

"Let's see. How can i possibly make it up 2 u?"

"u know how."

"u want me to sing u love songs?

"no."

"u want me to recite poetry?"

"wrong again."

"u want me to suck your big cock?"

"ahhhhhhhh."

"is it out now?"

"yes."

"i want it all the way out."

"it's all there for u."

His hands were off the keys. It had been so long since the last time that in just thirty seconds he was on the verge of climax. He touched himself with the left hand and fumbled through the desk drawer with the right, sifting through scores of photos he'd secretly taken of Peyton over the last eighteen months, searching for just the right one to spray with excitement.

A sentence was building on the screen, catching his eye.

"something's come up. gotta go now."

He dropped everything. "wait!"

"must go right now. catch me tomorrow nite in the movie chats."

"NO!"

"i promise. tomorrow nite for sure."

"u bitch!"

"tomorrow. i promise, i promise."

"Don't do this to me again!"

He stared at the empty screen. She was gone.

"Damn you!" he shouted, nearly rattling the windows. He yanked out the drawer full of Peyton photographs and hurled it across the room. Hundreds of snapshots scattered across the floor—Peyton jogging, Peyton walking to work, Peyton eating lunch at a sidewalk café.

Peyton on her way to Gary Varne's apartment.

With each hand he grabbed a fistful of hair and pulled till it hurt, grimacing to the point where he could no longer stand it, then screaming at the top of his lungs. He released his grip, ending the self-flagellation. A series of deep, noisy breaths followed as he calmed himself.

"That's it," he said softly, staring at the computer screen. "It's time."

61

PEYTON FELT CHILLS AS HER LAWYER ROSE TO SPEAK IN A PACKED BUT hushed courtroom.

"The defense calls the defendant, Dr. Peyton Shields."

After weeks of being portrayed as an adulteress in the newspapers, after being doubted by her lawyer and even her own husband, Peyton wanted nothing more than to tell her side of the story. That someday she'd vindicate herself had been her driving force through the lowest points. As she approached the stand, however, she was gripped by the dark reality that the world might never believe her.

"Do you swear to tell the truth, the whole truth . . ."

The oath had seemed so mechanical when she'd watched other witnesses swear it, but it was something else altogether to hear the bailiff put those words to her in front of the judge, the jury, her lawyer, her husband, her parents, a hungry press, and scores of spectators. With all those eyes upon her, she wondered how anyone ever lied on a witness stand. That nervous moment, on the verge of her personal plea to a jury of her peers, confirmed an unshakable truth about herself: She wasn't made of the stuff that liars were made of.

Her lawyer approached, cordial but professional. First he covered her background, particularly her decision to devote herself to children and pediatrics. It was a way of endearing the jurors to her while making her feel comfortable. Soon, however, the warm fuzzies were over.

"Dr. Shields, the last thing we heard from the government before the close of their case yesterday is that you owned a thirty-eight caliber handgun. When did you buy that weapon?"

"Last winter." Her voice cracked. The first substantive question, and already she had a lump in her throat.

"Why did you buy it?"

"One night, when my husband was out of town on business, I thought I heard someone picking at the lock on our front door."

"So you bought it for your own personal safety?"

"That's correct."

"Did you ever discharge it?"

"I took a safety course that included target practice. My last class was, I believe, February. That was the last time I ever fired it."

"What did you do with it?"

"I kept it stored in a metal box that was on the shelf in my closet. I put it in there and, I swear, never touched it again."

"Why wasn't it there when the police came looking for it after Gary Varne's death?"

"I can't explain it. All I can say is that it must have been stolen."

Tony paused, as if to let the jurors absorb the testimony. Judge Gilhorn grumbled like a bear waking from hibernation, waving the lawyers forward. Both Tony and the prosecutor stepped toward the bench for a sidebar, outside the earshot of the jury. From the witness stand Peyton was close enough to overhear the judge's scolding.

"Mr. Falcone, I granted your pretrial motion to prevent the government from offering into evidence those so-called love letters that were found in the box when the police went searching for the gun. With this suggestion that someone tampered with the box and stole the gun, you're about one question away from making me change my mind. Understood?"

"Understood."

The lawyers retreated, Ohn to his table and Tony to his place before his client. He steered Peyton directly into her "other life" with Gary Varne, how they'd dated in high school and then crossed paths again at Children's Hospital— friendly, but just coworkers. Then it was time to explain how she'd ended up in Gary's apartment, starting with her surprise visit to Kevin in New York and the horrible mistake she'd made in thinking that her husband had been sharing a hotel room with another woman.

"What did you do when you got back to Boston?"

"The last thing I felt like doing was going home to our apartment. So I went to the hospital, a way of losing myself in my work."

"And you saw Mr. Varne there?"

"Yes. He happened to be on duty, and we started talking. He could see that I was upset. Like I said, we were friends, so we decided to leave work and cheer me up a little bit."

Peyton glanced at the jurors. One or two seemed to have their own damning opinion as to where this "cheering up" would lead.

"So you went to a bar?"

"First we went for coffee. That was my idea. Then we met up with some friends of his at a bar. That was Gary's idea."

"Do you recall how many drinks you had?"

"Not exactly. It didn't seem like that many, but in hindsight I can say that it was definitely one too many. I was tired and feeling pretty low. I had just flown back from New York thinking my husband had cheated on me."

"About what time did you leave the last bar?"

"All I remember is that I started to feel really bad around two A.M., so we left. From then on, I don't remember anything."

"What is the next thing you do remember?"

"Waking up in Gary's apartment. The next afternoon."

The crowd murmured. Steve Beasley's testimony had given some insights, but these were new details, juicy ones at that.

Peyton's pulse quickened. She dreaded the next couple of questions, but at last night's rehearsal Tony had assured her that if she was going to tell the whole truth, it was better to bring the sordid details out on direct rather than to let Ohn extract it on cross.

"Exactly where were you in his apartment?"

"I was in his bed, alone. Gary had slept on the couch."

"Were you dressed?"

"Yes. Partly."

"What were you wearing?"

"My panties. And one of Gary's T-shirts."

The crowd's rumbling grew louder. The judge gaveled them down. "Order."

Tony continued. "I have to say, this is starting to sound like an embarrassing situation."

"It's not what it sounds like. Gary explained everything the next morning. He told me—"

"Objection," shouted Ohn. "The witness has testified that she has no recollection of what happened after she reached Gary Varne's apartment. Her understanding of how she ended up half-naked in the victim's bed is based solely on what Gary Varne told her. That's hearsay."

"Sustained."

Peyton looked at Tony, distressed that the jury might not hear Gary's own admission that they hadn't had sex, that she'd gotten sick, and that he'd simply cleaned her clothes for her.

"But, Your Honor," said Tony, almost pleading.

"The objection was sustained. Next question, please."

Peyton caught the judge's eye, and at that moment she realized Tony had been right. He'd predicted that the jury wouldn't believe that she hadn't slept with Gary. Evidently, the judge was of the same opinion.

Reluctantly, Tony moved on to Gary's hostility toward her after their night together, the argument over the rose she'd found taped to her locker, the theft of her computer from the library. Then it was on to the heart of her defense.

"Dr. Shields, we heard Sandra Blair testify about the argument she overheard between you and your husband at the Harvard cocktail party. What was that all about?"

"Kevin had heard false rumors about me and Gary, and he confronted me in the hallway. I denied that anything had happened between us, but I didn't think a hallway was the place to discuss it. When I wouldn't get into it, he got angry and left without me."

"So you went home alone?"

"Yes. I waited up late for him to come home, but he didn't. Around eleven o'clock I got a couple of hang-up phone calls. It scared me, so I stayed up watching television till pretty late."

"Then what?"

"The phone rang, and I woke up in front of the television. It was after four A.M."

"Who was it?"

"I don't know. A man's voice that I didn't recognize."

"What did he say?"

Peyton braced herself for another hearsay objection from Ohn, but he seemed just as rapt as everyone else in the courtroom, too curious to interrupt.

"He told me to check my mail, then hung up."

"Did you check it?"

"Yes. I found an envelope in the foyer that someone had dropped through the slot. I opened it right away."

"What was in it?"

She swallowed the lump in her throat and said, "A lock of human hair."

That drew a loud crowd reaction. "Order," the judge said, banging the gavel.

"What happened next?"

Her voice shook as she recounted the lights going out and the call on her cell phone. "I found my way to the bedroom and answered it. It was the same voice as before."

"What did he tell you this time?"

"He said he'd kidnapped Gary Varne and demanded a ten-thousand-dollar ransom."

Ohn looked shocked, too stunned even to object. Peyton tried to ignore the crowd noises and stay focused.

Tony asked, "Pay him ten thousand dollars or he'd do what?"

She stole a quick glance at Kevin. Only she knew him well enough to see how much this pained him. "He said he'd kill Gary and tell my husband that we were lovers."

"What was your reaction?"

"A combination of fear for Gary's life and anger that I was being accused of being his lover, when I wasn't. Beyond that, pure shock. He gave me a couple of days to come up with the money, and then he hung up."

"Did you call the police?"

"No. He said that if I called the police, he'd kill Gary."

"So what did you do?"

"Kevin came home around dawn, and we talked it out. He was convinced from the get-go that Gary had staged the whole supposed kidnapping and had simply made the phone call himself, essentially trying to blackmail us. So we agreed not to pay."

Peyton saw her lawyer wince at her mention of blackmail. It was the added motive that he'd tried desperately not to serve up to the prosecution on the proverbial silver platter.

"Did you discuss the part about you and Gary supposedly being lovers?"

"I told Kevin it wasn't true. He said even if it was true, he'd forgiven me."

"Did you hear again from this supposed kidnapper?"

"Two days later he called me at work. Said I'd better have the money by midnight or he'd kill Gary."

"Did you get the money?"

"No. Kevin and I were still convinced that it was just Gary harassing us. But we agreed that if I got one more threatening phone call, we'd go to the police."

"Did you get another phone call?"

"No. Kevin and I waited till after the midnight deadline, but we never heard a thing."

"So then what? Did you and Kevin go to bed?"

"I think the stress was finally getting to us. We had an argument. Kevin went out."

"For how long?"

"The rest of the night."

She glanced at her husband, then at the prosecutor. Ohn seemed to be making a note of Kevin's second disappearance.

"What did you do?"

"I went to bed and didn't sleep very well. I had to be at work early, so around five-something I walked to my car as usual, got inside."

Her voice was fading. For eight weeks, Tony had downplayed the kidnapping as something he didn't want to talk about, and Peyton had suppressed it. Now, it was flooding back with her in-court description of the man's hand over her mouth, the image in the rearview mirror, the man in the backseat behind the ski mask.

"He asked if I'd gotten the money. I tried to tell him that I *could* get it, but he just wanted a yes or no answer to his question: Did I get the money? I told him no."

"Then what?"

"He told me, 'Good for you, Peyton. You made the right call.'" She paused, her voice shaking, eyes clouded. Last night's rehearsal had ended right there, but almost involuntarily she added, "It was as if he was saying that it was the right decision to let Gary die."

Tony paused for effect. "Tell us what happened next."

"He put a rag over my mouth. I could smell the chloroform. And then I was out."

"What's the next thing you remember?"

"Waking up in the hospital. Kevin was there. He told me the police had found me in my car with a spilled bottle of sleeping pills. And then the police came," she said, displaying a touch of emotion. "They said Gary was dead. His body was in the trunk of my car."

Tony took a step back, and Peyton prepared herself for the strong finish they'd rehearsed.

"Dr. Shields, did you have an affair with Gary Varne?"

"No."

"Did you kill Gary Varne?"

"No, I did not."

"Did you assist in any way in the disposal of Mr. Varne's body?"

"No, I did not."

"Do you have any idea who this man was who abducted you?"

She did a double take. At their rehearsal, he hadn't asked about the possible identity of her abductor, and the change unsettled her. "No," she said, feeling shivers across her body. "But he seemed strangely familiar."

"How so?"

Perhaps it was the courtroom setting, perhaps it was the fact that she was under oath and searching every ounce of her inner self for the truth. But she was suddenly convinced that the man in the ski mask was the "Good Samaritan" who'd pulled her from Jamaica Pond. She looked at no one in particular and said, "It was as if I'd looked into his eyes before."

Slowly, with all of the jurors watching, Tony turned his entire body away from Peyton and toward her husband, seated at the table, letting his judgmental gaze rest on Kevin.

Peyton replayed in her mind those final words—*It was as if I'd looked into his eyes before*—and nearly choked on Tony's implied accusation. She wanted to retract her testimony or explain what she'd meant, but it had taken a second too long for her to fully appreciate the stunt her own lawyer was pulling.

"Thank you, Dr. Shields," said Tony. "Nothing further."

Peyton looked at Kevin, saw the mortified look of betrayal on his face. She glanced at the judge, her eyes emitting a silent but desperate scream, *Wait! There's something I need to say.*

"Mr. Ohn," said the judge, "cross-examination please."

Her heart sank further as the prosecutor stepped forward. She took one look into his burning eyes and knew that it was too late to explain herself now, too late for backpedaling.

The easy part hadn't been so easy. The hard part had just begun.

62

PEYTON COULD HEAR HERSELF BREATHING; THE COURTROOM WAS that quiet.

The prosecutor walked slowly toward her and stopped, hands on his hips. He locked eyes with the witness and said nothing, as if sizing her up, a slithering python poised to take her in one gulp. Peyton met his stare for a moment, but she could feel herself losing the battle of nerves. She looked away and saw Kevin, confusion all over his face. She tried to send a silent signal that she had no intention of burying her own husband, but the sharp sound of Ohn's voice snapped her back to attention.

"Nothing happened." His voice boomed, then seemed to drift into a softer but sarcastic tone. "And you woke up half-naked in another man's bed."

Peyton wasn't sure if Ohn wanted a response, but letting his words linger only made her feel more uncomfortable. "Yes," she replied, her voice weaker than intended.

"You were not wearing pajamas?"

"No."

"Your pants had been removed."

"Yes."

"No bra?"

"No."

"You were wearing only panties."

"And a T-shirt."

"*His* T-shirt, correct?"

"Yes."

He flashed a thin, sardonic smile. "And nothing happened."

"I tried to explain. You wouldn't let me."

"Kind of speaks for itself," he said, glancing at the jury.

Anger forced the words out. "I got sick on tequila, and Gary washed my clothes."

He glared, as if to shove the little mouse back in her hole, as if threatening her with much worse if she ever jammed him like that again.

"Right down to your underwear, you got sick, huh?"

"I was very drunk, so I don't really know how sick I got."

"You have no memory, so you're giving us Gary's morning-after explanation."

"That's correct."

"Which is why the judge sustained my objection earlier. But now that it's out in the open, let's deal with it. You didn't make love to Gary Varne that night, did you?"

She was taken aback, confused as to why he suddenly seemed to be on her side. "That's right. I didn't."

"But he wanted to have sex with you, didn't he?"

"I don't know."

"He was your old boyfriend, right?"

"Yes."

"He took you out to drown your sorrows."

"I guess you could say that."

"He got you so drunk that you don't even remember how much you drank."

"We had too much, yes."

"He took you back to his apartment."

"Right."

"And all you know is that the next morning, you were practically naked in his bed."

"That's true."

"And he told you that you'd gotten sick on tequila."

"Right."

He started to pace, then came to a sudden halt, as if a thought had come to him. "Now, you didn't go home and tell your husband about this, did you?"

"No."

"In fact, you didn't tell him anything until that night Sandra Blair overheard you two arguing, when your husband confronted you."

She lowered her eyes. This was the part she wasn't proud of. "That's true."

"You didn't tell him, because you knew he would be angry."

"The whole thing looked like something it wasn't. I was afraid he wouldn't understand."

"And when you finally did tell him, he was indeed angry."

"Yes."

"He was so angry that he didn't even come home from the cocktail party that night."

"True."

"And that was the same night this supposed kidnapper called to say he had Gary Varne."

She hesitated, but there was only one truthful answer. "Yes."

"And a couple days later, you and your husband had another fight."

"An argument, yes."

"He got so mad that he left the house."

"Right."

"That was the same night Gary Varne was found dead in your car."

Again she hesitated, knowing that things weren't looking good for Kevin. "Same night."

"What a night," he said, sneering. "The night Varne was killed. The night your husband stormed out of your apartment. That was the night you told Kevin the truth about Gary Varne, isn't it?"

"I told him that we hadn't done anything."

"You told him you'd gone drinking with Gary."

"Yes."

"You told him you went back to his apartment."

"I admitted that."

"You told him that you didn't remember anything but waking up in his bed."

"That's the truth."

He moved closer, eyes burning. "You told him that Gary Varne had tried to rape you."

"I object!" shouted Tony. "There is no evidence in the record to support an accusatory question like that."

"Join!" said Jennifer.

Peyton was aghast. A buzz filled the courtroom.

"Order!" shouted the judge. "Counsel, in my chambers!"

The judge walked angrily off the bench, and the lawyers followed him through the side exit.

Judge Gilhorn was leaning back against the front of his huge desk, arms folded across his chest in anger. He was glaring at the prosecutor.

Tony could barely speak. "This has to be a mistrial."

The judge raised his hand, silencing him. "Mr. Ohn, explain yourself."

He seemed perplexed by everyone's anger. "Dr. Shields testified that she had no recollection of the night at Varne's apartment. Obviously I wasn't aware of her lack of memory until she testified here at trial. So it was only today that I made the connection between her memory loss and other evidence that Mr. Varne drugged Dr. Shields with the intent to rape her."

"What other evidence?" asked Tony.

"The police search of Varne's apartment after the recovery of his body turned up an opened bottle of Rohypnol."

"Roofies, the club drug?" said Tony. "Why weren't we told before trial?"

"Because it wasn't relevant to any of the issues in the case. Until now."

Tony nearly exploded. "My client was found unconscious in the front seat of her car. How could *any* drug on the victim's premises not be relevant?"

"Its only relevance is to show Mr. Stokes's motive for murder."

Jennifer jumped in, appalled. "So now *my* client is the triggerman? How many times do you intend to change theories in this case?"

Ohn ignored the lawyers and addressed the judge directly. "Your Honor, this theory didn't jell till today, but it's clear now what happened. Mr. Stokes was furious to hear that Varne had drugged his wife with the intent to rape her. He killed Varne with the help of his wife. Dr. Shields tried to dispose of the body and ended up trying to take her own life with sleeping pills, driven probably by a combination of depression from the date rape and guilt for her role in the murder. Together the defendants then fabricated the existence of a mysterious kidnapper as their defense. Mr. Stokes was the triggerman. Dr. Shields is at the very least an accessory after the fact, probably an accomplice."

"This is absolutely prosecutorial bad faith and misconduct," said Tony.

"It's what happened," said Ohn, snapping. "I've acted in complete good faith."

The judge drummed his fingers on the desktop, thinking. "I suppose there really is no way for Mr. Ohn to have known about Dr. Shields's memory loss until after she testified."

"They should have told us about the roofies. It's a mistrial at least."

"I'd ask for a judgment of acquittal," said Jennifer.

Again the judge raised a hand, quieting them both. "Mr. Ohn, you really should have told them about the roofies."

"But—"

He stopped him, then continued. "This case has come too far

for me to do anything hasty. Therefore I will allow the prosecution to pursue this line of questioning within limits. Mr. Ohn can argue that Dr. Shields was drugged with the intent to rape. But there is to be no mention of the bottle of roofies found at Mr. Varne's apartment."

Tony groaned. "Judge, that's not enough."

"It's as far as I'm going. For now. Everyone back in the courtroom."

"All rise."

Peyton felt a strange sense of relief as the judge and lawyers returned to the courtroom. During their brief absence she'd felt on display, like a scorned adulteress locked in the stockade in the old town square. Five minutes had seemed like five hours. She'd been alone on the witness stand, no one to talk to, the obvious object of everyone's speculation.

She caught Tony's eye, hoping for some signal that the cross-examination was over. A tightness gripped her chest as she watched him return to his seat beside Kevin and Jennifer. Ohn reassumed his position before her and, with the judge's approval, resumed his attack.

"Dr. Shields, you are a medical doctor, are you not?"

Her throat had gone completely dry. "Yes."

"You've heard of date-rape drugs, haven't you?"

She glanced at Tony, confused. "Of course."

"You're aware that they are easily dissolved in cocktails."

"Some are."

"A person could drink it with a mixed drink, never even taste the drug."

"True."

"Most women don't even realize they've been drugged until it's too late."

"That's true."

"Isn't a loss of memory consistent with the effects of certain so-called date-rape drugs?"

She hesitated, now sensing where this was headed. "It can be."

Ohn took a few steps closer to the jury, as if they were on the same side in this contest, with Peyton as the lone opposition. "Getting back to that night you went drinking with Gary Varne and his friends and ended up back in his apartment. Was one of Mr. Varne's friends a woman?"

"Yes. Liz was her name."

"Let's assume, as you say, you got sick on tequila. Didn't you find it the least bit suspicious that Mr. Varne took you home himself and undressed you himself, rather than enlisting the help of this female friend you met at the club?"

"I don't know if he did or not. All I know is what Mr. Varne told me. I don't remember what happened."

"Precisely," said Ohn, his voice rising. "And isn't that loss of memory consistent with the effects of the club drug roofies?"

The courtroom was still. For Peyton, it was as if the lights had finally switched on. She couldn't speak, and she knew it was written all over her face—the realization that perhaps she had been drugged by Gary Varne. Still she was cautious, figuring it was information that Ohn intended somehow to turn against her.

"As a doctor, don't you think I would have known I'd been drugged?"

"Without a doubt," said the prosecutor. "And as a wife, you would have shared that information with one very angry husband."

Peyton, the judge, the jurors—everyone—followed the prosecutor's eyes as they cut across the courtroom. It was as if Peyton had built her own huge house of suspicion. And then dropped it squarely on Kevin.

Ohn started toward his chair, then stopped. "Just one more thought. Your husband had a set of keys to the car, I assume."

"Of course."

"A key to the trunk?"

"Yes."

"Thank you, Dr. Shields. You've been very helpful."

Before her very eyes, Kevin seemed to shrink beneath the weight of suspicious stares. She looked away, toward the back of the courtroom, and froze. She'd only seen it for a split second, an instant that had passed so quickly that the image had barely registered in her mind. She blinked, not quite comprehending, then took a deep breath to stop herself from shaking.

What she'd seen had chilled her. Or at least what she thought she'd seen.

63

AT THE END OF A HORRIBLE DAY, PEYTON JUST WANTED TO BE ALONE. Tony insisted on a strategy session back at the office—a joint meeting with both defendants and their lawyers.

They rode in the same car from the courthouse, but the show of solidarity was only for the benefit of the press. So far they'd managed to keep it out of the newspapers that Peyton had moved in with her parents, but riding in separate cars would have been a clear sign of division.

On Tony's order, no one talked in the car—for about thirty seconds. Jennifer couldn't contain herself. She reached over from the passenger seat and switched off the elevator music Tony had been playing in the hopes of calming everyone down.

"This whole thing started with your boneheaded direct examination," she snapped.

Tony kept his eyes on the blinking taillights ahead of him. "It wasn't boneheaded."

"You clearly were trying to create the impression through Peyton's testimony that the man in the ski mask was Kevin."

"Not *was*. Could have been, might have been. All I'm trying to do is create reasonable doubt."

"But you keep doing it at my client's expense."

"What I did is entirely consistent with your opening statement: If the jury concludes that either one of the defendants might have done it, they have to acquit. At the close of the government's case, the balance was tilting too heavily toward Peyton. I just shifted it a little."

"A little!" said Jennifer, nearly shrieking.

Peyton interjected from the backseat. "Can we please stop the bickering?"

An uneasy silence fell over them as the car stopped at the red light.

Peyton looked at Kevin and said, "I want you to know that I had nothing do with pointing the finger back at you. I don't mind saying this in front of my own lawyer, but his conduct in that courtroom came as a total surprise to me."

Tony grumbled, "Sharper than the serpent's tooth . . ."

"Tony, shut up," said Peyton.

"I saw it on your face," said Kevin. "I knew it wasn't your doing."

She left it at that, and so did the lawyers. The traffic light changed, and they continued their ride in silence. Tony battled the Friday evening traffic without so much as a cross word at a road-hogging cabbie. Peyton opened her window a crack, breathing in the cool autumn air.

Finally Kevin said, "I wasn't totally surprised by the roofies."

Jennifer shot him a hush sign. Peyton pretended not to have seen it. "Why do you say that?" asked Peyton.

"Because of Varne's background."

"Oh, jeez," said Jennifer, obviously trying to convince her client to shut his mouth.

He continued. "I ran a background check on him after that first call from the kidnapper. I wanted to see if he was the kind of sick puppy who might pull this kidnapping stunt."

Peyton went cold. "If you're about to tell me that you knew he was a rapist and still let Ohn paint me as an adulteress, Tony will be defending me on another homicide."

"It's not that at all. But knowing what we know now, it might be something you'd construe as predatory conduct."

"What?"

"Gary had a history of hitting on married women. My investigator got all excited about it, thinking he was on the verge of proving that he had a pattern of blackmail. But after interviewing a few of his past conquests, he concluded that Gary simply got off on the thrill of sleeping with other men's wives."

"Why didn't you tell me this before?"

"Because I honestly didn't start to think of that behavior as predatory—at least not to the degree of date rape—until after Ohn mentioned roofies." He lowered his eyes, then added, "And because if I had told you, I also would have had to tell you that . . ."

"Enough," said Jennifer. "As your lawyer, I'm advising you not to go there."

"Tell me what?" asked Peyton, pressing.

He looked at her soulfully. She could see in his eyes how tired he was of all the half-truths, the concealment, the suspicions inherent in being codefendants. "Do you remember the other day when I said I couldn't tell you where I went the night Gary Varne was murdered?"

"Yes."

"And you thought it was because I'd gone to see Sandra."

She suddenly felt sick, now wishing he *had* gone to see Sandra. "Don't tell me."

"The reason I couldn't tell you where I'd gone is because I went to Gary's apartment."

"Before or after he was dead?"

"About one A.M. After you and I had our argument, I went for a beer. That's when my investigator called me on my cell and told me about Gary's past. I decided I wanted to talk to Gary myself."

"Are you saying you actually saw him the night he died?"

"No. He wasn't there. So I waited outside. For hours I waited for him to come home."

"What did you intend to do?" Peyton asked tentatively.

Jennifer said, "You've said enough, Kevin."

"I didn't kill him, I swear. But my investigator told me what an operator he was, and you'd told me how you'd turned to him as a friend in a time of distress and ended up drunk and practically naked in his apartment. Well, like I said, I didn't kill him. But in hindsight, I'm glad he wasn't there."

"I understand."

"But hear what I'm saying. I wasn't going to kill him, but I didn't go there to talk to him either. Surely you can appreciate how a jury might get the wrong idea from that."

"I'm your wife. You should have told me."

"Oh, absolutely," said Jennifer, sarcastic. "That way, when the prosecutor asks you where Kevin was on the night of the murder, you can happily say that you refuse to answer the question on the grounds of marital privilege. That'll make you both sound very innocent, won't it?"

"Obviously it was something that Jennifer thought I should keep to myself," Kevin said, as if apologizing for having followed his lawyer's advice.

Peyton touched his hand and said, "I'm glad you finally told me. But there's something else everyone here should know too."

"What?" asked Kevin.

"Gary may have been some kind of predator, as you say. And I may have been drugged. But I wasn't raped."

Tony said, "That's probably because you really did get sick. Rape is more about power than sex, but tequila vomit has a way of turning a guy off, even a rapist."

It was typical gruff Tony-style delivery, but no one disagreed with the logic.

Tony steered into the parking garage, then pulled into his reserved spot and killed the engine. All four of them stayed put for a moment, as Tony seemed poised to say something.

"Let me be brutally honest," he said. "From the day you two came into my office, I didn't buy this kidnapping defense. I still don't know if you're being truthful or if the two of you are deserving of Academy Awards. I do know one thing, though. If you don't come up with some convincing evidence of exactly *who* this kidnapper is, come next week your theory is going straight down the jury room toilet. And you're both going down with it."

Peyton was reluctant to speak up, still not sure of what she'd seen. But time was running out. "I think I might have seen him today."

"When?"

"At the end of my testimony. While just about everyone in the entire courtroom was looking at Kevin, I had the strange sense that someone was staring intently at me. I looked up and for about a nanosecond I could have sworn I was looking into those same eyes."

"Whose eyes?"

"The man in the ski mask. The Good Samaritan who'd pulled me from Jamaica Pond."

"Are you sure?" asked Kevin.

She shrugged weakly. "It was from all the way in the back of the courtroom, but that's the way it hit me."

"I got a better question," said Tony. "Even if it was the same guy, does that give you any sense of who the hell he is?"

She looked out the window, seeing her weak reflection in the dark sedan beside them. "I'm afraid not," she said, her voice fading.

64

KEVIN WAS DISAPPOINTED BUT NOT SURPRISED. HE'D HOPED THAT THE truth-telling session in the backseat of Tony's car would have restored some of the broken trust between him and Peyton. He sensed that it had, but unfortunately not enough to bring her back home. At least not tonight.

For him, of course, Sandra was a mistake from what seemed like another life, many months ago in the lowest point of their marriage. It had been over and done with in one night. He was ready to be forgiven because he'd been punishing himself since it had happened. But he had to remind himself that, for Peyton, Sandra was a new wound. She'd only found out about it three days ago. He couldn't blame her for being standoffish. In truth, he couldn't blame her if she never forgave him.

That was what really scared him.

He ordered a pizza for dinner and watched a few minutes of the evening news while waiting for delivery. He braced himself when the scales of justice graphic appeared on the screen. Their trial wasn't the lead story anymore, but Kevin had learned the hard way that you didn't have to be charged with the crime of the century for it to be the crime of *your* century.

"The Shields-Stokes murder trial took a strange twist today," said the anchorwoman, "as the prosecution turned its sights on the husband, Kevin Stokes. Prosecutor Charles Ohn grilled Stokes's wife on the witness stand, and date rape emerged as a possible motive—"

Kevin switched off the set with the remote. He'd heard enough from the talking heads for one day, for one lifetime.

The pizza arrived. Kevin paid the deliveryman and brought the steaming box to the kitchen table. It wasn't what he'd ordered, and he made a mental note that, should he end up on death row, he'd order his last meal of pepperoni with extra cheese from someplace more reliable.

He was reaching into the refrigerator for a cold beer when the phone rang. He grabbed it quickly, hoping it was Peyton.

"Hello."

"Is this Kevin Stokes?" It was the voice of a woman, but not one he recognized.

"Who is this?"

"Someone who can help you."

Suspecting a crank, he was a half-second away from disconnecting, then reconsidered. "Who are you?"

"I'm a cyber-detective."

"A what?"

"A detective who specializes in online computer investigations."

"I never heard of it."

"That's because you never needed one before. You need one now."

"What do you do?"

"Basically I hang out in chat rooms and eavesdrop on people who think they're having cybersex in private. I track down the screen names of the participants and, if they're married, I contact the spouse and turn over all of my information. For a reasonable fee, like any detective."

"Are you saying . . ."

"I've been following your case for about two months, ever since the prosecutor released those transcripts of the chat-room conversations between Gary Varne and your wife."

"Those weren't between Gary and Peyton."

"I know. They were between someone else and your wife. They're still going at it."

Kevin froze. "I don't believe you."

"They chatted as recently as last week."

"How do you know that?"

"I'm a cyber-detective."

"I still don't believe you."

"Then let me prove it to you."

"I'm not interested."

"You'd better be. Because they have a date to talk again tonight at eleven o'clock."

"That can't be."

"Believe it, friend. I told you, I eavesdrop."

Kevin was silent. "Why should I trust you?"

"The real question is, why should you trust your wife?"

"Who put you up to this? Are you some kind of swindler?"

"Look, here's the deal. No risk to you. You and I meet up at eleven o'clock. I know the screen name your wife uses, and I know the screen name of her lover. I have the technological ability to pose online as your wife's lover. I'll just use his screen name. You can watch the whole chat as it unfolds before your eyes on my computer screen. We can ask anything you want. If at the end of the chat you're not convinced that we're talking to Peyton Shields, you pay me nothing."

"And if it's her?"

"Fifty bucks."

"What?"

"Cheap, huh? See, where these jobs get expensive is when you want me to find out who the lover is."

Kevin was suddenly struck with an idea. He didn't want to believe it was Peyton online, but if someone in cyberspace was pretending to be her lover, it might unravel the kidnapping.

"All right," he said. "Where should we meet?"

★..★..★

Peyton heard noises from the living room.

Twenty minutes earlier, she'd gone straight from her car to the upstairs tub in her parents' guest bathroom. Her father's car was gone when she'd arrived, and she'd assumed that he and her mother had gone out to dinner. She was actually pleased to have been alone.

She peered out the window, and the car still wasn't in the driveway. Still alone, she thought, until she heard it again—that noise from the living room.

She put on her bathrobe, opened the bathroom door, and stood at the top of the stairway, listening to the noises coming from below. It was a buzzing, rather constant but of varying volume. It was getting louder again, and she thought maybe it was a fan or appliance. The longer she listened, however, the more certain she was that it wasn't mechanical. It sounded human. Like humming.

She started down the stairs, then stopped about halfway. In the foyer she could see the glow of the lights from the living room. She had no recollection of having switched them on before heading upstairs. Instinct told her to run back upstairs, but on impulse she charged down the stairway another five steps, just far enough to peek below the ceiling line and see into the living room.

"Who's there!" she shouted.

That drew a loud shriek, then a quick turn and an angry glare.

Peyton sighed with relief at the sight of her mother.

"Why do you do that to me?" her mother asked in an angry tone.

"I'm sorry. I didn't see a car in the driveway when I got home, so I thought I was alone."

"Your father ran to the store."

Peyton slumped into the sitting position on the third step, leaning against the carved balustrades. "I'm sorry. I'm still pretty wired. Wasn't one of my better days."

Her mother turned her attention back to the built-in shelves adjacent to the fireplace. Peyton rose and joined her in the living room. She noticed that several framed photographs were stacked on the couch. Her mother pulled another from the top shelf and placed it on the couch beside the others. It was Peyton's wedding photograph.

Peyton checked the stack. They were all photographs of her and Kevin—wedding, engagement, vacation.

"What are you doing?"

"Just putting some things away."

"We aren't divorced yet."

"After the things that were said in that courtroom this week, I thought having these things around the house might make you uncomfortable."

Peyton gave her a quizzical look. "Are you glad Kevin and I are split?"

"Of course not," Valerie said with an awkward chuckle. "I just want you to be happy, that's all."

Peyton took a seat on the couch and examined one of the dethroned photographs. It was from one of their first vacations together in Martha's Vineyard. The two of them were wrapped in each other's arms on Menemsha Beach, just the two of them, a bottle of wine, a couple of boiled lobsters, and the blazing orange afterglow of an amazing sunset over Vineyard Sound. It was one of her favorite photographs of them for a lot of reasons, not the least of which was the memory of Kevin wading into the water up to his thighs and sprinting to the shore after she'd told him that this was where they'd filmed the movie *Jaws*.

She wondered if the two of them would ever laugh that hard again.

She looked up at her mother and said, "Dad told me about the problems you two had."

Her mother froze. "What do you mean, problems?"

"The kind of problems that Kevin and I are going through right now. And I don't mean a murder trial."

Her voice tightened. "He told you that, did he?"

"Don't get mad at him. I guessed it, actually."

Valerie dusted off an old framed photo, and put it back where Peyton and Kevin's wedding shot used to stand. Ironic, in a way. It was one of those high school shots that Kevin used to tease her about, mother and daughter dressed in the same outfit like a couple of teenage girlfriends.

"So, what brought this on?"

"I guess I'm searching for answers."

"As in whether you should forgive him?"

"Yes. Like Dad forgave you."

"He *forgave* me? Is that what he told you?"

"Yes."

She nodded slowly, but clearly wasn't in agreement. "That's interesting."

"Why do you say that?"

"Because what saved our marriage is the fact that we forgave each other."

"I don't understand. What did you forgive him for?"

She averted her eyes. "Peyton, why do you want to dredge this up?"

"Because it's important to me. I need to understand."

"It wasn't about sex," Valerie said, struggling to answer. "It was about adventure."

"There's always mountain climbing."

"Don't be smart."

"I'm sorry. Go ahead."

"I got married to your father way too young. I went through my twenties and early thirties thinking I'd missed out on all the fun. By the time I was thirty-five, I was . . . well, I'd say I was desperate."

"Is that when you strayed?"

She didn't answer, but it was a silence loaded with admission.

"I still don't understand. What was it that you forgave Daddy for?"

Valerie's look was incredulous, as if Peyton should have been smarter than that. "For nearly suffocating me. I was a twenty-year-old college girl with all kinds of dreams, dreams exactly like yours. I had so many opportunities. And then—bam. I'm dating your father, and I miss my period. You can imagine the reaction of my parents. But your father was right in the same camp. From that moment on, it was as if I had no more opportunities, no choices. We got married. My life was set. End of story."

Her voice trailed off, her eyes misty. Suddenly she came to Peyton, sat beside her on the couch, and gave her a tight embrace. She was sniffling, her head buried in Peyton's shoulder.

"That's why I always told you, Peyton. Don't make the mistake I did."

Peyton hugged back, but it wasn't from the heart. It *was* what her mother had always told her—when she'd first started dating, when she'd gone away to college, when she'd fallen in love with Kevin as a college student. The memory of those mother-daughter talks and the same old warning made Peyton want to pull away, made her want to grab her mother and shake her. Instead, she just held her trembling mother in her arms, trying yet again to understand that Valerie's insensitive message had been delivered in the twisted name of love.

"It'll be all right, Mom," she said, still holding on. "Everything will be all right."

65

THEY MET AT 10:45 P.M. IN A COFFEE SHOP ON NEWBURY STREET. THE cyber-detective had sounded nice enough on the telephone, but in today's world of wackos it seemed prudent to meet in a public place, rather than just the two of them at his apartment or hers.

The coffee bar was an old converted drugstore. The walls were unfinished red brick, and a well-preserved century-old soda fountain stood as the bar. Small round tables filled out the center of the room, and the back wall was lined with booths. A young woman in the corner strummed an acoustic guitar, the weekend entertainment. No one seemed to be listening to her. The place was about half full, a few people on dates, some college students, and a few loners with nothing to do on a Friday night but drink coffee and read a day-old newspaper.

Kevin had no idea what the detective looked like, but he spotted her easily at the booth in the back. The giveaway was the notebook computer up and running on the table before her.

"You're Daisy?"

"Yes," she said, no handshake.

She seemed slightly awkward in person, or at least not as smooth as she'd been on the telephone. She wore baggy jeans and an oversized sweatshirt. Her eyeglasses were black-framed and unflattering. Kevin figured it was par for the course for someone who virtually lived online as a cyber-detective, and he was actually relieved. Things the way they were with Peyton, the last thing he needed was to be spotted out on the town with a Beyoncé Knowles look-alike.

Kevin took a seat opposite Daisy, who positioned the computer at the end of the table so that they could both see. The back of the computer faced the restaurant, so no one could steal a glance.

"You nervous?" she asked.

"Should I be?"

She shrugged, then turned straight to business. "I'm going to use the screen name RG. That's the name your wife's cyber-lover travels under."

"Except that it's not my wife."

"Sure. Whatever. Did you bring the fifty bucks?"

The down payment was so low that Kevin had almost forgotten. He dug the bills from his wallet and handed them over. Then Daisy got started.

Kevin watched as she logged on and moved straight to the chat rooms. "Sometimes they meet right in the private chat room, but last time Ladydoc asked to meet in the movie chat room, their usual place. So that's where we'll go."

Daisy sounded so sure of herself, he was beginning to have doubts. *Could this really be Peyton?*

"How will you know when she checks in?" he asked.

"She's already here." Daisy pointed to the box in the upper-right-hand part of the screen, which listed a series of screen names. "Ladydoc," she said, reading the fourth name from the top. "That's Peyton."

Kevin checked his watch. It was two minutes past eleven. "Right on time," he said, remembering that Daisy had said eleven o'clock.

"How do we know Ladydoc is Peyton?"

"Just watch."

On the screen, typed messages were being traded back and forth among other chat-room visitors. Daisy typed in her own message, which appeared on-screen after her assumed screen name, RG.

"private chat, ladydoc?" it read.

A few irrelevant lines of script from other chatters followed, the cyberspace equivalent of everyone talking at once. But finally the response came from Ladydoc.

"ok."

Kevin had an uneasy feeling as he watched Daisy maneuver from the public to the private chat room. In a just a few seconds, he was staring at a white screen with just two names, RG and Ladydoc.

Daisy looked at Kevin and said, "Now, the show's about to begin."

"I'm not here for titillation. I want you to show me who Ladydoc is."

"She'll never come out and say she's Peyton. But watch the dialogue carefully. You'll see it's her."

Daisy typed the first line. "not very nice the way u left me last time."

"i wasn't trying to tease. my husband was coming. almost caught me. had 2 log off immediately."

"he's always in the way, isn't he?"

"nothing i can't work around."

"maybe. but i think u been holding back with us because of kevin."

Kevin started at the sight of his name. Daisy was getting right down to it.

"what makes u think that?" came the reply.

"i know everything."

"what r u, a detective or something?"

Off-line, Kevin and his detective exchanged glances. Daisy returned to the online chat. "i don't understand why u ever married that dweeb."

Kevin shot her a cross look. "Bear with me," Daisy told him.

The chat response came back from Ladydoc: "it's complicated."

"he's the problem, isn't he?"

Off-line, Kevin watched as his detective seemed absorbed by the chat, as if enjoying her role as Peyton's online lover.

"what do u think?" wrote Ladydoc.

"if it weren't for him, this whole mess never would have started. we would have been 2gether a year ago."

"sad but true."

Kevin interjected. "Why are you making her say those things?"

"I'm not making her do anything," she snapped.

"I don't like this."

"Deal with it." The detective typed another line to Ladydoc: "don't u wish sometimes that he would just go away?"

Kevin scoffed. "You're a troublemaker."

The detective didn't answer. She just stared intently at the screen, waiting for an answer. When it didn't come, she typed again: "don't u wish kevin would just go away?"

There was a few seconds' delay, then finally the typed response built across the screen. "don't u know it."

The detective looked up from the screen, looked straight into Kevin's eyes. A verbal response to Kevin came simultaneously with the typed response to Ladydoc.

"Consider it done."

Kevin froze. The woman's voice was suddenly deeper, and instantly Kevin knew from the evil look in those eyes that this woman was a man and this man was no detective.

Before Kevin could react, the man in the disguise lunged forward, reaching across the table, leading with an eight-inch blade. Kevin let out a loud cry as the metal pierced his skin, broke through a rib, and ripped through his chest. He locked eyes for an instant with his attacker, long enough to see the utter excitement in his face. The blade twisted, then exited as the man pulled away. A hot gush of red blood soaked through Kevin's shirt. He tried to reach for his attacker, but he slumped in the booth and fell to the floor.

"She's got a knife!" someone shouted.

Kevin could hear people screaming and running in every direction. He reached for his chest and felt the bloody hole between his ribs, and knew he was badly hurt. He tried to cry for help, but no words came. He raised his head a few inches from the floor and saw his attacker flee out the door with the computer under his arm.

"Stop her!" he said, trying to shout but it was little more than a whisper. The room was suddenly a blur. He rolled on his side and could feel the blood pumping from his body, feel his life oozing into the puddle beside him.

"Stop *him!*" he said weakly.

It was his last conscious thought before his head hit the floor.

Peyton rushed to the Brigham and Women's Hospital in response to the phone call. It took her only minutes to get there from her parents' house in Brookline, and she arrived not long after the ambulance.

"Where's Kevin Stokes?" she shouted to the ER nurse.

"Trauma One, but you can't go in—"

Peyton flew past her before she could finish the sentence. She turned the corner and entered the trauma room.

Inside was a flurry of activity. Two ER physicians and four nurses, all working furiously over the man on the table. Forceps, sponges, and bandages rested on trays all around them. Blood was everywhere, on the table, on the floor, and the physicians' gloved hands. Fresh blood was being transfused. One physician was checking Kevin's throat for blood and possible intubation. Another was checking his breathing with a stethoscope.

"My God, Kevin," she said, nearly in shock.

She rushed to the table, but a nurse gently pushed her aside. "Please, we need room."

"That's my husband!"

"We have to get him to surgery."

The physicians were calling out orders. "Breathing sounds good, no pneumothorax, thank goodness."

"Blood pressure ninety over sixty and falling."

"Gotta stop this bleeding!"

A police officer was standing on the other side of the table, crouched down and talking directly into Kevin's ear. Kevin was at best half-conscious.

"Kevin!" shouted Peyton. She squeezed his hand, and his eyes blinked open. For an instant Peyton was sure they'd made a connection.

The officer leaned closer and put the question to him more loudly. "Who did this to you?"

Kevin swallowed hard, his eyelids fluttering. His voice was barely audible. "Said . . . was . . . Peyton."

Peyton's mouth fell open.

"Let's go!" shouted the ER physician.

Kevin was whisked away on the table, nurses and physicians at his side. The pneumatic doors swung open, then closed, and the room was suddenly quiet, just Peyton and the police officer.

"Do you know who Peyton is?" he asked.

She dug her hands into her pocket, her expression falling. "That would be me."

66

PEYTON WAITED OUT THE SURGERY IN THE HOSPITAL LOUNGE, WOR-
ried for Kevin, worried for herself.

She kept telling herself that no news was good news, but as
the procedure dragged into its second hour, she found her nerves
fraying. This was one of those situations where being a doctor
didn't necessarily help. She knew everything that could possibly
go wrong on the operating table, and being alone in the waiting
room only fed her wild imagination. In her mind's eye she saw
them frantically working over his body and cursing the ER physicians for having missed obvious pneumothorax. She saw frothy
blood spewing from his side with each breath, the doctors frantically feeding a chest tube into his punctured and collapsed lung,
the ECG suddenly tripping the alarm as the tracer showed a flat
line. She heard the doctors calling a shock trauma code as one of
them grabbed the defibrillator pads and gave Kevin a jolt to the
chest—once, twice, then up to a full blast at 360 for one final,
futile attempt. "*Time of death . . .*"

"Dr. Shields?"

Her fearful thoughts evaporated. Standing before her was the
same officer who'd questioned Kevin in the ER, who'd heard that
curious fragmented sentence, and who'd made careful note of his
incriminating words. He'd brought a detective with him, and he
had a few questions for Peyton.

The detective quickly introduced himself, very polite—so polite that it made Peyton immediately suspicious. After a couple minutes of what seemed like meaningless banter, Peyton finally said, "What is it you want to know, Detective?"

He paused, as if taken aback by her directness. "Seems your husband was having coffee with an unidentified woman. Any idea who it would have been?"

"What did she look like?"

"So far, we don't have much. Blond hair. Anywhere from five foot six to five foot ten inches tall. Twenty-five to thirty-five years old."

"I would imagine that a lot of people fit that description."

"Yes. Including you."

"Like I said before, I was at my parents' house when this happened."

"Parents make convenient alibis."

Her look was incredulous. "Someone tried to kill my husband. You need to find her."

"That's what we're trying to do," he said, eyebrow arching.

"Are you saying that I'm actually one of the people on your list of possible suspects?"

"Right now, you're the only one on our list."

"Because of what Kevin said in the ER?"

"He did mention your name, Doctor."

"He also could have been delirious."

The detective didn't answer.

Peyton said, "We'll just have to wait and see what he says when he wakes up, won't we?"

"Sure," he said. "Let's hope he makes it."

The insensitivity galled her. "Excuse me," she said, rising. "I need some air."

Jennifer's information about her client's condition was thirdhand, but the chain from Peyton to Tony to her seemed reliable enough for her to take action before Kevin regained consciousness. She waited till 5:00 A.M., still an obscene hour on a Saturday morning, to call Charles Ohn.

He answered on the first ring, which surprised her. The moon was still hanging in the dark sky outside her kitchen window, and she was seated alone at the granite counter in the dim glow of a night-light.

"Sorry to wake you," she said, assuming that she had.

"You didn't."

"There's been a stabbing."

"I'm plugged in already. How is he?"

"Touch and go. We're hopeful."

"So am I."

"That's why I'm calling. If—I mean when he comes around, no one is to interrogate my client until I've talked to him. I want the police out of the waiting room."

"I've already pulled them out."

She was so surprised that she fumbled the phone. "My, how uncharacteristically proactive of you."

"Are you kidding? You think I'm going to let husband and wife make up and get all kissy-faced, only to have Stokes retract those beautiful words he uttered in the emergency room? I'm perfectly happy to leave it right where he left it, thank you very much."

She'd been awake for all of twenty minutes, and already he had her blood boiling. "So it's true what they used to say about you, isn't it?"

"What's that?"

"You are the Ohn-anator," she said, then hung up.

"You can see him now," said the nurse.

It was almost 6:00 A.M. when those long-awaited words finally hit Peyton's ears. The police had left about an hour earlier, and she'd waited alone for Kevin to come out of recovery and be moved to intensive care. Peyton rose quickly from her chair and entered the unit.

The ICU was a large, open area with the administrative staff in the center and one bay after another lining the perimeter. They weren't so much rooms as three-walled stalls with beige plastic curtains for privacy. The unit was busy this morning, typical for a weekend. Kevin was in the fifth bay. Peyton pulled back the curtain and froze, trying hard not to alarm him with her reaction.

He looked groggy and weak but very much alive. The electric bed was angled slightly to elevate his torso. Painkillers dripped from an IV, and his heart rate chirped steadily on the monitor at his bedside.

"How are you?"

"Tired," he said, his voice still raspy from the anesthesia. "And lucky, I guess."

"Very lucky. The surgeon told me that the blade just missed your pulmonary artery."

He smiled weakly. "Actually, I was thinking how lucky I am to have you here with me."

She stepped closer and took his hand. Her eyes turned misty as she leaned toward him and kissed him on the lips. He reached to embrace her, then groaned with pain.

"Try not to move around too much," she said.

"What are you, a doctor?"

They shared a faint smile, then Peyton turned serious. "Who did this to you?"

He had to pause for breaths, but slowly he managed to tell her about the meeting with the cyber-detective, the eleven o'clock private chat, and his own too late realization that the woman wasn't what she'd seemed.

"Obviously she was a he, and I presume he was RG."

"Then who's Ladydoc?"

"That's what I was trying to tell you in the emergency room. He said that Ladydoc was Peyton."

"You know it's not me. Right?"

"Of course. He had me going for maybe half a second. But your mother summed it up a couple of months ago at dinner, when she made the point that you couldn't possibly have been chatting online three and four nights a week while doing your residency at Children's."

"So, RG and Ladydoc are the missing screen names for those chat-room conversations that the prosecutor said were between me and Gary Varne?"

"Don't you think so?"

"Yes. But if RG went to all the trouble of removing the screen names from those other transcripts, why would he have shown them to you?"

He glanced at the bandages on his chest. "I would imagine that he didn't think I'd live to tell about it."

Peyton tingled with fear. "We need to post a guard here. This guy already killed Gary Varne, and now he's tried to kill you. If he finds out you're still alive, he could come back."

"You think the hospital will go for a guard in the ICU? Half the patients here have already had one heart attack this weekend."

"The doctor says you're doing great. If I push it, they'll move you to a private room on the surgical floor. It'll be better that way. The guard will have a much easier time figuring out who belongs and who doesn't."

"I'm all for a guard, but how will we know if he comes back? We have no idea who he is."

"The only thing I can think of is to have Tony subpoena all the Internet carriers. They can tell us who RG and Ladydoc are."

"It could take weeks just to identify and serve all the possible carriers, weeks more to resolve the privacy issues."

She lowered her head, tormented by the same old question. "So for the rest of our trial, our best argument is that the guy who framed us is some cipher who has a thing for me. That's all we have."

"Maybe we've been looking at it from the wrong perspective."

"What do you mean?"

"Think of it in terms of RG and Ladydoc. We've been focusing on RG, and it's gotten us nowhere."

"You think searching for Ladydoc is going to make it any easier?"

"The only question we've really asked so far is who wants to have you. Maybe the real question is this: Who loves, hates, admires, or resents you so much that, in the make-believe world of cyberspace and for God only knows what reason, they might actually want to *be* you?"

Peyton felt chills. The way she'd heard the question—the whole bag of conflicting emotions seemingly mixed together in one twisted mind—had sent her thoughts racing in a direction that frightened her to the core.

"You think it's Sandra?" said Kevin.

She looked off to the middle distance and said, "There's one way to find out."

"Where are you going?" he asked as she started away from the bed.

"I'll be back as soon as I can. With an answer." She stepped out of the bay, gaining speed and determination as she left the ICU and headed for the elevator.

Rudy was riding on the subway's red line. He took a seat in the space reserved for the elderly and the handicapped, scowling as if daring someone to ask him to move. The train was almost empty, too early for most people on a Saturday morning. The dark tunnel was a blur outside the windows, but he was staring without focus, deep in thought.

He didn't understand it. He'd seen Ladydoc's wishes on the computer screen in black and white, and he'd done exactly as she'd desired. He'd gotten rid of that worthless husband, or at least he'd tried. And then she'd promptly raced to the hospital and waited at his side. Did she think that RG wouldn't learn of her deception? Was she so foolish as to imagine that he wouldn't follow through on a kill? Of course he'd waited for the ambulance to arrive at the coffee shop. After dumping the disguise in the alley, he'd easily blended into the crowd as just another rubbernecker. He'd followed the ambulance to the hospital. To his dismay, they'd taken Kevin to the ER and not the morgue. He'd seen Peyton sobbing in the waiting room, a look of genuine concern on her face. All this love and affection after she'd told RG in no uncertain terms that she'd wanted Kevin out of the way.

Two-timing bitch.

The train stopped. It wasn't his station, but Rudy got off anyway. He wasn't going home. If Peyton wanted to be with her beloved Kevin, so be it. Rudy had a job to finish.

Only now he had twice the work.

67

HER MOTHER WAS IN THE KITCHEN WHEN PEYTON ENTERED THE house, and she could smell the coffee. Throughout the night, by telephone, she'd kept her parents posted on Kevin's condition. Her father had gone back to bed after the last upbeat call, but Mom was dressed and ready for the day.

Peyton went straight upstairs to her parents' bedroom and woke her father.

"What's wrong?" he said, groggy as he sat up in the bed.

"I have to talk to you," she said.

"Is Kevin still okay?"

"Yes. He's going to be fine."

He squinted, trying to see the clock on the nightstand. "What time is it?"

"Early. Daddy, there's something I need to know. It's about our family."

"Sure. Just ask."

"This is so hard, because if there was one person I thought I could always count on to be honest with me, it was you."

"You can count on me, darling. Always."

"Really?"

"Yes, absolutely. What's this all about?"

"Kevin and I have had a breakthrough on who might be stalking me. He's been chatting over the Internet with someone who is impersonating me. She calls herself Ladydoc."

"Impersonating you?"

"Yes. Which made us ask who would resent me or hate me or in some sick way admire me enough to want to *become* me on the Internet. And that's when this image flashed in my mind."

Her father propped himself up on one elbow. "An image of what?"

"Some teenage girl whose life sucks. Who has no existence or meaningful identity except the one she creates on the Internet. And she has no life because her parents didn't want her and instead put all their energy and resources toward making her older sister a successful doctor. But for this poor kid, there's no hope of success. Maybe she's one of the unlucky ones for whom foster care or adoption is a nightmare."

"What are you talking about?"

"My sister didn't die, did she?"

His face went ashen.

"Answer me, Dad. The baby Mom made with her lover was given up for adoption, wasn't she?"

He looked away. For the first time in Peyton's life, her father couldn't look her in the eye. "I'm sorry," he said.

"So I'm right? I have a sister out there?"

"Yes," he said, his voice barely audible. "Somewhere."

She nearly punched him in the chest, but she didn't. "You lied to me. How could you keep this from me all these years?"

"How could we have explained giving up a child for adoption unless we told everyone that the child wasn't mine?"

"I'm not talking about *everyone*. I'm talking about me."

"You're right. I regret that. But at the time, your mother and I were in agreement: If we were not going to keep the child, no one could know about the adoption. So we moved to Florida to have the baby, and we told everyone that the baby was stillborn."

Peyton closed her eyes, then opened them, her head spinning.

"I can't take any more lies. That's the worst part of this. If you had just told me the truth, maybe I could have understood. It wasn't your child. You forgave Mom for her affair and took her back. Maybe it was asking too much to expect you to embrace the child that wasn't yours."

"Well, if you're going to know the truth, it's important to get the whole truth."

"What am I missing?"

"It wasn't my child, and I did forgive your mother. But I wasn't the one who wanted to give up the baby for adoption."

Peyton was silent.

"That baby was still your sister. I wanted to keep her. But your mother, well, she just didn't want to be a mother again."

"Oh my God."

"She wanted to be . . . ," he said, his voice quaking, "I don't know what she wanted to be."

Peyton was way ahead of him, thinking once again about Ladydoc. "That's okay, Daddy. I think I know exactly what she wanted to be."

68

THERE WAS A PIT IN HER STOMACH AS PEYTON WENT TO THE HOME computer in the den and sat in her mother's chair. She had called Tony before going downstairs. He had some helpful insights, things she hadn't thought about. Now the execution was all up to her.

"Mom, can you come here for a minute?"

Peyton waited anxiously at the computer. Finally her mother was standing in the open doorway. She looked tired, obviously having slept very little all night.

"What is it?"

"I have to go online. Can I use your account?"

"What for?"

"Kevin saw the screen names last night."

"What screen names?"

"My supposed online lover and alter ego. RG and Ladydoc."

Her mother hesitated, as if processing Peyton's words. "He saw them?"

"It's a long story, but I need to check this out right away. Can I use your screen name, please?"

Peyton gave her an assessing look, but her mother didn't flinch.

"Of course you can." Her mother switched on the computer, entered her password, and logged on to her Internet service. "There you go."

Peyton checked the screen name. There was only one registered to the account: Valerie51.

Her mother seemed smug. "What is it that you need to check,
dear?"

"Tony suggested that I send an e-mail to Ladydoc and see
what turns up."

"You don't expect an answer, do you?"

"No. In fact, Tony said Ladydoc is probably a blind screen name."

"Oh? What's that?"

"It's for people who go out of their way to keep their online
identity a secret."

"How do you mean?"

"Well, let's take your name, hypothetically speaking. When you
log on, the screen name that shows on your computer is Valerie51.
If you enter a chat room, that same name should show up on
someone else's computer screen. But if for some reason you're
really paranoid about concealing your identity, then you hire a
fifteen-year-old computer whiz to rig it up so that your screen
name is converted to something else in cyberspace."

"Seems like a lot of worthless effort. I can create as many
screen names as I want under my existing account."

"But the list of screen names shows up every time you or
someone else logs on. With a blind screen name, no one else who
uses your computer can see that you've created an alias. Not your
husband. Not even me, for example."

Her mother emitted her phony chuckle, something she
employed only when she wanted to sound older and less savvy
than she was. "That all sounds so complicated."

"It's not, really. The bottom line is, your computer at home
might say your screen name is Valerie51. But when you go into a
chat room, people will read Ladydoc on their screen."

"I see. Hypothetically, you mean."

"Yes, of course. This is all hypothetical." Peyton turned back to
the computer. "So, my plan is to send an e-mail to Ladydoc and
see what happens."

"But if Ladydoc is a blind screen name, won't the e-mail just be lost in cyberspace?"

"No. It's delivered to whoever created the name. People who use these blind names aren't hiding as well as they think they are. In fact, they're only fooling themselves."

Her mother seemed to freeze, speechless. "But there are so many Internet servers. You could be looking for Ladydoc at AOL, Ladydoc at Earthlink, and on and on. This hardly seems worthwhile."

Peyton detected definite stalling. "Why don't we just start with your server."

"Mine?" she said nervously.

"Yes. Yours."

Peyton entered the name Ladydoc into the address box. With one click of the mouse, the test message would travel through cyberspace and land in the electronic mailbox of whoever had created the name Ladydoc. Peyton understood that. From the look on her mother's face, it seemed that she understood, too. The coffee cup was shaking in her hand.

On the screen, the cursor hung over the send button. Peyton clicked her mouse, and the electronic message was off to Ladydoc. Almost instantaneously, the computer beeped and the familiar message was announced over the speaker.

You've got mail.

It had come right back to Valerie51.

For the longest time, neither woman moved. Slowly, Peyton worked through her own denial and disbelief, bringing herself to a point where she could speak.

"What have you done?" she said, her voice low but filled with anger.

"I never intended to hurt you, Peyton."

"Does Dad know anything about this?"

"No, *no*. And we can't tell him. He'd leave me for sure."

"You deserve it. You cheated on him before, you gave up a child that he was willing to keep, and you had cybersex with a psycho."

"I didn't know he was psycho. He sounded very nice."

"They all sound nice online," she said, incredulous. "They're all pretending to be something they're not. Just like you were."

"I'm sorry, Peyton."

"Why me? Why did you pretend to be me?"

"Because . . . you are me."

"What?"

"You're what I could have been. No, I take that back. What you could have been is what I *should* have been."

"What are you talking about?"

"Don't you see, darling? For all my warnings, you made the same mistake I did. I married a man who barely got his college degree and ended up a beat cop. You married that white trash who grew up in a Key West trailer."

A creepy feeling came over her. She recalled what Kevin had said about last night's chat. "That's why you told him to get rid of Kevin, isn't it?"

"What?"

"Ladydoc told RG that she wished Kevin were out of her life."

She hesitated. "I—I didn't think he'd stab him."

"He killed Gary. You knew the man's a killer."

"Yes, but . . ."

"That's why you kept this all to yourself. Even after I was charged with murder, you didn't go to the police."

"I swear, I've been trying to do the right thing. I tried to lure RG out into the open so you could catch him. I set up a rendezvous with him in the park, and I sent you an e-mail telling you to bring the police with you."

Peyton recalled the e-mail she'd received a day too late. "Very brave of you, Mother. Everything had to be done behind the scenes. Protecting yourself and your little fantasy world was paramount."

"I couldn't go public with this. I didn't want to hurt your father."

"Liar. You didn't care about Dad, you didn't care about me."

"That's not true.

"You didn't want me to make the same mistake you made. You always said that."

"Because I love you."

"Ladydoc wasn't about love," Peyton said, her voice shaking. "Ladydoc was out there to erase my mistake. You became me, and you wanted to be rid of Kevin."

Their eyes locked in a tense, icy silence. But her mother didn't deny it.

Peyton rose and started for the door.

"Where are you going?"

"To see my husband. And then we're calling the police."

"Don't, please. I have a plan. We can lure him out together. We don't need the police or your father or Kevin or anyone. We can do it ourselves." She hurried to the computer, nearly pushing Peyton out of the way. "Look," she said, typing frantically at the keys, pulling up a file. "I don't know what he looks like, but he sent me this photo. Maybe it will give us a clue, tell us how to catch him."

The image appeared on the screen. It was a an old black-and-white photograph of Rudolph Valentino.

Clenched between his teeth was a single long-stemmed red rose.

"The rose," said Peyton, recalling the one she'd found in the tube outside her locker, and the one Kevin had found outside their front door.

"That's why he calls himself RG—Rodolfo Guglielmi, Valentino's real name. Come on, Peyton. We're the smart ones. We can catch this psycho."

Peyton stopped and glowered, her expression a mixture of contempt and pathos. "No, Mother. *You're* the psycho."

Peyton grabbed her purse and headed for the door.

69

PEYTON PHONED TONY FROM HER CAR, STILL SHAKEN, BUT DETER-
mined to push forward.

"It was her," was all she said.

Tony didn't answer immediately. "I'm sorry."

"Should I call the police or should you?"

"Before we do anything, we have to come up with a joint strategy. All of us should meet—you, me, Jennifer, Kevin. Is he up to it
this morning?"

"I wouldn't think so. I'll be at the hospital in ten minutes. I'll
call you."

"Whatever you do, don't say anything more to the police till
we get this straight among ourselves. I want a unified front that I
can take to the district attorney and to Judge Gilhorn for a joint
dismissal of all charges against you and Kevin both."

"But there's a killer out there."

"Yes, and from everything we've seen, he's not very eager
to get caught. I'm sure he's lying low after last night's attack.
It won't jeopardize anything for us to collect our thoughts so
that we can not only help the police catch this guy, but at the
same time get you and Kevin in the clear. I'm only talking
about an hour."

"It took a lot less than that to stab Kevin in the chest."

"If you're that concerned, stay with Kevin in his room. I'll call the hospital and make sure they have a guard posted outside the door."

"I took care of that this morning before I left."

"Great. Then you have nothing to worry about."

"Sure," she said as she steered into the visitor parking lot. "If you say so."

A car alarm was blasting. For two solid minutes it echoed off the unfinished cement walls of the hospital parking garage. Then it stopped.

Vinnie Skovick looked up from his morning newspaper. As the security guard posted at the ticket booth and entrance gate to the garage, he was doing what he did best—reading the sports section. He finished an article about the Celtics' hopes for the new season, wiped a few dots of powdered sugar from his dark blue uniform, and walked slowly up the ramp. He was certain it had been just another errant alarm on some doctor's Porsche, but it was his job to check it out.

To the untrained ear, sounds could be tricky in a parking garage. Vinnie had been a security guard for all of six weeks, however, and he could pinpoint a blasting alarm with impressive accuracy. This one, he guessed, had come from section orange, row two or three. He would have bet his life on it.

The garage was less than half full today, creating a cavernous effect that made the click of his heels reverberate even more loudly, more lonely than usual. He cut through the purple section on his way to the orange. Orange was near the elevators, always the first section to fill. He strolled down row two and saw nothing out of the ordinary. He doubled back on row three, and there he found it. No false alarm this time. Pellets of shattered safety glass were all over the ground between a white van and a Lexus. The driver's-side window of the sedan had been smashed.

Strange that the alarm had stopped so soon, thought Vinnie.

He stepped between the parked vehicles and peered inside the Lexus. He'd expected to see a hole in the dashboard where the stereo once was, but it was intact.

Must have grabbed a briefcase.

He reached for his walkie-talkie. His head was hovering in the opening, surrounded on all four sides by the jagged edges of the shattered window. In a split second, he heard the side door of the van slide open, felt a hand on the back of his head as someone grabbed him by the hair. Before he could react, his face was slammed down onto the jagged shards of glass that protruded from the window frame. He groaned, unable to talk for the blood in his mouth, unable to see for the cuts to his eyes. He was only half-conscious as his head snapped back, more hair pulling. A jacket was quickly wrapped around his head, soaking up the blood, cutting off his air supply. His entire body jerked back toward the van, and he was thrown to the floor. He heard the side door slide shut, followed by a voice he didn't recognize.

"Nothing personal, Skovick."

His head rolled back. He tried to speak through the blood-soaked jacket, but it was futile, his voice silenced forever by the rope around his neck.

Peyton took the elevator to the surgical floor.

She felt a little better now. Before heading up to Kevin's room, she'd stopped off at hospital administration to confirm that security was on alert. It had taken her almost twenty minutes to get a personal audience with someone in authority, but the assistant administrator had assured Peyton that they were on top of things. Kevin was doing very well, and they'd moved him from the critical-care ward to a private room that was more easily secured. It wasn't the hospital's policy to provide armed guards, but Tony Falcone had agreed to pay an off-duty Boston police officer to stand watch outside Kevin's door.

Thank you, Tony.

The elevator doors opened, and Peyton stepped out. She was immediately relieved to see a security guard posted right outside the elevator. It was even more than she'd expected. Nice to see the hospital backing up the off-duty police officer with their own security guards.

"Morning," she said.

As he turned, Peyton caught the guard's name on the hospital ID badge pinned to his chest: *Skovick*.

"Morning," said Rudy.

70

RUDY LOST SIGHT OF HER AS SHE ROUNDED THE CORNER. HE KNEW exactly where she was headed, having circled the floor twice already. Room 516 was off the beaten track at the end of a quiet corridor. An armed guard was seated outside the closed door. It appeared as though the hospital had selected a room off the main hallway to avoid drawing attention to the fact that a patient was being guarded.

Skovick's uniform had turned out to be a good fit, and the jacket Rudy had wrapped around Skovick's face had kept the blood from staining it. Rudy looked authentic, but he wasn't going to push his luck too long. He gave Peyton just three minutes to get settled inside the room, and then he made his move. With all the confidence of the head of hospital security, he turned away from the elevators and walked down the side corridor.

Straight ahead was the lone guard seated outside Kevin's room. The uniform was that of the Boston police. Because the officer was alone, Rudy presumed he was moonlighting while off-duty. He looked bored, rocking back on the hind legs of his chair, whistling an unrecognizable tune. Rudy kept one eye on the cop's firearm as he approached.

"I'll take over now."

The cop looked up and said, "Says who?"

"Administration."

He glanced at Rudy's belt line, seeming to note the absence of the firearm. "I was told they wanted an armed guard."

"I guess they changed their mind."

He gave Rudy a suspicious look. "Let me check this out."

As the cop reached for his walkie-talkie, Rudy pulled a knife from inside his shirtsleeve, the same one he'd used on Kevin. Before the officer could react, Rudy had the tip of the sharp blade against his jugular.

The officer froze.

In what seemed like one motion, Rudy grabbed the gun from its holster and yanked the man up by the collar. He moved quickly, out of concern that someone might happen by in the hallway. With the gun to the officer's back, he pushed toward the door.

"Nice and easy," said Rudy, "we're going inside."

Peyton was at Kevin's bedside when the door opened. She was holding his hand while he slept, the painkillers doing their work. Two men walked in, the officer from outside their door and the security guard right behind him.

"What is it?" asked Peyton.

The door closed and neither man answered. Peyton noticed the gun missing from the officer's holster. Suddenly the security guard moved his arm, and the gun was aimed at the officer's head.

"Not another word or the cop is dead."

She squeezed Kevin's hand, but he was still out from the drugs.

"Step away from the bed, Peyton. Away from the emergency call button."

She took two steps backward, staring into his eyes from across the room. She recognized that crazed look, that voice, both from Jamaica Pond and the night Gary was killed.

"What do you want?"

"I came to kill you both."

Her heart skipped a beat.

He looked right at her, his expression angry but the eyes soulful. "But every time I'm about to give you what you deserve, I can't do it. Why is that?"

"Because you're a decent guy," said the cop, his voice shaking. "You're no killer."

"Shut up, idiot." He pressed the gun harder against the back of his head.

"Come on, man. I got a four-year-old kid and a pregnant wife."

"Please," said Peyton. "You don't have to prove anything to me, Rodolfo."

His eyes lit. "That's the first time I've heard you say my name aloud."

Peyton didn't know whether to tell him that she wasn't Ladydoc or to play the role. "It's a nice name," she said.

"Don't stroke me."

"I'm just being honest."

"You don't know how to be honest."

"That's not true."

"You'll never be honest with me or yourself. Not with *him* around," he said, indicating Kevin.

"What do you want to know? I'll be totally honest."

"Did you mean what you said last night?"

Peyton paused. She'd heard Kevin's version, but she wasn't very comfortable with the idea of RG quizzing her about what was said. "What, specifically?"

"Don't be coy. You said you wanted to be rid of Kevin."

She didn't answer.

"Say it again," he said. "Tell me that you want me to get rid of him."

"I can't do that."

"Come on, Peyton. You made the right decision with Gary Varne."

"You killed him," she said, wanting the officer to hear it.

"For us. And now there's only one more obstacle in our way. Tell me what to do."

"I want this to stop."

"It can never stop."

The thought disgusted her, but Peyton was going to have to play Ladydoc. "Rodolfo, if you love me, put the gun away."

"Don't try to manipulate me."

"Just put it away. We can get you help."

He laughed mirthlessly. "You think I need help?"

"Yes, I do."

"You're the one who needs help. I'll give you one more chance, Peyton. One *last* chance to make the right decision. Kevin doesn't deserve you. Just say what you said last night, and he's out of the way forever."

"Nobody has to die."

"That's where you're wrong."

With the butt of the knife handle, he gave the cop a quick blow to the back of the head. He slumped to the floor, unconscious.

"Stop!" said Peyton.

"Quiet!" He pointed the gun at her from across the room.

Peyton trembled.

"Come over here," he said. "Handcuff yourself to the guard."

Peyton crossed the room, and Rudy kept the gun aimed right at her at all times. As she knelt she checked the cop's breathing and pulse.

"Do it!" he said.

She removed the handcuffs from his belt and joined him at the wrist.

"Sit," he said.

She took a seat on the floor beside the cop. Rudy quickly moved in behind her and put the knife to her throat. With the other hand he opened the revolver's chamber and dropped five of the six bullets to the floor. He spun the chamber, Russian-roulette style. Then with the knife still at her throat, he jerked her head around so that she was looking him in the eye, face-to-face. He placed the barrel of the gun to her head.

"Please don't," she said, her voice quaking.

His stare intensified. He jerked the gun away from her head and placed it beneath his chin, pointing toward his own brain.

"Would Kevin do this for you?" he said, then squeezed the trigger.

She braced herself, then started at the sound of the click. He'd fired an empty round.

Rudy pulled the gun away, and spun the chamber again. "Now it's his turn." He rose and started toward the bed.

"Don't," said Peyton.

"Quiet," he said sharply. "One more peep out of you, and I swear I'll keep pulling the trigger till there's a bullet in Kevin's head."

"Don't be stupid. If that gun goes off, the police will be here in ten seconds. There's no way out."

"You're my way out. I can go anywhere with a hostage."

"I'm not going anywhere with you."

"Yes, you will. You want this as much as I do. You said it last night. You wanted to be rid of Kevin."

She feared that screaming might get them both killed, but she had to stop this lunatic. She was about to shout for help when she saw something protruding from beneath the cop's pant leg. It appeared to be a small leather strap just above the ankle, right at the hemline of his pants. Beneath the trousers, she could make out the outline of a holster.

He was wearing an ankle gun.

Rudy held the gun about a foot from Kevin's face. "Are you watching, Peyton? I want you to watch."

Peyton edged slowly toward the ankle gun, then in a final quick dive snatched it up and aimed at Rudy.

"Put the gun down!" she shouted.

He held his aim steady at Kevin's head, smiling thinly. "Are you going to shoot me?"

"If I have to."

"You think you can drop me in one shot? Because if you don't, I pull the trigger."

"Drop the gun, or I'll shoot!"

"Can you risk it? There's a one-in-six chance there's a bullet in the chamber. You deliver anything less than a kill shot, and it will go off. Kevin could be dead."

She glanced at Kevin, then back at Rudy. She adjusted her aim. She'd studied enough neurology to know that the most likely kill shot was at the bridge of the nose. A direct hit would drop him to the floor, instant death, no reflex action. "Don't make me do this," she said.

"You can't do it."

"My father was a cop. I'm an excellent shot."

"But I'm not a jar of cotton balls on the counter at the Haverhill clinic. I'm not one of those black-and-white targets you shot up in the training course when you bought your gun."

His words were yet more evidence how closely he'd monitored her life. They took her anger up a notch. "I'll do it, I mean it."

"You can't kill me."

She aimed between his eyes. Rudy stared back, as if challenging her. She had a clear shot, but she felt herself stalling at the final hurdle. It was the fear she'd had when she'd first purchased her gun, the fear she'd articulated to her lawyer after her deposition in the Haverhill clinic lawsuit. She'd devoted her life to healing. She'd never killed any living thing. She didn't want to be anyone's executioner.

He moved closer to Kevin and pressed the barrel more firmly to his head. "You can't kill me, Peyton."

"Drop the gun right now or you're dead."

"You can't do it.'"

"I will."

"You won't. Because you love me."

With that, she found the power within her.

Rudy's finger twitched on the trigger, and Peyton reacted. The whole room seemed to erupt as her gun discharged in a single loud clap. Rudy's head snapped back, but not before he was able to squeeze off his own shot. It was all one movement, but Peyton could almost see each segment unfolding separately. The bullet smashing through Rudy's skull. His head jerking back in a crimson explosion. His knees buckling. And through it all, his finger still managing to follow through on the trigger.

"No!"

She lunged forward, only to be tugged back by the handcuffs. The sound ripped through her, the awful click of the gun hammer.

And then she heard it—wonderful silence.

She raised her head from the floor and looked through tears. Rudy was in a bloody heap beside the bed. Kevin was stirring in the bed, unscathed. Rudy had fired an empty chamber.

The door flew open. A nurse screamed, then wheeled and ran back into the hall, shouting for help.

Peyton dug the handcuff key from the officer's pocket, unlocked herself, and rushed to Kevin's side. In seconds the panicked nurse was back with a security guard and a doctor.

"What happened?" shouted the guard.

"This crazy guy had a gun!" said Peyton. "He's dead. Help the downed officer. Blunt trauma to the back of the head."

As they hurried to the officer, Kevin groaned, rousing from his drug-induced sleep.

Peyton touched his face. "Are you all right?"

His eyes blinked open. The doctor was calling out orders over the injured officer. Kevin looked barely coherent. "Man, it's noisy as hell in this place."

She had to chuckle, a release of emotion. "We had an incident."

"Is it over?"

She glanced at Rudy's twisted body on the floor. His eyes were still open. A pool of blood had oozed from the gaping wound in his head.

"Yes," said Peyton. "It's finally over."

Epilogue

FOUR DAYS BEFORE CHRISTMAS, PEYTON AND KEVIN WERE DOING their one-stop shopping. It had been a long time coming, but Kevin's novel was finally in bookstores.

A light snow was falling in the late afternoon, and a fresh, clean layer of white marked the east side of the bare tree limbs along the Boston Common. The storefronts of surrounding shops were decorated for the season with wreaths, twinkling lights, and menorahs. Peyton took Kevin's arm as they crossed the street, passing right in front of a horse-drawn carriage. It was a magical time of year, and the thing she loved about Boston was that if you squinted your eyes and blocked out the traffic noise, you could, for a dreamy moment, put yourself in another century.

The trial, thank heaven, was already beginning to feel like another era. Most important, Rudy was gone. Right along with him went the criminal charges against Peyton and Kevin. Even if the cop in Kevin's hospital room hadn't heard the confession, Rudy's apartment and his computer were filled with self-incrimination. Records, photographs, computer files, and maps created a veritable scrapbook of everything that had happened in the past year—his stalking of Peyton, his murder of Andy Johnson and Gary Varne, and his first attempt to kill Kevin. They even found Peyton's gun under his bed, which he'd used to kill Gary.

Peyton didn't like to think of the last two months as "getting back to normal," since it was hard to know what normal was. Her mother had yet to be charged with a crime, but in Peyton's mind she'd been convicted. Her father had filed for divorce, and neither he nor Peyton had spoken to her since. She was tempted to track down her half sister, but in the end she decided that it was up to the child who was given up for adoption to seek out her biological family, not the other way around. That the girl was still a minor made it even more sensitive.

On a more upbeat note, she was happy to be back at Children's Hospital for her residency, and she'd forgiven Kevin for his night with Sandra Blair. Kevin was working at a small litigation firm, part-time lawyer and part-time writer. He was just happy to be published, but their trial had turned him and Peyton into minor celebrities, boosting the book onto the Boston best seller list.

"There it is," said Peyton as they entered the bookstore.

On the table right in front: LYING WITH STRANGERS, A NOVEL BY KEVIN STOKES.

She felt tingles for Kevin as they approached the display. He picked up the book and held it carefully, as if it were breakable.

"I've waited so long for this," he said.

"Let's buy a copy."

"Kind of crass buying your own book, isn't it?"

"There's worse crap you could buy in here."

"Thanks a lot. Maybe you can give me a blurb for the paperback: 'It doesn't suck'—Peyton Shields."

She reached under the table and grabbed the stack. "Here, let's get all of these."

"Peyton," he said, groaning.

"What? We have to buy gifts for our friends anyway."

"Do you think the CEO of McDonald's gives his friends Happy Meals as gifts?"

"Yes, I do. And it's not the same thing anyway."

"We'll buy one copy," he said.

He started toward the register. Peyton acquiesced and put the rest of the books back—not under the shelf, where she'd found them, but on top, prominently positioned with the display copies.

Kevin watched with a boyish grin as the young clerk rang up the sale. He'd been playing it so cool, but Peyton knew that he couldn't possibly walk out without taking at least one feeble stab at triggering some recognition.

"This is my book, you know," he said proudly.

The clerk gave him a stupid look. "Yeah, it will be. When you pay for it."

Kevin was about to speak up, but Peyton stopped him. "We've had our taste of fame. Let's enjoy the anonymity."

He smiled, wondering if the clerk would match the author's name to the name on the credit slip. Just in case, he signed it *Mickey Mouse.*

Peyton snickered. The clerk didn't even check. He just placed the book in a bag and passed it over the counter. "Seems like a lot of people are buying this book. Must be good."

"Best book I ever—"

Peyton pinched his ribs, knowing that he was about to say "wrote."

"Ever bought," he said. "Best book I ever bought."

The clerk gave him another stupid look.

Peyton took Kevin's hand and led him to the door, smiling. "Come on, Ernest. We've got a bullfight to get to."

Acknowledgments

IN THIS WORLD OF REVOLVING DOORS, I'M WHAT YOU MIGHT CALL A professional anomaly. From the very start of my career, I've had the same agent (Richard Pine and, until his death in 2001, his father, Artie) and the same publisher (HarperCollins). I've also had the same editor (Carolyn Marino) since my second novel. I treasure these relationships. It is because of them that I am able to do what I love for a living.

Lying with Strangers marked the beginning of some new and exciting relationships. I'm eternally grateful to Markus Wilhelm, CEO of Bookspan, who tells me that he picked up one of my "Jack Swyteck" novels at an airport and was a fan for life by the time the plane landed. It was Richard Pine who suggested that he might like a non-Swyteck novel that I had in the works. The rest, as they say, is history. I'd been a "Main Selection" only once before in my life—my wife told me I was hers when she married me—so I'm deeply honored that *Lying with Strangers* was the first of my novels to be a Main Selection of the Book-of-the-Month Club, Literary Guild, and Doubleday Book Club.

Carole Baron should also take a bow. They say that an editor has done her best work when you can't tell she's been there, but trust me, Carole's mark is all over this book. She is a real pro, and I can't thank her enough for stepping out of her role in senior management and cutting on my manuscript, pushing me as a writer to another level. I'm also grateful to my reliable early readers, Dr. Gloria M. Grippando, Janis ("Conan the Grammarian") Koch, and Eleanor Rayner.

A huge thank-you also goes to David Weinstein, M.D., and the staff and administration at Boston Children's Hospital who allowed me to shadow David. It was some of the most educational and enjoyable research I've ever done.

Dr. Weinstein is now at the University of Florida, which has given him the opportunity to create and direct the ideal program for children with glycogen storage disease. Dr. Weinstein's program is now the largest in the world, and the University of Florida has more researchers looking for a cure and new treatments for this rare disease than the rest of the world combined. One of the patients Dr. Weinstein treats is a boy named Jacob Gordon, whose family has provided critical support for the program. In honor of Jacob, and in a show of appreciation to the Gordon family, Dr. Peyton Shields's favorite patient in *Lying with Strangers* is named Jacob Gordon.

Finally, I want to thank my wife, Tiffany, who helped me bring this story to you through the eyes of a female lead. Admittedly, it took me years to get it right. I started *Lying with Strangers* in 1999, and I can still see Tiffany looking up from the early manuscript, rolling her eyes, and telling me, "A woman would *never* say that!" *Lying with Strangers* is now one of her favorite James Grippando thrillers. I hope it will be one of your favorites, too.